HEART-SIDE UP

OTHER BOOKS BY BARBARA DIMMICK

In the Presence of Horses

Heart-Side Up

BARBARA DIMMICK

Graywolf Press

SAINT PAUL, MINNESOTA

Publication of this volume is made possible in part by a grant provided by the Minnesota State Arts Board, through an appropriation by the Minnesota State Legislature, a grant from the Wells Fargo Foundation Minnesota, and a grant from the National Endowment for the Arts. Significant support has also been provided by the Bush Foundation; the Lannan Foundation; Marshall Field's Project Imagine with support from the Target Foundation; the McKnight Foundation; and other generous contributions from foundations, corporations, and individuals. To these organizations and individuals we offer our heartfelt thanks.

Published by Graywolf Press
2402 University Avenue, Suite 203
Saint Paul, Minnesota 55114
All rights reserved.

www.graywolfpress.org

Published in the United States of America
Printed in Canada

ISBN 1-55597-362-0

2   4   6   8   9   7   5   3   1
First Graywolf Printing, 2002

Library of Congress Control Number: 2001096556

Cover Design: Jeanne Lee

GRATITUDE

At various stages of this work, I found long calm days, good company, afternoon tea, and whisky at Hawthornden International Retreat for Writers and at The MacDowell Colony. The Dartmouth College Visiting Scholars' program opened the doors to the rich collections of Baker Library.

Two Benedictine enclaves in Vermont, The Weston Priory and the Monastery of the Immaculate Heart of Mary, lodged me in their guest houses, affording not just serenity and quiet, but insight into their way of life. The radical Shroveton Skete, the Monastery of Our Lady of the Snows, and the characters who inhabit them are entirely my invention.

Rabih Alameddine, Andrea Gordon, Pamela Harrison, and Bonnie Pierce read this work in manuscript. James Shepherd put the right shotgun into Zoe's hands, and Norma Forbrich has continued, with great patience, dragging me into the computer age. Elizabeth Peltier and Steven Cahill welcomed me and Gabriel, my large wet retriever, to their island in Moosehead Lake. The Gordon family, as well as Char Hanks and Steph West, added him to their household packs while I traveled.

I would like to thank everyone at Graywolf Press, especially Katie Dublinski, who has been a deft and perceptive editor. At Curtis Brown, Kirsten Manges and Mitchell Waters have been cheerful presences, and Dave Barbor a good and loyal friend.

In memory of Clyde Taylor, who ten years ago pulled some chapters of mine from his slush pile and saw in them promise and possibility—

Clyde was my agent, friend, and mentor. His great love for books and the people who write them, helped to light my way.

I miss him more than I can say—

HEART-SIDE UP

CHAPTER 1

Zoe scrapes her hair back from her forehead, frowns, and for the third time rakes a part along her scalp, a flesh-white meridian. She stares herself down in the mirror, reaches for a clip, gathers her hair, tries to anchor it. Still too short; the ends spring free. She tries some mousse, works it into the errant bushiness around her ears, up through her graying temples.

Now she looks like a spaniel with an ear infection.

An edge of jagged light flashes in her right eye. It's a tell, a flashback harbinger. The corners of her vision darken.

Don't stare. That's what Zeke says. Zeke, her baby-faced psychiatrist.

Move your eyes.

Move a body part.

She waves her arms. Her fingers move through space, fingerlings in an ocean of air.

Focus.

And she does. Suddenly sees that she has somehow managed to put a small hoop in one ear and not the other.

Comb in hand again, she leaves the bathroom and walks a rapid circuit of her apartment. It's March, chill and dank, but with effort, she inventories what she has loved about these rooms: the tilt and creak of the old plank floors, the fine, detailed moldings, the old-house smell, even the astonishment in some other-world of the sea captain who built this place 200 years before that a woman now lives in his upstairs parlor. She pauses before

an eerie pen-and-ink done directly on the wall above the mantel.
A fleet of sailing ships in a harbor.

—Harbor, she says, trying out the word.

Out of habit, she clenches her toes on the bare wood floor,
tries to feel something, anything, the delicate graininess of her
stockings on the soles of her feet.

Above the masted ships, the clippers and the whalers and the
freights, the figure of a woman rises among swirling clouds. The
Virgin Mary, she supposes. The Blessed First Mate, palms up and
out, casting mercy and forgiveness on all before her.

She casts her own hands up, palms and fingers held just so.

I miss my mind, she thinks.

Back in the bedroom she lays the comb on the bureau. Her
skin is numb and her vision skips from frame to frame. Careful
not to look in the mirror, she sorts through her jewelry box. A
necklace is knotted around a bracelet. She digs out a clump of
earrings, the hooks in a tangle, hefts them in her palm, wants
nothing but to fling them against the wall. Sick, she lets the earrings drop, feels the temptation to rip, literally rip, the orphan
hoop from her lobe.

She closes her eyes.

She has promised Zeke not to hurt herself. Nor to have suspicious accidents.

I'm too old for promises, she thinks.

Backing away, she sits on the edge of the bed, takes the comb
to her hair again. If only she could reclaim her old routine: get
up, dress, and go to work without fireworks, without theatricality.

Now, according to Zeke, this is normal.

She glances in the mirror. All the fooling with her hair has
made it fluffy. Perhaps she should call, something she has also
promised. She bargains. She's not hurting herself, and the idea
that she will call a psychiatrist six years her junior in order to get
dressed in the morning is far too much.

If she could just figure out the hair, or get it cut. She stares
into the mirror.

—If you were me, she says: Would you let someone stand behind you with a pair of scissors and a razor blade?

She'll grow it out. Who cares about it, anyway?

She wriggles her toes, feels the lace hem of her slip across her thighs. One more fatuous remark, and she will be one of those people who shows up at work with an AK-47.

Oh, Zoe, are you changing your hair?

Oh, Zoe, what a good idea to get a new look.

Her underlings in the academic center notice every detail. If she wears a bracelet, a scarf they haven't seen in a while, they question, they congratulate. Is she feeling better? She must be; isn't that a pretty necklace? She's not, of course, and she is amazed that female adornment means so much to all of them: they read portents in lip gloss and new sweaters.

The woman in the mirror unbuttons the high neck of her blouse, lays the collar open as she might have a few months before. The red worm of the first scar begins below her left ear, runs down her neck. Eyes fixed, she undoes another button, then another and another. Finally she shrugs the blouse off. The second scar runs its diagonal, straighter than the first; a cleaner, harsher cut, it vanishes like a comet into the top of her camisole.

Lucky he missed your breast. How often has she heard that?

Lucky he missed your face.

She lifts her arms. Slices and hash marks all along her forearms, still raised and red.

They say she screamed.

The room was nearly empty, but not quite. There was a rule about that, more like a decree that she herself had issued, as director of learning services.

And no, she never guessed, never saw it coming.

Adam was eighteen, all charm, all smiles, good looks, good manners. Slow about the work, subtly resentful of his learning problems, but sweet, a little too dependent.

Zoe had refused to coddle him, or anyone else for that matter. She'd held to the belief that, whatever their weaknesses, he and all her students must learn to be responsible, must learn to fail if necessary, then pick themselves up again and succeed on the second try, the third, even the fourth. Often she'd declared she was in the business of providing opportunity after opportunity to get it right.

That day, she'd been looking down into Adam's folder. From the corner of her eye, she saw him reach into his backpack. Fishing for a pen, perhaps. His assignment book, a cough drop.

She heard her name: Professor Muir?

She glanced up, saw the glitter in his hand, had no comprehension until after the first cut.

In the mirror, she tilts her head, fingers the scar below her ear. Sometimes she wishes he'd just cut her throat and been done with it.

Half-dressed, she crawls back into bed, pulls the blankets over her head, reaches out, drags the phone in with her. She will have to call Zeke after all, see if he has a free hour. The settlement allows for all the psychiatric help she needs.

Zeke has even joked about this. If you're going to get knifed, at least let your attacker come from a very rich family.

Very funny, she says bitterly.

Laughter? he says: Want to try it? Any memory of it whatsoever?

She scowls like a seven-year-old.

Sometimes they talk about what she will do with the cash part of the settlement.

Have a really nice funeral? she says.

Buy an armored car?

Start a new life? Zeke says.

I had a life, she always says: I just want it back.

He shakes his head: Sorry, sorry, sorry.

She hates him for his sympathy.

She'll have to call the dean's office, tell them she won't be in today.

The dean is being good about this, though she suspects he's terrified she'll sue. He puts up with her absences, and she tries hard to remember when she seldom called in sick, when she was so focused on her work that she could lie in bed each morning and recall her whole day's schedule without consulting her daybook.

She huddles in the dark under her quilt, thinks about the calls but doesn't make them. Knows she'd better do it soon or the police will be at her door to check on her. It's happened before, everyone in the academic center thinking she was lying dead when she was only in her pajamas, paralyzed in the kitchen with a cup of cold coffee in her hands.

Lifting the phone from its hook, she listens to the dial tone, puts it down again. All she needs is something to get her going. Some idiot spark. She tries to interest herself in an exotic lunch. Or in buying herself a gift. She could use new sunglasses. Perhaps she could walk down to the harbor after work. Sometimes a good weather forecast is all it takes.

Sitting up, she cocks her head, hears the postman down in the front hall, banging the metal lids of the mailboxes. She wraps herself in her robe. Maybe if she could wear this heavy old tufted thing to work instead of clothes and earrings, if she could go in her bare feet and admit she feels like dirt, admit she can barely do her job for staring every minute at her students' hands, then life would be easier.

Perhaps the lying is the worst of it.

At the front door, she looks through the peephole. Once she had thought it a disgrace, cut into the heavy planking of the reverse cross door. Now she's grateful for it, and after the mailman is gone, she sets about undoing her collection of bolts. Yes, she herself has further marred the door, had locks added when her landlord made the offer. She would have taken searchlights on the perimeter, guard dogs, razor fencing.

Out in the hallway, she glances over the banister, down the sweeping, elliptical stairs. She rushes down, no stately descent as she's imagined the young women of this house were wont to make, snatches her mail, scuttles back to her apartment, and bolts the door behind her.

At the front windows, she opens the tall, wood-panel shutters. Outside, another gray Rhode Island morning. She's often thought of the first women in this house, the chill murk of the weather a nagging reminder of their men at sea. Barstow, Rhode Island, is gracious, gritty, miserable, and Zoe had once guessed half the stones in the old burial ground marked the tragic graves of pneumonia victims. She looks up from the mail, thinks pneumonia is a good deal if you can get it.

And then among the junk and the bills, she finds a letter from Black Hill, Pennsylvania.

Home.

Or what remains of home.

The envelope is pink, the handwriting swoops in a precise way. Annie, her mother's friend, has admitted more than once that writing to Zoe makes her nervous because Zoe is a teacher. She imagines the old woman fretting over her sentences, perhaps writing them out first then copying them over.

Carefully, she slides her finger under the flap of the envelope. Then pauses. After the letter, what then? She needs to locate the next bead of activity, needs to be poised to string it onto her thread of time. Impossible to assume that there will be something to do next, something obvious and safe.

Her slasher is securely tucked away, or so Zeke tells her, but she mistrusts the information, thinks Adam wouldn't be the first walkaway from a psychiatric hospital. Each time Zeke sees her skepticism, he says: Trust me, he's behind more than one locked door.

Not enough.

She drags the corner of Annie's letter across the back of her hand, leaves a white line in the skin, then decides she will start over.

Shower.

Pull on jeans.

Call in sick, call Zeke.

She breathes. The next few steps under control, she opens Annie's letter.

She never expects much from these missives, though she appreciates them. This one begins with the latest chapter of Annie's ongoing feud with a neighbor over a willow tree planted on the border between their properties. Annie would like it cut down. The neighbor wants the tree to stay. In Annie's view, and she always has one, if the neighbor wants such a messy tree he should be willing to pick up all the leavings and the branches. Apparently Annie now gathers up the branches that fall on her lawn and piles them neatly at his garage door so he must move them before he can drive his car.

Zoe smiles at the fervor and the pettiness.

There's a paragraph about someone in the bridge club who brought her sister from Ohio instead of her husband, and how the visitor never once stopped talking, not even through the bidding.

Another paragraph discusses the flap at church over the arrival of new hymnals. The books are beautiful, but some of the new tunes are discordant and Annie misses her old favorites. Honestly, she mutters, her handwriting disintegrating, can Zoe imagine a hymnal without "Rock of Ages"?

Zoe's eyes glaze.

Near the end is a paragraph to the effect that Mr. Reed has died.

At first, it doesn't register. Annie's letters are full of births and deaths, which amaze Zoe since Black Hill is such a small town.

And then she is wholly attentive.

Zoe, dear, Annie writes: I knew you'd want to know because of Dayton.

Plenty of grist for Zeke.

Early on, she'd told him small shards of the story, thinking it pleasanter to talk of Dayton, Dayton Deming Reed, her first love, than to admit she had nearly died at the hands of a student.

She'd conjured the sweetness of him, the richest boy in town whose idea of a date was tubing in the river behind his house, or hiking up Hawk Mountain to watch the red-tails, the sharp-shins, and the kestrels ride the thermals. He was amiable, kind, unhurried. Waitresses and gas-pump attendants told him their life stories, the names of their mates and children, and while waiting for the go-ahead through road construction, he never passed up the chance to lean his elbow on the door of his battered Triumph and chat up the flagman. But as the weeks and months of therapy wore on, Zoe had refused to say more, had refused to say what had become of him, of them, and Zeke had doggedly theorized that, in his own way, Dayton must have done her every bit as much harm as Adam.

She struggles to fit the letter back into its envelope. Perhaps she won't mention this at all. And then she sees there's a clipping. Common practice for Annie. This time it's Mr. Reed's obituary.

Heart failure. Past director of Black Hill Savings and Loan, president of this, chair of that, back through the decades. No calling hours, service for family only.

Zoe's throat closes.

What family?

Dayton is the only surviving relative.

CHAPTER 2

꒱

It's five minutes after one, and even though Zeke is sacrificing his lunch break to see her, so far neither she nor he has spoken a single word.

I know this trick, she'd told him early on.

It's not a trick, he'd said: It's a technique.

She watches him now, neutral expression on his face, waiting for her to begin.

Zeke Polushka is shorter than Zoe, his hair so blond and fine it seems not to belong on anyone over the age of three. His cheekbones are high, his chin delicate, and she suspects he travels to Boston for the classy haircuts, knows he shops far afield from Barstow for the elegant shirts and trousers. The diplomas on the wall certify he's a full-blown psychiatrist, but sometimes she can't believe she trusts him with the fragile contraption of her sanity.

—You know, she says at last: Since I've started seeing you, I no longer do this to my students.

—What's that?

—This waiting game. They teach it to tutors, too. Force the student to take responsibility for first speech. Ownership, investment, all that crap.

—I think of it as a courtesy, he says: It lets you set the tone.

—It's aggressive, Zoe says, all at once looking for a fight.

Empathy plays across his face. He takes a pen, fools with it.

—So, he says: How are you feeling?

She juts out her jaw, blows out air.

—Murderous.

—You were murdered, he offers: In a way.

She rolls her eyes.

—You know what you could do for me?

He looks hopeful.

—Just sit there. Keep me company.

Protect me, she wants to say. For these fifty minutes, let me feel safe.

They sit a good ten, fifteen minutes in stubborn silence.

Zeke folds his hands, leans back, and Zoe wonders about the relationship between smarts and therapy. Right this minute, she hates his dapperness, his youth, his ergonomic leather chair, the numbered lithographs on the wall, and what does that say about her? Something, she knows. Would she like him better if he dressed in tattered chinos? That he's so successful gives her confidence, yet she's driven to find fault with him, thinks he would be a better person, perhaps, if he gave half his clothing allowance to United Way or hung his walls with ragged paintings by nieces or young clients. What's more, irony is hardly lost on her. After all these years of packing students and younger colleagues off to therapists, now she's the one being watched, evaluated, often annoyed by a man in a seventy-dollar haircut.

—May I ask a question? she says at last.

He brightens, leans forward half an inch.

—Why does this always go off the rails?

—This?

—Seeing you.

—And how does it go off the rails?

—For heaven's sake, she snaps.

Rage blossoms, nearly erupts.

She finds it terrifying, the way she swings from relative calm to insanity and rage. Abruptly she wishes for a nice, cleansing nuclear holocaust, patently desires to shoot, one by one, every single person on the planet, which includes all the men, just because they're men, and all the women because she finds them either smug or full of pity.

—Just *talk* to me, she says, desperate and fierce: Get *on* with it. Make me feel better. All I want is to get up in the morning, go to work, and do my job. How hard is that?

Zeke watches her a long moment.

—You're not a car, he says, calm, perhaps a little sad: You're not in for repairs. You need help getting well.

Zoe shrugs. The world is suddenly flat again. She looks out the window, senses a shifting in his posture, knows what comes next is meant to be a change-up. She glances at her watch, says:

—Isn't it time you asked about Dayton?

Zeke laughs, relaxes, and Zoe nearly weeps, then pulls herself together. He insists tears would be good for her; she insists tears change nothing.

His voice is low:

—Well, what about Dayton?

—You're kidding, right?

—Worth a try.

He flashes her a smile, watches his fingers twirl his pen like a miniature baton, then asks if she's read any of the books he's recommended.

—What books? she says, although she knows perfectly well. She hates how common they make trauma, as ordinary as pruning roses, rewiring lamps.

Zeke smiles, waits, takes up his pen with his other hand.

—Okay, she says: There's news of Dayton. Happy now?

Zeke's hand stills.

She nods at his pen:

—I was hoping I could make you drop that.

He lays the pen on the desk, folds his hands.

—You heard from him?

Zeke has sometimes mused that Zoe should consider calling or writing Dayton, and at least find out where and how he is. She can't avoid him all her life, or so he claims.

Watch me, she had said: You're the one with the fixation.

Zeke waits, face neutral.

—His father died, she says finally.

—He's been in touch then?

—Of course, Zoe says, airily: He's completely overwhelmed by grief and regret. First he sent a dozen roses. Then a telegram: *All forgiven?*

Zeke stills.

—Oh, for heaven's sake, she says: It's been eight years.

She turns her face away. There is simply no explaining how all those years of simple rightness could end in such a way. She doesn't even know what way that is exactly, except that she had planted her feet, waited for him to come to his senses.

—I'm here because I was knifed, she says after a long silence: Not because of some old love affair.

—Some old love affair, Zeke echoes.

Even Zoe knows the words are wrong.

—It's been eight years, she says again.

Her voice goes flat. Eight years is a simple fact even a cherubic psychiatrist cannot refute.

Yet again Zeke theorizes that Adam's abrupt transformation from student to maniac somehow reminds her of Dayton. Zoe barely listens, ignores him a good long while.

—Did he leave you for someone else? Another woman?

—Yes, she says at last, knows she's giving in, allowing herself to be goaded: He left me for the Mother of God.

—The Mother of God?

Zoe smiles at his bafflement.

—You heard me, she says, then sees he's somewhat shaken.

But so is she. This is one story she has vowed is off-limits, to Zeke or anyone else for that matter.

After a while, she steals one of his lines:

—This should give us something to work with in the future.

Zeke shakes his head.

—I don't like this mood of yours, he says and for once seems downright worried.

—That makes two of us, Zoe says.

⤵

Afterward, she props her elbows on the roof of her car and glares up at the old Greek Revival converted now to offices. She sees the light in his window, imagines him, the good student all grown up now, writing thoughtful, rapid notes on her mental whereabouts. She forces herself into her car, pounds the door lock shut with her elbow, considers calling him to apologize for her testiness. But how often had she told her students that their apologies were meaningless unless they changed their behavior, too?

Arms stiff, she grips the steering wheel. No guarantee she won't be rude to him again. Her breath catches then, and she feels lost, panicked, unable to think, and she hears him remind her to find a purpose, however small, a destination, anything to keep going.

She'll go to the beach. But this semi-decision casts up a host of confusing choices. Which beach? A broad beach, a town beach, a deserted beach, a beach with shells? Which matters more? A nice beach? Or a nice drive to the beach?

Elizabeth Beach, she thinks, seizing on one before she is rendered helpless with indecision. The trip is fairly short, complicated enough to require concentration, simple enough so that she will get there. And then the filthy gray Atlantic will roar in and out at her feet.

Gingerly, she guides the car out into the sporadic traffic, passes the pharmacy, the captains' houses, town hall and historical society, bookstore, gas station, tourist shops, fish restaurant, and pool hall. Their lights are bright, stoic, in the midafternoon murk.

She came to Barstow after she and Dayton split up. Two or three years here, she'd thought. She'd start a doctorate, gain some experience, then move on to greater challenges. But greater challenges had come to her, promotions, research, and increasingly troubled students. Younger and younger girls with babies, their sparse welfare grants ticking down to nothing. Recovering addicts. Domestic-abuse cases. Victims of industrial accidents. Legions of younger students taught to read in such airy and hodgepodge ways that they had no clue there's a logic to language, guides and tricks for its mastery.

At the gravel turnout for the beach, she stops, lets the engine idle. She's not dressed for this, the extreme of the ocean. Seabirds run back and forth, just ahead of the lip of the water. In the distance, a man in a hooded parka throws a ball for a Schnauzer. The tide is out, returning.

Zoe sighs. Once upon a time, she'd joked that her job was to stem the tide of ignorance and learned helplessness. She stares out the windshield, wishes for a fishing boat on the horizon. How can a whole damn ocean be so empty?

All at once, she pulls Annie's letter from her purse, then puts the car in gear and heads south along Narragansett Bay.

CHAPTER 3

For a while, she simply follows the water, then crosses the Jamestown Bridge. Occasionally, she taps her brakes, wonders if she should go back to the apartment for anything, fears this precious impulse might vanish. She hugs the coast through Charleston and Westerly, then angles inland on Route 2, heading for 84. The route is automatic, comforting, although she's not made the trip in the last four years, not since her final vigil by her mother's side as she drifted off in the sweet coma of kidney failure.

Now she drives west into the glare of coming headlights, and every once in a while, ducks her hand into her bag, clutches the bottle of Xanax, pushes the edge of need. She knows the point from which there is no return, a particular shallowness of breathing, a heartbeat so fast it never touches down, but for now she's all right, oddly relieved that no one knows where she is, that not a single passing driver knows her story.

The evening wears on, and Zoe falls in love with the companionable glow of her dash lights, turns the dark beyond her windows into deep space, becomes a woman with power in her hands. Highway signs flip by like playing cards.

Maybe I'll just do this forever, she thinks, never teach again, never assign another failing grade, see another shrink. Instead, she sees herself in her little blue Volvo, heading for the Pacific. She'll cross a desert, drive through hairpin mountain passes. She imagines racing west so fast the light of morning never catches her, invents a car that never runs out of gas. Crossing the

Hudson, high over the water in the dark, she touches her neck, fingers a scar, lets her hand fall away.

When she reaches Scranton, she drives past one exit after another, unable to give up following her headlights in the dark. Finally, thirty-five miles west of her destination, in the midst of the Endless Mountains, her strength evaporates.

It's too cold to pull off and sleep in the car, so she gets off the highway, heads back on a county road. She scouts for motels, tourist cabins, passes the sign for the state park at Ricketts Glen, but sees nowhere she feels like stopping. In time she's so near Black Hill she knows the place, an old inn on the edge of town.

Coal Country Bed and Breakfast, it's called now. On the sign are a shovel and a pick. The rambling flower-jungles of roses and spirea, poppies, larkspur, and hollyhocks have been torn out. Uniform lawns surround the old Victorian cottage, now painted pale red with gray trim.

She shakes her head. On all her trips home to nurse her mother, she saw the coal country reinvent itself for tourists. Steam trains were moved here from Vermont; federal money now protects them. Abandoned mines, both vertical and pit, are open to the public, and farther south, you can walk through the village of Eckly, now a national preserve.

They should have left this old inn the way it was, the bar a local watering hole, the upstairs rooms rented by the week to skiers and summer guests.

It's 2 A.M., but inside, a young woman with big gold bracelets walks a squalling baby in and out of the office behind the desk, reminding Zoe of the controversy in her department over whether or not young mothers should be allowed to bring their babies when they came for tutoring.

Zoe apologizes for disturbing her.

The girl jiggles the child, kisses its forehead, swings her hips.

—This one had me up anyways.

Zoe looks at the infant, sighs. *Anyways.* Another child who will someday be mystified by the yawning gap between his mother tongue and standard speech.

The baby flings itself in his mother's arms, but somehow the girl hangs on, all the while running Zoe's credit card through the machine.

—Room 8, she says, sliding the credit card and key across the desk: Up the steps and to the right.

—Still the front room, Zoe hears herself say.

What an odd thing to remember after all this time.

—Oh, you been here before? the girl says, looking into her child's face.

—I worked here one summer. Zoe smiles: Before you were born.

She climbs the stairs, thinks ruefully of Mrs. Kichline, a crazy-clean German woman. Zoe'd been flat-out desperate for a job. She needed money for books and tuition, there'd been a recession on, and every day she'd ridden her bike out to the inn, leaned it up against the back of the barn, and prayed she'd be handed over to Mr. Kichline for a day of mowing, gardening, and setting up the bar for the coming evening. Otherwise, Mrs. Kichline clucked around her all day long, remonstrating over the drape of a bedspread, a smear on a window, a loose carpet runner, even dusty lightbulbs inside lamps.

Zoe lets herself into the front room. A streetlamp glares through drapes so flimsy and dingy they're probably disturbing Mrs. Kichline's eternal rest.

Getting out the Xanax, Zoe scatters the little football-shaped pills on her palm. One will make her relax. One and a half might induce sleep. Two will surely do the job, but she hates the fog in her head the next day.

It's not for sleep, Zeke tells her again and again: There are better things for sleep.

But Zoe knows this drug, has no wish to try another.

She settles on one and a half, strips, and crawls between the sheets. They're cold, almost clammy, and she takes an odd pleasure in the fact that she can register this. For a moment, she

misses her familiar quilt and pillows. It feels good to miss something, value something back in Rhode Island—even if only the
furnishings on her bed.

By the time she wakes it is nearly noon. She lies in bed, in this
long-lost place, and feels as if she is no longer real. Hands behind
her head, she thinks of Dayton, smiles wryly over the one and
only time the Kichlines, called away to a funeral, had left her in
charge, Mrs. Kichline threatening to fire her if "that boy" spent
the night, and Mr. Kichline winking and saying there was nothing
like having a man around the place.

Out of the blue, she thinks of Dayton's father, wishes she'd
kept in touch with him. She turns her face down into her pillow,
ready to weep, then abruptly shuts it off, has no idea when or how
she learned to do this.

Edgy now, she watches the clock, waits for it to reach ten, fifteen minutes past the hour, then on the bedside phone dials
Zeke and gets his voice mail, which is exactly what she wants.
She's on a road trip, she tells him. An adventure. Would he do her
a favor and call her dean? He's offered to do this in the past, so
could he just say Zoe won't be back for, oh, at least the rest of the
week? She lies, says she'll call again in a day or two, then lies some
more, says she's fine, merely getting away for some rest.

Hoping she's sealed her privacy for a while longer, she goes
and stands under the shower.

What she will say when she sees Dayton, Zoe has no idea. She
makes her way along Main Street, vaguely registers that a health-
food store has opened across from the miners' union hall. The
Polish American Club and Eagle Hotel still exist, but the old A&P
is now a Shop-Quik. She drives as in multiple time zones, the here
and now, the years she and Dayton were together, and the long
gray years before, when she and her mother lived behind tiny
Makarios Store, where her mother clerked, mopped floors, and
helped old Mrs. Makarios nurse her disabled husband. Even Zoe
had had such long lists of weekly chores that she'd not needed

her mother's constant moaning about education being the only possible escape for her darling Zoe, poor fatherless miner's child. She had elbowed her way into college, put a hundred miles between herself and her mother's sorrow, and by chance, landed at the same school as Dayton, the boy who'd grown up in the big house on the river bluff back home.

Makarios Store is long gone, replaced by a Texaco station. She passes the corner in a daze, continues along Main Street, passing the great double houses now, some dark brick, some blond, some sheathed now in vinyl. At the Union Cemetery she slows. It's filled to the brim with miners, dead from cave-ins, explosions, black lung, emphysema. Her father's there, too, killed in a freak crane accident when Zoe was barely five, and it comes to her there was an even earlier, mistier time. A shelf of books in matching bright red bindings her parents read from in the evenings, pancakes served with bacon and hot syrup every Saturday, and union picnics where her father danced first with her mother then with her, the soles of her patent-leather shoes scraping on the rough concrete floor of the pavilion out at the lake.

She turns onto Willow Street, climbs the bluff above the river. The inside of her mouth is pasted shut, and her vision is so full of white she's nearly blind. Thick Pennsylvania scrub bends from the shoulders of the road, the early leaves are tatters of green, and soon she sees the stone pillars of the river house. As always, they remind her of the entrances to WPA parks built in half the towns in Pennsylvania during the depression.

Zoe brakes, bewildered. Formal drive? Or, as in the old days, follow the service lane up around to the back door? In an odd, dislocated way, she remembers Dayton telling her that when he was a little boy, the formal drive had been white Jersey beach sand. The gardeners had raked it twice a week. Now it's paved, and Zoe swings up it as if breaking through the glass of a museum diorama, inserting herself into a time gone by.

The house rises on its bluff. It's not foursquare; the main gambrel is broken by two others turned east and west. Two stone chimneys rise through the roof, and old-fashioned louvered shutters, painted gray, hang at the windows. One spring break Zoe had been scrambling to find a home from an earlier era that she could sketch and analyze, and Dayton's father had suggested his.

Be practical, her mother warned at the start of every semester: Zoe didn't want to spend her life waiting tables, did she? With some useless degree in her apron pocket?

But Dayton's father had pressed her to follow her love of art. If she had to marry it to practicality, why not architecture? At least something *calls* you, he would say, offering a wry smile over Dayton's roaming interests, his innocent wish to save the world.

Zoe's assignment had been to study period influences, and while Dayton lay around studying botany, sociology, land-use planning, who-knows-what, Zoe and his father had catalogued the hodgepodge of styles so common in the houses that rich men built at the turn of the twentieth century, the stonework in contrast with the French doors, the portico flung out from the side, even the path of the drive, the surprise of the river falling away at the foot of the gardens out back.

She parks the car, remembers how easily she and Dayton's father had taken to each other. She feels herself floating off somehow, and suddenly fearing her own sorrow, wishes she'd taken another Xanax. In the mirror, her face is white and horror-struck. She gives herself a ghoulish smile, smoothes her day-old turtleneck, hides her scars.

The front porch is as wide as the reviewing platform for a parade. She crosses it, grips her handbag, and rings the bell.

Dayton will still be tall, she thinks. Will still be blond, though perhaps graying, will still have the childhood nick on his chin, the odd quirk of squinting his left eye when up to mischief or under stress. Certainly, he will squint when he sees her, and suddenly she realizes there will be no need to speak. She'll know all there is to know the moment her presence registers on his face.

She closes her eyes, and filled with dread, hears footsteps coming, then rouses. If that light, uneven tread is Dayton's, something's wrong. He's ill, or injured, or his father's death has ambushed him. She just has time to think that perhaps he might actually need her again, when the door opens.

A short, boxy woman stands in the doorway.

Zoe steps back in surprise.

—Mrs. Kuzak, she blurts out, equally stunned by the woman's presence and her recall of the name.

The old housekeeper is dressed in a black coat and black hat with a scrap of dotted veil.

All Zoe can think of are the words freshmen-comp students so often use to describe their grandmothers. Velvety skin, parchment skin, translucent skin.

—I'm sorry to bother you, Zoe says at last.

The woman waits. Ancient now, she seems exhausted and annoyed.

—I'm Zoe Muir. You remember me. I came to. . . .

She falters.

—I came to see Dayton. I need to speak to him.

—We only speak to Dayton when Dayton wishes, the woman snaps: Isn't that right?

Zoe stares, then hears herself say:

—What is he? The Dalai Lama?

Mrs. Kuzak turns, seems to hear something behind her.

—Perhaps you should come in.

My god, Zoe thinks. Who would choose servitude as a way of life?

Then wonders how you would describe what she's been doing for a living.

She follows the housekeeper into the front reception room. Nowadays it's merely a foyer with marble-topped tables, mirrors, and doorways in all directions; Dayton's father's office lies to the left, living room to the right, stairs and hall straight ahead.

A man in a dark gray suit emerges from the office.

—Can I help?

Mrs. Kuzak announces that she's a friend of Dayton's.

The man shakes Zoe's hand. He's a cousin, several times removed.

—We've just returned from scattering the ashes.

He folds his hands before him like an undertaker.

—Oh, Zoe says: So Dayton is here then?

The housekeeper and cousin exchange a look.

—You've been out of touch, he says.

Zoe feels a falling in her bones.

—He's not dead, is he?

The cousin tugs an earlobe, shakes his head.

—But he didn't come to the funeral?

—No funeral, Mrs. Kuzak says, bitter: No proper one. We just dumped—

The cousin takes her elbow.

—We followed Mr. Reed's instructions. The ashes were scattered in the gardens along the river.

Zoe nods, tearful.

—He loved those gardens. He even rearranged the rocks. We used to joke about it.

She falters, remembers the sorrowful way he saw them off to college in the fall, rattling away distractedly about planting bulbs, dividing perennials.

The housekeeper's eyes soften and she pulls a floppy handkerchief from under her cuff.

—This young lady was a friend of the family.

The cousin touches Zoe's arm, says:

—Next time we write, we'll let Dayton know you stopped in. He can't just up and leave for these things.

He grimaces and turns away, heads back down the hall.

Zoe looks into Mrs. Kuzak's face.

—Where is he? Is he all right? Is he married?

Mrs. Kuzak's hands tremble, and Zoe reaches out and holds them. Deliberately, she drops her voice:

—Tell me. I need to know. You know how close we were.

She feels like a cheat, using Zeke's rich, tempting tone on the housekeeper.

—He's in a monastery, Mrs. Kuzak says at last.

Zoe nearly crushes the old woman's hands.

—Say that again?

—A monastery. The young man is in a monastery in Vermont.

Mrs. Kuzak pulls her hand away. Her voice is hard:

—His father missed him terribly.

Zoe remembers how she and his father had first kidded Dayton. He was giving up psychology, or engineering or pre-med or whatever it had been, for *theology?* And Zoe, dead wrong as it turned out, had figured it was just another curious fancy.

Leaning forward, she kisses Mrs. Kuzak's cheek. The skin is indeed hot and papery.

Mrs. Kuzak presses her lips together, picks at the hem on her handkerchief.

—I'll go up there, Zoe says, and asks for Dayton's address.

—Leave him, the old woman tells her, and refuses to say more.

—Oh, Zoe says, abruptly vengeful: I mean to have a little talk with him.

And then, sick with blindness, old betrayal, rage, she forces herself to ask, as if she doesn't already know the answer:

—What kind of monastery?

CHAPTER 4

≍

For a little while after leaving the river house, she drives around Black Hill, thinking she should call on her mother's friend Annie, visit her parents' graves, go back to the inn and contact Zeke. But within the hour, she is roaring past Scranton like a woman possessed, then turning north along the Hudson.

All the while, amid flashes of stress-white, she catches images of Dayton. His thick, floppy, blond hair is hacked into a tonsure. His tanned face, gaunt and pale. His eyes, fixed with fervor. She shakes her head. He's not a lunatic. He's a monk. Surely there's a difference. She sees him, the tallest of the lot, candle in hand, entering an ornate chapel for midnight prayers. Sees him lying face-down, arms out, in penance for some infraction. Sees his face turned away from hers, on the other side of a grill, allowed a visit once a decade.

She rubs her eyes. It can't be like that, she thinks. It's not the Middle Ages.

Looking for a place to cross the Hudson, she stops for a map, spreads it across the steering wheel. Eagerly she scans the state parks, forests, mountain peaks, ski areas, various tourist attractions, searches for monasteries. In that trick of mind, she convinces herself it might be possible. Hasn't she seen maps with monasteries?

She takes a two-lane road. She'll sneak up on Vermont, come in the side door. Everything assures her she is far from Rhode Island, the rolling hills of the Taconics, the farms and nurseries, the drive-in restaurants and riding stables. Even the names of roads: Rabbit Congress Hollow. Nine Wives Alley. Van Vliet Mews.

A Catholic monastery.

Her old hatreds come flooding back. The Church's stance on birth control is archaic and misogynist. Its treatment of women more so. And she's never been able to get past the idea of the infallibility of the Pope. Surely that's some kind of cosmic joke. Upon this rock, her ass.

At dusk, she breaks through a final flurry of New York State billboards and crosses into Vermont. At times, the road is promising. A sign on the right announces the Six Maples Inn, and for a moment, she thinks of stopping for the night, then presses on.

A few miles later, she enters Bennington. Her headlights pick up a sign for the battle monument, and Zoe frowns. When was there a battle in Vermont? Ahead, a classic white New England church thrusts its spire into the night; its burying ground is marked by an elegant fence with sweeping lines and lovely posts. At the corner, she hooks a right and coasts down a hill, past a museum with a sign advertising Grandma Moses, and finds herself on a little strip with motels and gas stations.

Tired, woozy, indecisive, she drives past one motel after another, finally pulls in under a sign advertising *Mud Season Special.*

Inside, a man in a denim shirt and corduroys is painting window frames.

—Been driving? he says, not coming down from his ladder.

—From Pennsylvania.

He fills the brush again with gray-green paint, rubs out a mistake with his thumb, then paints some more.

Zoe leans on the counter.

—I'm here to find someone, she announces, taken aback by her candor: He's in a monastery.

The man stops, looks down at her, brushes out the last stretch of the window casing, then hurries down the ladder.

—Up on Equinox?

She squints. Hunger and the remembered glare of traffic paint are addling her vision.

—There's monks up there, he tells her: If yours is, you can just forget it.

Zoe decides not to listen. She registers, takes her key, feeds quarters into a machine, loads up on peanut-butter crackers. Monks on Equinox. Light-headed, she steps over to a rack of flyers, and amid shiny brochures for ski areas, antique malls, and discount basket outlets, she notices a brochure for a toll road up Mount Equinox. She opens it and reads it closely, but the road doesn't open until Memorial Day. And there's no mention of monks.

The next morning, she's yanked from deep but turbulent sleep by sheer terror. She fights the bed quilt, screams, then wakes completely, lies exhausted against the headboard. Her mouth is dry, her eyes gritty. She touches her neck, glances at her forearms. Still scarred. She pulls a pillow over her face, lies still.

All of Vermont stretches to the north. How hard can this be?

She presses the pillow hard into her face, half-hopes she finds only Dayton's trail, hopes she'll need to follow him elsewhere. Perhaps he's moved to the Arizona desert, gone on pilgrimage to the Holy Land, and she can merely draft along behind him, an exhausted cyclist drawing energy and protection from a leader.

Shoving the pillow aside, she decides monomania, even foolish monomania, Dayton Dayton Dayton, beats terror and paranoia. She eyes the pile of clothes she's been wearing for two days straight, finally gets up, showers, then chokes down a cracker and some Xanax, and admits she needs real food.

On the way out of her room, she pulls her turtleneck up to her chin, but it sags, stretched out after two days' wear. The top inch of her scar wriggles free.

Farther down Main Street, she finds a small storefront place crammed with locals. The booths and counter seats are all occupied and Zoe sits stranded and apprehensive at a wobbly table clustered with some others in the center of the room. The place is packed with men in everything from work boots and down vests, sweaters, khakis, and three-piece suits, women in gym clothes, jeans, business attire. It troubles her to have people anywhere behind her, and she's edgy each time she has to scoot in her chair to make room for passing waitresses, but the Xanax leaves her calm enough so that she manages to eat some eggs and half a grapefruit.

Afterward, she drops her key at the motel, climbs into her car, and studies her map. Two routes head north, the old and the new, and since the old cuts past the foot of Mount Equinox, she decides to go that way.

She drives slowly, studies the bleak scenery. She looks closely at everyone she passes, as if she might just happen across Dayton, and she reads every road sign, on the lookout for any and all monasteries.

The town of Shallowbrook occupies a curve in the road, and when Zoe sees a woman in galoshes and a bright blue coat jam an American flag into its holder on the porch column of the library, she swerves into the pullout.

The building is tiny, old, built of soft redbrick. A miniature Monticello, the portico and columns gleam fresh white against the mud and gloom. All that labor, all that solidity for what? Six hundred square feet?

Inside, heavy wooden shelves, laden with books, line the walls, and the bulletin board is strewn with the habitual cheery posters one finds in public libraries. In the corner, at a small table, a young woman works in front of a computer. The librarian, still in her coat, empties a bin of returned books onto a table.

—I'm looking for monasteries, Zoe says.

The librarian glances up.

—Excuse me, Zoe says: I'm driving through and I saw that you were open.

—Any particular type of monk? the librarian asks: Trappist? Carthusian? Franciscan?

—Monks in Vermont, Zoe says.

The librarian fingers an earring, then asks if Zoe is headed north.

Zoe shrugs. How many directions are there from this corner of Vermont?

Well, then, if she stays on old Route 7, the librarian tells her, she'll see windmills on top of Equinox. Some monasteries make jams or liqueurs, they garden and bind books, but the monks on Equinox had experimented with wind farming. The librarian frowns. The scheme had fallen through, though she can't remember why. But the windmills are still there and they will show Zoe which mountain is inhabited by the monks.

—But I need a list of all of them, Zoe says: All the monasteries in the state.

—Suzette, the librarian says to the young woman at the computer: Can you help with this?

—There's Weston, Suzette says, more to the screen than to anyone: And somewhere there's a new Buddhist one, isn't there?

—Just Catholic ones, Zoe says.

The librarian rubs her arms, leads Zoe to a small reference section, finds only a listing for a priory in Weston, which apparently the two women know about already. Then she digs out a volume on havens for spiritual pilgrims.

I don't want to retreat, Zoe thinks automatically.

Then wonders.

She scans the entry for the Weston Priory, and for another monastery up north, then hesitates, bewildered.

—Why does this monastery have women? she says: Women are nuns, not monks, aren't they?

The librarian puzzles, too, then says that, if she remembers correctly, any contemplative person, man or woman, can be called a monk. A nun lives in a convent, and would be something like a teacher or a social worker.

—You should double-check that, she adds: If it's important.

—But the ones on Equinox?

The librarian is searching out another book.

—Oh, they're men, she says: Although I don't know how they get up there, and I've lived here for thirty years. In the winter, the road is closed.

—Call Father, Suzette says. Then she turns to Zoe: I'd let you use this, but I'm doing a course online.

Zoe smiles weakly, as if looking back a mere half-year at her own driven self.

The librarian hands Zoe another book, and she glances through it, then stops, riveted by a young man's account of entering a Carthusian monastery, of being, as he called it, "buried alive."

Vaguely, she's aware of the librarian dialing the phone, then finally speaking:

—Father, she says, glancing at her watch: I wondered if I might send someone along for information. That is, if you're finished with confessions?

That kind of father, Zoe thinks, unnerved. All at once she believes the old superstition that a Catholic priest might look into her soul and see the seven sins and more.

The church is just a little way north on the other side of the road. Zoe considers reconnoitering first, walking past it, but there are no sidewalks. She smiles grimly at her apprehension. How her mother had hated Catholics, the Saint Barbara medal her father wore into the mines that didn't save his life, the fierce way she'd fought off the priest who had wanted Zoe to go to the parish school, since surely her father would have wished it. Even at the public school, little Catholic girls on the playground threatened their peers with mortal sins and eternity in hellfire.

Zoe enters at the main door, finds herself at the back of the sanctuary. The altar and crucifix rise, softly lit, at the far end. A handful of votives flicker at the feet of the Virgin. Zoe guesses that the office is somewhere in the rear, and she is just turning to search for another entrance when a quiet voice calls from near the altar.

Slowly she faces the altar, then startles.

A broad-shouldered man in a black coat and clerical collar raises a hand in greeting. His skin is dark black, his palm a vulnerable pink. He comes toward her down the side aisle, then stops, bows slightly.

—You are from the library?

Although the light in the nave is soft and easy, Zoe covers her eyes. She is wobbly, disoriented. What's a black priest with a big square body and a lilting voice doing here in the land of mud and maple syrup? The back of her neck turns cold, and she fiddles with her turtleneck.

—I'm not a Catholic, she announces.

The priest inclines his head.

—Mrs. Watersen felt I might assist. Please, he says: If you will. . . .

Zoe follows him along the side aisle, stands wooden and remote as he crosses himself on the way out of the sanctuary.

The office is a simple room with dingy green furniture and an even darker green carpet, scuffed and worn. The desks are heavy old wooden things with mismatched chairs, and against one wall stands a rank of battered tan and gray filing cabinets. On the walls are photographs and, of course, a crucifix. In the air hangs the scent of old cigarette smoke and carpet cleaner.

They sit, and Zoe tells a vague version of the truth. She must find her close friend, because his father has died. And she's just learned that the friend has entered a monastery in Vermont. A Catholic one.

She pauses. Church roofs don't cave in on liars anymore; it's the end of the twentieth century.

Besides, Dayton had been her friend.

The priest sits upright near the edge of his chair. He unbuttons his jacket, lays an open palm on the desk, as if waiting for more.

—I am from Mozambique, he says at last: A missionary.

Zoe can't help but grin.

—I didn't think you grew up here, but why send you to Vermont?

—The parish priest passed on. Where I am sent, I go. Tell me, he says quietly: How does one lose one's friend?

Zoe sets her jaw.

—Hard to explain, she says at last.

He reaches up, runs his finger like a knifepoint from beneath his ear and down across his harsh white collar.

—You have been in the clinic?

She hesitates, nods.

—Your wound is still new, he says.

She nods again.

His eyes narrow. He says nothing, waits for her to speak, then finally glances at the battered file cabinets.

—The Kennedy Directory will inform us.

Delicately, he licks his thumb, pages through a folder, then hands a single sheet of closely printed text across the desk.

The heading reads: *Monasteries and Residences of Priests and Brothers.*

The Brothers of the Sacred Heart in Burlington head the list.

Then come the Carthusians. She runs a finger through the entry.

—Are the Carthusians in Arlington the same as the ones on Mount Equinox?

He nods.

—They live in silence and prayer, and devote their lives to bringing God closer to the world. A life more to be respected than understood.

What was the expression? Buried alive?

—Would he even be able to see me? she says.

—At times.

Zoe glances up sharply, then returns to the directory, on the lookout for him elsewhere.

The next listing is the Society of Saint Edmund in Colchester, and the same society again at Saint Michael's College. Beyond that only one remains, the Priory of Benedictine Monks in Weston, which the librarian has already mentioned.

Zoe schemes: Vermont is a state that runs up and down, so perhaps the most logical thing is to head north, take them in order. But what if she does drive up to the gate of each place? What then?

The priest glances at the clock, shifts in his chair.

—I'm keeping you, she says.

—No, no. I'd like to offer further assistance. Perhaps tea to begin? Or coffee? A soft drink?

—Anything, Zoe says: I'm lost.

He smiles, slow and sage. Then he leaves the room, and from an adjoining kitchen comes the surprising racket of a coffee grinder.

Zoe digs in her bag, then realizes she can't swallow a dusty pill without water. She holds the bottle in her hand, as remote as a cigarette when you have no match, and sits looking out into the gloom of the midmorning, wishing at least for sunlight if not warmer temperatures.

In time, the priest comes back with mugs of coffee and a sugar bowl. He asks if she would care for milk.

She shakes her head, fails to hide the pill bottle in her fist.

He looks at the medication.

—For your wound?

Zoe's face freezes.

—Yes, she says finally.

Without a word, he leaves again, returns with a glass of water. He lays his hand on her shoulder and leaves it there until, embarrassed, she gulps some water and the pill.

Back on his side of the desk, the priest, with great deliberation, drops cube after cube of sugar into his coffee. He stirs it contentedly, a small child in anticipation of a treat, then reaches across the desk, his sweet palm up and open.

—Allow me.

Zoe hands over the list. The priest scans it.

—And what was his name?

—*Is* his name, Zoe corrects: His name is Dayton Reed.

He writes it down. His handwriting is stately.

—Now then, he says, and turns the list just so, picks up the phone and dials.

Zoe stares. How precipitous. Just seven or eight calls, and she will know. What if they patch him through, summon him from the chapel or his cell? She closes her eyes, breathes deep, tries to help the medication.

The priest introduces himself:

—I have a young woman here.

Zoe smiles. He sounds like an elegant kidnapper.

—She is searching for her friend, and the friend is in one of our monasteries. His name is. . . .

Zoe feels sick. Somehow this has all become too real, too official, and all at once she remembers filling out the police reports after she was slashed, how the typed words and her signature made the attack something she could not deny, irrefutable.

—There has been a death among the family, the priest murmurs.

He pauses, listens, then says thank you.

—Unfortunate, he tells Zoe: I hoped he might be close by.

Zoe nearly weeps.

—You mean he's not a Carthusian?

—Regrettably, no.

Zoe's hands shake. She sets her coffee on the desk.

The priest makes another call and another, and soon Zoe feels that this is how life will be. She'll just sit here forever, with the priest murmuring Dayton's name into the phone. She reaches up, gently rubs her neck.

Finally the priest stops, swivels his chair, then scans the directory again.

—There remains a possibility, he says: But I hesitate.

The priest finishes his coffee. Zoe wonders if all that sugar makes his teeth ache. Finally, he says:

—The archbishop's office might assist.

At last, he looks up a number, dials, then stands, walks the phone away from Zoe so that all she hears is musical murmuring. His back is straight, and from time to time she sees him nod. When he sits back down, he tilts his chair back a moment, then sits erect, nearly presidential.

—You found something out, Zoe says at last.

—He's at Shroveton Skete.

—Shroveton Skete? I thought he was in a monastery. I don't even know what a skete is.

The priest doesn't respond. He closes his eyes, in time says:

—Shroveton is a source of much controversy.

Zoe remembers the housekeeper's remark about Dayton's father.

—It was back home, too, apparently. Or at least heartbreak.

The priest tilts his head, studies her.

—I promised you would write first, he says.

She nods. She'll agree to anything. What's an archbishop to her?

The priest writes out an address: Shroveton Skete, Shroveton, Vermont.

—Go home and write, he says: Your friend needs no more trouble. He and his companions have enough of their own making. The whole group of them. No abbot. No prior. Just five Catholic men and what strife. The letters among the clergy! Are they really monks? Can you follow Saint Benedict in such a way? More like Anthony. Or Pachomius.

Looking troubled and upset, he folds his hands around his empty cup.

—So, is that a skete? Zoe wants to know: That's it? No abbot?

The priest hesitates, shakes his head, mournful.

—They borrow the word from the East, from the orthodox, whose hermits sometimes lived near to one another for protection and support. Even so, a true skete has an abbot, a fatherly presence. But these men in Shroveton?

He exhales, makes a dismissive gesture:

—They refuse, claim they've offered their vows only to God, not to the Bishop. They govern themselves, according to the Rule of Benedict, but refuse to join the order. It's quite true that in those first centuries nothing stood between the hermit and his god. Some say the brothers at Shroveton are renegades, little more than a commune run by Catholics.

Zoe puzzles:

—So, is he a monk or not?

The priest smiles.

—I'm sure he believes he is.

—But is that enough?

He smiles again, entirely enigmatic.

—Your friend either takes us back to the old days. Or he is misguided entirely.

The priest walks her out to the altar, lays his hand on her forearm, then abruptly asks her to wait.

Votives flicker in their ruby glasses. The Virgin Mary wears robes of the bluest blue, and Zoe wonders why she is always dressed in this same color.

The priest returns with a small vial.

—Oil which has been blessed, he says.

Zoe holds out her hand, as if he is offering a souvenir.

He shakes his head, opens the vial, and when Zoe sees his hand come up, she shrinks away.

—For healing, the priest murmurs.

—I'm not a Catholic, Zoe says, unnerved.

The priest smiles:

—It won't hurt you.

CHAPTER 5

Zoe resumes driving north on old Route 7. After she crosses into Arlington, she pauses often, fearing she's missed the windmills, distracted as she is by country stores, roadhouses, signs for Norman Rockwell galleries. And by the touch of the priest on her forehead. But there, north of town, high on the uneven shoulders of Mount Equinox, are three tall shafts with picture-perfect windmill blades. She pulls off the road.

From this distance, the windmills resemble delicate, lopsided crosses, and Zoe cranks down her window. Cold air eddies in. She shivers, tries to conjure monks on that mountaintop this very minute, struggling to bring God closer to the world. Do remnants of sanctity and peace fall to the people at the draping hems of the mountain?

Then she can't remember. Do the monks seek to bring God closer to the world? Or the world closer to God?

She looks in the rearview mirror, searches for something revelatory, supernatural on her forehead.

Nothing.

Later, she coasts by the foot of Bromley Mountain, and the skiers are bright-jacketed dots zigzagging the slopes. In her younger years, she might have sketched them, tried to capture the play of color, but in the end she'd heeded her mother's injunction for practicality and had majored in art education. But two years of teaching art to the disinterested had been enough and, still opting for practicality, she'd begun a master's in special education. After what turned out to be the final night with Dayton, she'd landed the job in Rhode Island, working with college kids burdened by the quirky hardwiring of learning disabilities.

She goes on to Londonderry, ignores the outlet barns, turns north toward Weston.

The Rhode Island salary was so-so, but she'd scrounged loans and grants, had earned a doctorate in organizational dysfunction, had stayed long enough in education to hear nouns like *conference* and *partner* turned into verbs, heard students artificially transformed into *customers* and *learners*.

She passes toy stores, fudge shops, quilt and photo galleries. Perhaps Zeke is right about her taking a year off. She can live on the money from her slasher. Or rather her slasher's wealthy parents. But until the very minute she'd bolted out of Barstow Tuesday afternoon, she'd been unable to think of a single thing to do, or place to go.

In the center of Weston stands the barn-red Vermont Country Store, and a village green with gazebo. She parks, goes into a lunch place, opts for a sandwich made of Vermont cheddar and industrial-strength California tomatoes.

At the register, she asks about the Weston Priory.

For one mind-twisting moment, she tries to recall what her life was like a mere three days ago.

The clerk is a middle-aged woman with graying hair and heavy arms. She points sourly at a sign:

HOW TO GET TO THE WESTON PRIORY

Zoe is embarrassed.
—So, you get that question a lot?
—Worse in summer.
—Do a lot of people visit there?
The woman puts Zoe's drink and sandwich in a bag.
—I wouldn't know.
Zoe nods.
—How far to Shroveton, do you think?

The woman points again.

—We have maps.

Amused, Zoe leaves. Would the woman be happier with no tourists and no income? Or would she miss having a fresh crop of people to crab at every day?

Zoe eats and drives, following the road to Rutland, then Montpelier, then veering northeast. There are no direct routes, and the roads are ribbons curling among the mountains, along the rivers. As the afternoon wears on, the sun comes out, weak but evident, and she's considerably cheered.

Dayton is in Shroveton, and Shroveton is somewhere up ahead.

God's in his heaven, she thinks.

How does that go?

Above gritty walls of snow thrown up by plows, purple and green tubing drapes from tree to tree. After a while, she realizes these are for collecting maple sap. The era of buckets must be gone, the lovely pictures on maple syrup cans in gourmet shops now wholly a lie. No more draft horses, no more men in wool plaid.

Well, maybe the wool plaids are still left. She thinks she saw some in Bennington.

Along the road, the towns are gatherings of diners, gas pumps, and stores, lumber yards, gift shops, grange halls, and farms. Eventually she reaches Benton. Shroveton will be next.

Now what?

The hypnotic calm of driving abruptly vanishes. She crosses into Shroveton, restless in her seat.

Maintenance sheds mark the entry into Shroveton Center. Two trucks, with high sharp plow blades, are parked facing the road. The rest of town lies along a straight, narrow river plain.

She pulls in at the store, zips her jacket collar up to her chin. Soon the light will drain from the sky, and a raw breeze blows. Chill and shuddering, Zoe thinks Shroveton an utterly remote and godforsaken place.

Inside, she is circumspect. Behind the deli counter, a woman in a white apron asks if she needs a sandwich? Soup? Something from the case? Zoe declines, pumps a cup of Green Mountain coffee from a stainless-steel cylinder, and wonders when coffee became a part of Northeast agriculture. When she thought of Vermont, she thought of cheese, ham, syrup, and especially good pot. Not hazelnut decaf.

At the register, a young woman perches on a stool, going through a pile of invoices. She has red hair, spiky on top, long in back, and she's wearing so much makeup Zoe is surprised it's not against the law here.

—Look at you, she says to Zoe: You'd think it was cold out.

Zoe shivers, jokes:

—I should be used to this. I'm from Rhode Island.

The girl circles something on her paperwork.

—Oh, she says dryly: Do they have winter there?

—Some, Zoe says and laughs.

—We need the cold. If it doesn't freeze nights, the run stops.

—Pardon?

—Sap, the girl says: For syrup? It has to freeze.

—Oh.

All the while, Zoe is looking for a sign that gives directions to the monastery. Instead a hand-made poster announces *Shroveton's Pretty Good Grocery.* A hand-lettered sign announces that orders are being taken for case-lots of citrus fruit, and a variety of towns-people offer baby-sitting, computer help, roof clearing, custom slaughtering, and dance classes. A curling photograph shows the winner of last year's deer pool—the lucky fellow who brought down the largest buck and therefore pocketed the bets of all the hunters. Apparently another pool is starting up—this one to guess the exact date of ice-out on Shroveton pond, benefit to the rescue squad.

—I'll be with you in a minute, the clerk says: I have to get some totals off this machine.

While waiting, Zoe reads a notice headed: *Dream For Sale.* Then sees that someone has crossed out *Dream* and written in *Foolishness.* There's a photo of a curious unfinished house. Tidy, it has a metal roof, a wraparound porch and a third-story tower, like a Rhode Island crow's nest. Closed in, the advertisement reads.

Ready to finish. State-tested spring. Stream. Mixed hard and soft wood forest. South slope. Four hundred ninety acres. Off grid. Morning Hill Ridge.

The phone number has what looks like a Connecticut area code.

And a price.

Idly, Zoe thinks:

I could actually afford that.

The clerk rings up Zoe's coffee.

—Anything else?

Zoe hesitates, remembers the nastiness of the woman down in Weston.

—I'm sorry to have to ask, she says: But can you tell me where the monastery is?

The girl looks surprised.

—I thought it was closed. We haven't seen anyone in a while.

Zoe feels a wash of panic. You can't just close a monastery, can you?

The girl leans dramatically backward on her stool, her red hair swishes. She calls to someone coming down the aisle.

—Mrs. R., is the monastery closed?

—I'm waiting for those totals, the woman says.

She's carrying a large zippered bank bag.

—Are you expected? she asks Zoe.

In her late forties or early fifties, she has a sharp straight hair-cut, a deeply tanned and wrinkled face.

—A priest called ahead for me, Zoe says.

The redheaded clerk pipes up:

—But you're not one of them.

She giggles.

Zoe sips her coffee, frowns.

—Do they ever come to town?

—Do they ever, says the girl: Brother Luke is a total knockout.

She makes a show of fanning her face, then says:

—And Brother Dayton's not bad either, except for being kind of old.

Zoe's breath catches.

—What a waste, the girl says, camping it up with a dramatic sigh: We're kind of short on men around here.

—Unity, Mrs. R. says: That's probably enough.

Unity pouts, turns impish.

—Come on. You have to admit that Luke is gorgeous.

The girl's boss suppresses a smile.

—Luke is their cellarer, she tells Zoe: He does the shopping for them, runs their errands. And they all turn out for town meeting, sometimes for other things.

Zoe asks when town meeting is.

—Early March. Just a few weeks back. Personally, I think they're good neighbors. All the fuss doesn't make any sense.

Zoe asks again for directions, and Mrs. R. points through the plate-glass window. Zoe is to go back the way she came, turn onto North Branch Road, then after a couple, three, five miles, there'll be a sign. She catches sight of Zoe's car.

—Is that yours? You might make it, though four-wheel would be better.

Outside, Zoe sits a moment, looking at the clapboard town hall across the way. Dayton has been here not so long ago, casting his vote for who-knows-what. That hardly sounds as if he's buried alive.

She drives back along the state highway, turns onto North Branch Road, and climbs the first hill. The pavement is clear. So why the remark about four-wheel drive? She frets a moment, then reminds herself that she's slogged through plenty of hellacious weather on the Rhode Island coast.

The day is graying, but there will be light for a while longer. Zoe pats the dashboard. Just get me to the gate, she thinks.

Then what?

—God will provide, she says out loud, and finds that she is giggling.

It's an unfamiliar, almost eerie sound. She leans forward, looks at herself in her three-day-old clothes and shaggy hair, and knows she's no competition for the Virgin Mary. Giddily, she bats her eyes, wonders what in hell she's doing here.

Abruptly, she scrubs her forehead with her fist, and finds herself hating Catholics, Dayton, God too, just in case he exists.

The pavement changes, and the road is suddenly full of potholes the size of trash-can lids. She rides the brakes, creeps along, aiming the front end of her car in and among the pits. Soon a big red Blazer is crowding her back bumper, and when Zoe pulls off to the side, the Blazer roars past, weaving among the potholes with speed and precision.

A native.

She resumes her trip. The houses are a mixed lot, some bunched on smallish parcels, others scattered with great distances among them. Trailers with catwalk porches or neat, capped roofs stand this way and that. Large houses sheathed in clapboard with color-coordinated shutters are built foursquare to the road, and chalets point their steep roofs up through the evergreens. Every now and again an old stone house appears among the trees.

The road climbs. Snow lies deep among the trees, and alongside the road, a brook rushes over rocks and lunges through melting channels of ice. The North Branch of what? An old mill stands beside it, the long low building, the old wheel housing, and what looks to be the old pond and race.

Farther up is an antique schoolhouse. A raffish bell tower perches on top. The walls are stone, huge chunks of rock mixed with smaller pieces, built out from bottom to top so that the foundation is narrower than roof line. Zoe wishes she could recall the reason.

Form follows function?

But follows, too, the limitation of material.

Suddenly, on the right, a lane angles off into the woods. A small neat sign hangs from a post: *Shroveton Skete*.

Zoe is wryly disappointed. Why not a cross gouged into a tree? A chalice carved into a rock?

The lane runs along a ridge. Bare majestic trees line the edges: sugar maples, each neatly tapped with green plastic spouts and purple tubing. The car slews around a bend. Zoe brakes. A wide white gate blocks her way. Trembling, she hangs hard onto the top of the steering wheel.

Down below lies a long lovely pocket of a valley. No houses in view, no road, only woods in gray and green and open rolling land, muffled in white. The late afternoon shadows are turquoise, the light pearl-gray, luminescent, the mountains soft-shouldered and secretive.

—Well, Dayton.

It's as if she's found his hiding place in a children's game.

She gets out.

A neat chain and padlock tether the gate to the post. A small notice, sheathed in plastic wrap, states:

Shroveton Skete. On retreat until Palm Sunday.

On retreat from what?

Just living here, she thinks, ought to be retreat enough.

Suddenly exhausted, she leans her elbows on the gate, and stares down into the skete. The lane turns quickly and although she steps back and forth, she can't so much as glimpse a building. Above the trees, though, wafts the heavy white smoke and steam of a sugarhouse.

She brings her palms up to her cheeks, ruffles her hair, then pulls the collar of her turtleneck down to her collar bones, zaps her scars with frigid air, scours them with cold. The woods breathe around her, pines, balsams, birches. The half-circles of bare earth around their roots smell raw and full of rot and humus. She likes it here, feels an unusual calm. Dayton is nearby but she doesn't have to see him, couldn't see him even if she were ready.

She closes her eyes. Proximity is plenty. And she thinks not of Dayton but of the simple joys of summer camp, cooking eggs over homemade canisters of wax and corrugated cardboard, swinging a hatchet and splitting kindling, the heat on her face near the fire in the evening. She'd been good with a pocketknife, she recalls, adept at lashing stools and tables out of twine and saplings, had loved the tease of following a map and compass.

She smiles, sees Dayton as a child, camping out with God.

Somewhere down below, a bell rings, eddies in the trees.

What does it announce to Dayton? What prayers or chores does it call him to? And what he would do if he knew she were up here, clinging to his gate?

She straightens, surveys the lane, the trees, a late blue jay on a branch, the coming dark. Full of mischief, she suddenly knows what's next exactly.

CHAPTER 6

Zeke is adamantly opposed. Reckless, he says: Impulsive. Perhaps even dangerous.

—You're the one who suggested it, Zoe counters, half-flirtatious, mysteriously come back to life.

—I suggested you call Dave, he retorts: Because it seemed to me you hadn't let go of him.

—Dayton, she corrects, calm and sweet: And you were right. I haven't let go of him.

—But Zoe, he says, eyes narrow: This is. . . .

She knows he's upset; usually he avoids the use of her first name.

—Are you saying that I'm crazy?

He rocks forward, lets his chair fall to its casters with a muffled thump.

—Precipitous.

She smiles, securely out of his therapeutic reach.

—Correct me if I'm wrong, but wasn't it you who kept saying I needed to make a new life?

In the end, they talk logistics. He suggests she keep her apartment, put her things in storage.

To Zoe, he's suddenly very young, almost frightened, and she doesn't tell him that she's given notice on her lease, and that she'll fill the car with what she might need and sell the rest.

He writes a new prescription for Xanax, but warns her it will only last so long. Then he plucks a card from his drawer, writes on it every phone number he has, private line, home phone, pager, cell phone.

Zoe stands. Her time is over. Zeke remains seated, looking
up at her a long while. Worriedly, he shakes his head, gets to his
feet, says:
—I always thought you were remarkable.
—Crazy as a loon, more like.
He holds out a hand, wishes her luck, and as she's going out
the door reminds her to call.
—I'm sure they must have phones there.

In fact, there is no phone. No running water, no electricity either.
Only plywood flooring, untaped Sheetrock, a padlock on the front
door, a little wood scattered in the shed. There is an outhouse
though, and 493 acres, plus or minus. She has great affection for
the plus or minus, learns that all north country deeds include
this caveat, since surveying up and down and across the sides of
mountains has a distinct inherent inaccuracy. She's buying herself a forest, a small clearing, and a structure that can't quite be
called a house. It's a shell, weatherproofed, with a rubble trench,
concrete-block foundation, a standing seam roof, plywood sheath-
ing. There are windows though, a whole bank of them on the
south wall, and doors, insulation, a gas range and gas refrigerator,
a woodstove and an ocean-blue ceramic tile hearth. And for
amenities, that's it.

The realtor called it a camp, tried to interest Zoe in something
more civilized, a cottage or chalet, but if Zoe has one reason for
buying this particular place, she has twenty.

She thinks she'll like the solitude, although she guesses what
she really wants is the absence of other people's feelings.

She has the money, and she figures a project will be good for
her. The people before her sank every dime into it, every free
hour and free weekend, until it killed their marriage. But Zoe
thinks she can indulge her old interest in architecture, thinks
she understands the logic of the floor plan, mutters to herself
about primary space, secondary space. She will be one of those
latter-twentieth-century architects who lives onsite, learns the
place and its rhythms, and then she will redesign as needed, add

her own stamp. Before she buys the place, she stands alone on the porch and imagines a little architectural gem looming at her back.

And then there's this: she's twelve-point-two miles from Dayton's gate.

Plus or minus.

The closing turns a little tense. Zoe herself has inspected the house as best she can, but she wastes no money on an engineer since she plans to become one herself. She simply shows up at the appointed time with a cashier's check and an attorney recommended by a local bank.

The attorney says it's the second large tract to be sold like this in the last few years.

—Like what? Zoe says.

Sarah Michaels, nearly divorced, up from Connecticut, shifts uneasily. She has a simple and beautiful face, and fine dark hair pulled back from her face. She wears an elegant navy trouser suit, and Zoe can't imagine her using an outhouse, swinging a hammer.

—An out-of-stater with a checkbook, her attorney says, his words clipped.

Zoe smiles, icy.

Sarah Michaels takes a deep breath, releases it.

The realtor, a slightly plump woman in a tan corduroy blazer, muses that that's real estate for you:

—Whoever gets there first with cash in hand.

Again Zoe hears that a Burlington group had been hoping to build some fine, discreet homes. The forests would have been held in common, the old logging roads restored as walking and skiing trails.

—It would have been good for the town, the realtor sighs, straightening a ring on her finger: For the tax base and the builders.

Then she pats Zoe's wrist:

—Not that you won't be a good neighbor, too.

Zoe keeps her face still. She has no plans to be anyone's neighbor. She plans to hunker down in the middle of her acres, keep a low profile, mind her own business.

—We're glad it's you, Sarah Michaels says.

Zoe guesses this is true. The developers were just beginning the process of permits and hearings.

The Michaelses' attorney holds his papers loosely, taps them on the table, scowls.

—Other folks had ideas, too. People right here in town.

He gives Sarah Michaels a look:

—But you didn't give them time, either.

She looks a little frightened.

The realtor reaches over, touches the table in front of Sarah, tells her not to mind:

—Oh, it's plenty easy to talk about buying. Most people never follow through.

Finally, at dusk, Zoe sits in the main room of the unfinished house. A kerosene lamp smokes on the kitchen counter, and another in a wall bracket next to the stairs that spiral up to the second floor. She's been left with thirty pages of directions for the woodstove. The damper is easy enough to locate, but is it open or closed? Perhaps the best solution is to pull the bottom from the chimney pipe, shine a flashlight in there and have a look. But the footcap is stubborn, won't twist or jiggle off, and finally Zoe raps it with the heel of her boot. It clatters to the floor, and ash and soot cascade down onto her feet and billow up in a mushroom cloud of oily fine particulate.

Cold and tired, Zoe glares at her black boots, at the atomic ash drifting on the air, and knows if she carried some water from the spring, she could scrub the hearth, but she doesn't have a bucket, never mind a brush, and she would add these to her list of things to buy, but she can't recall right this minute where to find the goddamn pen.

She looks at her watch. Not yet six. The whole evening ranges ahead of her, and abruptly she experiences time, unmeasured by

radio, phone, friends, obligations, even music, as going on forever, and yet not moving, soothing and crazy-making all at once.

Eventually, she sweeps up the heaviest of what fell from the
chimney, wipes her face on her jacket sleeve, coughs, then realizes she's covered. What's more, the bristles of the lopsided broom
have left greasy tracks across the tile hearth.

Okay, she thinks, inhaling, holding her breath. She walks to
the bank of southern windows and looks out. Snow lies in patches
among the trees and hummocks, and it's so cold in the house the
walls feel icy. On a windowsill stands a small plaster image of
Saint Barbara. In the consignment shop where Zoe took her
teaching clothes and household things, even her briefcase, she
found the little saint standing near the register, and had picked
her up.

The consignment-shop owner looked up from cataloguing
Zoe's items.

—That's Saint Barbara.

Zoe looked the plaster saint in the eye.

—My father wore her around his neck. She didn't save his life.

—Sometimes, the woman said: Her job is to bring a good
death.

—Goodness, Zoe said: Then I should take her with me.

A moment longer, she regards the saint, and the delicate reflection she casts on the darkening glass. I wonder who's in charge
of chimneys, Zoe mutters, then kneels and shines the flashlight
up into the stovepipe.

There's the flue all right, open, the flat disk vertical in the
stack. She hammers the footcap back on, and page-by-page works
her way through the directions, opening baffles, air vents, shovel-
ing ash from the firebox.

But actually starting a fire eludes her. She scours the car,
crumples up old paper napkins and cardboard coffee cups,
scrounges oil-change receipts and shopping lists that have slipped
under the driver's seat. But the logs in the shed are far too big,
and she has no way to split them.

In the end, she gives up, stands over the kitchen sink and

splashes water from a bottle on her face. The leftovers thunder through the drain into a small trash barrel, standing in the cupboard below. There is no other plumbing. With a jackknife blade, she scrapes black grit from under her nails, then in the freezing cold drags her sleeping bag up into the balconied bedroom to the mattress and box spring the Michaelses left behind.

Next morning, light pours in through the acre of glass on the south wall and illuminates the layer of black ash on everything from the kitchen table and chair pushed against the south windows to the scarred top of the secondhand range, the fine granite countertop. Zoe rinses her face and arms, all at once sees what the Michaelses were up to. Anything permanent is absolutely top quality; anything temporary looks as if it has been dragged home from the dump.

Deciding it's pointless to put clean clothes on a filthy body, she heads down to the village.

A pay phone hangs outside the store, and Zoe goes inside to borrow a directory.

The young redheaded clerk is sorting receipts behind the counter. Today she wears a cropped turtleneck over her jeans; two wildly mismatched earrings dangle nearly to her shoulders. She gives Zoe a bemused look.

—Ask me, she says: I know half the numbers in town.

—How many are there? Zoe says, laughing: Fifteen?

The redhead laughs, too.

Zoe says she needs to call around and get a price on propane.

—You're not really going to live up there?

Zoe shrugs, and the girl hands over a directory the size of a second-grader's spelling book, says:

—There's only one propane place.

Actually there are two, but the first one Zoe calls is the company who supplied the Michaelses, and Zoe is taken aback when the female dispatcher assumes Zoe would like the driver to go on into the house and light the pilots.

Zoe asks what day and time that might be, and is stunned to hear the driver has a key. He'll just let himself in, that is, of course, if Zoe doesn't mind.

Zoe doesn't know if she minds or not, thinks she just might buy herself a new lock.

Back inside the store, she returns the directory, asks the red-head where to find a good bookstore.

—Oh, says the clerk, half-mocking: A *good* one? Hanover, Burlington, Montpelier.

—My god, Zoe says: They're what? Sixty miles?

The girl smiles, smug, dismissive.

—Life in the north country. Get used to it.

Outside, Zoe wonders. She's been up for hours already, light pours early through that half-acre of glass, and given the unending nature of the day before, she figures she can get to a bookstore and still have a good chunk of the day left.

On pure whim, she heads southeast to Hanover, easily finds her way, finds, too, that she hasn't lost her faith in books, in printed information, knowledge, history, insight, the feel of pages turning in her hands. She wanders all three floors, room to room, from one half-level to another, stocking up as if for the end of time.

She gathers books on woodstoves, solar power, alternative plumbing, finding out right there and then there is such a thing. Avoiding the psychology section like the plague, she strikes it rich among the building shelves, finds texts on house design, framing, and do-it-yourself engineering. A clerk recommends Willis Wagner's *Modern Carpentry,* tells her with the wistfulness of a would-be builder:

—Look, all the nailing patterns you'll ever need. And roofs. And decks. And everything.

At the register, when she sees the total, her vision muddies. Privately she recites the sum of her settlement, thinks $400 won't bankrupt her yet, and both fears and relishes her recklessness.

Abruptly she wonders what she would be doing if Dayton had moved, say, to Portugal or Bali.

Leaving the books in the car, she goes to a café for lunch, sees it's not eleven yet, orders only coffee and biscotti. In the rest room, against a backdrop of blistering white tile and chrome fixtures, Zoe, in shaken-out but dirty clothes, black soot in the fine pores of her skin, looks like a homeless woman.

She scrubs her face, sloshing around what seems an astonishing amount of hot water. By the time she finishes, two women wait impatiently outside, one a college girl with perfect skin.

Zoe drinks her coffee, smiles idiotically. She's a world away from homesteading, from monasteries, too. All around her sit professors grading papers, conferring with students. Friends share a morning break, students labor over laptops. Zoe watches, eavesdrops, both smug and full of sorrow.

Midafternoon, back in Shroveton, she makes her inaugural run to the building-supply and hardware. She parks in front of the wide wood porch, stairs in front, loading dock off to the side. Someone obviously suffers confusion over apostrophes. On various signs and notices, it's parsed three ways: *Rileys, Riley's, Rileys'.*

She hopes they're more knowledgeable about hardware.

The heavy plank porch thunders beneath her boot heels. Zoe stops in surprise. She's been geared up to meet old men without teeth, young laconic men with names like Bud and Mack, even square-built farm women or the occasional hermit come to town for a seasonal stocking-up trip. But she's not ready for the redhead from the general store, unpacking bread-making machines, displaying them with other kitchen gear.

—Back already? she asks Zoe.

—You work here, too, Zoe says.

The girl laughs.

—I'm everywhere, she says, eyeing the display, moving a coffee-maker an inch or two to the left: My brother manages this place.

—And the general store?

—They try to keep me out of trouble. I'm Unity Everett.

Zoe fidgets with her coat collar, gets down to business:

—I need a hatchet, an ax, a chimney brush. Some other stuff.

Unity twists her neck, tries to read Zoe's list.

—Might be late in the year for a chimney brush. What size you after?

Zoe makes a circle with her hands, approximates the diameter.

Unity shakes her head.

—It needs to be exact. I'll get Callum. Might be he remembers what they put in up there.

She hits a buzzer, two quick blips.

Zoe stares, marvels:

—You really know where I live.

Unity smirks.

—Sure. The hippie place.

Zoe remembers Sarah Michaels in her wool trouser suit, says she doubts it.

—You know what I mean, Unity says: Homesteaders. Airheads. Come to live the clean pure life.

Her mimicry is vicious and precise, and even Zoe laughs.

Unity turns cool.

—You sure pissed off a lot of people.

Zoe gives her a level look, says in an utterly flat voice:

—Tell them I'm sorry.

She catches sight of someone making the long trip from out back. Definitely related to Unity, same color hair, some years older, and while Unity is thin and angular, shorter, round beneath his belt.

He holds out his hand to Zoe, tells her he's happy to meet her.

—I need a chimney brush, Zoe says.

She didn't come here for the Welcome Wagon.

Callum nods.

—Only she doesn't have the specs, Unity announces, as if Zoe has sat down to play poker without cards.

—I can go up and look, Zoe offers, annoyed at the airing of her ignorance, but Callum goes behind the counter, taps at a keyboard, mutters:

—As I thought. Plain stovepipe, with collars through the floors and roof.

He suggests Zoe rip it out and change it to Metalbestos.

—Metalbestos?

She may have bought all those books, but she's only had time to skim the wood-heat section in one of them.

He quotes the price per foot, and right there and then Zoe realizes that anyone who thinks it's cheap to live in the woods is sadly mistaken.

—No, she says: I mean what is it?

—Insulated. We're pushing for it on the fire squad.

Zoe sighs. How in hell do you replace a chimney?

—Right now, she says: I just need to split some wood and build a fire tonight.

—She's in, Unity announces: Can you believe it?

—You and Spark will have to walk up, Callum says. To Zoe, he adds:

—My uncle lives in the yellow house above the meadow. Unity's there, too, for a while.

He punches his sister's shoulder, lightly, and her face turns dark red.

—You're the one that screwed up, he says, as if she has offered up some protest.

—Only once.

Callum teases:

—Only once he caught you, more like. He's the constable, he adds to Zoe: His own niece, the wildest kid in town.

—Not exactly, the girl mutters.

Zoe feels bad for her, embarrassed like this in front of a stranger. By habit she mentally begins drafting a memo of need, confidential of course, in this case warning Callum of the danger of letting a girl that age build up her grudges.

Unity stalks out toward the back and slams a door.

—She needs to learn to think, Callum says, sliding a ladder along the wall: Before she jumps in with both feet.

—Most people do, Zoe says dryly.

He gives her a curious look, then climbs up and hands down a cardboard box:

—Rods, too?

She says she's read that she can pull it through with a rope.

He comes down the ladder, slits open the box, and lifts out what looks like a metal porcupine with bristles at attention all the way around. On one end are threads for screws; on the other a metal eye.

—Sure, he says: But it'll be tight. That's how it clears the chimney.

Zoe nods, hopes that all this foreignness, this minutia, will forever clog her flashback channel. Of course, in the next moment her hands turn numb and she is squinting in the light. She swears under her breath, leans on the counter, puts her head down.

—Migraine? Callum says.

Laughter erupts somewhere in the back of the store. Unity and someone else. Zoe shakes her head, wishes they'd keep it down.

—I need an ax, she manages to say, reading her list: And a hatchet, an ash bucket, and some other things, like basic tools.

Callum presses the intercom, three blasts. Each reverberates up Zoe's spine, sets her molars vibrating.

A young man in faded skintight jeans, a tan khaki work shirt, and surprisingly neat hair, given the time of day, comes to the desk.

—Leland, Callum tells him: This lady needs some stuff.

Zoe lays her list on the counter like an opening bid in contract negotiations.

Leland glances at it, then gives her a charming but wolfish smile:

—Very cool, he says: One of everything in the store.

He has spiky, thin lashes, beautiful brown eyes.

—Let's do it, he says and snatches up a large empty box and sets off down the aisle.

Just then the front door opens, and a man enters wearing a red down vest over a gray three-piece suit. His tie is sober, regimental stripes; on his feet are heavy pack boots.

Callum chuckles.

—Bet you need that last gallon of paint after all?

The man shuffles his shoulders, mocks himself:

—Been wrong before. Then he turns to Zoe: You're new.

—Did I miss something, she says: Is this the community center?

The man laughs.

—Close, he says, and points to a sign Zoe hasn't noticed before, taped to the back of the cash register: *Radio-Free Shroveton.*

—Gossip Central, he says, offering a hand: I'm Hal Westerbrook.

Out back, the paint mixer clangs, and Zoe glances down the aisle, sees Leland putting one thing after another into her box.

—You bought that place on Morning Hill Ridge. From the Mitchells.

—Michaelses.

—I'll stop in sometime, he tells her.

She's stunned.

—Oh, he says, grinning: You wouldn't know. I'm your senator in Montpelier.

Zoe points toward Leland, moving off into the distance, the box clearly heavy now. In fact, he sets it down and goes in search of an empty one.

—Better catch up, Hal Westerbrook says: I'll stop by after you settle in.

Zoe chases Leland down the aisle, assuming Hal Westerbrook must be up for reelection and guessing that any second she will indeed have run out of money.

All the way back up the hill, she is dying to look into her boxes, see if she can even identify what she bought. Charming and eager, Leland has told her he selected a hammer with a leather grip because she's certain to prefer it, a hatchet, a splitting maul but not an ax, and wood- rather than plastic-handled screwdrivers. Running the register, Callum nodded and approved, added his honest opinion that on her next trip what she really needs to buy is a generator:

—You'll never get a damn thing done.

Almost home, Zoe pulls onto the meadow road, draws herself

upright, and decides she's way too much of a purist for a generator. Painfully aware that she might be no different from a college
freshman, determined that her learning disability will somehow
magically disappear now that she's in a new school, Zoe tells herself she'll become a craftswoman, a hand-tool aficionado.

Eager and excited, she leans hard on the accelerator, races up
the hill into the meadow, then slams on the brakes.

CHAPTER 7

In the middle of the road, arms folded, stands a man in a brown felt hat, green wool trousers and wool shirt, and tall, pull-on rubber boots. Zoe stops, a mere ten feet to spare, and he strides directly toward her door.

With her elbow, she pounds her door lock shut. The cords in her throat tighten so fast and sharp she nearly strangles. In the days after the attack, she was given a cylinder of mace and a body alarm. She ditched the mace, found it too frightening, and out here the alarm would be useless; only the chipmunks would hear it. Her hands tremble slightly on the wheel.

The man bends, raps a jazzy rhythm on the glass.

—I'm Spark Everett.

My god, she thinks. The constable. She cranks down the window a few inches.

—Driving a little fast, he says, his voice flat: For this road.

—Was I? she says idiotically: Fast?

Managing to get the window down the rest of the way, she leans an elbow on the sill, confesses she's been in a rush all day.

Spark Everett straightens, and she decides it might be good country manners to get out of the car, not make a man so tall lean down to speak to her. She shuts off the ignition, gets out, then without thought wraps her arms around her middle and stands, still trembling.

The constable's eyes are a mild blue, his cheeks hollow. White goatee bristles decorate his jaw. Zoe isn't sure if these are deliberate, some kind of backcountry fashion statement, or simply oversight.

—We don't shoot speeders here, he says: Not on the first offense.

She holds tight to her ribs, nods, then realizes this is meant to be a joke.

—You look like you could use a drink, he says.

He smiles, his lips thin.

Zoe can't sort his humor from his sternness.

—Do I? she says.

What she really wants is a fire in her woodstove and a warm place to sleep, but yes, she says, she'll come for a drink.

—Door's always open.

He gestures to the one and only house on the road, then turns away, hands thrust into his pockets, assuming she'll follow.

She pulls her car into his dooryard. What must be the original building now has an attached kitchen, then a shed, a barn, a garage, another shed, each added one to another. She imagines ten-foot drifts outside, a farm family inside, their wood in the shed, their livestock snug, their feed undercover too, doing all their chores without ever setting foot outside.

Spark Everett opens the kitchen storm door, then the inner door, and stands back, courtly. On the mat, she wipes mud from her feet, and when he comes in behind her, and sheds his coat and kicks off his boots, she does the same.

He wears classic country socks, salt-and-pepper gray, white toes and red heels. Ruefully Zoe admires her own bright pink footwear with purple toes and heels, shocking green ankles. She's a downcountry girl all right.

At the hulking kitchen range, he lifts a burner lid, throws in another chunk of wood, and then she moves close, too, rubbing her arms as if the residual cold of these last days will never leave her.

—Scotch? he says.

She hesitates. God knows when she last drank hard liquor.

—There's coffee? he says: Tea? And stuff Unity drinks, Cokes and what not. Maybe cider in the freezer.

Zoe recalls the girl, wonders what it's like for her to be here.

—Scotch is fine. Just a touch, though.

He nods, and she pulls out an old wooden chair, sits at the small rectangular table. At one end two apples sit side by side. She turns toward the heat, rubs her hands, and he brings a bottle and a pair of glasses to the table. Zoe's surprised by the delicacy of his fingers on the cap. He shows her the label, lifts his eyebrows as if giving her one last chance to choose otherwise. But it's twenty-year-old single malt. Not exactly rotgut.

He pours a small amount into each glass, and when she sees him relishing the scent of it, she sniffs hers too, thinks it smells like the woods.

—So you've come to grace our hillside. Any particular reason why?

Zoe risks a joke:

—I thought Yankees didn't ask questions. Then before he can answer, she says:

—You start. What brought you here?

His father met his mother overseas during the war. She was Canadian, in the volunteer corps, and she came home with him. His family on his father's side, well, they've been here since forever.

Tell that to the Abenaki, Zoe thinks. Or whoever.

He points down the hill.

—That burial ground is full of Everetts. All my people. I'll be put there, too, someday. My wife is there already. No kids.

Out front, a car door slams, and in a minute, the kitchen door swings open and Unity is stamping on the mat, kicking off her boots and dropping her coat and mittens on the floor around her.

—Unity, he says.

—What?

He nods at her things, lifts an eyebrow. The girl fumes, shakes out her hair, then settles her boots into a neat pair, jams the mittens inside them, and hangs her coat on a peg. Again Zoe has the urge to warn her family to treat her with more kindness. She reaches up, cradles her neck with both hands.

—I'm starving, Unity announces.

Zoe says she'll be going so they can eat.

—Stay, says Spark: There's always plenty.

Zoe glances at the girl, sees her looking deliberately neutral.

—I love your woodstove, she confesses: I've been freezing.

Unity gets a soda, wanders into the living room, glances at the television, then at her uncle as if she's not sure she's allowed to turn it on.

—So, Spark says to Zoe: I missed it. How was it again you got here?

Zoe sips her scotch.

—Midlife crisis, she says quietly: I needed a change of scenery.

He hesitates, nods.

—Man or woman?

Zoe stares.

—Unless I misapprehend, Spark says, then mimics the way Zoe cradles her neck in her hands: It was a little more than midlife crisis.

—It was a student, she says: A male student.

All at once she is grateful for the sheer commonness of it: Angry male student, female teacher.

—And where would he be now?

Zoe shakes her head, says nothing.

—Jail? Loony bin?

Loony bin: the words turn her furious, protective.

—I'd rather not say.

Her voice is clipped.

Spark goes to the freezer, pulls out a package.

—Lamb okay?

Actually, lamb is not okay. Zoe no longer eats baby animals, but before she can speak, Spark says:

—Good. Bill Barton raises it.

She swallows hard. If it's home-raised, she'll manage. At least it hasn't been cooped up for its short life. And then it comes to her that if she's here in Shroveton to shed her past, or some of it, perhaps she'll have to shed some of her foibles, too.

He puts the package in the microwave.

—So you don't know if it was voluntary or not?

—What?

—The hospital.

Zoe balks, pours another half-inch of scotch.

—I was attacked, she says at last: And in time there was an agreement, treatment for the boy, compensation for me.

—Adele did say you had a pile of cash. We wondered where it came from.

Adele, Zoe recalls, is the realtor, and she gets a twist in her gut when she realizes she is a long way from the automatic confidentiality of academic services.

—I don't want this to be common knowledge.

—What did he use? Knife? Razor blade? Switchblade?

She looks down into her glass, then rolls a cuff back an inch.

—Something sharp, she says.

He lifts the bottle, pours her a more generous helping.

—Am I right to assume there's more than the arm?

He touches his neck. She looks away.

—I want to be hard to find, she tells him, surprised to hear herself say so.

He nods.

—But let's suppose you are found. No phone up there, he tells her: What about a gun?

The kitchen floor falls away beneath her chair.

—Get a shotgun, he says: Anyone tries to get in, just blast through the door. Don't even ask. I'll testify for you.

—You're scaring me, she says.

He gives her a flat look.

A bell rings, and he turns over the meat, sets the microwave again.

—Get a phone then. There's no poles, so you'd have to trench. Or get a cell phone.

He nods at the kitchen counter.

—I might get your calls on the scanner, but at least you could call out when you need help.

Zoe blinks, breathes deep.

—If you get sick, he says gently: Or hurt.

He pulls out the lamb, unwraps it.

—Unity! he calls: KP time.

He turns to Zoe, says:

—Uncle Spark's boot camp. Her brother lived here, too, for a while, until he straightened up.

—I'll help, Zoe says, but she's so unnerved she fears handling a knife.

—Sit. You'll get demoted down from company soon enough.

She marvels at the presumption of it, suddenly wishes to bolt for the safety of her cabin, even in the cold and dark.

Unity saunters through the doorway, says she doesn't feel like eating.

—Yes, you do. You were starving.

He points a knife at a bottom cupboard:

—Potatoes and onions.

Unity stands sideways at the counter, balances on one foot, the arch of the other pressed to the inside of her knee. She is deft with the knife, quick, yet there is pure insolence in the angle of her shoulders and the jut of her hip.

Suddenly her uncle bumps her with an elbow, kisses her cheek:

—I'll get the rest. Why don't you feed Gus?

She smiles.

—And try not to let that big galoot in here. Doesn't make it easier.

She goes out through a door into what Zoe presumes is a shed. Something clangs, a bucket, a gate, a feed-bin lid.

All at once, a red-gold comet flies through the door at knee-level.

—I'm sorry, I'm sorry! I'll get him, Unity is calling.

—I wish you'd learn to think first, Spark says, nearly automatic.

Meanwhile, what turns out to be a dog greets Spark with a quick bark, romps twice around the table, skids into the living room and back, then pitches to a stop in front of Zoe.

He tries to sit, but he has springs in his back legs. His butt touches down, bounces up, then touches down again. Meanwhile, he pokes his head into Zoe's lap, but when she tries to stroke his forehead, he leaps into the air, knocks the table with his shoulder, and sets the scotch lurching in the glasses.

—My god, Zoe says.

—Should I put him back out again? Unity says.

—It only makes it worse to have him in here, Spark says.

—Come, the girl calls, patting her thighs.

Gus's head whips around, his ears whap across his eyes, then he turns back to Zoe, presses his chin on her knee. Silky black feathers rim the edges of his ears.

—Could you hang onto him? Unity says: He's too smart to let me catch him.

Zoe holds him, leans her face down to his, and the dog laps happily at her jaw.

Spark and Unity stand there watching, stiff, a bit too still.

Zoe combs the fringes of his ears with her fingertips, then rubs underneath his chin. His nose goes up with pleasure.

—You are too sweet, she tells him.

Spark frowns, and Unity sidles in close, reaches for the dog's collar. He dodges away, snags a mitten from Unity's boots, then gallops into the living room, head high, joyful, mitten waving from his mouth like a pennant.

—That's the Higby dog, Spark says, watching Gus play keep-away, behind a worn recliner, and in and out of a pair of end tables. A floor lamp sways as he brushes past.

—He has to be destroyed.

—Oh, sure, Zoe says, taking pleasure in the dog's merriment. One of his Yankee jokes, she thinks.

—I'm serious, he says: The Higby boys surrendered him. It was either that or pay all his fines. They may look dumb but they're not. One more report of this dog stealing chickens, or taking a piece out of someone—

Zoe turns, makes a face at Spark.

—You're kidding. You can't tell me he bites.

The dog is clearly a mix, perhaps golden retriever and shepherd. He has a fine coppery red coat, elegant black fanny feathers, and black ears. One stands up, the other flops.

—Any dog will bite, Spark says: But I admit the stories about this fellow don't add up. He sighs: With dogs, they hardly ever do.

In the living room, Unity has cornered Gus, and she stands in front of him, hands on her hips. The dog flips the mitten this way and that, smiling, teasing.

—It's not fair, Unity says, eyes locked on the dog: He belongs to Arnie. Everybody knows that.

Spark sighs again, says, patiently:

—We don't know that.

To Zoe, he says:

—Arnie's the youngest of the four. A good boy. Works on the road crew. Only decent one in the bunch.

Gus bows to Unity, his front end stretching out and down like a circus horse. It's easy to see that if Unity takes one step toward him, he'll be off and running again. And easy to see that's exactly what he's begging her to do.

—Try this, Zoe tells Unity: Put your hand up, right in his face, and tell him to stay.

Instead, Unity steps toward the dog, and he bolts past her, skitters across the living room.

Zoe shakes her head. She'd once dated a man who had a young Chesapeake, and it had seemed that she'd been in training, too. How fussy the boyfriend had been that Zoe use the correct words and gestures.

—You shouldn't have stepped toward him, she says.

—You do it then, Unity snaps.

She stands in the center of the living room with the dog skidding this way and that, then adds:

—I still say he belongs to Arnie. Bart and Roger had no right to give him up.

The dog peeks out from behind the recliner, mitten still hanging from his chops.

—Gus, Zoe calls: Gus, bring.

The dog puts his head down, steps from behind the chair, comes toward Zoe, then stops six feet away.

Make me, says the look in his eye.

Zoe sighs, remembers that the young Chesapeake had sometimes been as tiresome as a two-year-old. She drops her voice, nearly to a snarl:

—Gus, come.

And he does, all the way. She rubs his chest, slips one hand under his collar, latches onto the mitten with the other.

—Give, she says, and tugs the mitten.

Gus tightens his jaw.

—Drop?

Gus whips the mitten away, holds it as far as possible from her grasping hand.

—Guess that needs work, Zoe jokes, then grabs the wrinkle on the back of the dog's neck, narrows her eyes, orders him to hand over the mitten.

—Careful, Spark says.

Zoe senses he is holding his breath.

—Oh, for heaven's sake, she says, and Gus gives up the sodden, misshapen mitten: He's just a great big kid. A marshmallow.

She lays her face next to his, feels the warmth of his furry cheek against her skin, his breath against her neck.

—A marshmallow who's about to be destroyed, Spark says: As soon as I have time to take him in.

—What, Zoe jibes: Is the vet so far away?

Unity stiffens, and Zoe wonders if she should apologize.

—The older boys seemed to think I should shoot him on the spot, Spark says: Dared me, in fact. So I impounded him. But it's no life for him in the run here.

Gus gives up leaning against Zoe's legs, and expertly lets his forepaws slide on the linoleum floor, then one by one turns his back legs out so that he is sprawled like a huge furry frog. He grins up at Zoe, pretends not to look at the mitten lying on the edge of the table over his head, then gets a whiff of lamb.

—Why can't Arnie get him back, Unity wants to know.

—Not while he's living with his brothers, Spark says: They're the ones who surrendered him.

—Maybe you can buy him a bus ticket, Zoe offers: Let him get a clean start somewhere far away, like Ohio? Colorado?

Spark sighs.

—The boy or the dog?

Zoe smiles down at Gus, says:

—Both?

Unity, a little hopeful now, crouches and strokes Gus's shoulder. He rolls onto his back, offering his belly to be rubbed.

—Arnie was a year ahead of me in school.

—End of discussion, Spark announces.

But Gus is allowed to stay while they eat, lying near the stove, chin glued to his paws, his eyebrows and nostrils working, tormented by the smell of lamb stew.

During dinner, Spark explains that the Higbys own about 150 acres, maybe a little more, an old family place, not so far away. Sort of kitty-corner to Zoe's property, only with some other land in between.

—So, they farm?

Spark draws a finger through the whiskers on his chin.

—What I would give to see their tax forms. They do everything and nothing. Drive backhoes and dump trucks, fix snowmobiles, plow snow, carpenter, cut firewood, trade old cars, you name it. One day I see them in a fancy sports car, stupid on these roads, and three days later it's some old beater I've never laid eyes on before. Then another fancy, brand-new something-or-other.

Unity giggles.

—They deal drugs.

—Really, Zoe says.

Spark shrugs.

—It could be why they were so eager to ditch the dog, get rid of any reason the law might have for paying visits.

—They burn down barns, too, Unity announces.

Spark gives her a level look.

—That was never proved.

—Yes, Unity says, loving a good gossip: But they can't get insurance anymore.

—Are they married? Zoe asks.

Spark gives her an amazed look.

—Who would know? Eldon, the oldest of the bunch, has been away for a while now. Supposedly in Florida working as an airline mechanic. What he knows about planes is a mystery to me. As for the other two? Women, kids, sheep, cows, chickens, they all just come and go.

Afterward, Spark offers Zoe a little more scotch.

She accepts, bends to whisper to Gus, who is now dozing by the woodstove.

—You can't have him killed, she says: It's not his fault he got mixed up with those Higbys.

Spark looks down at her a long while, his eyes narrow. Then he goes out through the shed door, and comes back with a worn, brown leash. He attaches it to Gus's collar, then holds it out to her.

—He bites anybody up to your place and we'll say it was self-defense. Maybe he'll eat that little punk who went for you if he gets out.

The leash lies across his open palm, an offering or a dare.

—I didn't mean I would take him, she says.

—It's either you or the vet.

CHAPTER 8

Gus dives into Zoe's car as if leaving on a European vacation, rides gaily home in the backseat, head high, eyeing the looming woods.

Zoe's glad for his company, more so when she pulls up to her dark house.

Heavy tire tracks gouge her pullout, and although she sits a moment and reminds herself of the propane man, she thinks, too, of those silly horror movies when a stranger shows up in a country village and is caught up in some kind of cabal, the townspeople's minds poisoned on some freak mineral in the water table.

Finally, she gets out, lets Gus out, too. The dog puts his nose down, charges along the path, up onto the porch, back down again, then bolts off into the darkness.

Terror overcomes her; she'll lose the constable's dog within ten minutes of taking it into her care; he'll run home, bite some-body. She'll be ambushed by someone hiding in her house.

House, camp, shelter, shack.

—Gus! She calls into the night: Gus, come!

A low, lean shape, the dog races at her out of the darkness, and she keeps him with her while she checks the shed and tiny con-crete crawlspace. Inside the house, heavy-treaded boot prints lead to the range and icebox, and Gus follows them a moment, then gallops around the great room.

Zoe sees about the propane. The refrigerator is far from cold, but the lining of the ice box is chilly. Somewhere beneath the huge refrigerator burns a pinpoint flame which, in a way she doesn't understand, will cool other elements which, in turn, will cool and freeze her food. It's too late to struggle with a fire in the wood-stove, but she strikes a match, lights a burner on the range, smiles with the delight of a child who has just had a silver dollar plucked from behind her ear. She opens the oven door, too; a steadfast pilot light burns in some deep recess.

At the foot of the spiral stairs, Gus walks his front paws up the first three treads then, with his hind feet firmly planted on the floor, looks back at Zoe and whines.

—Your guess is as good as mine, she tells him.

She brushes her teeth, reminds herself that at some point she will need to empty the barrel underneath the sink. Then she shines the flashlight up the stairwell, climbs a few steps above Gus, turns, pats her thigh, croons.

Gus whines again, gives a great heave of his hindquarters and, in sheer panic, clambers past her up the stairs and hits the second floor with a thud.

Zoe climbs more slowly. The stairs make her nervous, too. They're elegant, lovely to look at, they save on floor space, but she's not accustomed to the angled treads and turnings.

Gus waits for her. She points, and he races along the balcony, and dives like an acrobat onto the bed. Zoe laughs. The dog may have been living the straight and narrow life down in the constable's kennel, but this is a fellow who knows what beds are for. She lights the lamp, sets it on a high shelf, strips off her outer layers. The salesman who sold her the sleeping bag claimed she'd be warmest if she slept naked, but for Zoe this is too much a leap of faith. She orders Gus to move to one side. He rolls onto his back, offers his belly to be rubbed. His feathery tail splashes out.

—No one will pet your tummy if I die of frostbite. Move, she orders.

Her breath hangs in the air, a frigid cloud.

Still Gus smiles and flirts. She grabs the edge of the bag, rolls him off, and dives in. Instantly he plasters himself against her, breathes on her neck.

She pulls a hand up out of the bag and rubs his funny ears.

—I thought you were ferocious.

In the morning, she heats water on the stove, makes a mug of tea. She holds the door open for Gus, assuming he needs to go out, but instead he prances on the threshold, yodels, invites her to go out, too.

All this cheerfulness is way too much, and she gets the idea his history is a hoax. So much more dignified to surrender your dog to the constable because he's vicious than because he's too damn exuberant first thing in the morning.

Perhaps she should return him. Then again, she's had her first good night's sleep since the attack.

She pulls on a hat, reaches for her keys and wallet, looks at the grinning dog.

—Town?

Gus gallops toward the car, stopping once and, with an apologetic look, pees for a good two minutes against a tree then, natural as the air, leaps into the backseat.

Obviously he'd pile into any car and go anywhere. She thinks again about returning him, then smiles. Perhaps she should slip him into the backseat of a car with plates from out of state.

Passing the Everetts', there's no sign of Spark or Unity. Down at the store, she buys coffee and a sandwich, a couple cans of soup. Unity's not there either, and when the woman at the counter asks how she's settling in, Zoe only shakes her head and gives an enigmatic laugh.

In the car, when she unwraps the sandwich, Gus thrusts his head between the seats, leaning and leaning, his snoot seeming to grow longer, until Zoe, knowing better, breaks off half the sandwich, and hands it back to him. It vanishes in a gulp.

—Is egg salad good for dogs?

Gus grins, whaps his tail. Zoe's beginning to suspect that gaiety is his answer to everything.

—Gus, she says in a happy voice: Let's pull your whiskers out, one by one.

Grin. Whap whap whap.

She shakes her head, hands him the rest of the sandwich.

Rileys: Trip two.

Dog food, small bag until she decides for sure.

Kitchen utensils.

Woodstove tongs.

Out at the car, she runs into Leland, affable, how's-it-going, until he catches sight of Gus.

—Can't believe you have Bart's dog, he says.

Gus looks edgy, serious. His ruff raises.

—I haven't made up my mind, Zoe says, then adds: I heard he was Arnie's dog.

—They're my cousins, Leland says: Somehow or other.

He raps on the car window.

Gus growls.

—I don't know if I'd do that, Zoe tells him.

—I wouldn't be running home if I were you, Leland says to Gus.

Zoe looks down at the small sack of dog food among her purchases, says:

—You know what? I changed my mind.

Leland follows her in:

—That's smart.

—I think so, too, Zoe says.

She goes down the pet-supply aisle, picks up a few things.

Tennis balls.

Rawhide bones.

Water and food bowls.

Leather leash.

Brush.

Thirty pounds of kibble.

Well before nine, Zoe's home again. She carries Gus's food and gear into the house, remembers Zeke insisting that safety is a state of mind. And she had countered: So I was in the wrong state of mind when Adam sliced me? No, of course he hadn't meant that; he was only trying to say she might not need to be so wary of the whole world ever after.

She flips a tennis ball to Gus, and he leaps for it, races along the path, takes the porch stairs in two easy bounds, sails off them in one.

So now she has this doofy dog, who might or might not protect her, though by god she means to keep him since no punk kid is threatening her again.

Inside, Zoe gets the rope and chimney brush. In concept, chimney cleaning is a simple task. Tie the rope to the brush, drop the rope down the chimney, pull the brush through. Repeat.

No such luck.

The brush swings from the end of the rope as Zoe climbs the ladder, planting each foot as if the rungs will give way or vanish. Terrified, she clambers onto the roof. The brush snags on the drip edge, and she must climb partway down again, untangle it, climb up again. She crawls toward the chimney, wraps an arm around the metal chimney pipe, the classic pose of a drunk beside a lamppost. The joints in the chimney groan.

Her breathing stops.

In time she wonders how pioneers broke into the West without anti-anxiety drugs, then decides they were probably half out of their minds on rum and moldy grain. She focuses on the tops of trees, the far horizon, the ridges folding away to the south and west. Somewhere in those folds is Dayton.

At last, she drops the rope down the chimney, settles the brush in the top of the chimney, and crawls back down the ladder. Her wrists and fingers, even the arches of her feet, ache from so much clinging.

Gus waits at the bottom, front paws on the lowest ladder rung, tail wagging.

Celebrate the completion of each small step. And then go on.

How often had she told her students that? She grins, knows she was right, and patting her thigh, invites Gus to romp.

But once indoors, she can't find the end of the brush-rope.

Even shining a flashlight up inside the chimney, no rope. She swears. Obviously, it should have been weighted.

Livid, she storms outside, picks up a rock, wings it at a tree.

Gus cowers.

And just how often, when things had gone wrong, had she been philosophical, Buddha-like, asking her students what might be learned in the face of setbacks?

She heaves another rock.

Finally, after apologizing to Gus, she digs through her tools, selects a new monkey wrench, climbs the ladder again. Anger makes her bold, self-righteous. She yanks up the brush-rope, filthy now, ties the wrench to the end of it, releases the whole contraption into the top of the stack.

It falls away with a satisfying jerk, snaps the brush tight and straight in the chimney.

Rueful, she admits this is one lesson she won't forget.

Back inside, she leans all her weight on the rope, moves the brush a few inches, then rests, leans again. Soon her hands are sore, her eyes and lungs burning. The hearth and floor are covered with sparkling black flakes and dull ash. The bristles scrape closer and closer, like some odd percussion instrument, until finally she yanks the brush free in a final mushroom cloud of black particulate.

And she's supposed to do this twice more?

In the mirror the Michaelses left, her face is black, the rims of her eyes so red she looks deranged.

Too bad there's not some way to let her students know she's up here right this minute, sampling her own medicine. The infuriating fits and starts of learning.

She steps out onto the porch, and all at once Gus leaps up from the brook, barking and snarling. Gus tears down the lane, ears back, tail flat.

Well, she tells him in her mind: Bite this one and it's all over.

All at once the barking turns happy and gay, and Gus leaps into the air beside a figure in gray.

Spark Everett.

Christ, she thinks, thumping on her sternum. Don't these people have anything else to do?

She waves, waits for him in the road, rope and chimney brush in hand.

—This damn dog scared the petunias out of me, Spark says by way of greeting.

Zoe smiles, eyes and skin burning with soot.

—It's in his contract. Here Gus, she says.

On the strength of one chummy night and one egg-salad sandwich, he comes immediately, sits, leans against her leg, pins her foot down with his paw.

—Last night, Spark says, studying the dog: I was wondering if this was a good idea. But for now it seems so.

He nods at her tackle, then at the chimney:

—My Christ, you're right into it. You need a hand?

Before she can answer, he heads along the back of the house, and Zoe follows, dumbfounded and annoyed. He resettles her ladder, announces he'll hold it steady, and Zoe climbs, safer with him as spotter though miffed at the way he takes over, changes the pace of her work.

Every time she'd tried to plumb the psychology of the boy who knifed her, Zeke had stopped her.

We may never know, he'd say.

Or, don't make excuses for him.

Now she wonders if she gave Adam enough privacy or time.

She settles the brush in the chimney opening, lets the wrench drop the rope. She does the dirty work, which suits her fine, Spark stands by, and when they're finished, he helps Zoe find the chimney thimble where it's fallen in the underbrush, waits while she carries it up the ladder and coaxes it into place. Then he excuses himself, mysteriously promising to return. Meanwhile, she tackles the house, sweeps, scrubs, makes trip after trip to the spring with her inadequate water bottles. When she's finished, the place is not so much clean as livable, though she herself is filthy, from the whites of her eyes down to the spaces between her toes. But it's a convenient filthiness, and she keeps right on going, brings in firewood, tops off lamps, lays a fire.

When Gus launches himself roaring off the porch, Zoe leaps once more with fear. It's Spark again, carrying a small pack, and Gus, woofing happily now, ushers him to the house.

Heart still running fast and light, she wonders if she'll ever have solitude and calm.

Spark invites himself up onto the porch, sits on the top step, pulls bottles of water from his pack, oranges, too, a block of cheese, a sleeve of crackers.

—Lunch? he says.

Zoe goes inside a moment, scrubs her hands in the sink, tries to squelch her irritation. The poor man is only being neighborly. Outside, she musters up a smile for him, sits one step below him on the porch, drinks quite a bit of water. Silently Spark offers an orange, and she peels it slowly, deliberately. Gus drills his jaw-bone into her thigh, drooling, eyes riveted to the orange.

—Dogs don't eat fruit, she tells him.

His tail thumps.

She glances back at Spark, holds up half the peeled orange. Half his mouth lifts into a grin, and he points his jackknife at the dog.

Zoe shrugs, orders Gus down the steps, and tosses him an orange section.

He catches it in his mouth, experienced infielder getting a glove around an easy pop-up.

—You'll be sorry, Zoe tells him.

He chomps down hard on the orange, gulps, races up the stairs again, begs for more.

Zoe laughs, hears Spark chuckling behind her.

They sit in the lukewarm sun, and Zoe feels the pull of her muscles, eats cheese and orange slices, bemused by her stark black fingernails. She teases Gus, pretends to hypnotize him, waving an orange slice slowly left then right while his eyes follow it exactly until she tosses it for him, watches his easy joy at snapping it out of the air. She and Spark say little. He cuts cheese with his jackknife, she peels another orange, they swap back and forth.

When his pager sounds they both startle. The noise of it is scouring, alien.

He glances at it.

—Could be I'll need to head on out. If it goes off again.

—Trouble? Zoe says.

He shrugs.

—Could be, but it always could be.

—It can't be too bad here, Zoe says, calling Gus beside her, slipping him a piece of orange, gratis.

Spark slips the pager back onto his belt.

—No worse than anywhere else, he says.

Zoe holds Gus by the collar, traces the fine feathers of his ears.

—Did Unity mean it about drug dealing the other night? And what else was it? Arson?

She looks back and up at Spark.

He resettles the brim of his hat.

—Oh, sure, he says, voice flat: Also kidnapping, murder, rape and racketeering.

—I came to the wrong place, Zoe says, hears edginess in her voice.

The pager sounds again, and Spark gets up.

—I'm joking, he says: It's no more here than anywhere else. No less. We have our bad actors, sure. So doesn't any town.

Midafternoon, consulting the directions, turning this handle and that air vent, shaking the grates and crumpling all the paper she can find, Zoe lights her first fire. The little arrow moves on the stack thermometer and minute-by-minute she consults it with all the attentiveness of someone conducting a risky experiment in a lab.

In time, she leaves it long enough to lug more water from the spring, heats a kettle full of water on the kitchen stove.

Each step requires that she stop and think. Should she wash her hair or body first, bathe in the kitchen or, more romantically, in front of the woodstove? Finally she's clean, or cleaner, and she pulls on fresh jeans, fresh turtleneck and sweater, then stands in front of the woodstove, turning this way and that, roasting her aching body parts. She feels an astounding kinship with other homesteaders, pioneers, registers an odd sense of entitlement and worth. She's tired, clean, and warm, her body hurts, all the result of her own industry and effort.

Abruptly, she checks the time, rushes for her coat and wallet, whistles up Gus, then remembers the fire.

The temperature on the stack says "clean burn" but she has no idea if it's safe to leave, then wonders how people go to bed at night and leave such a thing on its own. She feels nearly pre-historic, sees the fire she's built as self-animated, necessary, dangerous. She wonders if the real punishment of Prometheus was his own divided opinion about the plain good sense of putting fire into human hands.

Glancing through the stove directions, she guesses things will be okay, hopes so anyway, then sees Saint Barbara on the window-sill, and leaves the little saint in charge. Later perhaps she should find out Saint B.'s precise areas of expertise.

Rileys: Trip three.

Deck chair. Then a second, in case she ever has company.

Propane lamp and extra tanks.

Swedish bow saws, bright red, their curved backs a familiar memory of summer camp.

Two five-gallon water jugs.

Rain suit.

Heavy leather work gloves.

Plastic pitchers.

Towels, sponges, dish soap.

Mop.

Broom.

Insulated boots like Spark's.

Next stop, the store. It's after five and the turnout is parked full. A woman in a nurse's uniform loads groceries into a pickup truck. Two men, one a carpenter she guesses, the other a logger,

stand and talk, each with a six-pack dangling from one hand
Inside, all of Shroveton seems to be in search of food, drink, and
videos. A mother bargains with two crabby children, a man in
a fuel-oil uniform orders coleslaw and a steak, teenagers pick
through magazines, and an older man in coat and tie parks his
cart crosswise in the narrow aisles.

Zoe fills her basket and, at the checkout, stands behind a tall
man in a frayed quilted jacket. His hair curls over his collar and
he smells acrid, of wood smoke or perhaps chemicals. He turns
once, gives Zoe a flat look, turns away again. In his arms are a
loop of sausage and a case of Ramen noodles.

Unity's at the register, fingers quick on the keys, a greeting, a
scrap of conversation for everyone who comes by. Zoe smiles,
guesses you can tell which men are single by the way the girl
turns on an extra sparkle.

The man in front of Zoe lays his things on the counter, asks for
cigarettes. Unity reaches up to the rack overhead, glimpses Zoe,
gulps, fumbles the pack.

—Don't crush them smokes, the man says, pulling wadded
ones and fives out of the pockets of his work trousers. He fishes
for still more bills, asks for lottery numbers.

Poor man's tax, Zoe wants to tell him, but only sighs, and the
man turns toward her again, then gathers up his bag and lottery
slip and moves away.

—I have that wild dog out in the car, Zoe jokes by way of
greeting.

Unity's eyes widen, and she says nothing, weighs the coffee
and vegetables, glancing several times at the previous customer,
standing in the open doorway a moment, answering some friend
who's asked how the hell he is.

—Did Spark say if he was going to tell the Higbys he placed
Gus with you?

Placed. The word is false.

—I don't know, Zoe admits.

Unity bags her order, counts out change, then leans over the
counter and whispers:

—That was him. Roger Higby. Right in front of you.

—So? Does it matter?

—I don't know, Unity says: I guess not.

Outside, Gus is grinning in the driver's seat. Zoe loads her groceries into the trunk, notices Roger Higby leaning against a pickup, talking to a second man, stabbing his lit cigarette in the air, making a point.

Zoe calls softly to the dog, orders him into the back, coaxes him to lie down. Then she climbs into the car, and, feeling as if all of Shroveton is watching as she drives up the hill with Bart, or Roger, or Arnie Higby's dog in her backseat.

That night, halfway into her second glass of wine, warm and sleepy, Zoe stands at her bank of windows. Behind her, Gus dozes in the patch of yellow light that falls from the tempered glass of the woodstove door. Candles flicker in their holders, the two new deck chairs stand empty and inviting. Saint Barbara with her mysterious sword stands watch.

Outside, the pointed tops of trees anchor the edges of the sky. A new moon waxes, the stars burn hot, and she remembers a long-ago night when Dayton called, 3 A.M., saying something about a solar storm, northern lights. She'd been cranky, snappish, lying in bed with the phone to her ear, glaring at her alarm clock because she could not glare at him, standing at his window, begging her to get up out of bed, look outside, see for herself. She had said she loved him, wasn't that enough, had finally put down the phone while he still rhapsodized about fountains of rose and green, beauty beyond words.

CHAPTER 9

※

Zoe is so taken with being warm that, although it's only April, it's clear her next task is to fill the woodshed. Book in one hand, hatchet in the other, she wanders among her messy trees. Some hang, caught in the limbs of their neighbors; others thread their straight branches into one another like spiky turnstiles. According to her book, these are mainly soft woods, pine, fir, balsam, hemlock, dangerous to burn in the woodstove. Occasionally a maple, ash, or birch lies dead, uprooted or struck down, and these she marks with her hatchet for later cutting, entirely unready to harvest living trees. She frowns to read that white birches, despite images of country inns with great white birch logs crackling on the andirons, produce too much creosote, although if she can find a way to split them, it's fine to burn the other birches. Yellow, gray, paper, river.

Soon she lives a fairy tale, eats a little breakfast at first light, splashes water on her face, gathers her bow saws and, cheerful, humble woodcutter, steps out into her forest. First she saws small branches, works the stiffness from her forearms, wrists, and back, eases out of the bad habit of bending saw blades, gets rid of the greenhorn curve and veer in her cuts. Slow, painstaking, in time her cuts run straight and true. She picks up speed, moves on to larger limbs, full trunks, resting, working until midafternoon, when she lugs her bounty, some to the shed, some to the house. After supper, she snoozes by the woodstove, Gus dreaming at her feet.

The weather might be raw, chilly, damp, but drizzle no longer sends her indoors. Nor light rain, overcast, or gloom. All that drives her in is heavy rain, the real thing, and it surprises her how seldom that occurs. True, she slips on mud as slick as ice, falls through patches of weakening crust. She dirties her new rain gear, makes it workmanlike, but her feet are dry in her new boots, and often in the mornings she is struck by the beauty of ice crystals blossoming up from the earth.

Whenever she goes to town, for supplies or mail, and someone asks how she is, she says she's fine, settling in, "putting up wood." She loves to hear herself say that, and one day when she sees Spark Everett in his dooryard, she turns off her car in the dead center of the road, and gets out to talk. This seems to be a local custom, one that infuriates her when she's the blocked motorist and the stalled-out drivers glance back at her with indifference, then keep on talking.

—Been wondering how you were getting on, he says.

Both hurt and grateful he's not stopped in again, she bobs her head, says:

—I've been putting up wood.

He looks surprised.

—Haven't heard you.

She frowns.

—What's to hear?

—Your saw.

Zoe chuckles.

—They're pretty quiet.

Spark runs his forefinger through an eyebrow, gives her an odd look.

—I have bow saws, she tells him: You know, with the curved backs.

—My Christ, he says: You'll freeze to death.

Zoe hesitates, then braves a question. How will she know when she has enough wood for the coming winter?

—You won't, he says: Not using toys.

Zoe's back goes up.

—They're not toys.

—I'd like to see you get five cord up with those things. And soon enough so it seasons.

—I'm cutting deadfall, Zoe says, again with a little burst of secret pride over this term.

His face is still.

—No, she tells him: Not soft wood, either. Maple, ash, birch. Those woods are a mess. And not white birch, either.

—Mind if I come up sometime, he says.

Zoe shrugs, then in a wild moment invites him for dinner.

—Supper, she corrects: How about tonight?

She's on her way to town. She can find some food, go to Rileys, get more kitchen stuff if she needs it.

—Tell Unity to come, too.

—She can't, he says.

—She working?

Zoe's amazed at how many hours the girl puts in between the store and Rileys.

He shakes his head.

—Gone.

Zoe grins.

—She's off probation?

He scowls, resets the brim of his hat, looks down the hill a moment, and Zoe regrets joking about his care of her.

—Nah, he says: Run off to Burlington with the Emerson boy.

The flatness in his voice surprises her. No anger, disappointment, censure. He might as well be mentioning the weather. Rain today, clearing tomorrow.

—You mean with Leland? Zoe asks.

—Good Christ, no. Tony Emerson's not as bad as that.

—Oh, Zoe says, then asks again about supper.

Sparks declines, says that unless he misremembers, the select board meets tonight.

—But I'll tell Callum to be selling you a chain saw. Save your toys for when your friends visit and need to feel useful.

荃

Zoe fights the idea of a chain saw by avoiding town altogether. In the mornings she still cuts wood, but after a few days, she admits Spark is probably right. She's not on a camping trip; she's proposing to keep warm for an entire winter in the north country. When she drives past people working on their woodpiles, she rolls down her window, listens to the angry buzzing of their saws, wants no such monstrosity in her quiet woods.

One day, she threads her way to the interstate, and heads toward Burlington, tries to imagine Unity running off to the big city with the Emerson boy, whoever he is. But as she weaves through town, she has the sickening feeling she could be in any college town with its outlet mall, upscale rehabs, and cleverly named delis. Except for the ferries on Lake Champlain, the city's a vague, boring blur.

Certainly it isn't fair, her easy dismissal of the place. Just how often had she railed at her students, tried to get them to set aside liking and not-liking, to learn some other, less self-centered means of evaluation? She finds a road leading south along the lake, decides she's on sabbatical from the role-model business.

Another afternoon, she takes Gus to the vet for shots and a thorough going-over. He barrels into the waiting room, sniffing eagerly at the floor, the coffee table with magazines, the basket of dog treats high on a counter. Zoe drags him to the chairs and sits, and he does too, barely, his rear end on springs, his head whipping left and right.

When the door of the exam room opens, and the vet steps out, in her blue scrub top, khakis, and hiking boots, Gus braces his front feet and his ears fall flat.

—You must be kidding, Zoe says: You? A coward?

The vet gives him a second look.

—That's not the Higby dog, is it?

Zoe sighs.

—Yes, it's the Higby dog. I wish everyone would stop saying that.

The vet bends, skritches Gus's chest, then takes his lead and drags him into the exam room. Zoe lags behind, explains why she's brought him in.

The vet scrubs her hands in a stainless-steel sink, asks Zoe again if it's really the Higby dog.

—It was either me or have him destroyed, Zoe says: It's not his fault he belonged to idiots.

The vet dries her hands, regards her.

—Dear god, Zoe says: Don't tell me you're another relative?

The vet laughs then, says no, she's not a Higby. She opens a refrigerator, finds the vaccines, loads a syringe.

—You have to admit, she says: This is a new wrinkle in dog control.

Gus is so busy trying to lick the vet's face that he doesn't notice the injection, wriggles with pleasure while she checks his eyes and teeth, listens to his heart.

—Here's what I want to know, Zoe says: Does he bite?

—Any dog will bite, the vet says, shrugging: Rumor has it this character really did bite someone from the humane society.

Zoe winces, says:

—Bad move.

The vet gives Gus a final pat, says he looks good, then adds:

—You never know. Some neighbor called the humane society, claimed the dog was tied out in all weather without shelter, barking constantly, never fed. That's against the law here.

She gives Zoe a narrow look, as if Zoe might be the next Shroveton scofflaw, then goes on:

—Someone from the animal shelter stopped by, just to look, or so she said, which was foolish without the dog officer. And supposedly this ragamuffin bit her.

Gus whaps his tail.

—So, she was trespassing? Zoe says.

—Technically. And it was a bite with no broken skin.

The vet shrugs:

—Who knows?

—He's been sweet with me, Zoe says.

From a back room comes a bloodcurdling howl. Zoe shudders. The vet stills, listens.

—That's a beagle, she tells Zoe: He's coming out of anesthesia. We set a broken leg for him this morning.

She gives Gus a final pat:

—You, my friend, have certainly lucked out.

Afterward, Zoe drives up toward the skete. Like her own hill, the road is slick, especially on curves and through dark hollows. Until this spring, she'd only thought of mud as a little extra-wet, squishy dirt in a bad patch of sidewalk, or clots of saturated earth in a flower bed too sodden to work. But here it's three, six, eight inches deep, sometimes bottomless. She leans hard over the steering wheel, her ankle rigid on the gas pedal, and follows the ruts until they grow so deep the undercarriage of the car scrapes. Then she wrenches the steering wheel, jerks the car free, and it skids across the road like a train off its tracks.

There's no choice but to keep going, not a chance she can stop or turn back now. Mortified, she prays for a gravel base at the gateway to the skete. If necessary, she'll pretend she's lost. Desperately she prays not to meet up with Dayton. Sometimes she thinks that surely something remains between them; other times, she scoffs at her own nostalgia, tells herself she's followed not Dayton but Dayton's lead to Shroveton. Often she considers how to break it to him that she's here. Call? Write? Or play emotional roulette, waiting for the inevitable moment they cross paths? She guesses he's far from Radio-Free Shroveton, but in a town this small, certainly they must meet someday.

Just not today, she prays. Not today.

On the last rise up through the maples, she notices that the sap tank and the lines have been taken down, and the gate's still locked. Chin forward, she brings the car to a landing on a patch of gravel, like a pilot touching down after a hazardous flight, and she half-expects applause from the passengers in the cabin.

Gus grins in the rearview.

Nosing the car to the edge of the gravel, she backs carefully around. If she can just get pointed downhill and keep going she will make it all the way to the paved road.

If there is a God, she wonders, what kind of humor is He partial to? Irony? Farce? Something subtler?

White flashes in the corner of one eye. She breathes deep, suddenly fears the sanity of her attachment, fears releasing her impacted history into the light of day.

She opens her door, walks in front of the car, double-checking the exact path of the lane. The ground underfoot seems solid enough, though it's surrounded by a sea of mud, and while Zoe gets her bearings, calms her nerves in the cool air, Gus slithers between the front seats.

She yells, but too late. The dog is free.

He gallops toward her, she bends to call him, but he gives her a wide berth, galloping through the mud like a horse in surf. He woofs, he romps, his tail flags with joy. Furious, Zoe stands with her hands on her hips, dreads the idea of putting the sopping dog back in the car, even though it's already become more country car than she might have imagined. He grins and dodges, long legs reaching, ears flying, and she figures he might as well get the kinks out while she gathers up her patience.

Leaning on the front fender, she breathes in and out, practices identifying trees. Ash. White birch. Gray birch. Pine. Maybe spruce. Or is that hemlock?

All at once Gus's nose goes to ground like a divining rod. He runs wide circles, head down, in mysterious hot pursuit. His head flies up, he poses, shoots Zoe a look over his shoulder, then swerves, wriggles between the post and the gate, tears down the lane into the skete, and vanishes.

Zoe stands at the top of the lane calling:

—Gus, come! Come on, Gus! Gus? Gus!

She tries a range of tones:

Sweet.

Beguiling.

Time-to-go.

Commanding.

No response.

She imagines a hundred scenarios. None does much for her pride. Her great big galoot knocking over sacramental wine, disrupting prayers, jumping up with muddy feet onto clean robes, squatting in the herb garden.

And then down along the lane, laughter rises. A voice says:

—Hey, buddy.

Zoe strains. Is it Dayton? She leans over the top of the gate, cups her hands, calls:

—Hello! Hello? I think you've found my dog.

The voice comes again, laughter gone:

—Easy there. Easy. No one's going to hurt you.

Definitely not Dayton.

—His name is Gus!

The voice says:

—Gus? Hey, Gus. Be nice, Gus.

—Should I come down? Zoe calls.

The voice is quiet, edgy:

—That might be nice.

Zoe climbs through the locked gate, awkward, then hurries down the lane and, just around the first bend, finds Gus growling at a man who's standing very still. The dog looks for all the world as if he's about to leap at the man's throat.

—Gus, she snaps: Get over here.

She slaps her thigh to get his attention, makes her own flesh sting.

To her surprise, Gus drops his eyes from the man's face, and trots straight toward her, tail down, ears flat. He sits uneasily beside her, his shoulder ruff standing up. His muscles are taut, spring-loaded.

Zoe gets a death grip on his collar, says:

—I'm so sorry. I haven't seen him do that before.

The man smiles, still a little nervous.

—So it's only monastics he doesn't care for?

—You're not a monk, she says.

The man holds out his arms, looks down at his heavy denim coverall.

—This is it, he says: No halo or anything.

Then he smiles.

—At least not while we're working.

She gives Gus a good shake by the collar, apologizes again, especially since the sign says they're on retreat. Then she adds:

—Although I can't think what there is to retreat from.

—Lots of things, the monk tells her: Trips to town, all unnecessary business, even people who come for prayers or hoping for spiritual direction.

Zoe does a double take.

—We don't offer that, the monk says: Prayers, yes. Direction, no. It requires special training.

Down below, a power tool starts up, whines at its work.

—I'm Brother Luke, the monk says.

Zoe smiles, can't help but chuckle.

The brother's face lights up, asks what's amusing.

Zoe shakes her head:

—There's a young woman in town with a major crush on you.

Then she remembers that Unity has run off.

Brother Luke rolls his eyes, groans.

—Not that. People think monks are so romantic. It's foolish, it's a hard life.

Gus is steadily relaxing, though he keeps his eyes on Brother Luke.

—I have an old friend in a monastery, Zoe says: I only recently found out.

—Someone here?

Brother Luke looks utterly delighted, offers to pass on her greetings.

—Oh no, Zoe lies: Somewhere else, but maybe you can tell me if it's okay to write to him.

—Why not? he says.

From down the lane comes the sound of hammering. Brother Luke glances in that direction, turns to Zoe:

—Time to go. Brother Dayton and I are repairing a roof. He's a stickler. Rock steady though, while I myself am forever wandering off.

Somehow she makes it back down to the main road without sliding into a tree or down over the bank into the brook. At the foot of the hill, she kills the engine, rests her forehead on the steering wheel. In the backseat, Gus whips his tail. Overhead, bare trees, in a hundred subtle shades of brown and gray, send ever-finer capillary-branches into the washed-blue sky. Her hand reaches for the Xanax and the water bottle, then falls back into her lap.

They were in the old trundle bed in the west attic of the river house. He was home for the weekend from graduate school, in the midst of one master's degree or another. She was dead on her feet, in her first unhappy months of teaching art, his car was in the garage, and she'd gone to pick him up for a rainy Saturday afternoon of errands in Scranton.

But he'd put clean sheets on that bed they'd occupied so often when they were younger, telling their parents they were at the library, had smuggled fresh pillows from a linen closet, a little wine from the cellar. Surrounded by steamer trunks and odd lamps, military uniforms hung with cloves, and some worn, leather club chairs, they'd entered freely into lovemaking. All this time and they still seemed a piece of each other, still full of their own great, grand seriousness, eternally grateful to have found each other so easily in life, so soon.

And what exactly had they been doing when he said it?

Force yourself, Zeke used to say when trying to get her to speak of the attack: It's like sucking poison from a snakebite.

They've been dozing and making love for hours, rain on the roof, the wine pretty much untouched. She lies beside Dayton, drowsy, tracing his ribs, convinced they'll love each other just like this when they are forty, fifty, sixty.

He touches her hip, and she props herself on one elbow, then lifts herself and straddles him, feels the tired roll of his penis against her. Leaning forward, she pins his shoulders to the bed, teasing him a little. He touches her breasts, makes a great show of not being able to lift his head. She releases him then, settles her weight back a little on his thighs, and he sits up. She feels him kiss her breast, amazed for what must be the thousandth time that what brings pleasure to one seems to bring pleasure to the other.

Then he rests his cheek against her, says:

—I promised I wouldn't do this anymore.

She thinks he's joking, takes his head and turns it, runs the tip of her ring finger along the uneven ridge of his teeth, offers him the finger to suck.

He gives it a gentle bite.

—Am I hurting you? she whispers.

She shifts her weight, but he holds her hard and soon she feels him sobbing.

—What is it? she keeps asking: Tell me. I'm sure it's all right.

Finally he answers, his voice raw:

—I've been going to confession.

He's been questing, sampling churches on Sunday mornings, reading this and that, visiting a local ashram.

She fingers the architecture of his ear, whispers:

—What's there to confess?

He looks up at her in horror.

—Dayton, she says: You've been telling a priest?

She gestures, including the entire attic:

—You've been telling about this?

He gulps, nods.

—He says that we should marry.

She feels seduced, tricked.

—You're not even Catholic, she hisses, pushing at his shoulders.

—I think I am.

—You think you are.

She holds him hard, her voice flat:

—Have you been confirmed? Look at me. You haven't even been baptized.

He shakes his head.

—Marry me, he says, voice soft, nearly frightened.

She yearns to say yes, of course, right this second, wants to say as far as she's concerned they're as good as married, that she meant it that night years ago they'd recited what they could recall of wedding vows.

Instead, she says:

—Not yet.

—You mean not until I grow up.

—I mean not until I get through this year, not until you feel more settled.

Despite her mother's nagging to marry him before he changes his mind, she's fearful, after all this time, to seem to be marrying him for his money.

—But meanwhile you'll have sex with me, he says, angry, somehow hollow.

And that does it. She lifts herself off him, reaches for the sheet. Shocked, she watches him hand it to her, as if indeed yes, under the circumstances, she ought to cover her nakedness.

CHAPTER 10

≈

For the next few days, Zoe gives up working in her woods. In fact, she gives up doing much of anything.

Brother Dayton. Brother Luke has confirmed that Dayton is here in Shroveton, caught somehow, in the clutches of God at the foot of that little valley, and repeatedly Zoe creates images of the skete, however foolish. A southwestern mission church. An abandoned Italian villa, like those in old war movies. Thermal shelters like those occupied by scientists at the South Pole, the last survivors of some global disaster.

She walks endlessly in her woods, every bit as remote as in the first days after her attack. She touches the trunks of trees, forces herself to memorize the difference between a white pine and a red. With Gus at her heels, she takes inventory.

A grandmotherly river birch.

A particularly fine ash.

A stand of beech.

She climbs jagged ledges, burns her lungs clean with the effort.

One night, she writes: *Dear Dayton.*

Crosses it out, pauses, writes again: *Dear Dayton.*

Tries: *Dear Brother Dayton.*

Then as she called him when they first fell in love: *Dayton Deming.*

Crosses that out, too, bites the pen top, stares into the oily lamp flame.

There's a diagnostic term for this restarting in the exact same way, but her eyes are filled with tears. Why did she ever put so much faith in terminology?

She tosses sheet after sheet into the fire, wonders what time Brother Dayton goes to sleep, wonders what became of their old attic bed and whether he now sleeps on a pallet. Ruefully, she recalls Brother Luke saying, *He's a stickler.*

One day, out wandering with Gus, Zoe cuts back and forth across a ridge. This high up, the trees are shorter, stubbier. Black spruce, balsam, white pine. She names them automatically.

Gus tears through the underbrush, doubles back, checks on her. She stops.

A stone wall runs firm and true across the slope. A stone wall, all the way up here. Zoe marvels just as if she's in Europe, standing outside a thousand-year-old cathedral.

Some time ago, some long time ago—a hundred years? two hundred?—before the advent of Green Mountain coffee, the telephone, and the horrific chain saw, someone labored all the way up here, pried up rocks, lugged them, turned them one way and another, and built this long, true straight wall.

Who were you? she wonders.

Until this moment, the stone walls of Vermont have been nothing more than a pretty backdrop, the peculiar thumbprint of the state.

She taps a rock with her boot toe. Not a wobble.

Hopping down, she finds her way to the top of the ridge then steps out onto a bold out-thrust of granite. She sits, traces a fingertip along the granular rock, muses that something once molten holds her up.

Gus leans against her, tongue hanging, panting. She looks out across the ridges and valleys, imagines the webs and grids, the miles and miles of stone walls. Monasticism, she thinks, is older than all of them. Much, much older. She tries to imagine this country full of panthers, virgin timber, ancient native tribespeople.

A chain saw is suddenly a measly thing. Noisy, smelly, and yes, dangerous. But she doesn't have to paddle all her worldly goods up some river, nor fell trees with an ax, nor pile rocks in order to build pasture. All she has to do is go to Rileys, work up a little nerve.

First though she has to eat humble pie. She'd often told her students that ignorance is merely lack of exposure, never to be confused with stupidity, nothing to be ashamed of. But how she hates going to Rileys one more time, admitting to still more ignorance. She hates that it makes her vulnerable, easy to dupe, humiliate.

But whatever she expected, she doesn't get: a knowing smile, a smirk, a remark. Not even a hint that Spark has said how foolish she has been, whittling away at her woods with a mere Swedish bow saw.

Instead, Callum asks what she had in mind, which make?

The question surprises her, and for a moment she wants to say, Don't you remember who I am? The queen of flatland idiots?

Instead, she asks what he recommends, and recalls a time when she wouldn't have bought so much as a toaster without studying *Consumer Reports*. Now, on the say-so of a backcountry store manager, she's about to buy a saw that can take off one of her limbs.

He walks her to an annex, and she confronts a whole range of gas-powered terrors. Generators, chippers, snowblowers, lawn mowers, log splitters, weed whackers, brush hogs. And saws.

Callum leans a fist on a hip, asks how much she plans to cut.

Zoe can't resist a joke.

—I did buy 500 acres, she says meekly.

He shoots her a look.

—Planning to clear-cut?

They laugh, then he reaches for a saw and lifts it off the shelf. Zoe backs away.

—That's way too big, she says, pointing to a saw with a short chain bar: I was thinking of something more petite.

Callum dismisses the idea, holds out the saw he has chosen for her.

—This one's safer.

She jams her hands in her pockets.

—Why? Because it's so damn big I'll never be able to pick it up?

And he gives a lecture he's clearly given before: That with a small saw, she will be tempted to reach up and cut branches overhead. That a small saw is more prone to kickback. That a small saw's just not built for the kind of beating she'll be giving it.

He holds the large saw out to her.

She hefts it, grabs the top and side handles, thinks she'll have forearms like a gorilla before the month is out. By summer's end, she won't even need a saw; she'll be able to break four-inch saplings with her bare hands.

She smiles, gives in.

—If you say so.

—You won't be sorry. And it's easy to adjust. The carburetor, and everything.

Carburetor, Zoe thinks: I'm taking something home that wants me to adjust its carburetor?

—There are directions?

Callum laughs, vanishes, comes back with the box the saw came in. The instruction manual is fully half an inch thick, the separate safety manual just as hefty. Digging through the box, he shows her a wrench and screwdriver gizmo, a cover for the chain bar.

—Sell me the rest, she tells him: Everything I might need.

Callum sets the saw on top of its box, and Zoe gives it a wide berth, as if passing a dozing alligator.

Rileys:

Helmet with face screen and ear protectors.

Safety chaps.

Sharpening files and templates.

Extra chain.

Bar lube.

Gas cans.

Oil additive.

More gloves.

Zoe makes a show of lugging the saw out to the car as if dragging through a bus terminal with a suitcase that is far too heavy and large. Callum follows, loaded down, tells her he'll stop at the pumps to fill both gas cans.

—What, she jokes: I have to buy that, too?

He offers to have Leland come out, get the saw started.

—I can probably figure it out, she says.

—Let Leland.

Callum buzzes for him, and without a word Leland helps himself to the saw and other gear in Zoe's trunk. Gus watches him with a steady frown; a low growl rises in his throat.

Leland ignores him, dumps some additive into the gasoline, and when Zoe asks how much to use, he ignores her, too.

—Must be in the book, she says.

No answer.

Zoe wonders if he's being rude on purpose or if he grew up with small engines just as another child might grow up with books or a saxophone.

He pours a thick red liquid into a well in the saw, fiddles with one adjustment and another, then braces the saw against his thigh. He pulls the cord until the saw mutters once, then pauses.

—Before she ran off, Unity told me and Callum about how you got cut. Horrible story.

—I guess you miss her, Zoe says, her voice quiet.

—Interesting, he says, deadpan: That a student could make a person run like that.

Zoe stares. The skin on her arms turns to ice. She pulls her cuffs down, anchors them with her fists.

Leland yanks the starter cord twice more, and the saw bursts into a wild snarl. He makes an adjustment, lets the saw run, grins.

She can see he is saying something, but she squints and turns her face away, eager to put her fingers in her ears, but ashamed to do so.

The racket fazes Leland not at all.

No wonder Yankees are laconic. Zoe thinks: They're all deaf as posts.

CHAPTER 11

❧

Back home, Zoe lugs the chain saw to a stump behind the house. Like a girl just home from the shop, eager to model new prom clothes, she slips on the chaps, thin layers of nylon meant to choke the saw teeth if they come too close to her legs, and tries on her new helmet. When she snaps the ear protectors down, the outside world falls silent and the inside world of pulse and breath is amplified. She pulls the screen over her face, sees her forest through a veil.

She grins.

With this gear, perhaps she could have continued in her profession.

Gus comes roaring back from the woods, skids to a halt ten feet away, then leaps up into the air, snapping and snarling.

—Gus, it's me.

Uncertain, Gus hunches down. His ears are back, his face full of mistrust and suspicion. Zoe doesn't like the still way he holds his tail.

—For heaven's sake, she says, slowly reaching up and lifting off the helmet: It's me.

The dog rises, sheepish yet wary. Zoe shows him the helmet, puts it on her head. Again he crouches, growls.

—Before you rip my throat out, Zoe says: You just might want to remember that the Higbys don't live all that far from here.

She holds out her hand, and in time Gus comes to her, allows himself to be petted. She likes the feel of the helmet on her head, but takes it off for him, lays it on the ground, lets him sniff it, sits on a damp stump.

Cold soaking through her jeans, she opens the saw manual, happens upon a list of dangers:

Kickback.

Dull chains, loose chains.

Cutting at low speeds, cutting overhead.

Poor footing.

Alcohol, drugs, fatigue.

There's risk of serious injury.

Risk of death.

And she's only on page one.

The next page is a diagram of the saw. Some of the parts are evident: front handle, rear handle, on and off switch. But she marvels over the rest. So that's what a carburetor looks like. And that's a brake, a spark plug, a choke. Zoe can read a dipstick and an owner's manual, and that's it. But now, here at her feet, is an engine, miniature and exposed, with a lethal chain attached to it.

Gus wanders off, finds a stick, hoists it like a trophy, chases in and out among some trees, pausing every now and again to look at her.

She flips through the remainder of the manual. Perhaps she'll start it, see how it feels alive and roaring in her hands, then turn it off again. That done, she'll find some simple things to cut. Later, she'll study maintenance, sharpening, the finer points of sawing.

See, she thinks, as if she has every last one of her students lined up before her. I'm following my own advice.

Divide any task into small manageable steps.

Chip away at your fears.

Gulping, she jams on the brake, slides the ignition switch, moves the choke, sets the throttle. Then as if about to be launched, an ill-prepared astronaut, she glances one last time at the manual, pulls the starter cord.

The saw mutters.

Behind her face screen, Zoe raises her eyebrows.

Three pulls, the book instructs, then close the choke.

Zoe pulls a second time, a third.

The saw suddenly snarls and rages. The air reeks of gas and oil.

Don't let go, the book had said, and Zoe crouches beside the saw, as if pinning down a violent child. She stares at the wildly revolving chain. Isn't she supposed to do something else?

She gropes for the throttle trigger, sets it free; the saw calms. Abruptly Zoe turns it off.

Closing her eyes, she staggers toward the house, rips off the helmet, lets it fall. Inside, she hoists herself up the winding stairs, curls up on the foot of her bed, cups her hands over her face. Her nylon chaps rustle on her legs; sweat drenches her back. Her wounds feel set on fire. She wishes for meds, knows she's too far gone for them to be of use.

After a while, Gus trundles across the porch and into the house. His tags jingle as he circumnavigates the kitchen, and Zoe imagines him nose-down, tracking her. She hears his front paws on the spiral stairs and then, having no wish to test his loyalty further, she calls his name.

He bounds up the stairs, slides crazily along the balcony. His tail flags and he leaps up onto the bed. Zoe pats the mattress. Gus circles and sighs, and Zoe wonders if it's true that genetic memory tells him to flatten grass, carve a den in snow.

CHAPTER 12

꓇

Later, woozy and detached, she puts the saw and helmet in the shed as if picking up after someone else, whistles for Gus, heads to Rileys:

Compass.

Field glasses.

Map of the Shroveton quadrant.

It's lovely, a geodetic survey with swaths of green and beige, and swirling lines of altitude, the gradual intervals of slopes, the tight dark ranks of steep inclines and small cliffs. Mountain peaks are full circles, tidily identified. Brooks are threads, ponds small puddles of pale blue. Roads are often dotted. Zoe smoothes the map across the steering wheel, finds what she's looking for, a road beyond the North Branch, and one particular black square of many, indicating a man-made structure.

As she drives, navigating is more difficult. She passes the turning for the skete, finds another dirt road, turns on to it, watching for a small brook, then an old, class-six logging road. A faint trace appears, an overgrown opening with a log across it, and Zoe pulls off as best she can, fearful of getting a wheel off the roadbed.

She hangs the padded strap of the field glasses around her neck, then the compass on its blue nylon cord.

Gus grins, gets to his feet, the air passenger who cannot wait, on landing, to unbuckle his seatbelt.

—Nope, she tells him, and holds up the field glasses: I'm going birding.

Best be consistent with her alibi.

On the hood of the car, she spreads the map, lays the compass on it. The needle settles north, and she turns the map to match, crooks her thumb, marks off four lengths. Then, glancing up at a weak April sun, she steps into the woods.

How she had loved orienteering at summer camp, with trails and puzzles set up by counselors, turns to make, markers to find, maps to draw of turns and lines, of distances from dining hall to swim dock, sunrise ledge to campfire circle.

Today's jaunt is less interesting in a way, since she will follow a single bearing, yet infinitely more exciting, certainly more risky. Every so often, she pauses and sights on two landmarks, one nearby and one distant. It's slow going. Bogs, fallen trees, dense thickets, crumbling ledges force her into detours. Vaguely she recalls something about a regular length pace, but here she must duck out of the way of whipping branches, watch where she puts her feet.

Often she glances at her watch, gives herself an hour, and then no matter what, she will turn back. This is the hard part, trying to hit a particular point. On the return, all she needs to do is come out somewhere on the road, and then go looking for her car, the new birder in town, heading home. That is, of course, as long as she doesn't break an ankle, and die of exposure in the night.

Then she cocks her head, listens, cuts a little to her right, stops again.

Could be.

As if she might come around a tree or outcropping, and fall right into the place, she tries to walk with stealth. Impossible. A displaced rock tumbles down a slope. She steps in mud, and her boot makes an obscene sucking sound.

Ahead, the wood-shadows lighten. Regretting her bright jacket, she slips it off, moves to the brow of the hill. She smiles, slow and satisfied. They were right to award her all those cheap little camp trophies. There, below her, is the skete.

For a while, she leans against a tree looking down into the bowl of it. What she heard was a chain saw. She walks back and forth until she finds a small clearing on the ledge, hunkers down, lifts her field glasses.

Not a chain saw.

Three men work together. One picks up a huge round of wood from a pile, places it into the bed of a machine, then stands back, pulls a lever. The wood falls away in split stove chunks, and the other two men gather it up, lug it to a pile, and stack it.

She studies each of the men. All wear ear protectors and the one running the splitter sports a helmet much like hers. One is short, round, and bearded, one a redhead, and one might be Brother Luke.

No Dayton.

She sits, scrutinizes the place through her glasses, then lays them aside, grips her arms around her legs, rests her chin on her knee. What had she expected? All she's looking at is a run-down farm. A rambling house with dingy, peeling paint, faded green shutters, a tilting porch, plenty of outbuildings and sheds, room for gardens. Behind the barn some tiny pigs scuttle in a pen, and hens parade. Two goats pull hay from a rack.

Not a single cross or shrine.

She grows uneasy. Where's Dayton? She should be getting back soon and, glancing at her watch, she hopes Gus hasn't eaten the interior of her car.

Down below, the gnomish man looks at his watch, too, shuts off the splitter. He removes his helmet and the other two slip their ear protectors down around their necks. They seem to be waiting, listening.

As if cued, the back door of the house opens, a man comes out, stands a moment. Tall and gaunt, he's not Dayton either. He reaches up, hands above his head, then pulls down with his whole body. The lead circles of a bell eddy across the skete, flatten, fade entirely.

A figure appears in the barn doorway.

Dayton.

Zoe glues her glasses to him.

Like the others, he's wearing khaki work clothes. His hair's still thick, though lightening with gray. Nice healthy color in his face. Same easy walk—except he's making his way toward the house with his hands cupped together before him.

Zoe grimaces. Some fanatic ritual, no doubt. Then she sees that his hands are full. She fiddles with the focus on the glasses, laughs softly at herself.

He's not doing penance. He's carrying hen's eggs.

With his head, he gestures for the men near the wood splitter to follow, although they're already setting aside their equipment, moving toward the house.

They climb the front stairs in sloppy procession, Dayton in the lead with his bounty of eggs. The others bend, take off their boots. Dayton lifts his cupped hands up and away, looks down at his own boots, tries to hand the eggs to the gnomish brother.

He thrusts his hands behind his back, shakes his head, says something.

The others laugh, Dayton too.

With a flourish, Brother Luke stoops, unties Dayton's boots, then Dayton pries them off, heel to toe, still laughing and cradling his eggs.

Through her glasses, he's too tall, too familiar, too close. She studies his face, can't read his mood. Happy or just bemused? And beneath that? Calm? Sad? At peace?

The gnomish brother opens the front door, holds it for the others. Zoe watches those shoulders she so loved disappear through the doorway.

That night she sits beside her fire, tries again to write to him. Her hands are stiff, her few words crabbed and choked, and after a while she simply sketches: a lanky figure with a cache of eggs in cradled hands, a distracted smile almost like Dayton's. Then a woman's hand and an unscarred arm, holding an out-thrust cross the way people in cheap movies drive off vampires.

CHAPTER 13

Zoe seeks to conquer her chain saw the way a pioneer woman crosses the Great Divide; she goes forward every day, tucks in her shirt, ties her boots extra tight, pulls her lengthening hair into the stub of a ponytail. Then she swathes her legs in the chaps and, as if heading out to round up livestock, she steps out onto the porch, whapping her gloves against her thigh.

Days pass. She grows accustomed to how the saw bursts into life. She makes it roar, quiets it, by adjustments of choke and throttle. In time, she pulls the start cord with a little flourish. Like a boy in a fairy tale with an enchanted sword, she lops up deadfall with mere touches of the blade's rotating teeth, branches the size of her thumb, her wrist, her upper arm. She finds herself ankle-deep, shin-deep, knee-deep in what she has cut, discovers that a forest takes up a whole lot more room when you cut it into pieces and pile it on the ground. Learning settles in her hands and shoulders, in the way she bends her knees, lessens the rattle of the chain saw in the small of her back. Her arms ache, her hips and her elbows, too. Finally ready to cut hardwood, she selects a half-downed red maple. It lies at a thirty-degree angle, its up-turned roots an exposed capillary system, its branches caught up in the fork of a nearby tree.

She snaps down her visor and Gus backs away. For the hundredth time, she thinks perhaps she ought to get a cell phone after all, then starts the saw anyway, riles it with a few squeezes of the throttle, puts the chain to the maple. She'll cut it near the roots, let it fall the rest of the way, then saw it to stove-length.

107

No such luck.

The saw strains and labors. The teeth revolve, but churn out only the finest sawdust, and blade cuts into the wood in seeming slow motion, a fraction of its old speed. All at once the trunk falls in on itself, clamps down on the chain bar, freezes the chain.

Zoe yanks.

Yanks harder.

The saw is seized.

Zoe kills the engine, rips off her helmet. The corners of her vision whiten.

She stares at the saw buried in the tree, can't believe she yanked back on it. What if it had come free? She could have gone flying backward, lost an arm, a leg, her life if the saw had landed on her, still running.

Gus roars up, barking insanely. Numb, she rubs his ears. He noses her gloves, and she simply hands him one. He mouths it happily, flips it into the air, flaps it around his face.

Eventually she goes back to the tree, bends like a weight lifter, wraps her hands around the trunk, straightens her knees.

The cut opens a hair's breadth. Not enough.

Again she lifts, grunting this time, nudging the saw with her knee. It tilts an inch. Again and again, she lifts, sobbing with the effort, nudging the saw, swearing at herself, trees, chain saws, life in general, her life in particular. Just as she resigns herself to having to go down to Spark's for help, the saw falls free.

She straightens, exultant, giddy, terrified. Next time she might not be so lucky.

Trembling and light-headed, she abandons the half-cut tree, carries the saw and helmet to the shed. She mills around inside, brews tea, takes it out to the porch, soothes her nerves by stroking Gus's silky lopsided ears, then finally admitting she's had enough for one day, she goes indoors for her compass and her map, thinks she'll stalk serenity at the skete.

On the way she idles, field glasses heavy around her neck. Patches of snow still lie in especially cold spots, but elsewhere the ground is wet and spongy. Deep green ferns are springing up. Gus races ahead, races back, wildness and joy incarnate. His ears fly, his silly dog lips flap, his tail helicopters.

Nearing her vantage point, she calls him close, and while she stands watching, Gus rolls onto his back, writhes with ecstasy, coats himself with mud, dried leaves, last year's pine needles.

Zoe laughs. The dog she understands, but life below her in the skete?

This afternoon in the bare orchard, three men stoop, pick rocks, toss them into the back of an old truck. They clang on the metal bed. The men take sporadic turns moving the truck forward, amble this way and that, loosening rocks with the heel of a boot, a pry bar, bare hands, whatever works. Sometimes they jostle one another, joke, pause and stretch their backs. One points to a hawk drifting overhead. They all look up, watch a moment, get back to work.

Then she spots Dayton. Behind the barn, he's painting the fences a dark, oily brown. His progress is methodical and distinct, the top then bottom of each board in the section, then the post, the faces of the boards, a second coat on the post, then onto the next section.

She smiles. Whatever he did, he did thoroughly. His back is toward her but she can just imagine the half-abstracted look on his face, what she once laughingly called his Teutonic stubbornness. What had Brother Luke said? *He's a stickler.*

Her chest tightens, and she buries her hand in Gus's wet ruff. All those years ago she'd been right: if he ever found what he was meant to do, there'd be no stopping him.

He crawls beneath the fence, pulls the bucket after him, starts on the other side, his face toward her now.

She lifts her glasses, finds first the cherry-russet of some swelling buds, a slash of a woodpecker's red, then zeroes in on Dayton, focuses.

Down below, the bell rings.

Zoe startles, tears the glasses from her face.

Gus woofs at her alarm.

She shushes him.

The men in the orchard stretch a moment. Dayton ceases painting, carries his bucket and brush into the barn. Soon the four of them make their way to the house, shed their boots on the front porch. For a moment Dayton stands, sock-footed, toes curled over the edge of a step, looking out across the skete.

That evening, she spreads newspaper on the kitchen floor, carries in the saw. She works quietly, late into the night, studying its innards, following the manual's suggestions on adjustments, then sharpening the chain, drawing the flat file and the round file across the teeth just so.

Finished, she carries the saw out to the shed, then goes up into the folly with the manuals under her arm. For hours, she studies up on hung trees, bent saplings, plunge cuts, back cuts, felling wedges, pee vees, winches. From time to time, she gazes out the folly windows. Around her, the planets move at speeds she can't discern, across distances she can't comprehend. She glances down at the diagrams in the manuals, then up again at the stars.

What comfort in simple physics, in immensity.

In the morning, she returns to the hung-up maple, starts the saw, steadies herself. What she hadn't understood was the relieving cut. Carefully she reaches the saw beneath the maple, guides it up into the trunk, the killer teeth gnawing toward her.

When the trunk shifts, she feels it, the changing kinetics of it, and when finally the tree falls free, she lifts the saw away, smiles behind her screen, tries to memorize the satisfying thump that comes up through the soles of her boots.

CHAPTER 14

⸗

Skills and patterns, Zoe thinks. That's all life should be.

She falls under their spell.

Trims lamp wicks with sharp scissors every morning, nipping off the corners.

Fills the kerosene reservoirs every other day, polishes the globes.

Goes for water before the last drop has been drunk, carries a five-gallon jug in each hand because two are easier to balance than one.

She reads about her outhouse, discovers everything they did to the latrines at summer camp, in the name of cleanliness, is what made them rank, scrubbing them with milky, harsh pine cleanser, dumping powdered lime down the holes until it billowed up in fine, choking clouds. Outhouses need organic matter. At Rileys she buys a bale of kiln-dried pine shavings, keeps a bucketful in the corner of the outhouse, flings golden pine confetti down the hole after every use. Soon the place smells sweet.

How simple.

How surprising.

She imagines including this in a letter to Zeke.

And laughs.

How remote he seems.

How irrelevant, insignificant, unimportant, inconsequential.

Adam and Dayton, too.

Around the house and around her clearing, she takes to wearing flannel or denim shirts, with the necks open and the sleeves rolled up. She doses her skin with weak spring sun, thinks of the word tonic, the scars nothing more than the cartography that led her here.

All day every day, she cuts wood, lugs wood, stacks it in the shed. In the evenings, she sharpens the saw, drinks a beer or a glass of wine, cooks a simple supper. At night she sleeps, hard, deep, exhausted, somehow convinced the long slow days will last forever.

In September, she cleans her chimney, hunkers uneasily on the roof, her gaze drawn out across the ridges to Dayton's valley. Her vision whitens. Trembling, she goes through the business with the rope, the brush.

What is it Zeke would have said?

She's here, she's this close.

But think of writing, calling, visiting?

She turns away, frightened, idiotic, panicked.

And let her stack more wood? Or admire the red-gold beauty in the heart of a slab of oak?

She calms entirely.

Approach.

Avoid.

Mid-November the deer hunters come, and Zoe, who hasn't posted, feels violated, invaded, put-upon. It astonishes her the free and casual way they wander across her land. Poor Gus, cooped up indoors, goes mad barking at the windows. One man intercepts her while she lugs water from the spring, asks if she might be so kind as to point him toward where the bears are denning. Another time, she spots a hunter coming out of her outhouse, buckling his belt. Rage brews up in her, goes flat, brews up.

Callum is the only hunter who knocks on her door, thanks her rather formally for allowing them all to continue hunting there. His cheeks are bright red in the cold, and red-brown curls rim the edges of his hunter-orange cap. He invites her outside to admire his buck. Clomping down the porch stairs, he admits his feet are cold, happily announces this is his first deer in three, four years.

Zoe zips into her parka and teasing, says she didn't know any man in town would admit such a thing.

Callum puts his head back, laughs, then gestures with pride.

The dead deer is lashed onto the hood of the Jeep. A plastic tag skewers a stiffening ear. The fine head is flopped onto the fender, the surprisingly delicate legs bound with rope.

Back inside, Zoe sits, puts her head between her knees.

The first snow comes just after Thanksgiving, a magical eight inches sifting from a low, soft sky, and Zoe tries her new skis. Gus cavorts around her, barking, but all she can do is shuffle. For a day or two she practices pushing off her edges, bending her knees. Then it rains and freezes, and on the radio she hears that power is out everywhere, the roads impassable, the interstate closed, the state police begging people to stay home.

Spark comes up to check on her, finds her in a pair of gym tights and a denim shirt, big fluffy socks stretched toward the stove, a mug of tea on the floor beside her.

—You said you'd get a phone, he says, gruff, annoyed.

Zoe smiles:

—I didn't say when.

He looks around, lays his gloves on the table.

She asks what she can get for him.

—Tea? Cocoa? Whisky? Wine?

He takes her up on tea, and she gives him Earl Grey, lashed with whisky.

He examines her books, stacked in neat piles by subject matter along the walls, raises his eyebrows once in a while, but says nothing.

She asks what he does all winter. Does he ski?

—Nope.

—Not downhill, she says: I meant cross-country.

—Nope.

—Snowshoe?

—Nope.

—What do you do all winter then?

—Beats me, he says, sitting at last, opening his down vest, balancing his mug on his knee: Plow, answer calls. Mostly keep the house warm.

Zoe gets up, feeds the woodstove a chunk of oak.

—Will we ever get snowed in?

—No doubt.

—No coming in and no going out? No mail, no guests?

She nudges Gus with her toe.

—That's pretty much it, Spark says: We're damn close to that right now.

Then he gives her a long look, studies her little house, sips his tea and whisky.

—You'll be safe, he finally pronounces: If that's what you're asking.

—I guess, Zoe says.

And when she thinks of Adam, she does feel safe, relieved.

But when she thinks of Dayton, sorrow and something else well up in her.

Cowardice?

Impatience?

CHAPTER 15

Never in her life has Zoe had a winter off. Determined to enjoy it, she sleeps later in the mornings, sometimes curls up in bed and reads, feels as if she's getting away with something, as if there will be a knock on the door, a summons back to meetings and other miseries, back to gainful employment of some kind.

Gus, too, lounges on the bed, sleepy and luxurious, begs for Zoe to massage his face, his forehead.

Finally up, Zoe stirs the coals in the woodstove, revs the fire, eats a breakfast of tea and fruit, then gets on with the chores, cleans the ash drawer, splits wood if necessary, fills the kindling box and wood rack, lugs water from the spring, tends her lamps. All that done, she sweeps the floors, eats a second breakfast, which is so late it might also be counted as lunch except she has grown quite fond of breakfast food, oatmeal, muffins, eggs, potatoes. She learns to make pancakes, tries her hand at baking waffles, fries tiny links of sausages.

In the afternoons, she snowshoes, or tries the skis.

In the evenings, she dozes, reads.

Christmas Eve brings the first distinct whiff of unease.

At noon, a mug slides out of her hand, an accident, but when she picks it up, she flings it full force into the sink, takes bitter pleasure in the way it shatters.

Shaken, she steps outdoors, listens, nearly suffocates with anticipation. It's the eve of comings, isn't it? Babies in mangers, magi, fat saints in white beards and red suits. Scanning the sky, the light, she expects a portent, seeks surprises, secrets, gifts.

In town, she buys a newspaper, scans bulletin boards. Every hamlet for miles has a grange party, a vigil, a mass, a pageant.

None appeal.

What is Christmas anyway? In Rhode Island, the end of fall semester, a respite, a party or two, church if someone thought to invite her. In Pennsylvania it had meant parsimonious gifts and her mother's fresh, late-night grief for her father.

Back up on her ridge, Zoe tramps her woods. She carries her hand saw and clippers, searches for a Christmas tree. What she will hang on it when she gets it home, she has no idea. She marks the candidates with snips of surveyor's tape, can't decide which to cut, finds herself nipping a branch, the end of a spray, and in the end that is how she celebrates: she spiffs them up, trims them, turns them into little conical Christmas trees, lets them grow another year.

That evening, snow blows slantwise past the windows. She paces, yells at Gus, rearranges jackets on the nails by the door, tells Gus she's sorry. She lights every lamp she owns, goes outside, admires the place all lit up. Shivering she comes back in, digs through her books for a Bible, vaguely recalls that the Christmas story begins the New Testament. She finds some chapters in Luke and more in Matthew, reads them aloud, admits she is entirely the outsider.

At last, with great reluctance, she selects a pen, a fresh bound notebook, sets a semicircle of fat candles on the table. One by one she lights them, solemn as a druid, and finally begins:

Dayton.

Brother Dayton.

Brother Monk.

Failing to find more words, she draws:

The candles, their reflection in the dark window, the snow outside. Labels it: *Christmas Eve.*

Then Gus, sleeping on his back like a pasha on the hearth rug. His hips fall away to the left, his belly fur gleams, his forepaws flop in the air. She smiles at his ear, turned inside out, the loose drape of his lip. Labels it: *The Higby dog, so ferocious.*

From memory, she sketches the house from the outside, block-wall foundation to third-story crow's nest, sketches it again, buried in snow drifts, only the crow's nest showing.

Sketches a monk, portly, barefoot, rope belt at his waist.

Then her arm, hash marks and all, labels it: *Self-Portrait, Christmas Eve.*

That winter, whenever the universe threatens to skid out of alignment, Zoe fools in the notebook. She details the day's snowshoe trip, charts early morning temperatures, describes splitting oak, the fine red-gold wood laying open with the sound of tearing paper. She notes that Spark keeps an eye on her, admits she starts her car almost every day, keeps herself shoveled out, but has more or less given up going to town, having decided there's no mail of import. What she doesn't write is that she's afraid of running into a certain tall, stickler monk, however remote the chance.

One night she sketches Adam, recalls the cut of his hair, but not the shape of his eyes or mouth. She draws his backpack, his sneakers, his expensive ski jacket, his hands, with their bitten nails.

She does gesture drawings of the attack, the arc of his hand coming out of the pack, the quick glitter of the blade, the two slices, the hacking at her arms.

She sketches Zeke, measured, cool, fancy clothes, leaning back in his chair.

Then a picture of a whole pile of books on trauma, and Zoe herself torching them. Labels this one: *I play Savonarola.*

She writes a line, a half-page, explaining that after Dayton left that last night, she had waited for him. Waited patiently, faithfully, until at last she wrote him off for good, since it was he, after all, who had finally walked out.

Distracted, she sketches interim boyfriends.

A man preparing French feasts in his cramped galley kitchen. Another with a dog.

A third at the tiller of a sailboat.

And then she grins, turns the page, sketches herself naked against her pillows, bare feet on a man's shoulders, her hands in his hair, his face hidden between her legs.

The covered pages curl at the edges, accumulate, yet she never looks back. She's bailing out a fast-leaking boat, stopping arterial bleeding with the simple pressure of her hand.

One night, in a complicated mood, she turns to the inside front cover and writes: *In the event of my death, please help this book find its way to Dayton Reed at Shroveton Skete.*

CHAPTER 16

In early March, the day before town meeting, Zoe drives to town. Warnings for town meeting are tacked to the doors of Rileys and the grocery store. At the post office, Zoe's box is crammed with months of mail, and among the letters is one stamped in red.

From the Town of Shroveton, it hereby notifies the recipient that the taxes on the Muir land and homestead are in arrears.

Terror shoots through her. She has whiled away the winter, believing the world entirely bounded by woods, weather, and sky, and now she discovers that this entity, this town, has some claim she has ignored.

The foot of the bill spells out the interest penalties, the process for appeal, the town's right to auction off her property.

Sick with fear, she trots out to her car, gets her checkbook. Luckily, the town clerk is in his lair beside the post office; Zoe's not the only one in a last-minute rush to pay her taxes before facing the neighbors in a full day of activities, town meeting in the morning, the library's benefit lunch of red flannel hash, then school meeting in the afternoon.

While she waits, she rifles through her other mail, finds letters from Annie, the college, and Zeke, all hoping she is well, all concerned about her silence. There are other bills, dunning notices, too, no doubt, but as long as she keeps her land and home in tact what else does she have to lose?

A man comes out, jamming a checkbook into the pocket of his wool car coat, and the clerk steps out behind him with a heavy marker, stands before a bulletin board, and crosses a name off

119

the list of delinquent taxes. Zoe has plenty of company; names, addresses, and amounts due are all carefully recorded.

While the next miscreant settles up, Zoe scans the list, certain that Spark and the town patricians would never allow themselves to appear on it.

Then she startles. At the bottom of the list are properties whose time has run out. One name she doesn't know; the billing address is Massachusetts.

The other is Shroveton Skete.

Zoe steps up to the desk, lays the bills on the counter like the cards of a failed poker hand. Her hands tremble and her chest is numb.

—Guess I should get the mail more often.

The town clerk peers over the top of his half-glasses. He's no Norman Rockwell; on his desk are a computer, fax machine, and miniature Zen garden. Water drips from a tiny height onto some glistening stones, then is apparently pumped underneath and drips again.

—I'm Zoe Muir, she says, though she met him when she registered to vote, which she never remembered to do. Sometimes she listens to public radio, but news and calendar events seem as disconnected from her life as old radio waves, still intact, carrying news of the armistice out toward Pluto.

The town clerk thumbs through a file, marked in red.

—Guess I got here just in time. Her voice quavers: Before the tax sale.

—There'd be buyers, the clerk says.

He's blunt, abrupt. An age spot punctuates his left cheek.

—Rumor has it I'm eroding the tax base, Zoe jokes.

The clerk finds what he's looking for.

—I'd buy your place, he says: If I could.

—I'm sorry, Zoe says: Were you in on the development?

—Cash or check? the clerk says, then adds: No, that was a terrible idea.

—The development?

—I wouldn't have minded the timber and the hunting. The quiet, you know. Just take care of the place on weekends, leave it wild.

Despite the water garden, which was probably a gift, she'd pegged him wrong.

—You're welcome to come up, she says: Anytime. To hike or whatever.

He smiles, says no thanks:

—Plenty of other room for that.

He watches her write her check, as if she might forge the signature. When she hands it over, she points to the delinquent list, feigns idle curiosity:

—What's the story on the skete?

The clerk looks up.

—The story on the skete, he says crisply: Is that you can't just declare yourself exempt from taxes.

—They did that?

He squints.

—Word is their church won't even own them. Word is they haven't even asked.

—Own them?

—I'm not a Catholic, dear. Some look at them and see monks. Some look at them and see hippies.

—What do you think?

—They're hard workers. Good to their land. But the town? The town looks at them and sees a long delinquent tax bill.

He rips a receipt off his pad, goes out in the hall, and with his marker crosses Zoe's name off the list. He pauses in the doorway, nods toward the warning on the wall:

—It's in the articles, he says: To sell at auction.

Back in her car, Zoe fumbles in the glove box for Xanax. She keeps one stash here, others beside her bed, in her kitchen, in her pack when she's out walking. Leaning back, she lets her head clear, imagines going straight up to the skete and giving them all a good talking to. For as hard as they work, and Zoe knows since she still goes and watches them, why have they done nothing about their taxes?

Explain to me the difference, she wants to demand again of Dayton, between passivity and faith.

There is a difference, he had said: Faith is active, willful.

No, it's not. It's not willful, she had countered: It's . . . it's . . . .

And she had not been able to find a word that would not finish them off for good.

Finally he had asked if she could just believe in something like providence? Or in anything larger than just the two of them?

She points the car south, brakes at the foot of their road, can't add up how defying the town and standing outside the church helps their cause in any way. She can't bear to have their valley threatened, can't bear to give up watching them from above, their labor as common and mesmerizing as fish swimming in a tank. She tries to imagine the brothers holding late-night strategy sessions on raising funds, building an endowment. Nonsense. At night they're probably silent, well into their dreams or private prayers.

On the interstate, she hits eighty, and heads straight for Montpelier. So what if it's the only state capital in the country with no McDonalds? Certainly it has its fair share of attorneys. Once in town, she parks the car and simply goes down the line of offices in old restored houses, presents herself at one reception desk after another until she finds someone who has time.

It turns out to be a young woman in a smart navy blue suit. For a moment, Zoe, briefly awkward in her ratty clothes tainted with wood smoke and kerosene, glimpses how foreign her life is to others. But she refuses to apologize, merely explains what she wants.

That night she goes back to full doses of Xanax, terrified that she's been so content and smug when so many things were threatened.

In the morning, she's not certain she can face town meeting. But she can't stay away, either. Town meeting brings people off their hillsides, keeps some of them home from work, reminds the gardeners it's time to start tomato seeds on their kitchen windowsills. Cars are parked everywhere and trucks; a rank of snowmobiles has materialized behind the store. People in all manner of attire wander in and out of the store, mill on the town-hall stairs, gossip in the parking lot.

Way behind the school, she finds a place to park, goes up the town-hall stairs, feels the tide of people pressing at her back. With some irony, she checks her mail again.

Nothing.

Oh-so-casually, she glances at the list outside the town clerk's office, then hears the town clerk say:

—It was a cashier's check. That's all we know.

Zoe leans around the corner. Five men stand at the desk. She recognizes the slope of Dayton's shoulders. The back of his neck is lightly browned and weathered. Gray lightens his hair, tied back neatly in a ponytail.

I knew you in tennis whites, she shoots at the back of his head.

I knew you in a dinner jacket.

I drove that convertible your father gave you for your birthday.

Someone says:

—Was there a postmark?

Zoe ducks away, hears the town clerk answer:

—It came by messenger.

Outside, men stand here and there, talking, glancing at their watches, the sky, at a pickup truck cruising by. A woman with a rolled-up magazine in one hand races up the steps, her pink wool scarf sweeping out behind her.

Zoe leans against the building. Across the road, two covered metal sap buckets hang from spouts drilled into a schoolyard sugar maple. She breathes the raw, wet air, in time hears the town hall quiet down, and follows the other dawdlers indoors.

She stands at the back, just inside the doorway. A man glances over, snuffles, looks away. One third of Shroveton seems populated by men of indistinguishable age, somewhere between thirty and sixty, in outdoor work clothes, various hats and caps, beards and unshaven chins, rough hands and loud voices. This one looks familiar, but somehow now they all do, the hunters, the men at the store buying beer and sandwiches, the guys at Rileys. A woman in a pale blue cardigan and page boy turns around, catches her eye, offers her an empty place two rows from the back. Zoe smiles, shakes her head.

Up on the stage, a sixty-year-old man with a shock of white hair and a weather-beaten face explains preliminaries. He wields a gavel the size of a baby sledge hammer. Zoe lets her gaze drift to the brothers.

There they sit, halfway up the other side, all in a row like mismatched bachelor farmers.

Zoe examines them, their backs, their partial profiles.

Sitting on her ledge above the skete, like a naturalist in a foreign land, she's given each a name as if the brothers are a new, unfamiliar species.

The Ex-Dentist is on the end, wearing a neat navy blue sweater and blue pinstripe shirt. He watches the moderator fiercely. Balding and lean, like a marathon runner, he has fine, surgically deft hands.

Next to him is Luke, the brother who caught Gus, the blond, good-looking cellarer Unity fancied before running off to Burlington. In flannel shirt and turtleneck, he ducks to the right, listening to Brother Red, the youngest, with his baby face, freckles, and gawky body.

On the far side of Brother Red is Brother Gnome, with his full dark beard, basketball belly, and slow sad way of walking.

And then Dayton, bending toward Brother Gnome. Zoe half-expects him to lay his arm around the shoulders of the other monk.

Her throat closes. She blinks and sniffles, suddenly sees herself at eighty-five, still pining for some silly love affair, her life squandered on nostalgia.

Hate floods her heart.

I bet they think God saved their bloody skete, she thinks.

The moderator calls for a vote.

On what, Zoe has no idea. Next is a long, unbearable debate over the purchase of a new truck for the town road crew. As far as Zoe can tell, every man in town has an opinion.

Buy one secondhand.

Take goddamn better care of the ones they have.

A tiny, hunch-shouldered man expounds for a full three minutes, filthy hands waving wildly, his speech unintelligible.

The moderator gavels, says:

—And thank you, Tim. We're much enlightened. Next year try to remember to put your teeth in.

The meeting rocks with laughter. Bored, Zoe wonders if she can edge her way along the side of the hall, get a look at Dayton from another angle. For all the times she's watched him through her glasses, it's dangerous, a thrill, to be in the same room.

When discussion finally ends, Zoe votes for the new truck, solely to prevent the agony of having to sit through this same debate another year, but the numbers are so close that the moderator calls for a division of the hall. He gestures; the ayes will stand on this side, the nays on that. Zoe stares. She's never seen this form of democracy. It reminds her of gym class, divvying up for games, and she plasters herself against the wall behind some of the other ayes. The monks come to the same side, far enough toward the podium that she is well hidden.

There's some joking back and forth across the hall. A man near her calls to a buddy across the way:

—You old cheapskate.

The moderator gavels.

The town gets its new truck by three votes.

A young man leaps into the air, arms lifted, and whoops for joy.

The moderator laughs, gavels:

—Control yourself, Arnie Higby. We vote later on whether you're allowed to drive it.

Laughter eases the sharp muttering among the losers, and Zoe realizes that it's true; it's the people from away who change things. Without her and the brothers, there'd be no new road truck.

The hall resumes its seats. Dayton moves with that old ease in his limbs. How easily he occupies his body; how she wishes God had diminished him somehow, dampened his smile, his appeal.

The next articles are the tax sales. The house votes to proceed against the landowner in Massachusetts, though there are some extenuating circumstances about a recent death, so perhaps it will get sorted out.

Zoe, standing in the back of town hall, a man reeking of cigars on one side, a child crushing graham crackers underfoot on the other, half-remembers, half-relives, the first night she let Dayton open her blouse, lift away her bra.

Dazed by lust, she hears the moderator remark that they'll move on, since the other tax issue has been resolved.

Dayton raises his hand, discreetly, as if summoning waitstaff.

Zoe smiles. He's pure flatlander, all right.

The moderator hesitates, then gives him the floor.

—I'm Brother Dayton, he says to the podium.

From the back of the hall, Bart Higby shouts:

—Speak up, boy!

Then loud enough to be heard only by those around him, he adds:

—Fucking monks.

Faces freeze. Nervous laughter laps along the back row.

Dayton turns, faces the hall. Pink tinges his cheeks and forehead. He clears his throat, begins again.

—My brothers at the skete have asked me to speak on their behalf. I'm sure you've all heard what's happened in the last twenty-four hours. When we came in this morning, we knew we might lose our land. The tax status, and so forth.

His words trail off, and he looks down a moment, smiles, boyish, vulnerable.

If Bart Higby makes one more remark, Zoe will kill him with her own bare hands.

Dayton looks up, his face suddenly set, his voice strong.

—But as you know by now, our taxes have been paid. Not miraculously.

He smiles gently.

—But certainly by grace of some kind.

Zoe gags.

The other monks look around, nodding agreement, smiling appreciatively. The Ex-Dentist reaches across the aisle, accepts a handshake from an elderly man. Pure disgust crosses the face of Spark Everett. The woman who offered Zoe a chair beams as if she herself paid the tax bill. People lean toward one another, murmur. A young woman takes rapid notes in a stenographer's notebook.

Dayton folds his hands before him, elbows loose.

—I'll just finish by saying that we're deeply grateful. Our benefactor has chosen anonymity but we'll be holding him and all of Shroveton in our prayers.

Murmurs rise, the moderator gavels. Dayton nods his thanks, then sits.

Zoe fumes.

How dare you? How dare you presume I want prayers from you?

Bart Higby mocks:

—It'll take a hell of a lot more than that.

—You said it, Zoe mutters, then turns abruptly for the door and runs smack into a man in a gray three-piece suit and a maroon tie.

Hal Westerbrook.

—Miss Muir, he says: Hiding in the back?

—I'm not the only one, she snaps: What are you doing? Keeping an eye on your constituents?

He smiles, sheepish, as if caught out.

—Gives me a sense of things. What do you think of the Shroveton miracle?

Blood roars into her face; she pulls at her turtleneck, glances at her sleeves.

He asks if she needs some air. They can just come in for the votes.

—Pure democracy is a shock if you've never experienced it before.

—I couldn't believe it, she says: How long did they debate that truck?

—One year, it took three hours to decide to dig a drainage ditch along the edge of the ball field. It's all big money for Shroveton. Not everyone has it.

Outside, Zoe regains her humor, offers a joke:

—You mean not everyone lives in the same luxury I do?

Hal leans against the railing, jingles keys in his pockets, muses:

—That's the other thing about town meeting. All these people cooped up all winter long, cranky, cabin-crazed, and we put them in a room together and make them decide things. And this was an easy winter.

—I'm going to miss winter, she says: The quiet, the woods. Almost missed my taxes, it's been so long since I've gotten the mail.

He kicks slush from his hiking boots. They're hard-used, and not just from marching up and down the capitol stairs in Montpelier.

—You're living my dream, he says: Do you know that?

—It was never mine, Zoe tells him: I fell into it.

She thinks of Dayton and his brothers inside the hall, voting as a block about who knows what, wonders if they would say God brought her to Shroveton.

—Come for dinner sometime, she hears herself say: How about Saturday? Come while it's still light out.

She nods toward the silver snowshoe tack, holding his tie in place:

—That is, if you really snowshoe.

He looks pleased, surprised, and all at once Zoe prays he's not married.

—Bring your wife, she says: Or whatever. If you have one.

He shakes his head, smiles, holds up his hands as if to prove they're empty:

—I'm completely unencumbered.

CHAPTER 17

By three on Saturday, Zoe has spent the entire week cleaning. It began innocently enough, wiping the kerosene film from the insides of the windows. Standing on a ladder, rubbing the south-facing glass with wads of newspaper, she realizes that the square beams that hold up the second floor are covered with dust, as are the pegs for the post and beam. She brushes, sweeps, scrubs, and soon is after every surface in the place. Like a farm woman, she hangs her hearth rug on the deck railing and whacks it again and again; a winter's worth of dust and grit billow out.

She loads up every last piece of clothing and bedding, packs the car so tight there's no room for Gus. She barricades him in the kitchen and spends half a day at a Laundromat three towns over, rather than washing things in the sink and drying them on the rack by the fire. She turns out all the shelves in the kitchen, lugs carboy after carboy from the spring, scrubs the entire kitchen with Murphy's oil soap. She even takes the food from her freezer and refrigerator, carries it out into the cold, takes a deep breath, turns off the gas, lets the whole thing thaw out. All day she chips at freezer rime, then that evening, she lies on the floor and tries to relight the bloody thing.

The directions say something about pressing down a blue button, waiting for propane to pass into the line, then positioning a match, which she manages by squashing her face flat to the floor and holding a flashlight in her teeth. The propane ignites with rippling pops as flame runs through the ports. Zoe lies there grinning. This is the kind of triumph she would tell Zeke about, if only he would understand.

By Saturday, Zoe wonders what's come over her. She's tidied the woodshed, washed the window in the outhouse, swept the cobwebs, topped off the shavings basket. At the store, she rounds up some things for salad, an exotic treat since her refrigerator freezes lettuce into a solid block. She makes a stew for dinner, bakes a fresh loaf of bread, gets out a bottle of red wine, and around noon, heats a vat of water, and treats herself to a bath. Scrubbing all of her nooks and crannies, she's aware she's crossing the line from seasonal housekeeping to some other urge, then laughs and shaves her legs. Eyeing herself in the mirror, she dresses in silk long johns and turtleneck, will pull on another layer the minute she hears Hal drive up.

Or rather the minute Gus begins to roar.

And then, with an hour to spare, she wanders.

The house seems more hers somehow, now that it's clean, and less hers, too. She glances through her notebooks. Since town meeting, she's written and drawn nothing.

How could something she meant well have turned so bitter?

Inside the front cover, she reads her note about the notebook going to Dayton in the event of her death. All at once she snatches her pen, turns to a blank page, and writes in heavy, unambiguous letters:

I'm the one who saved your goddam skete.

Me.

Fucking Saint Zoe.

Not the hand of God.

She slams the book shut, angry to have duped herself.

The light grows thin, and Hal is late. She fumes, rubs her itchy shins. She had wanted to snowshoe up into the woods, hoping Gus could tag along, distracted by his love of snow and thus put up with a stranger.

Finally she pulls on her jacket.

Gus leaps up, prances. He loves tramps in the snow, expects

one every day. He brings her hat, mittens, gaiters. Flustered, he carries them away again, hides them behind the couch.

Zoe grabs her pack, checks her emergency gear, extra jersey, dry mittens, water bottle, matches, knife, snack.

Outside, Gus leaps around her in happy circles, She coils his leash, pockets it. She'll head through the woods along the lane. If Hal shows up, she'll flag him down. If not, she'll bear southeast to the beech grove. And will be eating stew every night for days to come.

In the shed, she slips her boot into a snowshoe binding, wraps the straps around her ankle. It turns out that the skis were a silly purchase. How she'd imagined herself in snow-shrouded woods, an L. L. Bean photograph, sleek and skilled. But a heavy crust cemented itself over the first snow, and she'd found herself skiing on glass. And she was too damn proud to kill herself ramming into a tree.

Stepping into the other binding, she fastens it, wishes the snowshoes were made of wood. Alas, they're aluminum, as alien in the woods as if fashioned from the carcass of a jetliner fallen from the sky. A trampoline of neoprene holds her up, not a web of rawhide, and while she yearns for the old aesthetic, these weigh a mere fraction and will take her farther.

She and Gus plunge into the woods along the lane. They haven't broken trail here, and the snow is unpredictable. One moment she's walking easily on crust, hardened now by thawing and refreezing, then a shoe breaks through and she grunts in surprise, sinks in past her knee. Her back wrenches. All winter she's been clambering up ridges, digging in her crampons, tobogganing on the shoe-tails down small inclines, but this is heavy labor, hauling herself up, inching forward, falling through again.

Beside her, Gus gallops, falls through, flails, gallops some more until, sheepishly, he follows in her wake, snuffling in the broken snow. He whines, stops, bites at balls of ice between his toes, then springs up, flinging snow into the air in a happy shower.

At the foot of the lane, she looks down toward Spark's. Clear, viscous smoke rises from his chimney. He's running a hot, steady fire, but outdoors there's no sign of him.

Or Hal either.

Ducking back into the woods, she follows the faint trace of a logging road along a stone wall. During the winter she's read that 100,000 miles of stone walls crisscross central New England, more stones in them than in the Great Pyramids of Egypt. She plants her shoes one beside the other, catches her breath, wings a snowball for Gus, who snaps it in his jaws, bursts it into a brief cloud of ice and snow.

Down a slope, a small waterfall collects in a chill, black pool. Ice sculpts the rocks. Zoe's spring feeds these open, chattering riffles, and it occurs to her that one day she might dig a little swimming hole. Sure there's the EPA, but who would ever know if she shoveled out a spot deep enough to paddle in on buggy summer days?

When they reach the clearing, Gus is walking just in front of her. He moves with a tired swagger, satisfied, tongue lolling. Overhead, frayed clouds are backlit with gray-pink. Zoe detours to the outhouse, kicks out of her snowshoes, goes in, sits for a while, thinking of nothing. Afterward, she slings her snowshoes over her shoulder, makes her way along the path, goes into the shed.

Then Gus roars. His whole body horripulates, and he launches himself out of the shed, teeth snapping.

Zoe grabs the kindling hatchet, prays Gus never turns on her like that, then sees a strange car parked besides hers.

Hal Westerbrook.

She finds Gus lunging at the front door, hurling his shoulders against it, snarling.

—Gus? she says, half-afraid to draw his attention: Gus? Come on, sweetie.

Her mouth is dry with fear, her vision skips a little, but still she laughs. She called this ferocious behemoth sweetie?

—Gus, she says, firm now: Enough.

The dog stops leaping, and Zoe takes him by the collar, pats his shoulder.

—He's a friend, she lectures.

Gus wrenches away, leaps at the window.

Hal looks out, horrified.

—Get away from the window, Zoe yells.

She collars Gus again and marches him, muttering and snarling, to the shed.

Inside, Hal is pacing back and forth in front of her cold woodstove. He's lit a kerosene lamp on the wall.

—I can't believe you still have that dog with you.

—I like him, Zoe says, a little shaken: He's all pussycat when it's just me.

She moves to build a fire:

—I'd almost given up on you.

Opening the stove door, she crumples newspaper, lays a tidy crisscross of kindling in on top of it:

—Actually I did give up on you. I couldn't stand it anymore, I had to get outside.

He gives her an odd look, explains that he was held up at the State House. He'd planned to do a little work in the quiet there this morning and, of course, something had come up:

—I would have called.

—Spark Everett wants me to get a phone.

—Not a bad idea.

Zoe strikes a match, holds it to the unlit scaffolding of her fire.

—Oh, she says airily: I have Gus.

Hal has brought wine, and she rummages for a corkscrew until she finds it on the countertop where she left it. She hands it to him, lets him occupy himself, finds some glasses, then hardly knows what to do. She blushes. All week she's concocted images of wordless couplings under the stars, in the margins of the woods, up in her lamplit bedroom, here by the fire.

How obvious, how idiotic.

His presence seems enormous, he occupies space in a way that amazes her. Fiddling with the corkscrew, easing the bottle

open, he's too real, too actual. And that plaid wool shirt, in so-
phisticated ivory and gray with a touch of salmon. Zoe's gut tells
her it was chosen for him by a woman.

Why on earth did she invite him?

She busies herself getting the stew from the refrigerator, putting it on the stove.

Hal pours the wine, hands her a glass, and she offers him a
look at the house. Making a joke of the hostess-doing-house-tour,
she spreads her arms, and says:

—This is the kitchen. She points across the counter, announces: And that's the rest of the downstairs.

He strides over to the refrigerator.

—Gas?

Zoe nods, tells him the ins and outs of propane cooling.

He admires the skylights, then cocks his head at the sink.

—I thought you didn't have water.

She waves to the line of jugs in the corner, tells him she carries it.

—How does the sink drain then?

Rueful, she explains that when she moved here water drained
from the sink into the bucket, which she carried outside and
ditched.

—Once too often, I poured water down the drain until it ran
out on my feet. Then she laughs: Or I pulled the bucket out and
emptied it into the sink.

Hal chuckles, leans as if to open the doors beneath the sink.
Zoe steps neatly in front of them, blocks his way.

—What committees are you on down at that State House?
Anything environmental?

She admits she's put in a pipe that simply runs through the
crawl space into an outdoor dry sink she's fashioned out of rocks.
She wrinkles her nose:

—Not exactly up to code. But it's only gray water.

He raises his eyebrows, though it turns out he's an engineer,
interested in so-called alternative technologies. They discuss com-
posting toilets, gray-water systems, the state's inflexible rulings

on such things. Technically, he tells her, it's illegal to be living here. She can't possibly have an occupancy permit and it's against the law to live year 'round in a camp.

Zoe feels a wave of panic:

—I can be evicted? How did the Michaelses get away with it?

He holds her arm a moment, reassures her:

—A good fraction of people in the north country aren't exactly up to code. You'll be fine, trust me.

And so they go through the house, discussing its orientation, its general design. On the second floor he talks about how she might wire the house for solar, perhaps just the first floor for water and lights, leaving the upstairs more primitive.

She bristles, leads him along the balcony, gives him a moment to admire the view, then goes into her bedroom, lights a lamp. The yellow flame flickers in the globe, and a warm nimbus of light brushes the rafters.

—I defy you to say this is primitive.

He stands at the balcony, studies the ceilings, walks toward the bed, asks about insulation.

All at once she wants him out of here.

—One more floor, she says, leading him to the stairs.

Up in the crow's nest, she opens a window, but the air is raw. A deck chair, piles of books, and an unlit lamp occupy the center of the room, and Hal is saying something about what a fine place to sit, perhaps they could bring up another chair and the wine?

But Zoe is watching her forest turn dark. This spring she'll attempt work she's studied over the winter: fell some trees and season them with their branches on, girdle others. It comes to her again that it's a paradox, cutting trees, killing some off in order to nurture others.

Hal touches her shoulder, speaks, but Zoe wanders farther off, sees herself as if from a great distance, a tiny gardener sorting out a forest. Laughable, really. One woman, one chain saw, and 500 acres.

—It amazes me you live here all alone, Hal says.

His body casts a zone of warmth into the folly air.

—I don't often feel alone, she says.

She turns back toward the window, and her heart, like a beggar, goes out into the trees, the dark.

They have a fine dinner. The stew is good, the salad a treat. When Hal gives up making lists of what she might do to her house, he tells funny stories about Montpelier, then stories about growing up on the coast of Maine. They compare notes on being transplants in a state where you are either a native or a flatlander. Afterward, Zoe asks if he'd like coffee. Tea? She hesitates: More wine? A touch of whisky?

He moves to the woodstove, turns himself around, bathing in the heat.

—Whatever you're having.

—I'm having whisky. But then again, I'm not driving.

Loneliness sweeps over her. She looks away.

—Whisky then, he says: If I'm not keeping you up.

She pours two glasses, brings the bottle with her, lets Hal get settled on the couch. Then she opens the woodstove door, and puts up the fire screen. High, fast heat pours out, and Zoe sits on the floor, leans back.

—Pure extravagance, she says: All those BTU's flying up the chimney.

Hal murmurs. She feels his hand in her hair; she leans against his leg.

—Do you get out much? he says after a while.

—Sometimes I get tired of getting out.

It's hot so close to the stove, and she shoves her sleeves up, has another sip of whisky. She is getting quietly, pleasantly drunk.

—There are interesting stories about you in town, he says.

Zoe tenses. So much for her illusion of anonymity, invisibility.

—About me? I'm not interesting.

—Of course you are. You and everybody else. The Williamses, the Higbys. Bill Sorensen and his sheep's-milk scheme, the Emersons and their hothouse tomatoes. The skete.

Hal chuckles, holds his glass up to the light a moment.

—I heard a great monk joke, he offers: Marriage is for people too weak for celibacy. And celibacy is for people too weak for marriage.

He laughs, and to her surprise, Zoe joins in.

—One of the brothers told me that, Hal says.

Zoe's heart pounds, and she waits before she speaks, prays for diffidence in her voice:

—So, how do you know the monks?

—Sooner or later, I meet everyone. I make a point to. I like them actually, they're good ecologists.

—And you know all of them?

—More or less. Stephen, Dayton, and Luke are the strong ones. I can't imagine what it would take to get them out of there.

Zoe smiles down into her glass, asks Hal what he means by strong.

Hal glances at her, teasing.

—Never mind them. They'll be in tomorrow's papers. You're the one everybody's losing money on.

Zoe stills, puts down her glass.

—What does that mean?

He rearranges his legs, and Zoe gets up, moves away from the fire.

—What do you mean, she says again.

—There's a bet, he tells her: I thought you knew.

He pats the other couch cushion, and Zoe perches on the edge of it.

—No, I don't know, she says.

Clearly abashed, he tells her there's a pool on how long she'll last up here.

—That's horrible. Like a deer pool?

—My bet is that you'll show up all the old boys of Shroveton. The young ones, too.

He glances at her, looks abruptly worried, sets his glass down.

—This didn't happen here, did it?

He studies her scars, and Zoe sees he's a little shocked, shaken. Finally she pushes her sleeves down, falters, says:

—It was a while ago.

He waits.

She asks again about the bet:

—So is that why people are rude to me?

—Only some people, he says: It's all harmless anyway. And you do have your supporters.

Zoe settles beside him, watches the fire. He puts an arm around her, tentative. The fire burns down, and the world shrinks to a circle of light and shadow around the hearth. Hal's hand moves on her arm, and while part of Zoe screams with desire, some other part of her is unsettled, vigilant.

Hal ventures a kiss on her temple, tells her he's glad she came to Shroveton:

—We were running short on eccentrics.

Zoe, on edge, turns too flirtatious:

—Me? Eccentric? Not in a million years.

He glances at her arms again, then around the room, points to a shelf by the woodstove:

—Take that, for one, he says.

—Saint Barbara, she tells him, enjoying his puzzlement: Though I'm not Catholic.

He leans back, examines her as if she is a mysterious fish he's reeled up out of the ocean.

—I'm a heathen, she says, then amends: Or pagan. I believe in something. I just have no idea what.

And then she looks him in the eye, lets her aching body have its way, kisses him in earnest. After a while, he murmurs, teasing:

—Very pagan.

In time, his hands wander beneath her turtleneck, stroke her back, and all at once Zoe realizes that any minute now he will try to lift the shirt over her head and that all her scars will be exposed. She holds his arms, stops him.

—Not that pagan.

He lets his head fall back, holds her. He sits with his legs apart and she feels sorry for his erect penis, crowded inside his jeans, and if only it wouldn't be so confusing, so contrary, she would befriend it.

—So what did happen? he asks.

Zoe has no wish to explain, and simply lifts her face, kisses him some more, then his neck, feels his hand brush against her breast. She's hardly being fair, she thinks. She'd like to screw with wild abandon, but refuses to undress, wants to slow him down but refuses to talk about getting sliced. Their breathing deepens, his hand moves again beneath her turtleneck and, desperate, Zoe says the only thing she can think of:

—Would it shock you to know I paid the taxes on the skete?

CHAPTER 18

≫

Sunday morning, Zoe buys one of every newspaper she can find.

Montpelier, front page: *Shroveton Miracle.*

Boston, second section: *Mystery Benefactor Saves Monks.*

New York, bottom inside corner: *Reprieve for Religious Community.*

Winter ends. Sap lines go up all over town, and telltale plumes of steam and smoke rise from sugarhouses. Zoe's Shroveton neighbors, and no doubt the monks, too, shore up failing roofs, tidy their woodpiles, order seeds. Roads thaw, freeze, pucker into washboards. One night, three feet of snow falls. Early morning, Gus lunges through it up to his neck, quickly flags. Zoe finds the trip to the outhouse tiring. Noon, the temperature's still rising, forties, fifties, and by dusk the new snow, fallen in on itself, is a mere six inches deep.

Cutting trees again is wonderful and familiar. How easily she takes the saw apart, how matter-of-fact down at Rileys, loading up on additive and chain-bar oil, arranging with Callum for a thorough tune-up. Soon she sees the world again through her helmet visor, hears it fall silent beneath her ear protectors. Her arms and hips ache every night.

What doesn't happen this year is her sense of completeness in isolation.

More and more often, she breaks in the afternoon, creeps out along the ridge above the skete. One afternoon, she watches Brother Gnome, watering in some stalks he's planting in a patch. Raspberries? Blueberries? Dayton goes by with a wheelbarrow, tools resting on the metal bed of it, no doubt banging, and Brother Gnome flicks the hose up over Dayton's head, light and quick. Dayton glances back at Brother Gnome, once again innocently watering. Dayton continues on. Brother Gnome sprinkles him again, and Dayton drops the wheelbarrow handles, rushes him.

Up on her ridge Zoe holds her breath, horrified.

He wrestles Brother Gnome for the hose, aims it straight into the air above them. The water comes down on them in jerky splats. Soon they're soaked and laughing.

She learns to come at certain hours of the morning and afternoon, when they're likely to be working, and a few days later Dayton and Luke walk back and forth along the edge of the pond. Brother Red and Brother Stephen follow. All four are pointing variously at the banks, then at one end of the pond, back to the dock. Clearly there's some disagreement. Brother Stephen and Brother Dayton square off, fists on hips. Brother Stephen's finger wags at the pond, then in Dayton's face. Brother Red pats the air, palms down, trying to make peace. Brother Stephen wags some more, takes Dayton by the arm, tries to turn him to look at something in particular, and Dayton snatches his arm away, faces Stephen down. Then all at once he wilts, and in a moment walks out onto the dock, stretches face down on the planks, stares over the edge into the water.

Baffled Zoe must to admit she has no idea what's just happened, has no way to follow the trajectory of his character from the past into the present moment.

Fine.

She'll mind her own business, get on with her trees and woods, go to bed at night too tired to think.

Then one June morning, the early light steals over her balcony, comes to her bed with the ease and silence of an old lover. Deeply drowsy, Zoe responds. Her legs scissor, the sheets slip across them. She cocks a knee out, feels the promise of lubrication. She touches her breast; her nipple springs upright eagerly.

It must be wrong to live this way.

Outside, ground mist still swirls among the trees.

An hour later she's splitting wood, green wood, which is hard, difficult, and just plain dumb. She swings the maul, sinks it halfway into the end of a log, then swings the log and maul overhead, the blade married deep into the wood, and pounds and pounds it on the splitting block.

The impact jars her hips and elbows, her wrists, the base of her neck. The newly opened wood drenches the air with tannin, burning her throat. Her nose drips, her head rings with the metallic screech and whomp of the maul.

According to the books, abstinence focuses the mind.

How does Dayton do it? Does he take himself into his hand in the late-night privacy of his cell? And then confess?

Right this minute if a halfway healthy man stepped across her little bridge, she would leap at him, no matter who he was. For the hundredth time, she wonders if Hal can possibly cure her of Dayton. She stretches, runs her hands from her waist to her hips, amazed that she can still contain a part so wide awake, so voluptuous, so needy. Oh yes, she thinks, abstinence focuses the mind.

That night she sits at her kitchen table, so mad she gets nothing down on paper. She reaches for Saint Barbara, walks her around, considers tossing her into the fire to see if her house comes down around her ears. She pokes idly through her books, scowls at the ones on monasticism. So what if the monks gave us table manners?

This is one tidbit she's picked up in her reading.

The early monks ate two to a plate, two to a goblet, and the table napkin all but invents itself. Each monk has his own, blots his lips before drinking from the shared cup.

They gave us wine, too. And saved the whole of Western Civilization, shivering in their scriptoria, copying books.

They all but invented the hospital, tended lighthouses, offered sanctuary at the foot of their altars.

They were rigid, holy, sybaritic, alcoholic, inspiring.

When a monk asks what else he might do besides pray and fast and tend his soul, his master holds his ten fingers up to heaven and says:

—Be a comet against the sky.

Zoe smiles sardonically.

Then again, the Rule of Benedict requires all the monks to sleep together in one room, lights burning at all times, two older monks on watch, assuring that the young lusty ones lie each alone in his own bed, chaste the whole night through.

She begins to draw, cartoons now, outrageous caricatures.

She sketches a mythical game board. A plain little Protestant church stands in the shadow of a lacy buttressed cathedral. Around the corners are a mosque and reedlike minaret, a stucco synagogue, a temple with a bright-bellied Buddha. Then she sketches herself, age twenty-five, twenty-seven, innocently watching Dayton roll dice.

On another page, she draws the State of Rhode Island, neat and tidy borders to the north and west, the ragged coast to the south, the east side cracked open with bays. And she puts herself at the western border, defiant, arms folded, leaning against a billboard that says: *All religious paraphernalia must be checked.* And she draws Dayton, too, a tiny miniature, standing in Pennsylvania, already in his monk's robes, looking dumbfounded.

In another drawing, she sketches an absurdly long church pew, broad-shouldered Dayton on one end, herself on the other in a profoundly silly Easter hat. And between them, a long line of children in ascending height, as many as she can cram in. Seventeen.

This one she captions: *I capitulate.*

There are things she can't even draw, flickers of troubling images, though she does manage a series of panels so raw and harsh they're almost pornographic. In the first, she kneels in front of him, his penis in her mouth. In the second, semen sprays through the air in great comic quantities, but in the third, he's the one kneeling, in front of a priest, saying, *Bless me, Father, for I have sinned.*

CHAPTER 19

≱

That summer Zoe digs a pool beneath her waterfall. She begins in her rubber boots and woods clothes, but soon wears only old sneakers, nothing else, disturbs rocks from countless years bedded down at just this angle, in just this spot. She labors a week, ten days, two weeks. What's time to her? Finished, she washes her hair with baby shampoo, floats, cools off. Gus runs back and forth on the bank woofing, but will not brave coming in.

At a yard sale she buys an old enamel pitcher, and sometimes in the early morning she carries water jugs outdoors, lets them heat in the southern sun. Late afternoons, she stands naked on her porch, knowing Gus will explode with barking should anyone stop in, and sluices water over her head and face, squeezes lemons into her hair, then lathers with Cetaphil, knows it won't drive her mad with itching. She's long given up makeup, hasn't worn earrings in so long the holes are nearly closed, but she knows, reaching the pitcher up over her head and feeling the water run in sheets down her breasts and along her hips and splatter with abandon, that she's never been more herself, never more female nor more sensual.

She engages in outrageous fantasies about letting Hal Westerbrook find her bathing in this way, or while she lounges naked in the sun, letting the summer air dry her skin, something far from innocence on her face.

And he does drop in, every week or two, having found that Zoe, despite his nagging and Spark's, still has no phone, and he always brings something with him, a nice steak or a bouquet of wildflowers, wine or a six-pack of Vermont-crafted ale, an idea of a place to go for a picnic or out to dinner. But the Hal Westerbrook who shows up, handsome enough in his jeans or khakis and polo shirts, is not the Hal she imagines sporting on her deck.

And as it turns out, she's no wanton either.

Hal is campaigning for reelection, and wants to talk about it. He's been reading about the European Green Party, and he wants to talk about that, too. He wants to talk about everything, Zoe thinks, and as he does she watches his hands, listens to the rhythm of his voice, knows he cares deeply about certain things, knows, too, he was cut out to be a senator. He touches her arm, her knee, and sometimes she thinks he's rehearsing a point to make at a podium. She admires his convictions, she really does, but she seldom listens, amuses herself by capturing his hand, derailing his train of thought. The weather's been so warm, he's seen her in open-necked shirts, has seen the scars on her neck, and he asks about them sometimes, does she want to talk about it, but talking seems more his job than hers. Sometimes he kisses her, and she certainly kisses him back. He touches her breasts with a hopeful look in his eyes, and Zoe's hands have more than once found their way inside his trousers.

But each time, Zoe, who's beginning to think lust, or sexual frustration, might be terminal, finds herself baffled, dull, remote.

She doesn't keep track of his coming and going, but Spark does.

—We're only friends, she says, and throws up her hands in innocence: He likes to talk about electric cars and gray-water filtration. And all you fusty old Republicans, she jokes, then adds: I like a little company once in a while.

After that, Spark comes up more often, invites himself for tea, brings freshly gathered mushrooms Zoe's not brave enough to eat, takes her for a drive along the river to see a pair of eagles nesting in what looks like a sloppy raft of flotsam caught in the high branches of a pine.

At the end of July, he invites her berry picking, shuffles like a schoolboy, jokes he's really only asking permission to pick on what's now her land.

Zoe finds a bowl, goes with him. Gus bounds along ahead of them.

—Knew you two were made for each other, Spark says.

She laughs.

—Saves me all the work of having to bite people myself.

Spark halts, asks, his voice wary:

—He hasn't bitten anyone, has he?

—Not yet, Zoe says, cheerful and flip.

—No unwanted guests?

Still laughing, Zoe shakes her head, then realizes the question is serious.

—Now that you mention it, she says: My car was egged once in town.

—Just yours?

She shakes her head:

—The ones on either side of mine, too.

—Well, then.

She shrugs.

—So, that's it? Spark says.

Well, no, that isn't it.

More and more often lately, she misplaces a tool, later finds it some odd place. A hammer is suddenly hanging from a shed rafter, the plastic sleeve for the chain-saw bar is resting on a stone near the spring, her pry bar leaning in a corner of the outhouse. And twice now, Gus has come trotting back from some private expedition with what Zoe believes to be a slick, fresh knuckle of beef.

But to Spark, she says nothing.

He pauses on the hillside and surveys the stumps neatly trimmed, all the brush piles built going the same way, the remaining trees straight and strong, opening their crowns into borders of light.

—You're careful, he says.

They move across the ridge into an area Zoe has studied

but not begun to thin. He points to a wolf maple, assumes she'll leave it, yet Zoe has been coveting a nice stand of young sugar maples coming in around it. The wolf tree is already dying, its top branches broken, its trunk carved out by rot. In five, ten years it will be gone. Or will be living on one last root.

But the trunk is far too stout to cut in a regular way. It's as wide across as her outstretched arms. She's read in one book and another how to plunge the nose of the chain saw directly into the tree, at some risk to herself, though professionals do it all the time, and she's caught up many nights, even in her dreams, about whether to cut the wolf tree or to leave it.

They get a good crop of berries, but Zoe declines Spark's invitation for shortcake down at his place. She's had enough company for one day.

He watches her a moment, then taps his hat back half an inch, bows sketchily, jokes:

—As you wish, madam.

He swings his bucket in a small salute, heads home.

That night, she sits out on her deck, surrounds herself with a fairy circle of citronella candles to drive away the mosquitoes, and in her notebook tells Dayton:

I'm luckier than you.

Impossible to imagine living as he does, tethered by the whims, wants, conflicts of four other men. Do they wake one another in the middle of the night, whispering of crises of the soul the way her college roommates needed to whisper about their boyfriends, ever envious of the insufferably happy, inseparable Dayton-and-Zoe?

She sketches Spark in his hat and sweaty shirt, sketches him again making a courtly bow, then her tidy woodlot, the wolf tree, her brimming bowl of berries. She declares today the Festival of Raspberries.

She's inventing an entire calendar. Who needs Christmas and Easter?

Perihelion and aphelion, the days the sun and earth steal farthest apart, closest together, were her first acquisitions, and, of course, the equinoxes and the solstices. With some affection she remembers bonfire parties at which she and larking female friends drank entirely too much homemade mead, then leapt over the flames. And then there's Beltane, a pagan holiday she's read about in books, featuring still more bonfires and lots of sex, although she can't remember the precise occasion.

Now if she could only pin down the exact day the blackflies disappear.

A week later, when signs go up in town for an open house at the skete, Zoe smiles to see that, in seriousness or jest, they've chosen the feast day of Saints Fiacre and Giles.

One is the patron of fertility and gardens.

The other of impotence and insanity.

CHAPTER 20

≥⟍

September first is sunny, still, and humid. Zoe wakes with sticky sheets, grumps her way through breakfast, snaps at Gus. She sits at the table staring out at the clearing, drinks herb tea in a vile mood, thinks it ought to be laced with something. Whisky? Cyanide? It's far too hot to work, though this is something of a lie: she's worked in worse weather.

Finally she grabs a towel, heads down to the brook. Her pool is shallower now, but still she undresses, climbs down into it, but can't relax. Vaguely, she recalls that once-upon-a-time she never started any day without a shower. But living in the woods, it's easier to throw water on her face, smear herself with sunblock and bug repellant, and get on with cutting trees, tramping the ridges, doing chores. Later in the day she bathes, a reward, a respite, a gathering of the day's threads, before settling in for her evening.

But here she is.

She washes her hair, splashes water everywhere, climbs out and wraps a towel around her. Mud congeals between her toes; she dunks her foot into the water. A fern sticks to her calf, a mosquito hovers. She swats, swears. She hates the bloody monks, hates Dayton, too. She imagines what it's like there this morning, hectic, tense, festive. She kills the mosquito, a dark smear on her thigh, and remembers the pleasure and irritation of getting ready to have people in, thinking through this detail and that, setting a table, lighting candles, mentally walking through the whole thing step-by-step. With no small jealousy, she assumes that's what the brothers are doing this very minute, except that Dayton can't possibly imagine she herself might show up.

Morosely, she waves at the hovering bugs, examines the scars on her arms. They have faded somewhat, but are certainly still visible, more now that she's come out of the cool water.

Off and on during the week, she's thought about showing up at the skete in disguise. She'd had a student whose mother was a movie star, and the woman had always come to visit wearing a wig, and had instructed her daughter to call her Aunt Liz. They had all gone along with it, pretended they were fooled, but every time Zoe thinks of going to Burlington for a wig or jet black sunglasses and outrageous lipstick, it makes her laugh. The monks are having an open house. Not a costume party. Certainly, she'll cover her arms and neck. Once or twice, she's wandered into the store in the T-shirt she's been wearing in the woods and there's no doubt that every person she's come across has noticed her—the lines on her neck, the tic-tac-toe hash marks on her arms.

Lucky he didn't get my face, she thinks. I'd stop traffic.

She gets up from her rock, her wet hair dripping down her back. She won't go. She'll work, make it a normal day.

But back at the house, she begins to sweat, and in a few minutes she's sitting naked on her porch, cooling off with a washcloth soaked in springwater. She feels powerless and deflated, and with a sickening jolt, remembers this same feeling, the complete inability to move or think. Desperately she tries to conjure what she might do. But her arms are too weak for the saw, and somehow her vision is off, out of kilter.

Gus scratches in the dirt underneath the porch, lies down with a thud.

In time, thoughts trail across her mind like advertising banners behind annoying little airplanes above a summer beach.

She should have gotten that phone.

She should have kept in touch with Zeke.

She should have taken Xanax before she came up.

Getting up, she finds a book on saints, rifles through it as if reading jokes: Saint Elmo who protects the seas. Saint Simeon who lived for thirty-seven years on top of a pillar. Saint Pelegrine, a whore who heard just one sermon, repented, and hid in a cave the rest of her days.

Zoe marvels. Even the book's author concedes that, in real life, saints are often disagreeable.

Harsh.

Irrational.

Certainly not sweet, patient, "saintlike."

And that does it.

She paid their goddamn taxes. She made this goddamn festival possible, and she'll by god show up.

At the sink, she flings water on her face, then pulls on shorts and a thin, long-sleeved shirt. Twisting her hair up beneath her baseball hat, she examines herself in the mirror as if dressing for a bank heist. She wishes she could find some jewelry, but the holes in her ears are gone, and her fingers are too callused and thickened for rings. She whistles for Gus, locks him in the shed; it's cooler than the house, safer, too. As an afterthought, she digs out a sagging woven shoulder bag, drops in her wallet, jackknife, water bottle, Xanax.

She takes them less and less often; she's running low and she doubts Zeke will give her anymore unless she finds a therapist in Vermont.

She doesn't want a therapist.

It's not her fault the world goes wrong from time to time.

The front gate of the skete is flung wide open, and buckets of heavy-headed geraniums blossom in buckets at each gate post.

Zoe brakes, looks for a place to park her car, preferably pointed so she can make a fast getaway.

A glittering blue pickup pulls alongside, and a familiar voice calls:

—You can just drive in.

It's Unity, hanging from the open window, waving.

—You're back, Zoe says.

Unity turns to the driver of the truck, hidden from Zoe's view, then speaks again to Zoe:

—Follow us, why don't you?

Too precipitous, Zoe thinks: What if Dayton is parking cars? She waves, says she'll see them later.

—You have to meet my new boyfriend, Unity calls out, impish, irrepressible: I dumped Tony Emerson.

Zoe sighs.

Somehow she had thought she could come here and see no one she knew. Except Dayton.

Picking her way down the lane, she steps into the margin of the woods as cars come by, most going down the hill but a few already coming up again. She's surprised by the traffic, didn't know so many people in Shroveton wanted to have a look at the place. But many of the cars are from out of state, and Zoe wonders how they found their way there.

Angling through a patch of woods, she regrets her shorts and sneakers, feels silly with a shoulder bag rather than a saw over her shoulder. She comes out behind the barn, touches the fences she watched Dayton paint. How eerie to be down here, inside the valley she's so often spied on. She feels shrunken, tiny, one of the miniature figures she's watched through her glasses, but feels enormous, too, obvious, an interloper in her baseball cap and dark glasses.

For a moment, she looks over at the foot of the lane. There must be a good hundred people here, and Zoe's stunned. Two people are indeed in charge of parking cars; neither is Dayton. And then she's hurt, furious, like a girl who misunderstood an invitation, thinking she was going on a date only to find a whole gang has been invited.

She steps into the barn. A wheelbarrow stands upended against a wall; shovels, rakes, and pitchforks hang neatly in a rack; the floor is raked. In a pen, laying hens peck and murmur, ruffle their feathers, bathe in the dust. Two stalls stand clean and empty. A third opens into a yard, and two pigs trench and snort in the mud near their water trough.

Out around the corner, an ancient Allis Chalmers is parked in the middle of a shed. Around it, tools are stored on rough-sawn shelves. The air's familiar. Oil, lube, gasoline. Zoe composes herself; this is just like her shed, only expanded, as if for the seven dwarves. On the lower shelves rest several chain saws, handles out. She lifts one; the bar is longer than hers, the saw heavier. She tries another, more her size, examines the choke and throttle, tries to figure out how it works, then puts it back. On pegs hang a row of safety helmets, exactly the same as hers. A peach basket tacked to the wall is full of leather work gloves. She takes a pair, tries one on.

A huge black-and-white cat tears around the corner. Startled, Zoe drops the glove, stoops for it. A little girl races in behind the cat, stops, turns and yells back over her shoulder:

—No animals in here.

She spies the cat, tail flared, hissing on an upper shelf. Fists on her hips, she scowls up at it, then at Zoe:

—Who are you?

—I'm picking up these gloves someone dropped, Zoe says, heart pounding.

—Amy, someone calls: Remember what you promised!

—My mom is working, Amy brags: She's very famous. She takes pictures and I'm helping.

She whirls away.

Zoe waggles the gloves a moment, then returns them to their basket as if she's decided against buying them.

Out in a long, open shed, she examines an old but apparently operational sawmill. She's studying the belts, the toothed blades, the guides, wishes she could see it run, and glancing up at racks full of drying boards, she's just wondering if there's some way to have lumber sawn from her trees, when she hears a series of delicate, fast clicks.

She flinches, gasps, reaches for her neck.

—Sorry to sneak up on you, a woman says, lowering a camera.

—You can't use those, Zoe tells her.

The woman apologizes again.

—They might be nice. All silhouettes if they come out right, a person, an old machine? This shed?

Zoe exhales.

—I still wish you wouldn't.

Amy comes tearing back from another direction, stops when she sees Zoe. Amy's mother hands her a small canister, says it would really help if she carried it to the car, and put it in the glove compartment.

Happily, the girl goes away again.

The photographer smiles at Zoe.

—It's just some wrong film. Anything to keep her busy.

She turns, follows Zoe's gaze out across the skete.

Zoe asks who she's working for.

—I'm a stringer for the *Globe.*

—This is really news down in Boston?

She waves at the place, the gardens, tangled now with squash vines and tomatoes; the apple orchard, which Brother Stephen has been pruning; the pond, with chairs around it, all occupied by visitors. Under some maples, tables have been spread with checkered cloths and set with huge ceramic crocks, trays of snacks, bouquets of flowers.

—Just an old hill farm, being brought back to life, Zoe adds.

—But that's just it, the woman says: Is it any different? Is it sacred? Just because they say so?

—They do pray, Zoe says: Probably a lot. There's a regular schedule.

—Admit it, the woman says, shooting up toward the visitors, who from this distance look like picnickers: There's money here. All these repairs cost something. All the gear.

—It's mostly elbow grease, Zoe says: Diligence. They do all of their own work.

The woman nods politely, moves away.

Zoe blots perspiration from her neck, kicks off her sneakers, wanders barefoot up toward the tables. The rich grass pricks her tender soles. At her place, there's no lawn, only the smooth path to the outhouse, the thick soil in her weed patch of a garden. Before she reaches the pond, a path invites her into a flower bed. She follows carefully set stones, finds herself face-to-face with the Virgin Mary.

The Queen of Heaven is in miniature, a tiny statue in a grotto, pale blue cloak, the downcast eyes, the outspread hands.

Zoe glares:

—Tell me this isn't pagan. You standing out here amidst your silly rocks and flowers.

She looks away, toward an alley of white birches, most newly planted. Her respect for the skete shatters. How suburban. Don't these boys know how short-lived white birches are? All but useless except as transition trees? Then she realizes they mark the stations of the cross.

To the Virgin Mary, she says, snidely:

—Couldn't they find an old bathtub for you? I think there's one in the barn.

Abruptly abashed, she realizes she's talking out loud, has become accustomed to doing so in her long days in the woods.

A gangly girl in red shorts goes by spinning cartwheels, and her brother runs behind her, pumping his arms like a machine gun, making shooting noises.

Zoe pulls her cap down over her eyes, scans the place. At least four photographers are hard at work. She feels caught out in the open, notices Brother Red and Brother Luke in their pale denim shirts, ladling tea and lemonade, all the while speaking to a man and woman, writing rapidly in notebooks.

Crouching, she pretends to admire the little statue, fingers the delicate flowers at its feet then, astonishing herself, casually palms the statue, drops it into her bag, murmurs:

—Why don't you just come with me?

☙

The Virgin Mary is only the second thing she's stolen in her life. The first was a Hershey bar when she was seven, and she got caught for that one, the storekeeper waiting for her at the door as she tried to slip away.

But now she stands, zips her bag shut, wanders studiously among the flowers for a long while.

Okay, she tells the Virgin Mary in her head: Let's see what you have for special powers.

She meanders up to the tables, thinks she and the Virgin Mary will have some refreshments, tea, perhaps a cookie. Then someone raises an arm, calls to her.

Hal Westerbrook.

Zoe clenches her hand on her bag, wonders if he saw her in the flower bed, suddenly senses Dayton everywhere, but doesn't see him. Sweat blooms between her shoulder blades.

Hal turns back toward the table, and Zoe scans the crowd, grateful as she'd been so often in the past that Dayton is tall, easy to spot. But she only sees some nuns in navy blue habits, families with children, older couples, small groups of women, a clergyman, some young people, one sitting near the pond with a guitar.

Hal comes toward her, paper cup in each hand:

—Tea?

She takes the cup, thanks him, but unable to keep her eyes on him, glances over her shoulder, thinks that if there still are miracles on this earth, soon her bag will begin to glow. Or the Virgin Mary will speak from among the clutter of Zoe's knife and water bottle.

—Good turnout, Hal says.

Zoe shakes her head, says she didn't expect it. Then she notices his name tag and ribbon.

—You did though.

He smiles, dismissive:

—Just making myself visible.

Then he admits the coverage is the real surprise:

—There are at least four or five media outlets here.

Zoe can't resist:

—Media outlets? Do they allow that kind of talk in Shroveton?
He shrugs, laughs at himself.

Zoe confides:

—They make me nervous, all the cameras.

She wishes they would move off somewhere, scans for something to stand beside, a tree, a stone wall, a building.

He leans toward her, whispers in imitation of old-time radio drama:

—*And in this episode? Will the mysterious benefactress of the monks be revealed?*

Zoe's face tingles, goes numb. She hands Hal her almost empty cup, says she thinks she'll be heading home.

—Busy later? he wants to know: I could stop by.

—Don't, she says, stepping into the shade, then hears herself add: There's someone else.

They're both shocked, Zoe especially, by this abrupt announcement.

—I didn't know, he says, reddening.

Someone calls Zoe's name, and down by the pond, Unity is waving. She's sitting on the grass with a young man, her hand on his bare thigh.

Zoe feels an upsurge of irritation, feels her head clear. She waves at the girl, then tells Hal she's sorry.

—There really isn't anyone else. Honest, she says.

He looks stung.

—Then why say it?

—Off day, she says, bewildered: It's hot. Forgive me. Come some other time, she suggests, knowing all at once that he won't.

—Wait! Unity yells.

Heads turn.

Zoe pushes her bag behind her, mentally tells the Virgin Mary it will just be a few minutes more, then they'll get going.

Unity marches up the sloping lawn, swatting grass clippings from her bottom.

—I'm home, she announces: I was in Burlington, but I'm back now, starting over.

Zoe smiles that, at age nineteen, life might already need to be started over. She half-wishes the girl had stayed away.

Unity's new boyfriend approaches.

Zoe lifts her sunglasses.

—Leland, she says, amazed.

Unity snakes her arm around his waist, laughs.

—Isn't this cool? We're living at the Slipney place. You know, right next to the Higbys.

Hal shifts uncomfortably.

—I sure wasn't going back to Spark's, Unity says.

Her face darkens, and like a small child she mutters something sulky. Then she brightens, asks Zoe why she's at the open house.

—I was wondering that about you, too, Zoe says.

Hal takes Zoe's arm.

—Zoe here is checking on her investments.

She shakes him off, and Leland and Unity exchange glances.

—Some people think they shouldn't be here, Unity announces, as if challenging any takers to a debate. She glances at Leland, adds: All these outsiders coming in and buying up the old places.

—I thought you liked them, Zoe says: So good-looking, so romantic.

Leland scowls at Unity, then wraps an arm around her, gives her a mild shake.

Unity rolls her eyes.

—They paid for the place like anybody else, Hal says, then adds: And Zoe here pays their taxes.

—Once, Zoe snaps: I paid them once.

Leland lifts his eyebrows.

—Other people could have bought this place, Unity counters: Your place, too. You people from away act like nobody here has any money.

Zoe knows the girl is parroting what she's heard in countless gossip sessions in the village. Frustrated, she says:

—I thought you were glad to get rid of the Michaelses.

Leland folds his arms, stands surveying the skete, and Hal joins him, the two of them making a slow study of the gardens, barns, and roof repairs.

—You have to admit they're doing a good job, Hal remarks, then turns to Zoe: Go inside. The light's nice, just like your place. Really, he says: Go on in before you leave, see what you're paying for.

Furious, Zoe snatches her cup from him.

He gives her a sad, apologetic look:

—Now we're both sorry.

—No kidding, Zoe says.

All at once, she catches sight of Dayton in pale blue denim, his hair even blonder in the sun. He's standing on the bottom stair of the front porch, head bent toward a reporter, speaking as if directly to the young man's pad.

—Hal, she says, barely able to hear herself speak: You're right. I think I should go in.

Behind her, Unity calls out something about Gus, Leland cracks a joke, but Zoe can't even conjure the dog, can't believe that any other geography exists, but for these thirty uphill paces between her and Dayton.

CHAPTER 21

꒷

She pulls off her sunglasses, lifts her cap, lets her hair fall free. Twenty feet away, she stands watching him through a scattering of visitors.

He breaks off with the reporter, abruptly glances up, as if having heard someone call his name.

His face is both his own and now his father's, too, the tall forehead and fine hair, the precise jaw and easy smile, the sternness, sorrow, kindliness. He's weathered, wrinkled, perhaps handsome, but something's missing. Mischief, joy, something once irrepressible?

She clutches the contraband in her bag, calls:

—Dayton?

Her voice is raspy, barely audible. She swallows, coughs.

He looks up again.

Suddenly she's crying, feels foolish, frightened. Nearby two nuns break off their conversation and ask if she's all right. Trembling, Zoe nods, stands where she is, wiping her eyes, watches him glance around, humiliated that they should meet again like this, in front of so many witnesses.

And then he hails someone, leads the reporter away from across the lawn.

Stunned, Zoe watches a moment longer, simply can't believe he didn't see her. Slipping her bag behind her hip, she retreats up the stairs into the house, imagines the Virgin Mary smiling.

꒷

The front door leads into a mudroom, and there's the same seven-dwarves feel to the tidily hung jackets, and the boots lined up, heels out. She passes into a dining room, strains to remember the word as if needing it to pronounce a curse. *Refectory.* The wood floor has been sanded and varnished. Two mismatched flea-market cupboards, painted dark green, stand guard along the walls, and in the center of the room is a scarred trestle table. Candles, burnt halfway down, cluster in their holders, and along the sides are table settings, the plates upside down. The head is empty, for Christ, she bitterly surmises.

A book resting on a lectern at least gives the appearance of *lectio,* the reading aloud at meals from inspired texts. She saunters over, half-expects to find a salacious Henry Miller novel.

But it's *Abandonment to Divine Providence,* by De Caussade.

The real thing, she concedes grudgingly.

Her anger falls away and, suddenly exhausted, she pokes her head into the kitchen, which is definitely still in need of work. The metal cupboards are banged and dented, the porcelain sink and drainboard chipped and cracked. Verging on the antique, a refrigerator hums and rattles in a corner.

Other visitors enter the dining room, and Zoe goes out another way. A dark narrow stairway leads toward the second floor, but the way is blocked by a sign on a ribbon: *Private.*

Leaning this way and that, peering up, she sees nothing but bare treads and bare walls, then a landing where the stairs turn out of view.

What she would give for a glimpse of his cell.

Then she startles, gasps.

Behind her Brother Red, flushed pink with embarrassment, is stammering:

—I didn't mean to sneak up on you. I'm only coming around to say it's time for *none.* Well, not right this minute. But in a few minutes. And not in the chapel. But outside. Out back. I mean, usually it's in the chapel but there are too many people. It's fifteen minutes. I mean it lasts fifteen minutes. Or you can just go see the chapel. Or not.

—It's okay, Zoe tells him: It doesn't take much to set me off.

He tells her again he hadn't meant to frighten her, then backs away, distinctly unnerved.

The chapel is a double room, formerly the living room and parlor, Zoe guesses, the wall between torn out. From the doorway she sees exactly what Hal meant. Clear, clean light emanates through three windows on a long north wall. A single eastern window is shaded now, but a matching window to the west lets in a dappled blaze. It gleams along the waxed, wide-planked floor, brightens the cream-painted walls, warms the oiled wood of simple, mismatched wooden chairs. Shadows gather beneath the plain table at the far end of the room. Above it, a cross throws an elongated image of itself across the wall.

Zoe steps in, closes her eyes, breathes long and slow, the way Zeke taught her. She can't pretend she feels a holy presence, even with the Virgin Mary held hostage in her bag, and she cracks a funny smile. Even if by some wild chance she had a conversion, a true call, she could never stay in this very place. She feels the first thrumming of rage, then looks up as if someone's come in behind her.

No one.

Unsettled, she mocks herself. She's not in the market for conversions.

In the next moment, she thinks of Adam. Perhaps he attacked her because she was the keeper of a world in which he was forever the outsider. Hadn't he once said he wanted to be a welder? A sculptor? But common wisdom, in the guise of parents and teachers, had held that he needed academics first, had thrown his language handicaps in his face again and again, supposedly for his own good.

Through the windows, Zoe sees visitors streaming toward the backyard. They drop paper cups into barrels, jostle, whisper, laugh. In the distance, Unity leans back against a tree, her hands slipped into Leland's hip pockets, pressing him against her.

Zoe shakes her head, finds her way to the door, follows the crowd out back.

The hours, the offices, the daily schedule of prayer are at the heart of the monastic day. She hopes Dayton doesn't look up and catch sight of her during his devotions.

Behind the house, chairs are set in careful rows, the seats too close together, molded blue plastic things, no doubt borrowed from a school or bought as an odd lot at an auction. In front of the chairs stand five tall stools, and in front of them a small altar with a crucifix and a bouquet of late-summer asters.

The chairs are quickly occupied, and Zoe stands off to the side behind a young couple with a child. Beside them is a reporter, looking at his watch, pulling a cell phone from his pocket.

You wouldn't dare, Zoe thinks.

Instead, he presses a button, puts it away again.

The kitchen door swings open, and the visitors fall quiet, rustling a little, rearranging themselves in order to see. Out come the brothers, and Zoe hears the click of camera shutters. The monks' feet are quiet across the porch and down the stairs. They're still in jeans but have donned large muslin shirts. Zoe notes their footwear. One pair of Birkenstocks, one of Teva sandals, two pairs of work boots, and Dayton in running shoes.

Her lips twitch.

Not a single bare or bleeding foot.

Each brother stands in front of a stool, bows as if in prayer. Brother Gnome carries a book; the others seem empty-handed.

Zoe watches fiercely.

Dayton's face is pink, a little flushed, but now he exudes a boyishness, though at the same time he seems older than before. She cocks her head, studies him. Is it age? He seems removed, calm, assured.

Her eyes sting with tears, and she slips her hand into her bag, gropes for the Virgin Mary.

Brother Gnome opens the book, speaks a line.

Unable to comprehend, Zoe squints, at first thinks he's reading Latin.

A colleague in Rhode Island, nostalgic at the ripe old age of forty for the old language of her childhood faith, used to sneak off to Latin Masses now forbidden by Vatican II.

Dayton produces a pitch pipe, sounds a low, steady note. The brothers hum, then chant. She listens, watches, sees that while there's some unease among them, perhaps defiance, or vulnerability in praying before strangers, there's also something serene about the chant, comfortable and practiced.

The young father in front of her shifts his child from one hip to another and cuts off Zoe's view. She elbows a little to the side, sees Dayton's eyes are nearly closed. Shutting her own eyes then, she tries and fails to identify his voice among the others. Occasionally she makes out a word or two, English after all, but when chanted somehow foreign, too.

Mystified, she imagines *none* circling the world like a children's round. The globe turns, and at least one enclave in each time zone, hour after hour, picks up the thread of these brief prayers.

CHAPTER 22

After the open house, the newspapers are full of articles and feature stories on the skete. Zoe haunts the Shroveton store, a newsstand in Montpelier, spends a frenzied afternoon at the state library, then races guiltily home, eager to gorge on what she's found.

Except that once she's back on her hilltop, papers and photocopies stacked on the kitchen table, she only circles the pile. She builds a fire, reads a snatch or two, then shies away. Feeds Gus, puts him out, reads a little more. A swath of an interview, the tail end of a feature story, the captions of photographs, a sidebar.

One piece seems to be about their life as a tiny community, full of clever stories and amusing quotes.

Brother Luke explains that if people want to support the survival of monasticism in the north country, they should pray for an early spring. Cabin fever, not property taxes, is the real threat.

Brother Red, apparently blushing, tells the story of half a roast chicken, meant for the next day's sandwiches, that went missing mysteriously one night. With a straight face, he tells the reporter:

—And not a single one of us has ever admitted to it. We're not saints.

There are long philosophical discussions about the history of monasticism, about why the brothers feel the need to purify what already exists. Brother Stephen, refusing to name particular monasteries, though apparently almost provoked to do so by the interviewer, speaks of wanting to boil the day down to work, prayer, rest, and study. And to last as long as possible without pandering to the public, through the sale of baked goods, or whatever.

Brother Dayton breaks in:

—With all due respect, I don't think pander is the best word. Whatever others choose is not for us to judge. This life is the one we five have chosen.

He goes on to speak of a woman named Mary Ward, who founded a similar movement in England, centuries ago, where no vow was made to a bishop, and where the focus was on work and Ignatian theology.

Zoe reads and rereads his words, admits the man who spoke them is certainly her Dayton.

Some interviewers seem to be looking for chinks, and the brothers open these willingly, charmingly to the public view. Besides the missing roasted chicken, there were trees taken down by mistake, inedible meals, pranks, arguments and disagreements, the strain of their chosen life, accompanying doubts.

Brother Gnome curiously admits that while they're scheduled for two to five hours of prayer a day, he probably only manages a minute or two.

Only a minute or two? The interviewer asks what he does instead.

—Oh, I'm *trying* to pray, he says, forthright and somehow appealing: I'm not reading magazines. Pure prayer is harder than it seems.

There are inevitable questions about celibacy.

Brother Luke quotes Saint Augustine's infamous request:

—Lord, make me celibate, but not yet.

Zoe smiles, knowingly.

Brother Stephen says that his wife of twenty-three years passed away, and so that celibacy is different for him than for younger men.

Brother Gnome's marriage failed.

Brother Red admits he only ever wanted to be a priest when he grew up.

Only somehow he landed at Shroveton first.

Brother Luke concedes he finds it a struggle, just tries to think of it as a test of strength, or cleansing, or the only way he can stay focused:

—Sometimes I think of it as a sacrifice I offer up.

Then he shrugs:

—There are any number of mental tricks, or ways to frame it.

Brother Dayton, even when asked directly, has nothing to say, then grudgingly admits there were two heartbreaks for him on entering the life. One was that his father was unable to understand, although in the end he gave his blessing, an act of grace if not of acceptance.

And the other?

Brother Dayton is silent, and the reporter describes his face as pale and still.

—Was it a woman? the reporter prompts.

Brother Dayton refuses to speak, and Brother Luke rescues him, explains that the men are required to have their lives in order, sort out their affairs, before taking their first vow.

—And did you? the reporter asks, still zeroed in on Dayton.

—I did my best, he says.

—You don't sound convinced, the reporter says: Is there someone out there?

But Brother Dayton says no more.

She reads the passage over and over, the questions and answers, but the monks move on and talk about their families.

With tears in his eyes, young Brother Red admits he's sometimes homesick. He misses family Christmases, his brothers and sisters. He's the youngest, so there are already plenty of nieces and nephews whom he hardly ever sees, and he knows it's hard for everyone, never being able to celebrate a christening, Thanksgiving, a parent's birthday, together as one tribe.

Brother Gnome mentions that faith gets them through, the conviction that their work and life here do connect them with their families, and with the world at large.

And he's the one who tells of Dayton's father dying, at least she's certain that's who he must be talking about. That it was difficult for all of them, that in fact, they would have allowed the particular brother to travel home to attend the death itself, since there was no other family, except the end had come too quickly and there had been no time.

The interviewer apparently asked Brother Gnome to say more, perhaps indicate which brother, but all Brother Gnome will say is:

—He's a stickler. Principled. It's not for me to say if he would have made the trip or not. Of course he's grieving. We're human. We grieve. But he'll be fine. He's very steady. The steadiest of us all.

But Brother Luke had added, curiously:

—Although sometimes those are the ones who get hit the hardest.

Brother Gnome reaches a finger into his beard for a subtle scratch, agrees:

—The rest of us have mini-crises all day long. We're used to being tested.

CHAPTER 23

꙳

A few days later, Spark Everett calls on Zoe. On official business:

—I understand you were at the skete on Sunday.

With some deliberation, Zoe reaches down, tosses a stick for Gus to get him to stop barking.

—Is that a crime?

Spark rubs his jaw, sits on the porch stairs.

—I admit. I should have been there myself. Or so I'm told.

Zoe jams her hands into her pockets, puts one foot on the stairs. Frankly, she's amazed by her calm.

The Virgin Mary is up in the cupola, Zoe's hostage.

Spark slaps his thigh. Gus bows and woofs at his feet, and Zoe realizes Spark's ill at ease, off-kilter.

—I'm told my manner could use some work. He sighs, irritated: They called yesterday, but only after the five of them tramped all over hell's half acre, looking at one thing and another, touching things, moving them.

Zoe raises her eyebrows.

—Hell's half acre?

He looks annoyed.

—Apparently someone poured sugar in their gas tanks. The saws, he says: The brush cutter, the generator in the lumber mill. Even two of the vehicles.

Zoe squints.

—All their stuff is wrecked?

Spark shakes his head.

—Just the saws. This Brother David figured out everything might have been tampered with.

Zoe gulps for air.

Spark snaps his fingers for Gus, but turns his head, watches her, waits.

—I was in the shed, she admits: There are even photographs of me taken by some woman from the *Globe*. I was drooling over their sawmill.

She shrugs, makes fun of herself:

—It's not a crime though, is it? Jealousy?

Spark watches Gus snuffling for a stick, looks perturbed.

—I sure wish they'd called sooner. They didn't start the other engines, which was smart, but first they held some meeting or other.

—Oh, Zoe muses: So they have chapter.

—You know what it's called? I never heard of it.

She gestures toward her door.

—I have stacks of books. You saw them.

He leans his elbows on the stair behind him, casually stretches his legs.

—I had an interesting talk with Hal Westerbrook.

Now Zoe panics.

—I wouldn't pay too much attention, she says.

—So Westerbrook was lying?

Zoe fumes, hates these dances.

—No, she says: I hurt his feelings. I was rude. I wish I hadn't been.

—What's your investment then? If there is one?

—Look, Zoe says: If I did have an investment there, I'd hardly be the vandal.

—I don't know, he muses: There's been trouble there off and on since town meeting. Slashed sap lines and whatnot. So I'm asking.

—Fine, Zoe says: I'll tell you. I paid their taxes. Happy now?

Spark smiles to himself, as if he's just forced her to lay down trump:

—That's what Westerbrook said.

—You should have been there Sunday, she says, sighing: They have a lot of supporters. From everywhere. From all over New England. Anyone could have written that check.

—But it wasn't anyone, he says: It was you.

—Yes, it was, she tells him: And I'd be glad if you lived up to your Yankee reputation and kept it quiet.

—They don't contribute to the town, he says.

—But who exactly are they hurting?

He gets to his feet.

—They're taking up my time, for one.

Zoe softens.

—Look, I paid their taxes because I thought it was the right thing to do. And, she adds, turning huffy: The person who's taking up your time is the jerk with the sack of sugar.

All at once she remembers Unity and Leland, so involved with each other as the crowds passed by them for *none*.

—How long would it take?

—Only a few minutes, if you had it planned.

Zoe looks at him:

—Fifteen?

—What is it?

She sighs, looks out into her trees, rubs Gus behind the ears.

—Unity was there. I don't know if you know that. She and Leland. They didn't go out behind the house to listen to the afternoon prayers.

—And then what? Spark says quietly.

Zoe falters.

—I don't know, I left right afterward. I just couldn't take anymore.

Spark's shoulders relax.

—Too much popishness?

—It wasn't that. They're hardly popish. It was. . . .

—Never mind, Spark says: Probably you came home for the same reasons I didn't go in the first place. It was stinking hot and I was in no mood for crowds.

—Talk to Unity, Zoe says.

Spark narrows his eyes.

At times, Zoe revels in the autumn. The light's delectable, clarifying, like reading that Dayton still thinks of her. Then she thinks, no, he doesn't miss her, he was merely goaded by the reporter. And then all she notices are the lowering skies and the red-black leaves on diseased maples, the hemlocks and spruces killed off by acid rain.

She hears nothing more about the troubles at the skete, and when she stops in at Spark's, he's polite but curt.

From the pay phone at the store, she calls Hal Westerbrook to say hello.

—How are things?

—Fine.

—Beautiful fall.

—Been walking?

—Some.

When Zoe ventures an apology, he thanks her, but says they might as well not see each other anymore.

—So much for your interest in eccentrics, she says.

—I wish you well, he says: Honestly I do.

She tries to be sad, but it doesn't matter.

Sometimes she wonders when she turned into a loner, recalls that certainly she'd been all-too-vocal in meetings at her college, once had actually asked the board of trustees to explain when education had segued into a money-making enterprise. Whatever had happened to public trust?

She takes to climbing ledges, scrambling up with her toes and fingers, Gus whimpering far below. She scrapes her hands, tears her trousers, scuffs her sturdy hiking boots.

One afternoon, she slides down a ledge so slick and crumbling she shouldn't be on it, loses her balance and goes into a headlong tumble, comes to a rest convinced she's hurt.

Gus whimpers, licks her face.

She moans, moves, drags herself home, back wrenched, shoulder and arm bruised.

Nothing liniment won't fix.

Another day, she puts on all her rain gear, goes out into a howling thunderstorm as if she hears her name in it. Gus sticks close to her, tail down, dubious but loyal, shoulder against her leg, squinting in the downpour. High winds whip the trees. Branches fall like spears, trees uproot. Lightning halves the sky.

What relief, what calm, having her mood matched, stroke for stroke.

When she works again, she's unstoppable. She cuts trees where they hang, reaches the saw overheard and whacks off limbs, even plunge-cuts the old wolf maple. Then late one afternoon, long after she should have quit for the day, dropping one last tree, then another last tree, another, for the pure pleasure of watching them fall, not bothering to limb them, cut them to length, she attacks an oak, fourteen inches in diameter, cuts it recklessly, no wedge cut, no back cut.

Instead of falling, it twists up off its stump.

Appears to hover.

Then spins, flips over backward.

Zoe dives.

The tree catches her shoulder hard, knocks her off her feet.

There's simply no way around it. She should be dead. She's not, but she certainly is terrified. What's more, she stays terrified. Sobers up.

Every night, she sits on her hearth, draws the tree launching up, spiraling down.

And she finally remembers their last evening together. A Thursday, and she was lying on her couch. That afternoon a fight broke out in the back of the junior-high art room near the end of last period, and she had five minutes flat to get the perpetrators to the office and write the incident report before attending a teachers'

meeting at which it was announced they would be translating
the entire curriculum from one set of fancy, meaningless terminology into another, just as fancy, just as meaningless. Afterward
she still had to clean the art room, prep for the next day's classes,
and now it's half past ten, and she's too exhausted to drag herself
to bed.

Dayton appears at her door, haggard, full of longing and his
mysterious sadness. But at least he gives her a reason to get up,
turn off the television, and once they are in bed, he kisses her
neck, unbuttons her pajama top, then stops, reaches over, turns
off the light.

Zoe reaches up, turns it back on, snaps:

—Let's give that God of yours a ringside seat.

Dayton stills, and that instant she hates him, hates herself even
more. She sobs, all the wear and tear of the day, and the knowledge that she hates her job, that she has it only because she
wants to be near Dayton, even though she won't marry him until
they're through this God-thing.

By now, it's nearly midnight, her alarm will go off before six.
She touches his face, tender, frightened, whispers:

—We can't go on like this.

He says nothing.

—Can we? she whispers.

Sadly, she snaps off the light, and digs in beside him, tries to
get more comfortable, asks if they can please sleep now and see
this in a new light tomorrow.

Dayton is more quiet than he's ever been.

Finally when Zoe whispers that maybe they need counseling,
she's desperately relieved to hear him agree.

But then it turns out she means a couple's counselor, and
Dayton is thinking of a priest.

She sighs, finds his hand, kisses the back of it, hates how the
God-thing turns them into strangers, says nothing more, tries
to sleep.

Of course, she can't and finally she climbs back onto her couch,
curls up and dozes off in front of some old movie. In the morning,

she's wakened by the distant clangor of her alarm and, neck and shoulders stiff, she heads back to her bed, wondering if she agrees to speak with one of his God-friends, he'll agree to see a counselor she might choose, surely there must be a way to fix this. But Dayton is gone.

No note.

No token.

No anything.

CHAPTER 24

⚘

Late October, in the midst of a stretch of overcast days and lingering showers, Gus wakes abruptly before dawn, woofing long before his eyes are open.

—Oh, for heaven's sake, Zoe mumbles: Like you haven't heard that before.

Rain, drumming on the propane tanks.

She digs back into her pillows, sleeps forever.

Finally, when she does get up, the house is chilly and her head is full of wool. She builds a fire, heats water, feeds Gus, and lets him out into the rain. Perhaps she'll go to town, stock up on a few things for the winter, kerosene, bar lube, dog food, and whatnot. It seems like a good day to get out, go for a drive.

Outside, Gus thuds across the porch. Zoe runs a comb through her wet hair, without thought opens the door for him.

Then stares, pulls back.

Gus is prancing on the deck, paws flipping up, some treasure in his mouth. He bows, stretches out his forelegs, grins, invites her out to play with his new toy.

Which is dripping onto the deck.

Zoe screams.

Slams the door in his face, leans her shoulders against it, shuts her eyes.

This is no prize stick or long-lost tennis ball, no mysterious, fresh knuckle of beef.

She bolts the door, huddles on the couch with her head between her knees. White flashes in her eyes. Trembling, she yanks her sleeves down over her hands, reaches up and holds her neck.

Finally she draws a deep breath, opens the door. Gus wriggles happily, snatches his toy, trots over to her, lays it at her feet. She snags his collar, hangs on tight, drags him away, and locks him in the shed.

By the time she gets to Spark's, she's incoherent.

Words present themselves in nearly random order:

Head.

Gus.

Legs.

Pile.

Entrails.

Spark has her sitting down by now, is handing her a glass of water, looking out the window for her car.

—How did you get here?

—Ran, she says, shocked and blank: How else?

—Is it a doe?

She stares. The picture is clear as day to her: just behind her parked car, four legs and a heap of red, black, purple entrails. Dirt and bits of leaves stick to the drying membranes.

He shakes his head with disgust.

—Jackers, he says, and goes to the phone, dials a number without looking it up.

Zoe swishes water in her mouth, thinks she should dash it on her face. She hears him say "poached." Hears her own name, the plan to meet at her place.

Then they get into the car and drive on up.

Spark asks where Gus is and she tells him.

He taps the brake.

—Did he bring it down?

Zoe squints, gives Spark a weird grin.

—I don't think Gus carries a knife.

Spark shifts his shoulders, moves his hands on the wheel.

—If it was Gus, he says: I'll have to shoot him. Which I most likely should have done back at the get-go.

Zoe registers this remark the way one more cannonball hits the ground in the midst of battle. Winces, automatically.

—He's not this neat, she says.

Spark pulls in beside her car, and Zoe stays in the truck. She wraps her arms around her middle, presses her face against the cool window glass. Once she glances over her shoulder, sees Spark staring down at the legs and guts, then looking around.

In time another vehicle charges up the lane, as fast as if there is a bleeding victim who might yet be revived.

The fucking thing is dead, she thinks, and trembles all over again.

Over in the shed, Gus roars.

The two men greet each other, camaraderie in their voices, the two guys in charge of keeping things under control, and Zoe's abruptly angry.

It's not her fault the fucking deer got itself jacked on her property.

Not her dog's fault either.

Then the image of the head in Gus's mouth, the doe's gray tongue and thin bloodless lips, hangs in the air before her. She opens the truck door, tumbles out, desperate for fresh air. Perched on the running board, she puts her head between her knees.

In a moment, she hears a voice:

—Ma'am? I'm Jim LeFebvre. The game warden.

—Gus didn't do it, she tells the ground between her feet.

There is silence, then Spark's voice saying:

—Gus is the dog. He pauses, adds: The Higby dog.

—She has the Higby dog?

Spark laughs.

—It's okay, he's in the shed.

After a moment, the game warden says:

—Just about perfect for up here, isn't he?

Then it's clear they want Zoe to stand and walk over to the

heap of deer parts with them, as if she is immediate family, asked to verify the identity of a corpse.

The questions begin, and Zoe has no answers.

No, she heard nothing. Well, just the rain.

Yes, Gus did bark but that's not unusual.

Maybe after midnight, again before dawn.

No, she hasn't seen anyone odd, no traffic, no one even hiking through. Not that she knows of, and anyway, Gus would have heard.

Spark watches her steadily, as if waiting for something but the warden's not surprised.

—Lots of guys know this land to hunt across. All these old logging roads.

The two men walk off, shoulder to shoulder, examining one thing and another, the dirt road, the brush beside it. Zoe leans against her car, wonders when they'll move the pile of guts. She wants to remind them to get the head off her porch.

When they come back, the warden rattles off a list of eight or nine names for Zoe. Has she seen any of them?

By name, she recognizes only Leland and the Higby brothers. And she'd know only Leland by sight. Possibly Mike Higby. She shakes her head, shrugs an apology, doesn't say she can't tell apart the young working men of Shroveton, the loggers and hunters, the carpenters and laborers. The ne'er-do-wells either, for that matter.

Spark jerks his head at the deer guts:

—What do you think about that though?

The warden doesn't know.

—Usually they like to hide that stuff. Leave it in a ditch, kick leaves over top of it.

—What about that young man of yours, Spark asks Zoe: Could it be him?

She squints up at him.

—What young man, she says, then adds, stupidly: Hal Westerbrook?

Spark looks up into the trees.

—He runs crossways to me, but I don't think he's a jacker.

—Jesus, the warden says: The senator?

—Friend of Zoe's, Spark says, then corrects himself: I meant your slasher.

Outraged, Zoe stares at Spark, feels a tirade loose itself in her brain, doesn't speak.

—Miss Muir was attacked before she came up here. She's one of those delightful folks who think you can get away from it all up here to Vermont.

Vur-mont, he says, landing hard on the first syllable, mocking her and every other living person who failed to have the good sense to be born north of the Massachusetts border.

—Doesn't seem to know it's practically the best place in the country to hide out from the law, he adds: Not enough police, and we leave our neighbors be. Can't even get her to keep a gun.

Zoe cannot move.

—This was done by a hunter, the warden says.

—Someone good with a knife anyways, Spark adds.

—I don't like this, the warden says, waving an open palm toward the back of the car: Why put the entrails there?

—And the legs, Zoe says.

—Where was the head? Spark says.

Zoe stares.

—Gus brought it to me.

—So we don't know if it was here with the rest.

The game warden's voice is low and shocked:

—What are you saying?

—Seems like a message, Spark says: Who's going to run over this mess with their car? I wouldn't.

Desperate for medication, Zoe tries to move her hands, but they jerk like the appendages of a robot whose wires are loose.

—You ever file that report? Spark asks Zoe: About that boy?

Zoe shakes her head.

—No.

—Do you know if he ever hunted? the warden asks: With his dad or anything?

—Show him your arms, Spark tells her.

She won't.

—They're cut, she mutters, and clamps them tight.

—I see her neck, the warden says: That's enough.

Zoe glances up, sees a softness, fear almost in his eyes, and for a moment she thinks the one thing she hasn't done since the attack is lie in someone's arms and sob her heart out over what's become of her. And she won't do it now, either, instead becomes that pioneer woman on the trail, who has buried her husband just after dawn, said a prayer, read from her battered Bible, now harnesses her team and gets going because there's ground to cover, today like every day, before the sun goes down.

—You're hurting your own case, Spark says: I'll ask one of the boys to stop out and take a statement.

Zoe grimaces.

—A trooper, he adds.

—Not if you don't want to, the warden says: Not if the report's been filed in some other jurisdiction.

—Rhode Island, Zoe says: And he's under lock and key.

—Last we talked you didn't know how long. You didn't even know what kind of admission.

Zoe watches her feet. Her head feels as if it is being pressed in from both sides.

—Fine, she says, knowing she'll have to call Zeke anyway and beg for more drugs: I'll ask.

Spark shrugs, gives the warden a meaningful look.

—Anything else, Jim?

He fidgets.

—I'm wondering about the situation here in town. Aren't you the lady who bought this place out of the blue? Just showed up one day with a check?

Zoe swallows.

Jim LeFebvre glances at Spark.

—Any connection?

Spark shrugs, disgusted, turns to Zoe as if this is all her fault, and tells her again to get a phone.

The warden watches Spark, then says:

—I'll go pay some calls on my usuals. See who has what hanging in their garage today.

Spark gets in his truck, heads down the hill, offers one slow wave behind him out the window.

—What's up with him? the warden asks.

—You wouldn't believe it if I told you.

What would she say? I used to see Hal Westerbrook? I paid the taxes on the skete? She has run crossways, as Spark would put it, to Spark's iron will, and she has a sudden flash of empathy for Unity. In Spark's world there is a narrow band where thoughts and actions meet approval. Outside that band, all is bad behavior.

—Then I'll ask this, the warden says: Are you safe?

Zoe smiles.

—Once upon a time I thought I was, yes. Then I wasn't. Now I think maybe none of us are.

She looks into his eyes and wonders if he knows what it's like to live in a world as dangerously balanced as her own, where sometimes all that gets her through the day is the knowledge, and she can take a deep breath and verify this, that right this minute no one has sunk a knife into her flesh.

—You want me to move this? the warden says.

Zoe feels a wildness in her eyes. What she wants is to keep him here. Maybe it's the uniform, maybe it's the eyes so brown they're nearly black, maybe it's the fact that he makes his living in and about the woods.

—You go on in, he says: I'll take care of this, then I'll come in and wash up if you don't mind.

—The head's over by the deck, she says, not budging.

The warden takes a plastic bag from his truck.

Mechanical and dazed, Zoe goes indoors, refusing to look right or left. She puts water on, blesses her morning instincts to tidy up, and in a little while there's a knock and she calls for him to come in.

The door opens an inch.

Gus is roaring again out in the shed.

—That dog's not in here, is he?

Zoe smiles.

—In the shed.

She leads him into the kitchen, gets out the mixing bowl she uses for a basin, pours in some boiling water, then some cold, tests it, points him toward the soap and a towel. He kicks up a little storm in the basin as he washes, lathering up to his wrists. She likes the vigor of it, sees his hands as two friendly wrestling fish, hands him a towel.

Two hours later she's sitting in his office, a cubbyhole of a place, reading notices stabbed onto a nail driven into the corner of the bulletin board. He'd asked if she had someone to call and she'd said yes, although she has nowhere to call from. There's no one she can impose on, and no way is she standing outside the front door of the Shroveton store, trying to reach Zeke on the public phone. For a moment she thinks of the skete, wonders if they'd loan their phone and grant a little privacy in exchange for payment of that tax bill.

Instead, Jim LeFebvre, after some mulling, offered her the use of his office. He'll write the call off as pursuit of information. He's going out on a limb for her and, in exchange, Zoe's promised to tell him if the boy is still in custody.

He's pulled out the banged-up office chair, shown her where to get coffee down the hall, and told her that she can't have anyone call her back because when he's not in, the state police dispatcher gets his calls, contacts him on the road. He looks at his watch, says he has to dash, and overcome by his own kindness, shuffles out of the office. Zoe wonders if he's unaccustomed to dealing with human victims, isn't more accustomed to criminals and scofflaws.

She waits to call Zeke, hopes to catch him in the magic ten-minute breather that supposedly exists between one patient and the next. Zeke has faded into some netherland of history, has become someone she once knew, some long-lost baby cousin. Often she thinks of telling him about trees she's felled or seeing a fox or finding the entrance to a bear's den. But she knows these would mean nothing; she's slipped into a world beyond his limits.

Closing her eyes, she tries to imagine what shirt, what tie he might be wearing that day, then knows she's been gone so long he's no doubt acquired a new wardrobe. She wonders if he still has the leather desk chair, the prints of Chinese characters?

She looks down at her work boots and saggy sweater, fingers an earlobe, pulls her hair over her shoulder, eyes the ends. A trim wouldn't hurt, and while she waits, she opens the warden's desk drawer, finds a comb, and fiddles with her hair, does it up in a French braid. More interesting than reading memos on the State of Vermont's sexual-harassment policy, the notice of the next state employee union meeting, or the new, and stricter, policy on taking a personal day.

I'm taking a personal decade, she thinks: Maybe I'll make my whole life personal.

At ten minutes before the hour, she dials Zeke.

Gets the machine.

She is silent a moment, then says, trying to sound happy and diffident:

—Hey, it's me. Zoe. Just calling to check in.

She gives the time, says she'll try again for the next fifteen minutes. She has no number to leave.

Her heart is racing now, and snow whitens her vision. Her hands turn numb. She'd felt safe in this office, hidden. For a moment, she tries to think of other places no one would ever find her.

On a rifle range, she thinks.

In a convent.

In a classroom, she adds bitterly.

She dials the number again.

Still no Zeke.

She leaves a shorter message, watches the clock, feels a sudden terror that he's out of his office, away on vacation, at a conference, getting his own silly hair cut.

The next time she dials, she gets the number wrong, is informed the line is out of service. Breathing hard now, she tries again, lets out a gasp when Zeke answers.

—Dr. Polushka, he says, in a voice low and modulated as if ready to hear anything, soften any blow, empathize with the impossible.

Zoe can't speak. Her eyes well. All she wants is to listen to his voice, doesn't care what it says.

After a moment, he says:

—Zoe?

—Yes, she manages: Yes.

She takes a deep breath.

—It's just such a surprise to hear your voice, she says, and then she's sobbing, sobbing and apologizing, suddenly laughing, too: You always wanted me to do this.

—Do what? he says, his voice wary and full of caution as if she might be about to light the fuse on a Molotov cocktail.

—Cry, she says, wiping her nose on her sleeve.

—You called for a reason.

Silence.

And then:

—Someone jacked a deer and we need to know if it's a message.

—Zoe, Zeke says: I'm having trouble understanding.

—Do you have someone at eleven?

—They've just come into the waiting room, he tells her.

She smiles at this penchant for professionalism; even at this distance, he won't disclose the gender of his waiting client.

—Can I call again?

—Not like this. Let's make an appointment.

—I'm not driving to Rhode Island.

—On the phone, he tells her: Can you call back at three? I have a cancellation.

—Okay.

—You'll be all right until then?

—Sure, she says, wondering what in hell he would do if she said no.

CHAPTER 25

꙲

As promised, she writes Jim LaFebvre a note and locks the door behind her. She can't talk to her shrink for an entire hour on the game warden's phone; she's seen enough of those state notices to figure there'd be trouble.

For a while she sits in her car, wondering what to do. She'll check into a motel; that's the easy part. But which motel? Finally she heads to Burlington and finds her way to the Radisson. Hadn't she said it was a good day to go somewhere?

Her room has a view of Lake Champlain. Across the water, the hills of New York are curtained with fog and clouds.

She spends pretty much forever in the shower, regrets having nothing to put back on except her woods clothes, and in a fit of inspiration, does a little shopping at an outdoor gear place, buys a clean one of everything except boots. Back in her room, she pops the plastic anchors off the price tags, pulls on stiff new jeans and a soft sweater with a slight, brand-new chemical smell, new socks, and her old, damp boots. And then she heads out again, finds a haircutting place that will take her as a walk-in.

—Just trim the bottom, she keeps saying: I'm in a hurry.

She tells herself Zeke will worry if her call is even a few minutes late, but in truth, this is her first haircut since the attack. When the young woman offers to cut some layers into her hair to give it shape, Zoe nearly bolts out of the chair.

By ten to three, she's back in her room, sitting at the small table by the window, fingering the clean blunt edges of her fresh haircut, rehearsing what to say to Zeke and how to say it. Lately, her voice is sometimes rusty, from disuse she supposes, though it seems to her she talks all day long, though mostly to herself and Gus. She clears her throat, sips some water.

Down on the lake, a ferry boat blasts its horn, churns away from the slip.

At three, she dials.

Zeke, of course, sounds calm as anything, deliberately so, a man with his feet braced on the deck of a rolling ship:

—Dr. Polushka.

While Zoe sounds like the idiot who's been washed overboard, screeching for help:

—Zeke? It's me. It's Zoe. You said I could call at three. It's three now, isn't it?

She clamps her mouth shut tight, knows she sounds frantic, not casual, composed.

—Zoe, he says: How have you been?

And never mind the rehearsal; she tells her tale all in a jumble, the deer guts this morning, Gus carrying the head to her, the game warden letting her use the phone only now she's calling from a hotel. She'd meant this last to sound as if she's calm and full of forethought, but to her ear she sounds like a refugee. It's the constable who's making her call and find out about Adam. Should she file a report with the state police? What does Zeke think? Was Adam admitted voluntarily or otherwise and where he is now, because even the game warden thinks the way the entrails were left was some kind of message, though she guesses it could be anyone. After all, she's ticked a few people off because she's paid the taxes at the skete and it wasn't just developers who wanted to buy her place.

Zeke interrupts:

—Zoe, he says quietly: Tell me if you're all right. I can't understand any of this.

—I need more Xanax, she says: I've been hoarding it, I'm nearly out, but I'm okay really.

Even as she says this, she suddenly admits, though only to herself, that even before the deer was jacked, she was careful to be indoors before full dark, that she can't even say when the last time is she left her property in the evening. If she's out in the open of her clearing when a plane passes overhead, she steps into the protection of nearby trees; certainly she's grateful for the infamous Higby dog, hopes it's true he's vicious.

—Okay? he says: Okay in what sense, exactly?

—You know, she says: Okay.

—Are you sleeping?

—Yes.

She has a dog now, he's quite protective. She should have gotten one back in Barstow. She doesn't have a gun though. Or a phone.

—A phone sounds good, he says, his voice warm yet measured, as if talking someone down off a ledge: But a gun?

—The constable thinks I should get one.

—And what do you think?

—Not a great idea, she tells him.

He asks about depression, flashbacks, the white flashes in her eyes.

—I got a haircut, she volunteers.

He sighs.

—And how often do you do that?

Silence.

Then she admits today was the first time.

—One haircut in how long?

Zoe doesn't know.

—You've really been out of touch, he tells her.

—I talk to you in my head, she says cheerfully, means it as a joke, though in fact it's true.

She adds:

—Though mostly I can't imagine you would get what I'm talking about.

—And why is that?

She remembers how much she hates this therapeutic questioning, this interrogation essentially for her own good.

—I have a dog, she says: I cut trees. I heat with wood. Do you really want to know how nice the outhouse smells with kiln-dried pine shavings?

—Oh, Zoe, he says, as if she is a child who has just spilled her milk.

—Anyway, I'm doing pretty well. Only now there's this trouble. Someone jacked a deer and left the entrails. . . .

—Jacked a deer, he says gently.

—Poached, she says, her voice ragged: Gus brought me the head. All that blood.

—And Gus is?

She begins to sob.

—The fucking dog.

—And why do you think this has to do with Adam?

—I don't, she says, angry: Everyone else does.

—Everyone else? And who is that?

—The constable. The game warden. I'm supposed to call you and find out where he is. Where is he?

Her voice is full of terror and of begging.

—Zoe, he says: Do you remember that your part of the settlement means you're supposed to keep this as confidential as you can?

And she blows.

—Confidential? Confidential? My body looks like someone couldn't get the hang of the knife trick at the circus. This is a small town. By now she's shrieking: A goddamn small town.

Someone in the next room raps on the wall.

Her voice drops.

—I drove fifty-five fucking miles so I could call you on the phone. In private.

For a moment, there's silence.

And then Zeke asks her to do her best to listen. Can she find something to focus on, perhaps the hand that doesn't hold the phone? Perhaps she can try to touch something with that hand and focus on it?

—Okay, she says, ignoring her hands altogether and staring out at the lake. She longs to be back in her woods, safe from all of this.

Then she remembers the deer guts.

And the head.

Quietly Zeke explains that Adam is still in the hospital, though he's now allowed out on furlough.

—Furlough?

—You'd said you'd listen.

She narrows her eyes, fumes.

—First he was allowed out for a few hours, accompanied by a staff member. Now I believe it's a day. But he's closely supervised. Whatever happened up there couldn't have been him.

—Was he in the hospital last night? Is he there right now?

—I don't know.

—Can you call?

—I can, he says: But I don't like the way you sound.

—What if the police call you? The ones from here, I mean.

—Are you giving me permission to talk with them?

—What do you mean? It's not about me.

—Some of it is, he says gently.

She wonders what strength of glass they use in these picture windows, guesses that five stories up she couldn't actually hurl the phone through it.

—All right, she says, her voice measured, too, icy cold: I'll just finish my statement by saying that I don't know whether he was in the hospital and accounted for at the time.

There's a stretch of quiet, then Zeke asks:

—Do you think Adam knows how to poach deer?

—No, she snaps: I don't. Or I didn't. It's the constable.

—So let's just leave it at that. If it will get him off your back, give him my number. I won't say anything about you, but I won't say anything about Adam either.

—What kind of admission was he? Involuntary? Or—

—Right at the moment, Zoe, I don't think I should tell you.

—Fine, she says: How about more Xanax?

As far as she's concerned this is an even bargain. If he won't give her information, he can at least give her drugs.

He sighs.

—You know I can't.

—Sure you can, she says, and tries to make a joke, wonders where their old relationship got to, anyway: You just get out your little pad, you write my name at the top—

He interrupts:

—I'd ask if you had a new therapist up there, but it's obvious you don't.

—Obvious? Why? Do I sound nuts?

In fact, she fears she does sound nuts, fears that maybe she is, just a little, not too bad, no more eccentric than anyone else who lives alone in the woods.

—I didn't say that, he tells her: It's just that you wouldn't have to call down here for meds. You'd have someone there who could get them for you.

—Oh, she says: Well, I don't. I just wanted to leave myself alone.

—And is that working?

—I run a mean chain saw, she tells him: Not only that. I own the whole goddam top of a mountain.

—And what about Dayton?

—Dayton?

—Yes, he says: Dayton. Have you seen him?

Zoe turns cagey:

—Yes, I've seen him.

—And what was that like?

—It's only been twice. Or a couple of times, I forget.

She figures she'd best leave out the part about spying on the skete.

—How did it go?

—I don't know, she says: I haven't talked to him. Only seen him.

—I guess I don't understand, Zeke says again.

How different from the old days when Zeke seemed to understand her most bizarre symptoms.

—I haven't had the chance to talk with him, she says: Though I write to him. He is a monk, remember.

Zeke's voice lightens.

—So you're corresponding? Well, that gives you some support. He pauses, then adds: So he wouldn't know about the deer yet?

Zoe hesitates. She simply cannot say she's never mailed a single letter, that mostly she draws him pictures, so instead she ponies up a confession:

—I'm still a little in love with him. And well, it wasn't all his fault.

—What wasn't?

But now she's sobbing:

—I'm just glad to have whatever contact I can manage.

—I'm proud of you, Zeke tells her, his voice rich, expansive: You had to come to some kind of resolution.

Resolution.

Zoe stares at the lamp on the table. Touches the shade, the little fake key that turns it on and off. Tries it. Turns the light on, turns it off. Resolution isn't what she wants.

Zeke chuckles:

—I must admit I never thought living up there was a good idea.

Vaguely, she hears him moving back into the old easy arena they once occupied.

—We're almost out of time, she says.

—Zoe? he says: I shouldn't tell you this, but I often wonder how you are.

Then he offers her a deal. He'll send one scrip for Xanax, not renewable, if she'll write him one good long letter and tell him more about her life.

—Will you send it right away? I'll start my letter to you tonight.

—I'll trust you for it.

She asks if there isn't anything more he can tell her about Adam, but all he'll say is that he's concerned; he'll make some calls. Meanwhile she also has to promise to find a therapist. He'll send a list along with the prescription. Then he jokes:

—I gave you a list once but you probably used it to start a fire in your fireplace.

—Woodstove, she corrects.

She's eager to be off the phone, to end the posturing, the bargaining.

—I can't tell you how happy I am that you've begun to reframe your relationship with Dayton.

Reframe, Zoe thinks: As if Dayton is a painting on a wall.

But then Zeke takes her by surprise:

—Is there something else? I feel as if there's something else.

—Nope, she says with great cheery finality: Absolutely nothing.

CHAPTER 26

Just before deer season starts, Zoe stands in front of a stack of *No Hunting* signs down at Rileys, hands thrust in her pockets, mulling. Maybe she can post a good five acres around her house, a demilitarized zone, and hunker in it for the duration.

She asks Leland again how the posting should be done.

—Can't up there.

She bristles.

—Oh, really?

With pleasure he recites the law. She needs a sign every so many feet, and each sign must be mounted on a separate board and hung. She must sign and date each one. They're not valid just stapled to the trees, and she'd better check them often because if one goes missing the whole place is as good as not posted.

—You know, she says, sarcastic: If you weren't so discouraging, you could have sold me a whole pile of these. Does Callum know you're bad for business?

She picks up a Safety Zone sign.

—What if I put up some of these?

—Might's well not, Leland says: Everybody knows you're there.

Zoe shudders, gives the idea up, but when hunting season begins she must force herself to go outside. She imagines getting shot on her way back and forth from the outhouse, hears the story of a woman "from away" killed in her own backyard, hanging laundry, hears, too, the widespread condemnation, not of the hunters, but of the woman herself. How stupid, wearing white mittens in November. Or maybe it was the white baby clothes she was hanging they mistook for the deer-flag.

Every time she steps outside, Zoe dons hunter-orange. At Rileys, she buys a second vest, and every day pulls it over Gus's head, tapes him firmly around the middle. He's so goofy he thinks it's fun, doesn't fuss with it at all. It's better than just an orange collar, though frankly she wishes she could dye the whole damn dog fluorescent.

Within days, her hair-trigger startle reflex returns. The slam of a car door, a man's shout across a ridge, a shot, and she flinches, throws her arms up before her face. Each time she reacts, Gus explodes into barking, and she knows he's taking cues from her. More and more often, he barks on his own now, too, and that sets her off as well. Her nights are worse again and she wakes, every ninety minutes, every sixty, every forty-five. She goes to a drugstore, gets some over-the-counter stuff for sleep, then won't take it for fear she'll sleep through danger.

She spends her days sitting at her windows, sketching the cars coming up the road, the men in their plaid killing clothes, armed with their deer rifles and knives, hot seats flapping at their butts. When she can, she sketches faces, mentally matches them to men she's seen around town, tries to capture the way they walk through her woods as if they own them.

One Saturday, when the traffic has been heavy, and Gus, cooped up, has been barking at the windows like a madman, slow footsteps cross the porch.

Gus roars across the room and, blind with righteousness and frustration, he stumbles through the hiking boots Zoe has left lying, hurls himself anyway, but misses the door, and slams hard against the mirror.

It explodes into shards.

Zoe flings her arms up.

Now there's knocking at the door, and Gus leaps and barks, again and again, landing in the scattering of jagged mirror shards. Zoe swears, snatches his collar, hauls him off to the side. He leaves a trail of bloody paw prints.

When the caller knocks again, Zoe closes her eyes, actually hears Gus's jaws snap, knows the floor will soon be slick with blood.

The caller knocks a third time, harder now. Through the window, Zoe sees a tall thin hunter in red plaid, shoulders hunched up around the ears. Jesus, she thinks. Another jackass who isn't dressed for the weather. Fuck it, she says, lets Gus go, opens the door.

He lunges out, lips drawn back, an eager lion ready to devour a Christian for a midmorning snack.

Zoe doesn't care.

All around her on the floor is blood. What's a little more if Gus chews up a hunter? Maybe then people will leave her alone.

Outside, the barking stops, and Zoe hears Gus doing his happy footwork. Puzzled, she leans out, sees the visitor bending toward him, ruffling his ears.

—Jesus, Zoe says: Unity.

The girl looks up. Her skin and lips are bluish gray.

—My god, Zoe says: You're frozen.

The girl nods, a little dazed.

—Come on, Gus, Zoe says: Let her in.

Gus comes in, looking over his shoulder the whole time, making sure that Unity is coming, too. He's happy as a car salesman with a live one.

—Who's bleeding? Unity says.

Gus cavorts around the girl, whips his snoot into her hand, demands to be petted. He circles this way and that, leans his shoulder, his flank, his neck, hard against Unity's legs.

—Gus, Zoe says: Stop bleeding on her boots.

Then she goes into the kitchen, finds the Xanax. Fifteen to twenty minutes, she tells herself. And more reliable than prayer. But she has trouble with the cap, pours a few tablets into her hand, picks one, drops it, finally gets it into her mouth. She isn't fast enough with the water. The pill chokes her with its bitterness, and she wonders whoever got the idea in the first place that such vile chemicals can ease the mind.

Unity's skin still has a bluish cast, and when she speaks to Gus, her speech is slurred, disjointed. She flaps her hands against her upper arms, pats her thighs, wanders back and forth, keeps Gus stirred up.

With the backs of curled fingers, Zoe touches her cheek.

—You have to get by the fire, she says: Sit.

She orders Gus onto the hearth rug. If she can just get him to bleed in one place, that will be an improvement.

—'S pretty cold, Unity says.

—Sit, Zoe tells them both again. Zoe's read that hypothermia victims should hold still, and warm up slowly. Too much moving, and the cold blood from the extremities stops the heart.

—You can help me, Zoe says: Get here by the fire and hold Gus. I want to look at his feet.

She opens the stove door, throws in a hunk of oak.

—Either that or I can just run you down to your uncle's.

Unity glares:

—You wouldn't.

—Then do what I say.

Unity sits, clamps her hand on the dog's collar.

—'M only cold, she says.

Zoe brings a dish pan of warm water and a towel, kneels in front of the girl and dog.

Gus grins at her, full of joy to have company, then puts his head back in Unity's lap.

Zoe touches Unity's leg, squeezes her foot in her boot.

—Can you feel this?

Unity shrugs, plants a kiss on Gus's forehead, lets him kiss her back.

—Let's get these off anyway, Zoe says, and gently unlaces the boots.

One at a time, Unity surrenders her feet.

—These aren't even insulated, Zoe says: You need pack boots. Something better than this, anyway. Spark would kill you.

—So?

She puts Unity's feet in the warm water, drapes a blanket around

the girl's shoulders, then crouches, and lifts one of Gus's paws.
It's sticky. Blood oozes between the pads, mats the paw fur.

Zoe shudders, thinks she should have taken more than one
Xanax.

—Bad? Unity says, anchoring the front edges of the blanket
with her fist, pulling the back of it up around her neck. Then she
whispers, horrified: Your arms. What happened to your arms?

Zoe stares. Snow drifts across her vision; the old invisible band
crushes her chest. Finally, she gets up and on sheer instinct,
maneuvers up the stairs, followed by her own footsteps on the
wooden treads.

Dazed, she wanders along the balcony, desperately tries to
focus, feel her feet, her hands. She opens drawers, pulls out silk
long johns, top and bottom, thick wool socks, turtlenecks, a flannel shirt, hears herself call down to Unity:

—I'm getting you some things to put on.

—Your arms, Unity calls back: What happened to your arms?

Zoe freezes. Is the girl being cruel on purpose?

She manages an answer:

—Nothing. An accident.

Wrapping the clothes in a loose bundle, she calls:

—I'm dropping these down for you. Get out of your wet things.

Below her, Unity stands with her arms out, like a fireman about
to catch a baby thrown from a burning window.

—His feet are real bad, she says: I think there's still glass in,
like, two of them.

—Hurry up, Zoe says: I'll be down in a minute.

In the distance a shot rings out, and down below Unity giggles,
then tells Gus:

—They're shooting Bambi's mother.

There's a stash of Xanax and a water bottle by the bed. Zoe
takes a second pill.

Piling her wet clothes on the sleek tile hearth, Unity dresses in
Zoe's diaphanous underwear. Without the shirts on yet, she looks
to be wearing a ghostly second skin. Gus snatches the socks, gal-

lops off with them, leaves still more blood, now in a new corner of the room.

Unity stretches up to pull on the turtleneck, and Zoe sees her small fine breasts, the almost boyish slant of her waist, and for a moment she wants to seize the girl, hold her still, wants to show her the face of the universe, and the tiny spot of it she occupies.

Instead she says:

—Gus, bring those socks back.

She collars him, forces him to lie down. The second pill eases in, sends in reinforcements.

—I knew you'd be here, Unity says.

Zoe glances up, says:

—I thought you were hunting.

Then she gets it:

—You don't have a rifle.

The girl unrolls the clean wool socks, lifts a foot, pulls one on, waggles it to show Zoe how big it is.

—I just came to visit.

—Then how did you get so cold?

—I walked, wandered around a little. I played in these woods when I was little.

Confused, Zoe tells the girl to hold the dog, then scrunches every muscle in her face, and lifts another paw. Two of the pads are shredded. She gulps, puts the paw down, says:

—I'll take him to the vet.

Unity makes a knowing face.

—Why don't you just clean them out yourself?

Zoe sits back on her heels, regards Unity, then rises, rummages for her wallet and car keys.

—Vets cost a fortune on the weekend, Unity announces.

Zoe blows.

She shoves up a sleeve, thrusts her forearm at Unity:

—See this?

By the look on Unity's face, Zoe knows she seems stark mad. She yanks down the collar of her turtleneck, too, snaps it up.

—Do you have any idea what this does to me? This fucking

dog. And all you fucking hunters. And the fucking jacker. And Gus carrying that . . . that head.

And then she realizes that Unity already knows the story of how she was attacked. Sickened and suspicious, she looks at the girl.

—I can't believe it, Unity is whispering.

—Get dressed, Zoe orders: I'm taking you down to Spark's and I'm going to use his phone.

Gus gallops to the door, and she turns on him and hisses:

—Haven't you bled enough?

Unity flinches, hurries into Zoe's jeans and turtleneck, then her own wet coat and boots.

—It would be better if you didn't leave me there, she says: My uncle—

—That's your problem, Zoe says.

Unity gulps.

Out at the car, Gus scrambles gaily into the backseat, leaving a trail of blood, and Unity climbs into the front, clinging to her wet clothes.

But it turns out Spark is gone, and the kitchen door is locked. Unity swears she doesn't have a key, and while Zoe doesn't exactly believe her, there's nothing she can do.

Glancing around Spark's dooryard, Unity says:

—It's always busy for him during the season. Just take me to our place. You can use our phone.

Zoe follows Unity's directions, down to the hard road, take a right, go slow. The lane is just ahead. But when Unity tells her to turn, Zoe brakes.

Hard.

In the backseat, Gus scrambles for balance.

—This isn't it, Zoe says.

A rusty mailbox with a cockeyed door reads *Higby*. Down the side, in various hands and colors of paint, black, purple, a little red, are the names of family and occupants, some old and peeling, some painted out, some new, as if the social history of the place is recorded for the benefit of the mailman.

—No, it is, Unity says.

—I thought you said the Slipney place.

—Same road. The Slipneys and Higbys go back a ways.

—I'm not driving in there, Zoe says.

—They're all out hunting, Unity says: It's no big deal.

Zoe looks in the rearview mirror at Gus, orders him to lie down.

He does, grinning at Unity all the while, whapping his tail, clowning to get her attention. Once in a while, she trails a hand back over the seat, and Gus is content.

—You do have a phone, Zoe says, then shakes her head, and knowing this whole enterprise is foolhardy and stupid, turns up the lane.

The place is totally hidden from the road. The new barn is pole-built with a forest green metal roof. All the doors are neatly closed. Around it stand various sheds and outbuildings, like the mailboxes painted whatever color seems to have come to hand, mint green, pale blue, battleship gray, even pale pink for what might have been a child's playhouse. Vehicles and equipment, snowmobiles, tractors, a motorboat, backhoes, a hay rake, and snowplows are scattered everywhere, like toys left by large, messy children. There's no engine hanging on chains from a tripod, but a collection of generators, antique gasoline pumps, and motor-cycles congregate near an outsized, stationary cement mixer.

Zoe aims the car toward the house, a peeling yellow saltbox with a tacked-on woodshed and a front porch loaded with picnic coolers, stacks of lawn chairs, and bags of trash.

—Not here, Unity giggles, and points to a lane tapering into the woods: Our place is up away from these guys.

Zoe follows her directions, asks:

—Why are you doing this?

—What?

—Oh, for heaven's sake, Zoe says: Living here.

—Leland and I are in love, Unity says, huffy and defensive.

—No, you're not, Zoe says: You're in love with mischief.

To her relief, the Slipney place is set still farther back in a grove of pine and maple, out of sight of the Higby base camp.

A square, tiny place built on concrete pilings, it's covered with some kind of asphalt shingles, textured to look like wood, though, of course, they don't and never did. But the dooryard is clean. No iffy vehicles or old refrigerators, only a pair of neatly covered snowmobiles.

Inside, the place is a surprise: small, of course, not much more than two or three rooms and a bathroom, but the carpet, coun-tertops, and appliances are brand-new, the windows and kitchen spotless.

—We've been fixing up, she says, proudly: Leland got a rent-to-own agreement. And a second job.

—Doing what?

Everything here makes Zoe edgy.

—I don't know for sure.

—Is it for the Higbys? Unity, Zoe says: Think about what you're doing.

—Of course it's not for them.

Unity flings a phone book on the kitchen counter, flounces out of the room to change.

Zoe clucks with disgust, hurries to find the vet's phone number, calls, gets put on hold by the answering service. She paces, looks out the kitchen window for signs of returning Higbys, shakes her head over the television set with the three-foot screen and the case of expensive beer resting on the floor near the refrigerator.

The answering service comes back on, and Zoe's told the vet's out on an emergency, but is due back at the clinic in less than an hour. Can Zoe get there?

She looks at her watch, says:

—You bet.

With no small relief, she calls to Unity that she has to get going.

The girl comes out in her own dry clothes, and tells Zoe she'll wash her things and get them back to her.

—You don't have to.

Then she notices the kitchen includes a tiny washer-dryer stack. Living in the arms of the enemy, this little snippet has far more comforts than Zoe does.

Unity walks her to the door, says thanks, and somewhat subdued says that, um, it might be easier for everyone if Zoe didn't tell Spark about this afternoon.

Or, um, Callum either.

—Or Leland? Zoe asks, trying to speed up her departure.

Unity shakes her head, sets swinging her hoop earrings, freshly chosen.

—Oh, I pretty much tell him everything.

On the way back out, Zoe understands Spark's frustration as constable. There's no legal way to have a look at what goes on in here, without just cause for an official visit. Nervous, she keeps ordering Gus to lie down, but without Unity to distract him, he keeps springing up, sniffing the air.

—You know where you are, don't you?

Gus wriggles, whaps his tail, and for a moment Zoe wonders if she should open the door, let him out, return him to young Arnie.

She watches the dog in the mirror, says his name.

His head whips toward her, his ears lift, expectant and alert.

—No way, she tells him, and they slip back out onto the main road, Zoe driving with a foolish, deliberate nonchalance.

The vet is brusque, annoyed, snaps at Zoe when she sees Gus grinning and whapping his tail.

—I was told this was an emergency.

Then she notices the patches of blood on the dark floor, and she helps Zoe drag him into the exam room. Bloody paw prints trail behind. They lift him onto the exam table, and Gus scrambles, the table loud as tympani as he rummages his hips and shoulders, tries to feel safe so high up off the floor.

—There's glass in his feet, Zoe says, more than a little nervous herself.

The vet examines a front paw, then glances at Zoe:

—I hope you're not squeamish. This one's mincemeat.

The corners of the room undulate, and Zoe grips the edge of the exam table.

—You know what, the vet says: I could just keep him.

—Keep him? Zoe says, abruptly more alert: You can't keep him.

—Just for tonight. I'll get someone in to help me, then you could come get him in the morning.

—No, Zoe says: Tell me what to do.

—It's a pretty hard floor when you hit in a dead faint.

But they get to work, Zoe steadying Gus's head as directed, keeping his snoot out of the vet's way, his tongue from her face. Once in a while she glances down, sees the vet with her eyepiece, picking at Gus's feet, looking for all the world like a jeweler who's lost a diamond.

Bits of glass rattle in a metal pan.

—How'd he do this anyway?

Zoe tells about him bouncing around because someone was coming and crashing against the mirror.

—A few weeks ago, someone jacked a deer. And now this. I'm so sick of hunters.

The vet murmurs, doesn't look up.

—Actually, I'm sick of people, Zoe confesses.

—Sometimes it helps to act as if you need them, the vet remarks, idly, zeroed in on her work.

—Embarrassed, Zoe thanks her for taking care of Gus on a weekend.

The vet glances up:

—I didn't mean me. Then she adds, gently: I see you've been through this once or twice yourself.

Zoe notices she's pushed back her sleeves. Sweat drenches the small of her back.

—I was attacked, she says, bending toward Gus.

He dabs his wet tongue on her ear.

The final tally is two paws cleaned of glass, a third merely cut.

To Zoe, the vet explains the care Gus will need, then ruffles his ears and tells him:

—You'll be sore, but you can still guard your mistress.

And Zoe remembers when her own wounds were fresh, when every time she made a fist, turned her head, took a breath or let one go, her cuts became hot pokers, reminders that she'd been knifed.

CHAPTER 27

≱

It's a joke that Zoe's supposed to keep Gus quiet. How? she wonders. Tie his legs together, lay him on the hearth rug like a roped calf? She slips his paws into the Gore-Tex boots the vet has given her, walks him on the leash, and he parades along the lane quite happily, prancing. But he refuses to urinate, or move his bowels, and in the end she runs out of patience, lets him go, and he shoots away from her like a rocket. Other times, she simply forgets, opens the door, and as he skids across the porch on bandaged feet, she remembers he's supposed to be an invalid. Still, when she takes him back to the vet, his pads are healing nicely, and Zoe hopes the tide of luck is turning.

The vet pauses while taping him back up, says that after Zoe left the last time, it occurred to her she hadn't asked if Zoe had reported the jacked deer.

—I hate that shit, she tells Zoe: I hope you called it in.

—I did, Zoe says: Though no one seemed to know what to make of it.

The vet glances up, waits, but Zoe says no more.

Life falls quiet for a week or two, and Zoe gets out her helmet and chain saw, tries to pick up where deer season left her. She'll ease into the work, walk the saw to her southern boundary, perhaps cut a snowshoe trail. Sometimes she does this, wanders and tidies up, a painter standing back from the wall-sized canvas, adding a dab here, smearing a color there. Somehow, she needs to reclaim the place.

The day is bright and cold. The bare branches of the hardwoods net the thin blue sky. Tucking a water bottle and apples in her pack, extra gloves, she makes it festive, a little picnic, then smiles to herself: an apple, a tank of gas, and thee.

At the sound of her whistle, Gus leaps up and they head off.

The air is still, no wind, and she and Gus are loud as elephants in the fallen leaves and dropped branches. Gus gambols on his new feet, his first sanctioned romp in ten days. He bounds around outcroppings, dives through thickets, digs at a squirrel hole, then charges off again, and Zoe thinks it a miracle he's never been hurt before. He'll sleep tonight.

Zoe hopes she will, too.

As she walks, the chaps rustle on her legs, and her helmet, with the ear protectors and face screen up, is comfortable as an old crown. Somewhat large and top-heavy, but snug, secure, familiar.

Gus puts his head down, charges off, single-minded, then halts, throws up his head, tests the air, shoots a look at Zoe.

—What? she jokes: Killer chipmunks?

He bolts away, and Zoe's pace slows. Up ahead the light is different, open, more diffuse.

Zoe sets the saw down.

Steps forward, hypnotized.

A logging site, ragged obscene stumps and a patch of open sky, has been gouged out of her woods. The stumps still have their step-hinges, and the trees have all been felled toward the southeast. The tops and branches have simply been left. Sawdust lies in mounds where the trunks were cut to four-foot lengths and hauled away.

She catalogues the loss. Maples, hard and soft, some ash, two yellow birches.

She tells herself perhaps she's wandered onto the neighboring property. One drawback to owning this much land, especially land that tilts and pitches, is that there are gaps in the natural boundaries of stone walls and line trees.

Trying to divert her nausea and rage, she strips off her chaps and helmet, goes looking for a marker. A red pin punctuates the end of the stone wall and, casting above the cutting, then below,

Zoe finds the next pin. Finds, too, the way someone's vehicle has gouged the fragile forest floor, wet, dark brown ruts spun deep, the shiny scrape of a truck's undercarriage across the earth.

She snatches up her saw and gear, marches home, then charges down to Spark's and bangs on his door.

He's surprised to see her, tentatively pleasant even, but she's off and running, ranting, vaguely realizing she's blown the chance to resume cordial relations.

His manner changes. He's cautious, defensive:

—Are your boundaries posted?

—No, they're not. But I know my line, and so should my neighbor.

—Easy on who you accuse.

And she knows that's true.

He asks if she has a recent survey, and she says no, but she has the deed.

—Even I can find my way from pin to pin, she spits out: And I'm nothing but a flatlander.

—It's not a backyard, Spark tells her: Someone needed wood.

—So, when I need wood I can just go onto anybody's land and help myself?

—If you want me to look, I'll look, Spark says: I'll file a report. The law says you're entitled to double the value of the wood, based on the size and species of the stumps. But only if you know who did it and you can prove it.

—And what about cleaning up?

She imagines standing over some local cretin, hands on her hips, while they fill in the ruts to her satisfaction.

Spark sighs.

—Like I said. Do you know who it was? Did you see them at it? Will you sign an affidavit?

Zoe fumes.

—I wouldn't take it so personal, Spark says: Someone needed wood.

🦗

A week later, she finds a cardboard box and a pile of other trash where her lane leaves the woods and heads out across Spark's meadow. Disgusted, she goes back up to the house, gets some trash bags. She makes Gus stay in the car and, wearing gloves, picks up bottles, cans, smelly trays from red meat. She feels like vomiting, tries to follow Spark's advice, not to take this "so personal," though she wonders why she's been here so long and so far has only had to pick up after hunters who, she thinks, leave a stunning amount of trash behind them in the woods. But when she comes down two days later, and finds still more trash, including a dead gerbil in a shoebox, she mentions it to Spark, gritting her teeth, keeping her temper in check, and all Spark says is that if she's going to complain about every little thing, it sure would help if she'd file that report with the state police.

—On what? she says.

—That boy. Your student.

Only a few nights later, she sits bolt upright in bed. Gus leaps up, barking, still asleep, and Zoe thinks it would be funny, Gus woofing automatically before his eyes are open, but out on the road headlights are creeping through the dark.

She gets up, throws on clothes, in the instant decides not to light a lamp. Downstairs, Gus flings himself at the door, snarling. If the car stops, she can always let him out, then has the sudden thought that someone very well could shoot him.

There are ways, after all, to stop a charging dog.

The car goes past and the woods are dark. Gus still barks, and Zoe shushes him, desperate to listen. All at once the car flies back down through the woods, fifty miles an hour, horn blaring, and, even over Gus's roaring, she hears something that sounds like gunshots.

The rest of the night, she stokes the woodstove, relies on the flicker through the glass door for light. In time she dozes on the couch, and in the morning, it takes some time before she works up the nerve to step outside. Gus hasn't forgotten any of it, rushes out to the road looking for some trace, someone left behind he might attack.

Tentatively Zoe follows, finds the remnants of fireworks.

She puts the pieces in a plastic bag, careful not to touch them, and in her journal makes detailed notes.

As if she has something to prove, she takes to going out more. She tries to remember why Zeke wanted her to get to work whenever she could manage. What was the term? Reality referent? And so she makes her way to town almost every day. She buys newspapers, picks up her mail. She purchases more fresh fruit, vegetables, and deli fare, once even a bouquet of flowers.

She travels to a far-off Kmart, staggers around the store with a big plastic shopping cart on wheels, squinting against the glare of the fluorescent lights overhead and the highly waxed floor underfoot. The music bothers her, and the announcements to the throng of shoppers. Still, she trails from department to department, with a list of objects to find and carry home. Underwear, bootlaces, waterproofing, bedsheets, rawhide bones, radio batteries, notebooks, a chocolate bar, skin lotion, new toothbrushes.

Another day she visits a genuine grocery store, attempts to load up on staples, but she abandons her cart halfway down the second aisle and flees.

She does manage another haircut, this time without Xanax, though she knows it's mere bravado, watching the shiny shears come at her head and neck, willing them away from her flesh. When the young woman delicately suggests she might like a manicure, too, Zoe is offended, although later she has a good laugh about the difference between her rugged practical hands and the long red nails and soft skin of the technician.

The first snow finally arrives. It begins before dawn, a leisurely, feathery storm, and Zoe scoffs at her instinct to stay put on her mountaintop. Midmorning, with two fluffy inches decorating the landscape, Zoe and Gus make their trip to town.

Shroveton seems positively festive. Callum is doing a brisk trade in snow shovels, de-icer, and winter windshield wiper blades. At the store, people linger, exchange their versions of the forecast, anything from a few inches to a foot. They discuss snowmaking at the ski areas, fender benders, the need to put on their snow tires, their plow blades if they haven't already. They tease one man who hasn't stacked his firewood yet, pass around the news that the emergency squad was called out just an hour ago because old Ettie Pitcairn fell and broke a hip, sweeping snow from her walk, too stubborn to let anyone help with her chores.

At the post office, even Hattie Mims, the dour postmistress, says hello to Zoe, remarks cheerfully on the weather, glad the snow will scrub germs out of the air.

—Green Decembers fill the graveyard, she recites.

In Zoe's box is a letter from Zeke.

Zoe thanks Hattie, as if Hattie is somehow responsible.

Deciding to make an occasion of the letter, she drives twenty miles to Benton, where there's a lunch counter. Still unable to sit with her back to anyone, not that she has much chance to practice, she'll enjoy the drive along the river, get some soup or coffee, perhaps stop at the swimming hole on the way back and listen to the water, stand out under the benevolent snow.

But the corner stool is open, and Zoe takes it, turns her back to the knotty-pine paneling, orders coffee, then pulls her jack-knife from her pocket and neatly slices open the heavily textured envelope.

She smiles with affection. Pure Zeke, she thinks, and wonders what his stationery bill is like.

But when she begins to read, her smile falls away, and within moments she's pressing her back hard against the wall, eyeing the door, wondering if she should throw money on the counter, and make a run for it.

For starters, Zeke is furious. Her sent her the Xanax prescription, but she never wrote the promised letter. He insists she find a counselor somewhere nearby, at least a doctor who might be talked into continuing the prescription. He'll give her no more medication.

But it's the second paragraph that really stops her breathing. Adam has been released from full-time custody, and is now in a halfway house. She covers her eyes, shields them from the dull light in the place, fights the iron terror cinching her chest. As far as Zeke can tell, Zoe is quite safe. Adam is making good progress, or so Zeke has been informed. And now Zoe regrets the whole deal she has made. At the time, all she wanted was to give the boy his best chance, and give herself some privacy. But now she gets a whiff of conspiracy. Aren't Adam's parents paying the doctors and the hospital who in turn are coming up with these reports? Besides how can anyone be certain that a sweet-looking boy who once pulled out a razor won't do it again? Zoe is suddenly done with second chances; he's wrecked her life; she wants him locked up forever and she's willing to admit it.

She goes out to the car, rattles a pill into her hand, then counts the remainder in the bottle. She'd better not. She'd better wait for real disaster. And in a clear dislocated way, she realizes there's some difference between actual danger and the warning of it.

Slowly she drives back toward Shroveton. The sky is darker, the snow heavier and faster. Concentrating on her driving, she feels sensation flood back into her feet and hands, keeps careful distance from other vehicles, reminds herself to brake well in advance of stopping.

At the swimming hole, she pulls over, lets Gus out to pee, follows him down to the river's edge. Snowflakes hit the storm-black water, vanish as if called home.

In her pocket, Zoe fingers Zeke's letter.

She wishes he'd said when Adam was released and whether he knew where she is. Has Zeke told Adam's parents where she's hiding? Certainly they must be enjoying a respite from paying for her therapy. She smiles. Now there's a reason to find a therapist, the petty revenge of psychiatric bills.

Eventually they turn toward home, pass through the center of Shroveton where people seem more hurried now, coat collars turned up against the snow. Shoulders hunched, they scrape windshields, dust off engine hoods, eager to get where they're going. Back up on their mountain, Zoe's glad to be finished driving and Gus, grateful for his own reasons, bounds off into the woods, comes back, tags Zoe as if inviting her to play. Yes, she thinks, they'll walk. The day is shot, although she feels modestly triumphant, reading the letter, managing without a pill.

She bundles up, straps on her snowshoes. It's half and half whether she needs them, but it makes the walking more consistent.

Wild with joy, Gus barks, he tears around her in circles, all his fringes and feathers flying. Then his nose goes up, he runs a bit, sniffing left and right, then halts, checks on Zoe's whereabouts. She smiles. Why not? She'll follow him, save herself a decision while she's still a little rattled, and off he goes toward the southwest corner of the property. He cuts back and forth, purposeful, brow furrowed and nose working, and Zoe more or less tags along behind, calms herself with the old rhythm of the snowshoes, the lift of the toe, the drag of the tail, the settling of the whole platform on the shallow snow.

She wonders what to say to Zeke. She will, by god, write to him, mail a letter tomorrow. She smiles. Hadn't she once harangued her students about the value of setting deadlines? She'll impress old Zeke, pretend to health, apologize, ask a few questions.

The woods and snow turn into a pleasant blur, and she remembers walking home from school on days like this in Black Hill, remembers betting her friend Phyllis a nickel as to whether or not there would be classes the next day. She remembers, too, going skiing with Dayton in the Poconos, he an expert, she thrashing on rental skis, and the snow coming down harder and harder, until they ended up staying for the night, swearing to his father and her mother on the phone that they would rent two motel rooms, and how silly they had been with that old your-place-or-mine joke, and how when her mother had asked the next day if she had slept in her own bed, Zoe been able to say yes, she had, and her mother hadn't asked if she'd slept alone.

And then Gus puts his head down in that I'm-hot-on-the-trail-of-villains way of his, and Zoe halts on her snowshoes, forces a smile. What had Zeke said, time and again? Just because something happened once doesn't mean it will happen again.

Probably Gus has found a hiker to have for a snack.

She calls him, his head whips back, then he ignores her and rushes on. She goes after him, finds him with his head down, gulping something out of the snow.

—Gus!

She runs toward him. This is one predilection of dogs she loathes, this scavenging and gorging, as if she isn't buying all that expensive dog food.

—Oh, Gus, she says when she gets closer, tries not to think about his snoot buried in the belly of this dead furry thing.

She snags his collar, braces her knees, flings him off to the side.

This dead furry thing is a raccoon, lying on its back, paws out in all four directions, belly open like a bowl on a sideboard. An odd kill. No packed-tight owl cast of bone remnants, no messy aftermath of a coyote banquet, or the circular strewings the foxes leave. She examines the raccoon, glances around, freezes.

Certainly she's hallucinating. She reels Gus in beside her.

The two of them are stranded in a sea of footprints, fresh ones, lightly covered by the last two inches of snow. Then she sees that the crisp golden bark of a birch has been slashed, and after a while she makes out the letter T, picks out other letters on other trees.

I hate this, she tells herself all the way back to the house. I hate this I hate this I hate this, as if hatred can counteract the rest, and despite Spark's remark about reporting every little thing, she locks Gus in the shed, drives down to his house, bangs on his door.

He's not home, and for a moment, she debates letting herself in. The door's not always locked; she could use the phone and call the state police. But then she tries to imagine a trooper huffing down the hill just so she can show him a dead raccoon, splayed out in the snow the way no wild animal would leave it, and some carvings on a bunch of trees.

Instead she leaves a note, goes on home, bolts the door, builds up the fire. She feeds Gus his supper, wishes she could make him gargle the raccoon flesh out of his mouth, then remembers a poster at the vet's about brushing a dog's teeth. Heaven knows she needs a distraction. Wetting an old toothbrush, she spreads a ribbon of toothpaste on it, sits at the table, summons Gus.

At first he isn't sure. His brow furrows, he sniffs, decides he wouldn't mind licking the paste off the brush. And then he offers just to clamp his teeth down and walk away with brush, toothpaste and all. Zoe's relieved to laugh at him, however weird and shaky, and she wraps her free hand around his snoot, manages to lift a lip and gently scrub his teeth. He gulps like mad, foam and froth cascading from his mouth.

And then there's a knock on the door.

Zoe's heart lurches.

Spark, she tells herself, and forces herself to go to the door in her sock feet, toothbrush in hand.

Gus, of course, is barking like a maniac, lips covered with toothpaste foam, stopping once in a while to swipe his tongue at the tasty stuff all over his face.

Zoe invites Spark in, and the moment Gus sees who it is, he grins and wags, bowing and licking his chops.

—My Jesus, Spark says, backing off: How long's he been like that?

Like what? she thinks: You knew what he was like when you gave him to me.

Then she realizes he's putting together the raccoon in her note with the foaming mouth. She holds up the brush, says:

—I was just cleaning his teeth.

This is a story that will make a nice feature on Radio-Free Shroveton.

Spark shakes his head in disbelief.

Zoe attempts to repeat a joke about cabin fever she heard that morning at the store, but loses the gist of it.

Curtly announcing that he has other business waiting, he asks for an explanation of her note.

Sighing, Zoe tells him everything, why she went that way, how the trees and the raccoon looked. She admits she's not keen to go back down there now, not in the dark. And anyway, once was enough.

She adds, trying to curry a little favor:

—I'm trying not to take it personally. Like you said.

Spark thinks maybe he'll get the light and go on down there before more snow falls. He'll check back before he leaves. Can he just follow her path?

Again she's rueful.

—I had on the snowshoes. I left a trail a mile wide.

It's more than an hour until he returns, and Zoe begins to fret about whether she should go and look for him. But in time his light flickers up through the woods. He knocks, lets himself in, and once Gus settles down, accepts her offer of a fresh cup of coffee.

She sits across from him, clanks her spoon in her mug. Finally she says:

—So what did you think?

—Don't know. Maybe harmless, maybe not.

Zoe blinks. She's been bracing for another speech about reporting every little thing.

—We don't get these shenanigans here that much, but I think it's just kids, playing on your nerves.

—You got the last part, she says.

He nods, sips his coffee.

—What about the skete? she asks: Are they having more problems?

—Thought you had friends there.

—In a way.

She shrugs:

—Did you ever question Unity and Leland?

Spark works his jaw, checks his watch, shifts in his chair.

—She was up here not too long ago, Zoe says quietly.

Spark says nothing.

—She seemed all right, Zoe tells him: As far as I could tell.

—She could choose better boyfriends, Spark concedes after a while: But she's on her own now, no turning back.

Zoe smiles, sympathetic:

—It could be worse.

—The raccoon was gone, Spark says.

Bewildered, Zoe wonders what raccoon? Then remembers the one down in the snow.

—There was one, she tells him, defensive.

—I don't disbelieve you, he says: Dragged off. Coyote, I'd guess.

—What'd you think? Otherwise?

He sighs.

—I dislike the word *death* carved into trees. Took me a little while to get it.

—Bad spelling. Took me a little while to get it, too.

They smile a moment, companions in slow-wittedness. Then Zoe wrings her hands.

—I guess that I should tell you I've had a letter.

Spark looks at her, sharp, alert.

—My slasher's been released from the hospital. Adam. He's in a halfway house.

Spark gives a long slow nod, stretches a leg.

—This actor ever going to acquire a last name? Or a description?

Zoe doesn't know. Her heart races and she must set her cup down.

—He's young, she says: My height, maybe shorter, slender, light brown hair. Good-looking.

—Last name?

Zoe shakes her head.

—Then get a gun, Spark tells her: If you're so damn stubborn.

Again, Zoe shakes her head.

—I'm serious, he says: Get a gun and just shoot through the door.

His voice is warm, fatherly. She glances at him.

—You're scared to death, he says gently: It's no way to live.

Her throat tightens and she forces a smile, looks at him through tears.

—You don't need to look, he says: Just call out and ask who's there and if they don't answer, shoot through the door. I'll vouch for you. I'll put in my report tonight I told you to do that.

—Is that legal?

He smiles, shrugs.

It comes to Zoe that he must be cocksure Unity's not involved. Either that or he's some kind of maniac.

CHAPTER 28

That night Zoe's determined she'll write to Zeke, raccoon or no
raccoon, refuses to admit this is the perfect excuse to avoid going
to bed at all. Pulling a chair close to the woodstove, she opens her
notebook. Gus lies on the hearth rug, glancing at the stairs like a
lazy husband whose ardor has worn off, wondering if he can slip
away to bed.

She catches him at it, says:

—Oh, really?

Sheepish, he puts his nose on his paws, lets his eyelids drift
shut.

Zoe slips her toes under his ribs, bends forward over a blank
page.

What would her students say to see her now, the time creeping past eleven? Hadn't she nagged them to keep regular hours,
get plenty of sleep, learn to live a healthy life? Now she admits
that, like them, sometimes she waits until the dam breaks.

Gus slides into sleep, woofing and whimpering at her feet.

Outside, snow still falls. By the way the stove draws, she knows
the cloud cover is low. No wind, or she'd be battling downdraft.
Nor is the temperature so cold that the fire gets drunk on oxygen,
rages on a fast draft.

Her eyes are gritty and her shoulders ache, and when she finally begins to write, she reveals her dismay over newspaper ac-
counts of the capture of a longtime fugitive from the law. His very
cabin, the way he lived, horrors, with no electricity or running
water, has been offered as evidence of insanity. She's even studied

the photos in the papers, relieved that she's more upscale. Her woodstove is more modern, her walls are Sheetrocked if not taped, and her kitchen has a sink, even if it does drain out onto the ground.

The fire sighs and shifts.

She glances at Saint Barbara on the chimney shelf, says:

—Is that you?

Then she nods toward the upper reaches of the house:

—Or Our Lady of the Crow's Nest?

She wonders who thought it necessary to rip the breasts off women saints, then lets her neck fall at an awkward angle, remembers that Adam's attack might not have had to do with her. She might simply have reminded him of someone else, some other situation.

But he planned it, she had always protested. He had the razor.

And she makes an old familiar leap.

If murderers and rapists choose victims along private, subconscious patterns, is there any way to keep safe from such encounters?

She thinks of Dayton. Is it just the abandoned one, the jilted one, who really suffers?

Pulling on a coat, she goes outside, lingers on the deck. Somewhere in the woods below, the last of the raccoon is being eaten, and snow is covering the misspelling of death.

She shines her flashlight up into the darkness, lets herself remember that Dayton had called her mother after that last night, asking if she was all right.

The flakes hurtle toward her, encased in light.

She never called him back.

CHAPTER 29

In the morning, Zoe makes it to the post office just before the mail leaves Shroveton. The envelope, addressed with the painstaking care of a woman who's been up all night, slides easily down the throat of the old brass chute.

Her letter to Zeke, written at dawn, is a careful concoction, not untrue, not a lie, merely artful. She lauds the joys of her new life while raising questions about the well-being and precise where-abouts of Adam. In a ragged postscript, she wonders for the first time whether it's worse to be a victim, reliving powerlessness, ter-ror, shock? Or worse to fend off the hideous self-knowledge of having hurt another human being?

In the hallway outside the post office, the town clerk is pin-ning up a reminder of the due date of property taxes. He greets Zoe cheerfully, congratulates her on getting down off her hill after the snow, stands folding and unfolding his reading glasses.

—Thought I'd come out of my burrow, she jokes.

Then as if to make it appear she's not interested in taxes, hers or anyone else's, she reads the notices of grange meetings, holi-day bazaars, the fire company's Christmas open house, the sched-ule for the regional hospital's exercise and education classes over in Benton, the agenda for the next trustees' meeting at the li-brary, an invitation to the candlelight service at the Shroveton meeting house.

She decides she'll call the attorney in Montpelier and find out the tax status of the skete.

Zoe's pleased, and embarrassed, too, at the speed with which she has a return letter from Zeke. He's surprised at how good she sounds, and she reads the line aloud to Gus and laughs.

—Took me all night to write four miserable little paragraphs.

Zeke assures her that Adam is well cared for, then adds that, of course, a halfway-house placement is always something of a risk, though it's a risk everyone deems appropriate.

Zoe's forgotten that word: *appropriate.*

Appropriate according to whom, she thinks, turning herself around beside the woodstove, rereading the letter, roasting one set of body parts after another in preparation for plunging back outside into the dropping temperatures to finish her chores before the arctic front fully descends.

Zeke doesn't comment on Dayton, about whom she's still been vague, or on her brief flirtation with the idea of laser surgery for her scars which, standing here in her thermals now seems ridiculous. But he's adamant that she needs to find a Vermont clinician, since in his estimation she is being unfair, leaning on him at this distance, when he barely knows what she thinks or what's happening in her life.

Unfair.

Now there's another word that seems out of place in her little universe, and she feels the first tiny starburst of rage, then damps it off, before one little thought ignites each of the rest.

She pulls on her boots and hat and mittens and face protector, carries her jugs to the spring, careful not to slip, knowing that she could die if she went into the bitter water in zero-degree weather.

In the days that follow, she often listens to the radio for reports on the weather as if for bulletins on an invading army. Already the ground is iron, and out in the woods, trees split, cracking and booming. Each night the stars are brilliant and the skies are clear, she wraps up in a blanket and stands in her crow's nest gawking at her swath of sky like an old astronomer.

One night, as the weather forecaster says, it "warms and storms," and they get a nice fourteen inches, and while Zoe has hoped this will soften the winter, the next arctic wave comes through within hours. The temperature plummets, the wind kicks up, then dies away to eerie silence.

Christmas Eve is a few days off, still early winter, and Zoe's following Spark's winter schedule; she keeps the house warm and the woodbox full, trims the lamp wicks and fills their reservoirs, gauges the best time each day to go out to the spring for water.

The car still starts and when she goes to town, it's reassuring that, even all the way up here, people say, by way of greeting:

—Cold enough for you?

When they see Zoe, though, the question is often kindly, tinged with concern:

—Keeping warm up there?

One day, when the temperature rises all the way to fifteen, she ventures out on her snowshoes, just a brief trek, and meets a man on her road, down near the gate, walking on the plowed surface.

He's muffled up in a black snowmobile suit, insulated boots and dark knitted cap. His eyes are an odd flat blue, and Zoe thinks she's seen him before, but after a while in a town as small as Shroveton, even total strangers sometimes seem familiar.

Still, she's leery, wants to challenge his presence on her land, when in fact he's on the public portion of the lane. She hangs onto Gus's collar, thinks for the thousandth time she ought to teach the dog more manners, and forces herself, in honor of the season, to be genial, asks if everything's all right. Is he having trouble with his snowmobile?

His face never changes, and Zoe studies it as if she might sketch it later. Strong cheekbones, dark wayward eyebrows, an empty earring hole in one lobe.

He doesn't answer her real question, the unspoken one: What in hell are you doing here?

Instead, he says:

—So what's it like, up here all alone?

She meets his eyes, the odd blue of them.

—Do you like dogs? she says, and smiles stiffly: You must know this is the Higby dog.

—Aa-yup, he says out of one side of his mouth, mocking her.

—I hear he bites, Zoe says, then adds: You do know the class-six road ends right up there? At that pine with the blaze.

And then in a show of bravado, she steps off into a patch of red pines, planted in their neat rows, circa 1930s, and lets go of Gus's collar.

The dog flies at the man, leaps and snaps, but from a safe distance. Then he freezes, sniffs toward the man's legs and, puzzled, wags his tail, one tentative swipe, then barks and barks around him in a half-circle.

Zoe counts to ten, then calls, and after a few more barks and snarls, Gus gladly follows her among the gnarled, shingled trunks, the air itself nearly red from the color of the bark.

The blue-eyed man walks a dozen and more deliberate steps onto Zoe's lane, then turns and makes his way back out.

Zoe writes the man's words in her journal and, really, they seem harmless. She sketches his face, can't get the eyes right, and wonders what, if anything, she should say to Spark. That she didn't like the way he walked onto her land when she's never posted, when during hunting season the whole mountainside crawls with hunters? For all she knows, he's one of those hunters she's condemned for not setting foot in the woods except when trying to shoot a deer, and now here he is and she doesn't like that either.

Still, when she passes Spark on the road, the two of them stopping their vehicles, rolling down their windows, leaning out briefly into the bitter air, the first thing Zoe says is that she's had a visitor.

She recites the incident, describes the man, and Spark is interested, but only mildly, and suggests that Zoe keep an eye out for him around town and see if she can identify him again.

—I made a sketch, she offers.

He tells her to hold onto it; he'll have a look sometime.

By Christmas Eve, there's no doubt in Zoe's mind. She'll go to the town's candlelight service. She already has mild cabin fever, and somehow thinks she should show the colors, prove that by god she's still holding out up on her mountaintop. And she can look for the blue-eyed man.

It's a typical Vermont gathering. People wearing everything from suits and dresses to corduroys and blazers, wool trousers, jeans, sweater vests, and flannel shirts make their way toward the stately stone meeting house, guarded on all four sides by bare, majestic sugar maples. The heavy double doors, with their ornate hinges and heavy thumb latches are standing open, and Zoe steps into the foyer. She nods and murmurs, shakes a hand or two. Callum stands in a corner, talking to Spark, dressed up in a striped shirt, corduroy jacket, and narrow tie. Hal Westerbrook, arm around the shoulders of a tall brunette in a turquoise coat, waves to someone across the room. Even Unity is there, arms folded, trailing along behind Leland through the crowd.

Steep stairs wind in ovals up both sides of the foyer, and Zoe follows the general throng upstairs to the meeting room, recognizes the meat cutter from the store, the old man who builds the neatest woodpiles in town, Hattie Mims, the postmistress, and the town clerk with a woman Zoe presumes to be his wife. The carpeted stairs creak and groan, and children skip ahead or hoist themselves hand over hand up along the worn wooden banister, then are restrained by parents, or by awkward adolescent siblings.

No blue-eyed man.

The pews are boxes, with paneled doors, and the backs meet the seats at perfect right angles. One does not come to the meeting house, even on Christmas Eve, in order to be comfortable. The kneeling benches, racked up now, have no cushions. Zoe slips into a center pew, a man hands her a bulletin, and asks her to move all the way in. She does, finds herself wedged against the center divider.

An armada of old ladies sails right in beside her, bumping one another as they shed their coats, saying hello to people all around,

picking up and dropping threads of conversations about grand-
children, choir directors, surgeries, and recipes for sour dough.
Up front, on a plain platform, stands an altar draped with one
lush rope of greens tied with a dark red bow. On each windowsill
burns a hurricane lamp with a small oil flame. No one in Shroveton
can be accused of going overboard. Zoe's old ladies, wearing
huge corsages or delicate-crocheted wreath pins, are more gussied
up than the entire church.

Zoe looks out into the twilight. The sky is gray now, edging toward black among the upraised limbs of sugar maples, and it
gives her a start to realize she can identify them solely by the telltale choreography of their branches. She wonders if, 200 years
ago, the town argued over the expense of planting them as bitterly as they argued last March over the new truck.

And then she glances to her right, and her heart abruptly jigs
and skips.

The man on the other side of the divider is Brother Luke.

Her throat catches. She coughs, sniffles discreetly, coughs
some more, then can't stop.

The old lady beside her offers her a hankie.

Brother Luke asks if she's all right.

Zoe takes the hankie, wipes her eyes, mumbles something
about allergies, then still coughing, reads her bulletin as if she
has never before in her life seen the words to a Christmas carol.
Her face is red and hot. She puts her head down and rubs her
forehead, glances to her left. No way can she crawl out over five
well-fed, fussy old ladies.

Again Brother Luke asks if she's all right.

She mumbles something noncommittal.

A young woman in front of her turns and passes back a roll of
LifeSavers, gives Brother Luke a second look.

—Aren't you from the skete?

He nods, and the woman smiles warmly, welcomes him to their
service.

Her husband glances back, says a curt hello, then turns away,
frowning with irritation.

His wife whispers to Brother Luke:

—Where are the rest of you?

—Only Brother Timothy and I were able to get away.

The woman's husband rattles his leaflet.

The older woman on Zoe's left is leaning forward now, smiling at Brother Luke, then turning to her friends and whispering that the monks are here.

To Zoe's relief, the organ starts, a little asthmatic. She feigns an itch, leans forward, makes a great show of scratching her ankle while glancing to the right. Indeed only Brothers Luke and Timothy are here. She guesses the others are back at the skete, feeding animals, cooking dinner, readying for the high holidays.

The service is simple and sweet. The local clergy do a kind of tag-team reading of the Christmas story from the New Testament, a chunk at a time, and in between the congregation sings hymns and carols.

On one side, her old ladies sing with antique, out-of-control sopranos, and on the other side Brother Luke spills out his modulated tenor, smooth as melting honey.

Zoe tries to remember if she ever heard Dayton sing.

With great community gusto, the congregation works its way through every verse of every hymn as if pitching in to stack firewood or raise a barn. No pretensions here, and Zoe feels a flash of warmth for the good folk of Shroveton. Near the end of the service, the lights dim and men walk along the aisle, counting out candles, one for each person in each pew. They're the heavy white wax candles sold in grocery stores for emergencies, and Zoe smiles to see that they have been used before.

The next tune is "Joy to the World" and the men make their way along the aisles again, lighting each end candle, and the congregants pass the flame, each to each.

Brother Luke reaches over the divider and lights Zoe's.

The last hymn winds down, and a woman pastor in a bright red corduroy dress offers a prayer. It's very short, perhaps because all these candles are burning up precious wax. Zoe finds it embarrassing when others pray aloud and, bowing her head, she tries and fails to fabricate some prayer of her own. When she looks up again, the candles around her are being blown out and the congregation is murmuring and reaching for their coats.

Beside her, Brother Luke wraps a gray wool scarf around his neck, pats his pockets for gloves, and before she has a chance to think, Zoe says:

—So, you're all still there. At the skete?

Her earlier panic at bumping unprepared into Dayton has been replaced by Christmas Eve nostalgia and the rising anxiety that he might no longer be in Shroveton.

—Yes, Brother Luke says, then gives her a puzzled look: Did you want me to pass greetings to anyone in particular?

—No, she says, then: Yes. Tell Dayton hello. Brother Dayton.

—And you are?

His eyes are grave but on the edge of mischief, too, and she's taken aback by the way the air around him fills with joy. No wonder the people of Shroveton are suspicious. Who has the right to be so damn happy?

Brother Luke places her:

—You're the lady with the dog.

She nods, smiles, suddenly full of her own joy and mischief.

—Tell him that, she says: Tell him a woman with a dog said hello. And Merry Christmas.

CHAPTER 30

꧂

The new year comes in bitter cold, and Zoe half-forgets the blue-eyed man. Life circles around her woodstove. She wanders only so far from it, to the outhouse and the spring. The winter light is thin, the skies brilliant blue, the air unbearable. She gauges the cold by how fast it sears the insides of her nostrils, dries her eyeballs, by the way the snow-squeaks change with every ten-degree drop. Even bundled up in all her gear, she's soon drawn back to the fire, to the safety of flame and heat.

Restless, she prowls her tiny house, admits she's been living like a squatter, driving in nails and hooks where it pleases her, camping out. She has a place to keep warm and dry, to eat, sleep, and dump her clothes, but wasn't she the one who meant to turn this place into an architectural gem?

And so she hits the books. The Michaelses have left her a nice building block: the careful post-and-beam saltbox with the extensive glass, the open upstairs with the balcony, and she reads in her texts, as if recalling a language heard in childhood, about primary space and secondary space, about the play of light, solar angles. Sometimes she thinks she should just finish the Sheetrock and lay a floor, cover the ceilings, but surely if she worked at it there would be room here for some touch of her own. Perhaps one day she'll go to Burlington or to White River to a salvage place, see what she can find for architectural details.

Meanwhile, it's high time to tape and mud the Sheetrock seams. She reads up on the job in Willis Wagner's *Modern Carpentry*, makes one of her trusty lists, and on a day she ventures to town for mail and fresh food, she leaves the car running outside the hardware store, in line with four others, steaming like horses tied up by their reins outside a saloon.

Callum loads her up with joint compound, tape, and taping knife, and Leland carries the heavy mud bucket to her car.

—Really need all this? he says: I heard you might be selling.

—Wishful thinking, Zoe tells him.

—Sheetrock's a miserable job. If you're leaving anyway.

—Oh, she says, half-cantankerous: The bet's still on, is it? By this time, the jackpot must be enormous.

Leland shrugs.

Back up the hill she lugs in the stuff, plans to ask Spark to come up and give her a lesson. Since the cold set in, they've traded a supper or two, drinks, coffee. Bitter weather makes good neighbors.

But that evening, impatient and unable to find Spark, she chooses an easy wallboard seam near the stairs, consults Willis Wagner yet again, spreads the mud as carefully as if icing a cake, wrestles with the paper tape, tries to knife it smooth. When she stands back, her work appears somehow messy and fussy all at once, certainly not potentially invisible beneath a coat of paint.

Often Gus interrupts. Bored in the bitter weather, he whines to go out, then turns and comes right back in. For hours, he listens fixedly to a mouse in the mudroom wall, cocking his ears, sometimes leaping up and barking with sheer frustration. He snatches the socks from her feet, carries her boots, her mittens around in his mouth. To distract him, Zoe puts down her tools and teaches him tricks. He's gullible enough, he'll work for bits of dog kibble, though he prefers orange slices or carrot chunks. They focus on the old standards, sit, down, stay, come, wait. They heel endless circles around the main room, figure-eights around the counter and kitchen table. Since he's always stealing things, she works on bring, though the treats she offers in exchange are not nearly as interesting to him as the sock, the mitten, the scarf he's hiding in his favorite spot behind the couch.

Clean the house would make a nice command, she thinks.

Fetch water.

Tape Sheetrock.

She teaches him to shake but not to bow or say prayers, draws in her notebooks, writes letters that are such odd fabrications that they must confound the recipients. She writes to Annie, her mother's friend, sends a note to her old dean, considers writing more to Zeke but isn't sure what to say. She reads her stack of books on monasticism, Benedictines, on saints and crazies and prayer. Contemporary writers laud the warmth, the serenity, the absolute hospitality of monastery guest houses. Zoe doesn't believe a word of it. What's this business about treating every stranger as if he or she is Christ? One day, as if to prove the whole thing a lie, a hoax, nothing more than a quaint tradition no longer practiced, she writes to Our Lady of the Snows, a community of Benedictine women near the Saint Lawrence River.

In her letter, she is blunt. She makes clear that she's not a Roman Catholic, probably not even a Christian. She leaves out the fact that her one true love has turned inexplicably into a monk, and fabricates the need for a few days of rest. Rest from what? she thinks. Going stir-crazy? Then, certain there's not a hope in hell, she asks if she might come and spend a few nights in their guest house.

Every day or two, Spark checks up on her and, in the face of fifty- and sixty-degree below windchill factors, she's pretty much glad he does. One evening she remarks that the mischief at her place seems to have come to an end.

—Too damn cold for mischief, he says: Outdoor mischief anyway.

Then he asks if she's heard about Hal.

—He's getting married.

—Not to me, she says, stating the obvious with chirping cheerfulness.

Later though, she writes a weepy, nonsensical note to Dayton in her notebook, then rips the pages out and throws them in the fire.

During daylight hours, she finishes taping the downstairs walls. They still need a lot of sanding, but she's fed up, goes outside more often. She swaddles herself in down and Gore-Tex, moves fast. In the shed, she splits wood into smaller slabs than necessary. In a sheltered lee, she sets up a makeshift snow gauge, tacks up a flag, records the weather. From her books, she continues collecting esoteric holidays.

Meteorological spring.

Purifications. In April, Rogation for the corn crop. In May, Lemuria.

Harvests, too. Lammas, Lughnassa, Succoth.

She collects the names of full moons like exotic buttons:

Snow, wolf, and storm.

Hunger.

Crow, sore eye, chaste.

Full sap, crust, and worm.

Cherries ripen.

Blood and falling leaf.

Moon of the long night.

One morning, she comes across a ceremony for self-blessing. It's broad daylight, but she strips, scatters salt on the floor, stands in the middle of it. Near the woodstove, she admits. Surely the powers of the universe don't expect her to freeze.

Gus rouses from where he's sleeping, in a patch of sunlight behind the kitchen counter, and he makes a beeline for Zoe's legs, laps at the body lotion she rubs on every morning, fighting an impossible battle with dry skin.

She does a little dance, shoos him off, and he backs up only a few feet, lies down, watching quizzically.

Like a new cook, she consults her book again, mixes water and wine. The salt is gritty underfoot. She lights the candle, feels like a high-school senior acting out the witches' scene in *Macbeth* for extra credit.

—Bless me, she reads aloud, then dips her fingers in the water and dabs it on her eyes.

Blinks to read the next line:

—Bless my eyes that I might see your glory.

She dabs wine and water on her forehead and sternum, sprinkles some on her feet, reading aloud the pleas for wisdom, heart, direction. Double-checking the incantation, she sees she has left out the anointing of the loins.

Better late than never, she flings some droplets at her crotch.

Next she's supposed to bask in the attention of the cosmos, but mostly she's shivering and feeling foolish. She shrugs, chalks one up for experience, and dives back into her clothes.

It's going to be a long day, when she starts it by casting spells.

Turning her hand to the chores, she sweeps up the salt, tends the lamps. Out at the spring, the air seems warmer. It has moisture in it, give, and by noon there's snow, heavy curtains of it, not the ice-fine snow of bitter cold nor fat indifferent feathers, but real snow, solid snow, genuine snow.

Midafternoon, it's still coming down hard, and Zoe eyes it, pulls on thermals, then debates. It's like handicapping a race horse. Too much clothing and she'll sweat, turn sluggish, then chill. Too little and she'll have to turn back. Warm and storm, she recites, then slips on heavy ski tights, checks the wind. It carries the snow slantwise past the windows. She reaches for her boots.

Gus leaps in the air.

He's been lying on the hearth rug, eyebrows knitting and un-knitting, but the boots confirm it. They're going out. He shimmies toward her, bows, grins, then dodges in circles, his tail whapping her legs.

Zoe gives a signal, and he throws himself down as if onto a trampoline.

—You can't have nerve endings.

He grins and wriggles. His back end slowly comes up on the happy hydraulics of his hips.

—Butt down, Zoe orders.

He flops over, thrusts his legs to one side, flaps his tail.

Taking her pack from a peg by the door, she stuffs in a second knitted hat, extra mittens, a water bottle. Considers a flashlight, but leaves it out. She won't be that long. She does throw in a neck warmer, an extra sweater, checks on her jackknife and matches.

Glued to his spot, Gus swivels, straining toward the door.

Zoe pulls on a wool turtleneck and an anorak, slings the pack up onto her shoulders, then winks at Gus, whispers:

—Free.

He leaps up, charges through the mudroom, then leaps out on the porch, a dancer going onstage in a grand jeté.

—Nice of you to humor me, she says, making her old joke that he'd really rather stay home beside the fire.

She steps out from under the porch roof. Snow sifts past, and she turns her face up into it a moment, then pulls on her hat. In the lee of the shed, the air is still and frigid. Zoe stands a minute. The wood is ranked left and right, the thick ends toward the middle of the shed, the stacks tight and balanced. Her first winter here, her woodpiles fell and fell until she learned the simple trick of tilting the wood, leaning it in on itself.

In the doorway, she laces into her snowshoes, watches Gus sniffling along a drift. Then she steps out into the snow.

Gus leaps into the air, lands already running, flat-out, hind legs digging way up under his chin. He goes thirty feet, skids to a halt, kicks up a cloud of snow, and tears straight back at Zoe. She prays he won't run into her knees. As always, he dodges at the last instant.

They go up the logging road. Her feet find their rhythm, her pack rustles on her back. On either side, the stone walls are nothing more than contours, and rocks and coverts lie disguised beneath capes of snow. She passes a rock cairn, drifted shut, where a fox had kits last spring, and where she learned to circle away to avoid making the mother snarl. Once or twice, she glances back. Their tracks are vague, impressionistic.

The storm is coming from the south. What a surprise to learn that snow sometimes comes up from the warmer states, picking up moisture over the Atlantic. And what a surprise, too, to learn she has her own private weather system up here on the ridge. She gets more snow than down in the village, sometimes gets snow when no one else does. Spark calls it shadow snow from a nearby peak and, while she never enters the competition at the store over whose place was coldest during the night, in the fall and spring, she takes pleasure in driving up the ridge, crossing from rain and mud into whiteness. It's an unexpected gift she never knew to wish for.

She snowshoes onward. The snow falls at a steady rate, a steady angle. Nothing in the forecast leads her to suspect anything else. She revels in the luminescent gloom, the silver, black, and brown of Vermont winter.

And then, as if the ball has stopped on the roulette wheel, she halts. Calls Gus. Zigzagging up ahead, he whirls at her voice, gallops toward her, tail winding like a helicopter blade, snow flying up in clouds around him.

She nods toward the upside of the road.

—What do you think?

He dives through the drift, clears the stone wall, plunges neck deep into the snow on the far side.

Zoe marvels at how well he knows her. Canine anthropologist, he's formed her speech and habits into patterns, often surprises her with her own predictability.

What do you think? means they're going bushwhacking.

Zoe heads uphill, climbs an hour, perhaps more. The mountain comes up beneath her snowshoes. The incline determines how she holds her shoulders, the fallen snow dictates the lift of her feet. A rhythm rises in her. She breathes, blinks under the brim of her hat. The world grows wide and small all at once, and as time passes there's nothing but this mountainside, this storm, this steepness beneath her, her joyful dog bowling on ahead. The snow thickens and Zoe's heart lifts. Gus's coat is shaken with white, his Groucho Marx eyebrows frosted over.

Finally pausing, she leans against an ash, drinks some water. She can't see far, but there down the slope are her tracks, clear enough. Putting her snowshoes together, she pats her thigh, and Gus climbs up onto the back of them, a swimmer resting on a raft. He leans against her legs, and she scratches him with her mittened hand.

Around them, the storm, the woods are seething. It doesn't rage. Or howl. All words are wrong. She knows this now. It breathes,

perhaps. It lives, and it's a privilege to be out in it. Vaguely she recalls her old life. How she and all her colleagues had pushed for
words, demanded articulation, details, insight. Or what passed
for it. They had actually believed that if you couldn't put it into
words you didn't know it, had no grasp of it. She looks around,
defies herself to describe this moment, thinks of the sad futility
of the sentence, the paragraph.

Rested, she resumes her route. Gravity reverses. There's no
downhill drag, no Isaac Newton, only a harmony she has entered
and cannot name. The mountain pulls her up. She wonders how
snow enters the valley of monks. Is Dayton on his knees in this
same storm? Does he pray before a plain chapel window, or in
front of a blank wall?

Gus interrupts, leans against her legs, bites at his foot. She examines his paw, fearing ice balls, but there are none.

—You're okay.

Then she realizes he looks tired.

He gazes up from beneath the snow-covered awnings of his
eyebrows, and she looks with longing up the mountain, feels the
pull of the slope, admits her thighs are hardening with fatigue.

What's more, no one knows she's afoot in this storm. It violates
all common sense, but then so do lots of things. Alcohol, drugs,
auto racing, rock climbing.

Celibacy.

—Okay, she says: Let's go back.

Gus knows these words, too. Usually he does a quick about-
face, trots toward home, but now he sits, looks up at her, waits.

For a moment, she stands, zipping and unzipping her anorak,
shifting her pack, wishing for still more time in the strange, full
vacuum of the storm. Then she turns and retraces the remnants
of her tracks.

Going down is harder than going up. Going up, the mountain
holds her. Going down, she slips. Her knees shake. Patches that
going up merely took a little extra effort now mean stopping,
parsing out a route. Fear taps Zoe on the shoulder, and she bribes

it with the promise never to go out again on snowshoes without carrying ski poles. Then for good measure adds that in the future she'll tack a note on her front door as to her destination.

As if having a destination wouldn't suck the joy out of this expedition.

Behind her, Gus hangs back, whimpers. Snow lies heavy on his coat, fringes his ears.

—Is this your Lassie act?

Clearly he wants to go another way.

The day is darkening now, the snow subtly shifts directions, shifts again. Seasick, she squints, spreads a mittened hand against a tree, then hefts her pack, comforts herself with the thought of matches. And all the while she grasps for logic.

Old logging tracks cross her property, and if she continues downhill, she's bound to find a trace of one. Then, if she follows it, sooner or later it will lead her out, preferably toward her house. But even hitting the paved road far below is better than wandering in circles.

Happy to be on the move again, she starts downslope, the past few minutes of near panic as long as the whole afternoon.

But Gus whimpers again, refuses to budge.

—Not now, she says, her voice strained.

Gus takes a step, whines again, halts.

—Jesus Christ.

She turns, goes back uphill, watches him as if they're playing some find-it game.

—This is wrong, Gus.

He looks up at her, sober, doesn't move.

She takes ten steps another way, checks his reaction.

None.

—I give up, she says, then tries again: Let's go home.

His eyebrows lift and, checking that she follows, he heads across the slope in entirely the wrong direction.

She swears.

Their tracks are sifting over now, and trying out one direction and then another has already bewildered her. She rucks her shoulders, shivers though she's not cold yet.

—Gus! One of us is wrong.

He poses but, when called, refuses to come.

She swears again, then gives up and follows him. Better to stay together, she tells herself, already imagining sheltering in the storm, huddling together for warmth. Dark visions come to her of cutting branches for a lean-to, getting doused with snow. She fears dropping her jackknife, losing it in a drift.

In time, she realizes Gus is headed for a spot well above where they entered the woods. If so, they'll at least get out of the hummocks and ledges. She calls for him to wait, but he trundles relentlessly across the mountain, as if late for an appointment.

—What's the matter? Zoe says, straining for a joke: Afraid you'll miss your supper?

No need for a watch when your dog has no doubt his food bowl will be filled at precisely 7 A.M. and 5 P.M.

Finally Gus halts, waits, furrows his brow.

—Now what?

Zoe snowshoes past him, calls, looks back.

He hesitates, weary abominable snow-dog.

—This is no time to change your mind, Zoe tells Gus.

Then she bargains with whoever's in charge of fools. Saint Barbara on the chimney shelf? The Virgin Mary up in the cupola?

Should she promise to carry not just ski poles but a compass? But why lie? Instead she offers up a meek appeal, tries not to be greedy, merely mentions to the universe that it would be nice to get home in one piece to her hearth and woodstove.

Looking into the snow as if into a gazing bowl, it comes to her to walk against the snow at a consistent angle. She laughs bitterly, needs no special powers to see that the slightest shift would send them off-course.

Finally, she forces herself to take ten strides, pause, take ten more. Panic rises in her, but she counts her paces, one to ten, reconnoiters, turns in the most downhill fashion. Victims to the vagaries of topography, she and Gus thread their way down through the bowls and across the ledges.

They come up over some drifts, and Gus slows, stares across the slope, watchful, quiet. He steps forward a pace or two. His ears pin back and he growls, tentative.

Zoe gasps, gathers herself, whispers to Gus:

—Here, to me.

Is that someone out ahead of them?

Gus glances back at her.

Then a figure comes toward them through the storm.

Zoe's hand goes into her pocket, but she's hampered by her mitten, and it's foolish anyway to think she can protect herself with a jackknife.

The figure is a man, his head down in the storm, his shoulders round. He wears a dark parka, hood pulled up, and some kind of dark trousers.

As casually as if they're meeting in a park on a sunny afternoon, he says to Gus:

—Here, fella.

Gus goes to him, the man pats his head, and Gus smiles up at him as if at a long-lost friend.

—Spark? Zoe says.

But the man's not tall enough.

Gus turns and gives her a loopy smile, pleased to have found a compadre in the storm. Zoe stares at him, her wayward goofball who chases mice and supposedly bites strangers.

The man looks up, and Zoe's relieved to see he's not the man with the flat, blue eyes. Truly a stranger, he's older, much older. His eyes are dark, his face deeply creased. Snow catches in his white, heavy eyebrows.

The wind shifts and tears another way.

—Do you know where we are? Zoe says: I'm a little turned around.

The man says nothing, claps his mittened hands together. The left thumb is beginning to unravel.

Zoe steps sideways, asks:

—Which way did you come from?

Her skin turns tight and icy, her vision narrows, and she throws back her hood, lets snow hit her hat, touch her face.

The stranger smiles, quiet, benign. He pats Gus, says:

—It's nothing to worry about.

—What's not? Dying of exposure?

—You're not lost, he says.

—I'm not lost, she echoes, disbelieving.

—Nor are you in charge of what happens next.

What's next seems pretty damn obvious to her. Find her way home and then stay put until it's safe again outside.

—I didn't know it would be this bad, she says.

He shrugs.

—Some moments we're meant to have. Might's well just accept it.

His eyes brighten. He watches her a moment, then points:

—Head that way. You're only a little way off. You'll get home fine.

—How do you know where I live?

He shrugs.

Stupid question, Zoe thinks: Who doesn't?

She thanks him, then suggests they make their way back together. She wants to keep him with her, not just for his sense of direction, but for company, comfort, sanity.

But he only smiles, waves her off, and within moments he's a diminishing gray figure in the storm.

In his absence, Zoe's little mountain once again turns enormous, assumes the size and mystery of the Himalayas. Then it shrinks again. What a small death, dying in a common storm. How she would be ridiculed, posthumously, for her stupidity and recklessness. Another flatlander forcing the boys on the rescue squad to risk their necks.

Idiot.

She considers her fellow snowshoer, his calm, his seeming benevolence. Some old-timer, is he a recluse? A nut? A soulmate out harvesting the ineffable from the storm?

Zoe follows his offered bearing.

—We'll get there, she tells Gus, a frightened parent reassuring a frightened child.

They march ten paces, Zoe checks the direction, they march ten more. The wind shifts again, the snow with it, and behind her Gus gives up. He walks head down, in the exact lee of her steps.

Fear and false confidence keep time like the two halves of a heartbeat, and Zoe clings to the stranger's directions, tries to recollect his exact words, ponders the inexplicable business of intended moments. Sometimes she conjures her warm fireside, the pleasure of hot soup, a good fire in the woodstove. She imagines Gus, konked out on the hearth rug, sees herself watching the flames, letting herself turn dreamy.

Around them the air darkens; the woods are downright eerie, the trees and underbrush sculptures of indistinct white. She wonders if they should look for shelter before too late, and each time she finds an outcropping with a cave beneath, or a hemlock with branches that brush the ground, she hesitates then hurries onward, remembering that the man in the storm said they would make it home.

And then they step into a long, high tunnel of snow-muffled trees. Disoriented, she stops, stunned at its soft architecture. All at once, Gus forges ahead and Zoe realizes it's her road. The snow's too thick to make out her half-buried house, but she knows it's there, knows smoke rises from the chimney.

That night, Gus sleeps hard in front of the stove. Zoe lounges in gym tights and wool shirt. Halfway through her second glass of wine, she stares into the fire, rests a foot on Gus's flank, lets his breathing raise and lower it. On her lap is her open notebook, but all she's been able to render is a set of sketchy snowshoe tracks crossing a plane of white. At the bottom she writes the date, pencils in a caption:

I have a vision in a storm.

Then hesitates, amends:

Or not.

Then finally adds:
Close call.

Three days later, a letter written in pale blue ink and wavering
script arrives from the Monastery of Our Lady of the Snows. Yes,
certainly, Zoe is welcome to come on retreat. The sisters will pray
for her safe arrival.

CHAPTER 31

꩜

Come between one and two, she's been instructed, but she leaves her mountaintop early, dropping off Gus with Spark then, against her will, heading first to Montpelier. Spark drove a hard bargain about boarding Gus; he'd only do it if on her way she picked up a cell phone. He's tired of her stubbornness. The technician takes a ridiculously long time programming it, and Zoe, impatient, wanders the store, irked by the glare of the linoleum underfoot, the displays of glitzy new computer gear. At last, the phone is ready. Zoe plugs it into the Volvo's cigarette lighter, and heads north.

For a while, the land folds more steeply, then flattens as she approaches the Saint Lawrence and crosses into Canada. It's just past noon when she glimpses the sign for Our Lady of the Snows, and she drives on by, finds a store, not so different from Shroveton's, and buys a ham sandwich and an apple.

Probably her last good meal for the next three days.

The monastery driveway winds through patchy, snow-covered fields. A row of old, bare oaks follows the gentle curves. In summer the lane must be a cool rustling tunnel. Zoe shifts in her seat, and one more time concocts an explanation of who she is, why she's here, recites her litany of half-truths and prevarications. Vaguely she remembers beginning to memorize her catechism before her father's death, stuttering an answer or two, sensing even then that getting the words right would make the priest happy, get her into heaven.

The driveway ends in a patch of gravel in front of an enormous stone-block building, a cross between a castle and a cathedral

243

dropped into Canadian farmland. Feeling like an intruder, Zoe parks her car. It's the only one in the place. She grips the steering wheel, closes her eyes.

You don't have to like it here, she tells herself.

In fact, she plans not to. Yet she's half-fearful that, because she has come, something will happen to her, too. She will be brainwashed, kidnapped by the Holy Spirit.

Don't say a word, she tells God: I'm not in the mood.

With that, she gathers her pack, gets out, and with no small sense of irony, carefully locks the car.

A heavy planked door in the shape of a bishop's hat is the only break in the monolithic wall. High overhead is a row of stained-glass windows, also shaped like bishops' hats. Zoe tries the door, rattles the heavy brass ring.

Locked.

A neat laminated sign announces the times for *Eucharist* and *vespers.* Just when she's considering going out to her car and using her new phone to call inside, the latch rattles and the door swings inward.

In a low stone passageway stands a trim man in black shirt and trousers and a long black sleeveless coat. He wears horn-rimmed bifocals, a tidy gray beard.

—You're here for retreat, he says in a measured, nearly soporific voice: I'm Father Frank, the chaplain.

Retreat is what Zoe would like to do.

Instead, she follows him through the chill passageway, a low stone arch overhead, flagstones underfoot. And then she hears her own quick intake of breath.

—It's your first time here, the priest says.

They're standing in a courtyard. The stucco walls are shell pink. On one hangs an elaborate crucifix. The others are covered with rich old oil paintings, their crazed varnish the color of tea. Pillars hold up a second-story gallery, and light streams in from a hidden clerestory. All that's missing is the sound of splashing fountains.

—It's beautiful, Zoe says, entirely surprised.

—It's not exactly to my taste, Father Frank says, dryly: But nonetheless.

He arches an eyebrow, then says that if Zoe will wait, he'll find Sister Clarice who will come take charge of her. He swirls off through some double doors.

In no hurry to be taken charge of, Zoe peeks down a corridor. Voices murmur from behind a closed door. Another door, ajar, leads to an inviting reading room.

Rapid footsteps come along the gallery overhead, then down some stairs. Sister Clarice, white hair slipping from her wimple, hands folded beneath her apron, apologizes for making Zoe wait.

Wait for what, Zoe thinks. The three days of her visit fall away before her, blank and bottomless as a glacial chasm. Milling around with the comforting weight of her pack slung over her shoulder is just fine with her.

Sister Clarice sets sail across the wide expanse of the courtyard, leads Zoe up some spiral stone stairs. They're steep and claustrophobic.

—Mind your feet, Sister Clarice calls.

—I have stairs like these at home, Zoe says, then adds: Though not so many. And not so dark.

They come out onto a gallery.

Zoe looks over the railing.

—It doesn't seem real here, she says, feeling as if she has somehow fallen back in time, or perhaps out of time altogether.

Sister Clarice looks Zoe full in the face.

Fine scars radiate from her left eye. The dark brown ring of iris is missing a wedge, as if the clear black pupil has chiseled it away.

She tells Zoe that the monastery building is 200 years old.

—The order fell on hard times and finally the house was sold to a private individual who used it for a country home. It was passed down through a few generations, and when the last of the line died, the place was left to a stableman, who as far as we know, lived solely in the kitchen. When he died, we were fortunate enough to acquire it and reconsecrate its use.

—Poverty and property, Zoe remarks: The historic cycle of monastics.

Sister Clarice says:

—The cycle of humanity, no?

Zoe has no idea if the sister's chiding her or agreeing.

Behind them a row of plain wooden doors stand ajar. The first is an office, the second a kitchenette where Zoe will find snacks and can make tea. Next is the guest dining room where Zoe will take her meals. Sister Clarice walks her along a line of cells, indicates the one she occupies as guest mistress. The other five are for guests.

She opens the last door but one.

Zoe steels herself, instinctive as an animal sensing a trap.

Then she chuckles. The room is charming. A rocker, a small desk and chair, good lamps for reading, and the smallest bed Zoe's had since first grade. It's covered with striped sheets and wool blankets, and the foot of it is pushed up against the sill of one of the stained-glass windows she saw from outside.

—Will this do? Sister Clarice asks.

—I love the window, Zoe says: It'll be like sleeping in the sky.

The sister sighs:

—At least there's a clear border, so you can look outdoors. If all that color drives you batty, we can move you to another cell.

—No, Zoe says: I'll like it.

Sister Clarice explains that in the desk drawer are a Bible and diurnal, the book of prayers and offices organized for the year. Zoe's entrance to the chapel will be through the southwest doors. A bell will ring for every office but *prime.* Her hands folded beneath her apron, Sister Clarice explains that it's Zoe's choice whether she attends.

—Guests come here and they don't go to chapel?

Sister Clarice dusts a spot on Zoe's headboard, dips her chin.

—People come to us for many reasons. We minister to guests and strangers.

At least they give it lip service, Zoe thinks: This business of receiving each guest as if he or she is Christ.

She studies the sister a moment, wonders if she is savvy enough to know that Zoe is only here in search of contradictions, flaws, and lies.

Then all at once she knows that she's the one who's lying. She's driven all these miles to pray the prayers that Dayton prays, to bow her head, crawl into bed, even eat her meals the same time he does.

Flooded with sorrow, revelation, she feels the urge to confess: I'm in love with one of you people.

She looks up at the sister, longing for comfort, recognition, solace.

Sister Clarice waits, as if giving Zoe a chance to speak, then merely explains the meals, and apologizes that Zoe must eat alone since at the moment there are no other guests.

—But I don't want to be alone, Zoe says: And what about *lectio*? The reading aloud at meals? Don't I get to hear that?

—I'm sorry, Sister Clarice says.

In her eye, the black wedge darkens.

—We are enclosed here, she says, her voice hard: By choice. I believe that was explained to you on the phone.

Then she excuses herself and, on her way out, closes the door.

Zoe flings her bag on the bed, then for a wild moment wonders if she's been locked in.

Cell.

What an awful word. Then it comes to her that a cell is also a part of a living organism.

It's already getting to you, she tells herself with disgust.

At the door, she tries the handle.

Unlocked.

She looks up at the colors of her window. Ruby, emerald, lapis, gold. But she's no princess in a fairy tale, vulnerable to charms and spells.

Paranoids don't go in for them.

She lies on her bed. It's so narrow that if she puts her hands under her pillow, her elbows stick out over the edges. She thinks dark thoughts about monks being like children, then wonders if only the guests get these tiny beds. Perhaps she should just turn around and go home.

First though, she'll have a look at the diurnal, the text by which Dayton measures his seasons and his hours.

She lays the heavy book open on the desk.

And is stunned to find it's been made by hand.

Literally.

Bound in stretched black cloth, its lefthand pages are Latin, its righthand pages English. All have been typed on an old manual typewriter. Zoe runs her fingers across the typing. Each *o* perforates the page; each *a* is black with extra ink. Four hundred pages. What labor. She conjures old film images of solitary monks with cold hands and feet hunched over desks in scriptoria, copying manuscripts.

The days of the week are painstakingly listed, and for each day, the offices. *Lauds, prime, terce, sext, none, vespers, compline, vigils.*

Zoe looks up Monday, looks up *none*, reads a few lines of the prayers, checks her watch.

Another half-hour.

She'll stay that long, at least.

Then out of the corner of her eye she catches a movement. Wheeling down the driveway on a bright red ten-speed is Sister Clarice. The hems of her habit fly, and Zoe's only thought is that she must feel safe in her vocation. Anyone else would worry about catching her skirt in the spokes, breaking her neck.

The sister coasts the last part of the way, gathers mail from the box, and with more effort rides back up the hill. Then it comes to Zoe that her own letter has been thus retrieved, by a sister in long black skirts and a snow white wimple, gaily riding a bright bike down the drive.

All right, she thinks: I'll be polite. I'll spend the night.

Tomorrow, though, if it suits her, she'll make up some excuse, a message on the cell phone, and will head for home.

In time, the tower bell rings, and Zoe snatches her diurnal and walks the length of the west gallery. Down below in the courtyard, a sister disappears from sight. Zoe turns a corner, swings a door back, finds the chapel entrance.

Heavy old pews march toward a richly rubbed wooden altar draped with a cloth. Statues in niches line the roughened walls, and subtle light falls from high windows. Overhead, hand-hewn beams hold up the roof.

The Rule of Benedict instructs all to go with deliberate but solemn speed at the first sound of the bell, and Zoe's grateful she's first to arrive, since she has no intention of genuflecting or dabbing herself with holy water.

She's not a Catholic, but a spy, an adversary, an unbeliever.

She smiles at herself. Then why not touch the water?

Clinging to her diurnal as if to a false passport, she sits in a pew somewhere just behind the middle.

A quiet scuffle of feet.

Zoe shudders, suddenly appreciates the implications of enclosure.

The chapel is L-shaped. Zoe has entered the south doors, and sits facing north. The sisters are entering from the east, hidden behind an elaborate wrought-metal gate. Both guests and sisters face the altar, but neither will ever see the other.

More footfalls, a whisper, a book bumping against a wooden choir stall.

Zoe listens as if in the woods:

How many are there?

What ages?

What do they wear on their feet?

Behind her, the chapel door opens, and in sweeps Father Frank. At the head of the aisle, he crosses himself, then moves to a high heavy desk with a tilted top, carefully straightens his robes before he sits.

A bell rings, a pitch pipe sounds, the chanting begins. It occurs to Zoe that if she sat right up front and craned her neck, she could get a look at the sisters.

Behind her, the door opens again, and Sister Clarice strides in, and without looking in her prayer book, joins what seems to be some kind of call and response.

Zoe runs her finger down the page. The Benedictines pray the Psalms. In more modern times the prayer load has been decreased, but once upon a time they prayed every psalm every day, knew them all by heart, and privately Zoe admits she likes the idea.

No threats, no hellfire, only praise and contemplation.

What good it does, she can't begin to fathom.

The sisters' voices rise and fall along the Gregorian scale. The words are Latin. In Zoe's text are three- or four-word prompts, followed by ellipses, cues for familiar prayers that will not be spelled out for the likes of her.

No earthly way to follow the service, she simply sits, observant. Father Frank and Sister Clarice rise to their feet, bow, kneel, sit upright again. Sister Clarice has repinned her veil so that it falls forward as she moves.

And then Zoe realizes that *none* is the exact same office she heard at the skete's open house. She conjures Dayton, eyes half-closed, perched on his stool in front of the listening crowd at the kitchen door.

Abruptly the chanting ceases. Zoe startles. Father Frank and Sister Clarice turn, come toward her down the aisle. They're business-like, matter-of-fact. What had she expected? Religious ecstasy six times a day?

Outside in the hallway, a peal of laughter sounds.

Dazed, Zoe leaves the chapel, too, finds Father Frank and Sister Clarice still chortling over some joke.

Sister Clarice asks Father Frank if he's had a proper introduction to their guest.

Here it comes, Zoe thinks: The Inquisition.

—Perhaps Miss Muir would care to see your shop, Sister Clarice says, then explains to Zoe:

—Father is a renowned appraiser of antique instruments. And a master craftsman, too.

—Really? Zoe says: You have a shop here?

—It would be more proper to say I'm skilled, Father Frank says, glancing at his watch: I'm sorry, dear. I'm running late. You're in good hands with sister.

He excuses himself.

—Father's dilemma, Sister Clarice explains: Is that his work is important to our community, since it's so well rewarded. But sometimes it threatens his prayer life.

Zoe tries to remember her readings:

—I thought work was prayer, she says.

Sister Clarice looks decidedly bemused. Or irritated. Zoe's so hypnotized by her eye that she can't tell which.

—And what will you do between now and *vespers?* Sister Clarice asks.

—Take a walk, Zoe says: Get outdoors.

—Let me give you a front-door key, Sister Clarice says: You don't need it to go out, only to come back in.

She laughs.

Zoe laughs, too, cautiously.

Is this an old chestnut of a monastery joke?

Outside, she walks along the high stone wall. Capped with slate, it closes off substantial ground around the monastery, seals the place from view. In two places are heavy wooden doors, one wide enough for vehicles to pass through, the other smaller, nun-sized. On each, a small brass plaque asks visitors to respect the monastery's enclosure.

In other words, *Keep Out.*

Honestly, she thinks, how is one to understand monastics if always held at arm's length, locked out?

Zoe wishes for a compass and map, a nice bluff with a view. Instead, she wanders the parklike woods, every bit of fallen wood picked up, and creates a Middle Ages image of the sisters, gathering fallen sticks for kitchen fires.

She comes across a well-worn path. Up ahead, a few slabs of rock have fallen in a promising way against a boulder, and hoping for a place to perch, a place where the earth feels inviting, Zoe quickens her step, but as she gets nearer, she finds the Virgin Mary has beaten her out again.

Zoe clucks with disgust.

For some, divinity rises from the earth. The Celts, the Greeks revered their cairns, their springs, their holy trees—until the Jews came along, and the Christians and the Muslims, insisting that divinity emanates from above. An old story, this Christian image plunked down in a some natural spot, usurping its earth-given holiness.

Our Lady of the Boulders, Zoe mutters, and turns angrily away.

Back at the front door, her key slips easily into the lock. Surreal to have in her possession the key to such a place.

Up in her cell, she stretches out on her bed, and is soon lulled by the piece-work colors of her window.

I've missed it, she thinks.

I've missed *vespers*.

Then: I've missed supper.

Groggy, she recalls the admonition to be on time for meals.

Then she hears Sister Clarice calling:

—May I come in? I've come to explain the next office. If you wish.

Zoe answers the door, says she doesn't know how long it's been since she slept like that.

Sister Clarice stands utterly still in the doorway.

—I should have let you sleep, she says gently: I could have fixed a tray with your supper.

—No, no, Zoe says, knowing that to the south, at Shroveton, Dayton, too, is readying for *vespers*.

—What do you people do out there? Sister Clarice says: In the real world, as you call it. Everyone comes to us so tired.

Zoe has no idea.

The sister bustles to Zoe's desk, sets down an ominous stack of books.

—It's a little complicated, she says, apologetically.

Zoe blanches.

Sister Clarice nimbly flips the pages in one text after another, slipping in ribbons of different colors, and Zoe nods along, doesn't confess she was utterly lost within the first twenty seconds of *none*.

But when the bell rings for *vespers*, she carries the little stack of beribboned prayer books to the chapel.

To her surprise, two old women from the community already occupy the back pew. They purse their lips as she walks past the holy water. A young woman in a neck brace sits near the front, precisely behind Father Frank, as if hiding, and a tall man with white hair and a scrawny, wrinkled neck has stolen her spot from *none*.

He notices her prayer books, nods, crosses himself, then slides forward onto his knees.

Mortified, Zoe dives into the pew across the aisle, then pins her eyes forward to give him privacy.

Soon the sisters enter, their feet scuffle, the pitch pipe sounds. Unable to follow the office, Zoe merely follows Sister Clarice's lead, wonders if she can fool the white-haired man, make him believe she's the real thing by opening and closing one book after another, rising, kneeling, bowing, sitting.

But he's oblivious, trying to chant along with the office, his voice falling flat, or groping clumsily, and Zoe's indignant at the sacrilege of it, his rough man's voice dragging at the light clear voices of the women.

That evening Sister Clarice serves stew and bread from her caterer's cart. Still disappointed to be eating in what feels like solitary confinement, Zoe tries to entice the sister into dawdling, but the sister's next stop is Father Frank, and then she'll feed herself, make the round once more for dishes, and do the washing up so she and Father Frank can be on time for the next office.

—We don't chatter over meals here, Sister Clarice says.

—I understand, Zoe says meekly, then mentions, by way of apology, that while she's here she hopes to follow the monastery schedule exactly.

What she doesn't say is that it's Dayton she hopes to follow.

Sister Clarice suddenly has time. Her hands slip beneath her apron, fold themselves. Solemnly she warns Zoe not even to attempt doing all the offices.

—But I thought that was why people came here.

Sister Clarice ducks her chin:

—You must come for your own reasons.

Zoe finds herself staring at the sister's chipped eye, the tiny web of scars.

—Forgive me, she says: I can't stop looking at your eye.

Sister Clarice reaches her hands out from under her apron, turns them up and out.

—I've noticed your wrists, too.

She hides her hands again.

—Oh, those, Zoe says and without thought pulls down her turtleneck, exposes the upper inches of those scars, too: I was attacked.

Sister Clarice searches Zoe's face.

—Father and I wondered if it had been a suicide attempt.

Zoe puts her arms up, as if defending herself.

—No. I was trying to stay alive.

Sister Clarice nods, approving, tells Zoe she herself was injured in a car accident while in college.

—I was a tad bit wild.

Zoe says nothing.

—You'd like to know if it led to my vocation, Sister Clarice says: Everyone wants to know that, and I always say what I'm going to say now. You have your blind eye. And I have mine.

She laughs then, says:

—And now that's enough penny-ante wisdom.

Pausing in the doorway, she reminds Zoe not to overdo the offices. The sisters spend between five and six hours in the chapel every day, but for them, the round has meaning

—But for newcomers? Much too much.

She suggests Zoe come to *compline* at eight, but not *vigils*, which are much longer and much later.

—But what will happen if I come to all the offices? Zoe says.

—Nothing will happen, the sister says: That's the problem.

Compline.

Candles illuminate the chapel.

In the corners, shadows drift.

Alone with Father Frank and Sister Clarice, and the fifteen or so sisters she can hear but cannot see, Zoe spreads her palm on the open pages of her diurnal.

The prayers wash over her, beautiful, incomprehensible.

That night she wakes, convinced that the sky's on fire, that she's having revelations. But it's only an outdoor light, shining through her stained-glass window.

Early morning, she can stay in bed no longer. Out along the gallery, no light slips from Sister Clarice's cell, and Zoe slinks past, opens the heavy front door. The night sky fades to violet. The last stars weaken. In the turnout, her old Volvo seems the flotsam of some remote life, and out along the road, a dairy barn, its lights ablaze for the first milking, seems no more real than a model on a train platform. Zoe passes a village school, dark, a library, also dark, some stretches of snowy fields and woods, and a few houses, one with a light in the kitchen and a car warming up in the driveway.

She frets over whether she should stay for her entire visit or whether she should bolt back to Shroveton. It's town-meeting day today, and she worries about the taxes on the skete. Unable to decide whether she should make a habit of riding to the rescue, she hasn't left directions for another eleventh-hour save. She walks fast, lets her heels strike so hard they jar her hips, remembers the attorney telling her there will still be time when she returns.

The bell for *lauds* rings just as Zoe unlocks the front door. She goes directly to the chapel, sits near the wall. Father Frank shuffles in, his ankles and back stiff in the early morning. Sister Clarice ignores Zoe as she passes. In the side chapel, a sister coughs, coughs again. Someone sniffles. It startles Zoe that they come before God this early in the morning, rumpled, grumpy, human.

Zoe feels suddenly at ease.

The prayers begin, the voices a little hoarse with disuse. These are the sisters' first words since The Great Silence began at last night's *vigils*.

How many relationships could be salvaged, Zoe wonders, by a daily dose of silence, which can only be ended with words of praise?

After *lauds*, Zoe showers, planning to be quick about it. The guest bathroom is a palace of modesty and hygiene. Striped canvas curtains cordon toilets, sinks, and showers into separate cubicles. Inside this labyrinth, Zoe strips, unwraps her body as if unwrapping dynamite and, while the sisters walk the grounds, tell their rosaries, meditate, she stands naked before a small mirror over a sink.

No full-length glass here.

Idly, she regards the scars quiet on her neck, her arms softer from the lighter work of winter, their scars quiet, too. On a whim, she wraps her towel around her head, tries to fashion the dark blue terry cloth into a wimple, then tears it off again, can't imagine for one second giving up sun on her arms, breeze in her hair, can't fathom trading jeans and boots for the cumbersome habit of a sister.

And then she showers, utterly profligate. Her quick rinse between *lauds* and *prime* becomes a bacchanal of bathing. She lathers up, scrubs her arms and back and legs and buttocks, runs soap-slippery hands up over her breasts, her neck. All the while she offers little pagan prayers of thanksgiving for heat and steam, scented soap, water without end.

Afterward, when Sister Clarice serves her a plate of eggs and a cup of canned fruit from her cart, Zoe apologizes for missing *prime*.

—I just couldn't get out of the shower. I live way out in the

woods, in a tiny little house which I love. But it has no running
water.

She shudders with pleasure:

—There's nothing like a shower when you haven't had one in
a long time.

—So, you're a Daniel Boone, Sister Clarice remarks, ready to
move on and deliver breakfast to Father Frank.

—Not really, Zoe says, suddenly knowing she'll stay for her
entire visit.

She likes Sister Clarice too well to hurt her feelings.

—Could I have a job today? Zoe asks, by way of making herself
at home: Something to do?

—We have a modest library if you'd care to read. I'm afraid it's
too early for hiking.

The sister brightens:

—Do you ski? There's a place about an hour away. Or you can
go driving. It's very beautiful countryside.

—I'd rather work, Zoe says: I can cut brush, if you'd like. Run
power tools, split wood, almost anything.

Sister Clarice dips her chin.

—Then you must do something different while you're with us.

That evening, Zoe lingers in the doorway of the kitchenette while
Sister Clarice refills sugar bowls, salt-and-pepper shakers, answering the sister's questions about her day, telling about her drive
along a river valley but leaving out that she felt homesick for
her forest and her dog, oddly homesick for this place, too, for
any place where someone waits for her, expects something so
simple as her return.

Sister Clarice asks about her stay so far. Her eye glints.

—Did you smuggle in food?

—I thought about it, Zoe says, sheepish.

Sister Clarice laughs, holds out a cookie tin she's refilling:

—People don't know the joy of a place like this.

She snaps the lid back onto the tin. It sounds like a muffled
cymbal.

—May I ask why you've come? she says: If not because of your scars?

—It's complicated, Zoe says.

Her throat knots then, and she turns away, goes along the gallery to her cell.

When the bell rings for *compline,* Zoe doesn't move, but two hours later when it rings for *vigils,* she finds her way to the darkened chapel.

The service is long, and for a while, she thinks it can never be long enough. What is it here? The calm? The bells? Being tended once again by women? In time, her back and knees are aching, and finally she slumps forward, exhausted, rests her head and arms on the back of the pew in front of her. Father Frank and Sister Clarice rise and kneel and bow, and when it finally ends Zoe rushes out ahead of the others, crawls into bed.

That night, safe and undisturbed, she sleeps beneath the hot blanket of colored light.

CHAPTER 32

≈

Our Lady of the Snows, day three:

Walk.

Lauds.

Shower.

Prime.

Breakfast.

Drive.

But this time she returns for *sext* and lunch, reminds Sister Clarice she wouldn't mind visiting Father Frank in his shop. She spends the afternoon on her bed rereading the Rule of Benedict. No summons comes from Father Frank and Zoe dozes, wakes in time for *vespers.*

That evening, Sister Clarice scrubs the guests' dining table, and Zoe sits by the window, thinking of Dayton and his brothers, doing their kitchen chores, envious of his family of brothers.

—Are all monasteries like this? Zoe says.

—Like what? Sister Clarice wrings out her sponge, begins to buff the table.

—Like this.

Sister Clarice bears down on her cloth.

—Why do you ask?

Zoe goes to the sideboard and with uncertain hands makes a cup of tea she has no wish for.

—I have a friend in a monastery, Zoe says, then blushes: From long ago. He's at Shroveton Skete.

Sister Clarice straightens, gives Zoe an astonished look. The cloth hangs utterly still in her hands.

—You know someone at Shroveton?

—I used to know him, Zoe confesses: I came here hoping to understand him better. Monks, I mean. Hoping to understand monks better.

Sister Clarice smiles wryly.

—You were going to understand monks in three days?

Embarrassed, Zoe can't meet the sister's eye. She sits, looks down into her tea.

—How's that for arrogant, Zoe says.

Sister Clarice glances at the door, as if to see if anyone is out in the hall. Then she gives Zoe a long look. Her chipped eye is clear and sharp:

—We've had some lively talks in the parlor about Shroveton.

—I'm sure you have, Zoe says dully.

—Your friend is right in the thick of what keeps faith alive. You should be proud of him.

—I just don't get it, Zoe says.

Sister Clarice glances out toward the hall again.

—I'm not sure this is the right thing, she says, then tells Zoe to wait: I have something for you.

Zoe swishes the tea bag in her mug, assumes the sister will return with a rosary, a holy card, something puzzling and useless.

Instead, she brings a sheaf of paper, stapled at the corner.

—It's from the computer, Sister Clarice says: I don't know how it works exactly, but it's a discussion we have, just monastics in the north country writing to one another. There's a patch in it from Shroveton. I'm a great fan of what they're doing.

She gives Zoe a conspiratorial look, then rifles the pages, finds what she's looking for:

—Too bad it isn't signed.

Day four.

The bell for *lauds.*

Zoe lifts her head, gropes beneath her pillow, feels the wrinkled printout, which she has read and reread all night long. She plants her face in her pillow, winces at the thought of all that Latin going on upstairs, closes her burning eyes, sleeps a little. When she wakes again, the sisters are out walking the grounds. Finally Zoe leaves her tiny bed, and, determined to be the good guest, makes her way on time to breakfast.

Sister Clarice serves her a stack of steaming French toast, then wheels away.

Zoe stares at her plate, drinks a little tea.

On her return, the sister's barely through the door when she asks if Zoe has perhaps found the time to read the newsletter.

—Discussion group, Zoe says automatically, as if she is teaching once again: Listserv.

—It's supposed to be private, Sister Clarice says, worried now: So we can be frank with one another. But you seemed so interested.

Zoe has nothing to say.

—I'm sorry, Sister Clarice says: Has it upset you?

Zoe musters a smile:

—Nothing that I didn't already know.

—And today's your day, too, Sister Clarice says: To go back to the real world, as you people like to say.

—I haven't said that, Zoe tells her.

—No, you haven't, the sister says thoughtfully, folding her hands beneath her apron. Then as if Zoe is a small child who must be consoled, she offers: I'll take you along to Father's shop.

At first, Father Frank refuses their visit.

He stands in the doorway of his workroom, wearing a light gray shop coat, sleeves rolled up. A dust mask hangs at the ready around his neck. With some annoyance he tells Zoe he can't get the sister to understand that while he's working he has no time for visitors.

—I understand, Zoe says, knowing how she herself, even living all alone, hates to be interrupted.

Sister Clarice wrings her hands beneath her apron.

—But Father, Miss Muir has a friend at Shroveton Skete. I do apologize for the interruption.

—At Shroveton? Father Frank says.

—I gave her the computer letters. Perhaps that was wrong of me, but she does have a friend there.

Father Frank steps to the side.

—Let's go in.

The shop is well lit, orderly to the point of fussiness, and Zoe's drawn immediately to several rosy-colored, fine-grained boards of wood lying on a workbench. She reaches to stroke the grain.

—Don't! Father Frank says, then adds, more quietly, a little desperate: Please.

Zoe's hand freezes.

—You have oil on your skin. We all do. If you touch that now, I'll be sanding for the rest of my life.

Sheepish, Zoe puts her hands behind her back.

—I see why guests are a bother.

—What do you hear from the Shroveton renegades? Father Frank asks.

—I thought they were monks, Zoe says.

And before he or the sister can respond, she tells Father Frank that she'd love to learn about woodworking some day, at least that seems it would be natural since right now she's occupied at an earlier stage in the process:

—I have 500 acres of woodlot. I spend my days cutting trees.

Both Father Frank and Sister Clarice are impressed.

—Now that's a job, the father says.

—Do you find it impossible to work and talk at the same time, Zoe wants to know: I mean, do you have to work from the part of your head where there are no words?

Father Frank considers:

—Possibly. I know I spend too much of my day talking, trying to manage things.

—Thanks for the visit, Zoe says, hoping to leave before he realizes he's been waylaid.

—I just wish I knew what to think of Shroveton, he muses: Is it a legitimate purification or something else?

—It's a fine thing, Sister Clarice announces: That letter was just one more proof.

—I thought the point was that there is no proof, Zoe says, then gulps and gulps, manages to thank the surprised father again for his time, and flees upstairs to her cell.

Cramming her clothes and toothbrush into her knapsack, she thinks how hard it is to pack when leaving home, deciding what's necessary, what's extra baggage. Yet how easy to return; load up what's yours and drag it back. She strips the mattress, gathers her towels, and in keeping with the tradition of Benedict, prepares her cell for whoever will occupy it next. Zoe, whose usual idea of bed-making is to change the sheets once in a while and fling the free end of the blankets toward the head of the bed, takes momentous care anchoring the bottom sheet, adjusting the top sheet, smoothing the blankets.

The bell rings for *terce.*

She's been avoiding Mass, but now she goes out into the hall.

Sister Clarice waits, hands folded under her surplice.

—I apologize for Father's brusqueness. Sometimes he enjoys guests even if he says he doesn't.

Zoe avoids her eyes, says:

—I thought I might stay for one more office.

Sister Clarice inclines her head.

Light-headed, she watches Father Frank celebrate Mass, sees his profile, neat beard and glasses, his deft gestures as the sisters come up for the *Eucharist,* kneeling just out of Zoe's sight.

Do the wafer and the wine truly become the body and the blood? Whole countries have changed hands because of this same question but for Zoe, already queasy, the idea is repulsive, ghoulish, the imbibing of flesh. Distracting herself with distantly recalled remnants of college courses, she thinks of sacrificed kings, of corn turning to gold, fish to princes, but only for those who follow essentially nonsensical instructions.

Hop three times in the dark of the new moon.

Sleep with four magic pebbles under your pillow.

Carry a newborn upstairs first, never down.

Afterward, she gathers her knapsack, takes it to the car. Dodging the Virgin Mary, she walks the perimeters of a pasture in the first stages of turning back to forest. The junipers are spreading their branch-tentacles in all directions.

When the bell rings for *sext,* Sister Clarice greets her at the front door.

—I saw you walking, she says: I ordered lunch for you.

Midafternoon, Zoe's still dawdling, and sits through *none,* wondering what monastics prize. A beautiful voice? Amiability? Are there petty jealousies? Feuds? Love? She tries to conjure Dayton, right that minute, head bowed, blond hair falling forward as he bows his head, that old nick in his chin, the sound of his voice in prayer. Before she can render him completely, *none* comes to an end.

The sisters exit the chapel, return to their day's labor.

Dayton vanishes, too.

Zoe, however, cannot get up, get moving.

For a moment she thinks of the group of retreatants who are due here just after *vespers,* driving toward this very monastery even as she sits, immobilized. All at once she envies intensely their first hearing of the sweet evening prayer:

Grant us a restful night, and a peaceful end.

And then she's full-out weeping. She pulls the wadded-up pages from her pocket. Wiping her tears with her fingers, her fists, her sleeve, she squints in the darkness:

Nearly a decade ago, I drove someone from my life because I had an answer and she didn't.

More accurately, I believed I was right and she was wrong. Certainly she was stubborn.

Zoe gulps, sniffles.

Now I see that I was desperate and she was wise enough not to parrot what she didn't believe.

It isn't signed, but certainly she hears Dayton's voice again, the warmth of it, senses his presence, his scouring absence, too.

So it's not for me, as a brother at Shroveton Skete, to answer the constant question of whether we're true monastics.

I lost my mother when I was two, my fiancée when I was twenty-eight, my father a little more than a year ago. As you all know, here, as in any monastery, my avenues of escape are limited. Five men on an isolated farm have nowhere to go but into full engagement with their own characters and with the characters of the other four. We might disagree, distrust, dislike, even sometimes despise, but here we are, all day long, all night, the five of us, wearing away at one another's rough edges. Abandonment, escape, is a cowardice in the past I might regret, but which I cannot mend.

There's more, of course, lots more:

About the danger of language, how he personally turns away at every opportunity from debates on theology and doctrine, rejects therefore the politics of archbishops, how he's even writing this against his will, only because his four brothers assigned it to him as part of his work. Language gives the illusion of certainty where there perhaps is none. Language articulates, quantifies, divides, allows us to believe we have it in our power to comprehend the incomprehensible. And any fellow monastic who's spending time over the question of whether Shroveton Skete is real has perhaps been distracted from more serious matters of the soul.

It's Dayton all right.

Pure Dayton, entirely himself and no one else.

Zoe smoothes the article against her knee, slumps exhausted in her pew.

The bell for *vespers* wakes her.

Five P.M., and soon dark.

Stiff, she stands a moment, massages her neck. Outside in the hallway, Sister Clarice paces. Worried, she tells Zoe that Father Frank is waiting in his study.

—I told him you never left the chapel after *none.*

Zoe's face is clammy with dried tears.

—I'm fine, she says: I only need to listen.

But then she thinks: What on earth am I talking about?

Dipping her chin, Sister Clarice gives Zoe a suddenly impish look:

—God speaks in a rather loud voice.

Zoe pulls a face, laughs:

—I worry about that.

Off in the distance, five women enter the courtyard with their bags. Zoe hears them marveling.

—Your new flock is here, she says, looking into the sister's chipped eye.

—They'll wait, Sister Clarice says, then asks if Zoe will be all right driving home at this hour.

—I'll be fine, she says, abruptly kissing the sister's cheek.

Minutes later, sitting in darkness at the foot of the drive, waiting for a truck to lumber past, Zoe remembers Sister Clarice on the bicycle, skirts flying among the spokes. She smiles, considers staying a while longer, waiting for the bell for *compline,* as if it might bestow a kind of blessing.

CHAPTER 33

≱

The drive home is long, but Zoe has a quiet energy. It's ages since she's been on the road at night, slipping through the dark, headlights casting before her, taillights leaving their pale wash behind. The clutch is nimble beneath her left foot, the gear shift notches easily, and the moon leads her through the mountains. Right this minute the universe breathes around her, and she hopes, against all twentieth-century rationalism, that heavenly bodies indeed make music as they move through their orbits.

She recites:

Lauds, prime, terce, sext, none, vespers, compline, vigils.

Automatic, she turns here and there. The earth rises around her in slopes and ridges, falls away along riverbeds. Several hours later, when she reaches Shroveton, most of the town has gone to bed. A small light burns at the store and another at the fire house. By now the sisters must be sleeping in their cells. A century ago, they would be rising for *matins*, the night office.

On a whim, Zoe pulls off the road, slips and scrambles down to the river where townsfolk and tourists, with hearts strong enough to stand the jolting cold, swim in the summertime. The water, running gladly, breaks through scarves of ice. Zoe catches her balance against a birch, feels the fine branch-ends of a young fir whisper through her fingers.

She climbs up onto a rock, flat as a tabletop. The moon pleases her. Its glare shatters on the moving water. The blackness of the shadows pleases her, too, and the world shouldering in around her. Two years ago, she couldn't have concocted this moment if she tried.

Crouching, she holds a hand in the water, flings droplets across the water. They silver on the river's surface. She touches her cool palm to her neck, wets her eyes, puts her hand back into the water, splashes once more.

Lauds, prime, terce, sext, none, vespers, compline, vigils.

Quiet falls around her soul and, in the sky a curtain of light rises suddenly, comes from nowhere, everywhere at once.

Northern lights.

No explanation of solar storms and ions touches the sheer majesty of pink and green light, in balls and waves, undulating now, rising far above where the sky should end. Perhaps, just perhaps, some presence, unnamable and unknowable, powers the universe, and Zoe plants her two inconsequential human feet in this one little spot on planet Earth, and looks up into the cosmos. She watches the lights and wonders if any of the sisters are awake for this performance, thinks of her beautiful yet confounding stained-glass window, thinks, too, of Dayton with joy and sorrow both.

More greens, then rose.

So be it, she thinks.

Then tells the river and the sky:

—So be it.

And surrenders Dayton.

The lights flare to the north.

Absolutely numb, she makes her way back to the car. The night turns mechanical, and she wishes she had the courage to drive the rest of the way home without headlights, as if wanting something back from God.

She dips her chin, mimics Sister Clarice, and hopes for what? Strength? Grace? Guts? Common sense?

Dayton is gone. She will not storm. She will write, sane and calm, find out if there's anything he needs.

More tears come. He needs nothing from her, but regard at

some remove. Perhaps money for taxes. She'll go home and, in the next few days, read through her notebook one last time, then pack it away.

Turning on the headlights, she drives with care, and by the time she climbs her own road, she feels as if she's been away a century. It's so late, Spark Everett's is completely dark. Suddenly she remembers Spark was to leave Gus at her house first thing this morning. She loaned him a key.

She grits her teeth. She's lost herself in the chanting of the sisters, has handed over the one person in the world she loves most to an entity she can't comprehend. And she has forgotten her own dog.

Dreading to think of the chaos he can wreak in a long day on his own, she speeds up the hill.

Of course, the house is dark. The lane going up has been dark, too, the moon crowded out by the trees, and Zoe points the headlights at the front door, opens the glove box, finds the flashlight, and hurries along the path. She'll let Gus out first then light a lamp or two.

Her feet ring hollow on the porch, and the door pulls open. She shakes her head, useless key ready in her hand.

How could Spark not have locked it behind him? After all his fussing about her safety.

Of course, she's the one who came home a full twelve hours late.

She steps in, expects her old buddy Gus to be leaping at the mudroom door.

Nothing.

No bark, no woof.

The inner door opens easily, and her beam of light catches Gus lying in his favorite spot on the hearth rug, although the woodstove and house are stone cold. She flicks the flashlight around the room.

—Oh, Gus.

The cushions from the couch are strewn across the floor. Kitchen towels are strewn, too, and scattered across the floor are odds and ends from the table, lamp, salt-and-pepper shaker, a stray book. The lamp globe has been shattered; kerosene soaks into the floor.

—Oh Gus, she says again.

And then she realizes the dog is slow about getting up, comes toward her as if his feet are lead, then winds awkwardly back and forth in front of her, bowing and licking his lips.

—You should feel guilty.

She shines the light into the kitchen. Food containers, now licked clean, lie scattered everywhere. Then she sees that the rich red and black feathers of his tail have been hacked off. Only the feathers. Thank god he isn't bleeding. She snags his collar, flicks the light here and there, tries to get her mind around what's happened. Frantic, she drags him across the porch, along the path. He moves as if he has a basketball in his belly.

At the car, she opens the back door, orders him in. He gets his front paws up on the seat, then turns and gives her a look both humiliated and pained. She grabs his back legs, wheelbarrows him in, dives into the driver's seat.

She's just breaking out of the woods and into Spark's meadow when she remembers the phone on the seat beside her.

The dispatcher's advice is that she lock herself in her car and wait. Turning in the seat, she examines Gus. He draws his lips back, halfheartedly whaps his cropped tail. Zoe feels the end of it; whoever cut it missed the bone.

Just barely.

Twenty minutes pass. Headlights cut up across the pasture lane, and a car pulls up to Zoe's. A state trooper, gangly and crew-cut, unfolds himself from his car.

—Zoe Muir?

The sight of him is profoundly calming, and for a wild moment Zoe suspects they will get to her house and find everything in good order.

—My house was broken into, she says, tentative: I just came home.

She turns her car around, follows the trooper to her turnout, leaves Gus in the car.

The trooper plays his spotlight over the house, across the porch, up the lane, into the trees.

—Is it empty?

Zoe nods.

—How do you know?

Horrified, she stares at him, then at the house. Could someone still be upstairs? In the cupola? The shed? The crawl space?

He tells her to get back into her car.

Inside the house, his light moves across the windows, then goes up to the second floor, shines out through the crow's-nest windows like a beacon. In time, he comes back out, pulls a clipboard from his car, pauses to radio a message. Then they go in, and he instructs her just to talk her way through the house, describe what she sees, tell him if anything is different or missing.

—Missing? Zoe says, as if she has just gotten it.

And so they tour the house, and Zoe feels idiotic saying:

—The cushions were taken from the couch. The chairs have been turned over. Some plates have been thrown onto the floor and broken. The refrigerator has been emptied and all the food fed to the dog.

Soon she is recording everything:

—Most of the books look all right. The kindling box is still full. They left the stove matches.

Then back to damage:

—The lamps have all been turned over. And my saint.

Saint Barbara isn't damaged, only knocked down, and Zoe picks her up, carries her along.

—Let's go upstairs.

—I'm getting the creeps, she says: Is it bad up there?

—You'll have to tell me.

The bed has been tossed, and books, pages every which way, lie like a flock of colorful, broken-backed birds. Papers slide in messy heaps. Zoe stills, falls silent.

—Tell me what you're seeing, the trooper says.

—My notebook, she whispers finally: It's gone. I'm going to be sick.

—They say it's like rape. You'll feel violated for a while. Shaken up.

—There's no word for what I feel, she says.

The trooper makes a face.

Zoe looks at him stupidly.

—Who would want my notebook?

The trooper points his pen to the crow's nest stairs.

Snow whitening her vision, Zoe stumbles along behind.

He shines the light. The room is empty.

Completely.

—Anything missing?

Zoe gapes. Lies.

—No.

—Sure? Nothing?

She nods.

Nothing but the skete's Virgin Mary.

Downstairs, Zoe sits on the very bottom step, puts her head down.

—I should clean up this kerosene, she mutters.

The air is rank with it, sickening.

—Probably just kids, the trooper says.

—Kids, Zoe echoes.

She hoists herself up, picks her way through the debris, opens the door, whistles for Gus, then remembers he's in the car. A wide, scary moat of darkness lies between house and car, and Zoe asks the trooper to come with her.

He shines the broad beam of his light all around, walks her out.

Gus rolls down from the seat, halfheartedly rushes at the trooper's leg, snaps once, then turns his head to Zoe, face goofy with apology and worry. Once or twice he growls at the trooper, but only briefly, as if uncertain of his lines.

The trooper points.

—Was that dog here?

—Yes, she says, massaging Gus's forehead with her fingertips.

He pins down her foot with his paw, sags against her.

—The food, the trooper says, remembering.

—They cut off his tail, she says, vaguely aware her teeth are chattering.

The trooper shines his light up toward the woods again, along the path, then swings, gets a look at Gus's tail, makes a note.

—Would you feel better if we went back inside?

—I'll never feel better, Zoe says, miserable.

Headlights break through at the bottom of the lane; a bar of red lights glows across the top.

Zoe gasps, shamelessly moves behind the trooper.

—Constable Everett, the trooper remarks: Must have been listening to the scanner.

The truck stops, Spark opens the door, clear in the dome light of the truck's interior.

Zoe greets him:

—They win. I'm going to sell.

—It's not that bad, the trooper says: Let's go back in. The longer you put it off, the harder it gets.

Spark asks if she's hurt, and when she tells him no, just stunned, he says he tried to keep an eye on things, but he'd been up all the previous night, then had dropped off Gus and had apparently fallen asleep. The blue lights of the trooper's car woke him.

—You were at the accident? the trooper says.

Spark sighs, says yes, tells Zoe it was a car crash, a rollover, one dead, and he'd been at the scene until daybreak.

Again, the trooper suggests they go back in, and Zoe lets herself be escorted, the trooper in front, Spark behind, Gus alongside.

They step across the threshold, and Spark whistles.

The trooper's ready with his pen.

—Any idea who it was? Either of you?

—They had to get past Gus, Zoe says.

—Lots of dogs might go off-duty for the contents of a refrigerator, the trooper says.

Frowning, Spark examines Gus.

Zoe gives Spark a pleading look:

—But why hack off his tail?

—There's been a lot of mischief in this town these last months, Spark says.

The trooper looks around the room.

—I think we've begun to cross the line from mischief into something else.

CHAPTER 34

꧁

During the night, Gus repeatedly wakes Zoe from where she's dozing by the fire. He goes to the door, comes back, goes to the door. Zoe refuses to open the door for any reason before the light of day, refuses even to undress, never mind go upstairs and get into her bed. Spark had suggested that Zoe sleep at his place until she felt safer, but the trooper interposed; it's better for the victim to spend the first night in the house. The longer it's put off, the harder it is.

So Zoe slumps before the fire, clutching the cell phone, and finally Gus gives her a sheepish look and vomits by the door. She mops up, gagging, marveling that the calm she had—how many hours ago?—is impossible to recall. She marvels, too, that Dayton can believe in a God who thanks her for surrendering her obsession by allowing her house be trashed.

Quid pro quo might be a more reliable faith.

Off and on throughout the night, Gus is sick and, in the morning, when he refuses food, she knows it's serious. She's always imagined him growing old, even in his last hours finding the strength to snuffle for crumbs on the kitchen floor. But now he lies on the hearth rug beside the morning jack fire, flat on his side.

When she offers him a walk, he hoists himself up, so dutiful and pained, that she loads him in the car instead and drives to the vet's.

They suggest Zoe leave him for the day, but she's too shaken to part with him, and soon the vet passes through the waiting area, sees him with his tail hacked off and his head hanging, and simply takes him next.

By now, Zoe fears he's been poisoned, knows in some vague way that it's easier to fear for him than for herself.

No, the vet says. Dogs are seldom poisoned in break-ins. More likely in neighborhood feuds.

Same difference, Zoe thinks.

She tells the vet about the refrigerator food emptied out on the floor for Gus to eat, and the vet's indignant. She palpates his throat, his belly, asks Zoe about the vomiting, prescribes small portions of rice and chicken broth for a few days, and tells her to make sure he drinks enough water. She fingers the blunt end of Gus's tail, finds no wound, only the harsh ends of the hacked-off hair.

—Sometimes we're wrong about our dogs, she muses: We like to think they protect us, but sometimes maybe we have to look out for them.

She tells Zoe to get a gun.

For a mile or two, Zoe has her same old thought about this gun business: She can't. She won't.

Then all at once she's so damn mad, that back in town, she heads straight to Rileys. The store is quiet. Leland is nowhere to be seen, and Callum is flipping through some order forms. Nervous, Zoe saunters up, like a cowboy in a western, places her palms on the counter, and announces she means to buy herself a shotgun.

—Can't say as I blame you, Callum says: I heard about your place.

—Your uncle's been after me about this since the minute I moved in.

Callum looks diffident.

—Wouldn't have kept your house from being broken into.

Zoe shrugs.

—Your uncle tells me I should just shoot through the door.

Callum gets up from his stool, fishes a small ring of keys from the breast pocket of his shirt, and walks Zoe over to the gun cabinet.

—If it were me, Callum says: I'd make sure I had a damn good lawyer before I pulled a stunt like that.

Zoe is defiant, jittery, too.

—I have his permission. Under the circumstances.

Callum lifts his eyebrows, and all at once Zoe wonders if this is some bizarre piece of advice given to flatlanders to see if they're dumb enough to blow their kitchen doors to smithereens at the hoot of every passing owl.

—I think it's called country justice, Zoe says.

Callum frowns.

—Just pick one out for me, she says, pointing to the weapons behind the locked glass doors, muzzles leaning in felt forks.

—How thick is your door?

Zoe holds up her thumb and forefinger.

Callum nods, then selects a gun for her.

—Harrington and Richardson, he says: Break-action, single-barrel, twenty-gauge.

Zoe is reminded of buying the chain saw, only this time, she actually intends to do harm. Or at least scare the hell out of someone.

He holds it out to her, and her skin crawls as if he's offering her a snake. Callum's eyebrows lift.

—Show me how, she says.

And so he does. Demonstrates that she must cock the hammer before she fires, explains she only gets one shot at a time.

—That should slow you down.

Zoe smiles.

—Not an assault weapon.

—You can do a load of harm with this, he tells her.

She takes it from him, holds the stock to her shoulder, and Callum, as if giving a golf lesson, adjusts her arms, tells her to press the butt firmly into her shoulder. She does, looks through the sight, points the barrel at a paint sprayer, a toaster, a roasting pan, cans of paint.

—What do I put in it?

Callum hesitates.

—Shells.

Zoe lowers the shotgun, lays it over her left arm, points the barrel at the floor; after all, she watched enough westerns when she was young.

From a drawer, Callum takes a box of shells, metal caps on plastic cups, dull red.

—Don't they come in some other color? Teal? Baby blue?

She laughs.

—I'm kidding.

—A gun is a deadly thing, Callum says: It's not for jokes.

Zoe reaches for the shells. Callum lays them down some distance away.

—Store these separate, he says.

Zoe's eyes glint.

—Kind of limits the chances of scaring off the enemy, doesn't it?

Callum slides a form across the desk, goes back into the office to call it in. When he comes out, Zoe's also gathered lamp wicks, duct tape, mousetraps.

Benign necessities.

—So, she says: Would I press the barrel right to the door before I fire? Or hold it back a little?

Callum shakes his head.

—I'm not touching that one, he tells her, nodding toward the shells: No telling what will happen to the pattern as it passes through a door.

Zoe smiles, oddly enjoying Callum's discomfort.

—Blame Spark. It's his idea.

—Then get him to give you a lesson.

Zoe stops by his place, finds him rearranging the remnants of his woodpile, straightening up. When he sees the shotgun, he commends his nephew's selection.

But just as she's asking him for a lesson, his pager sounds.

—I have to run, he says.

—I'm scared, she confesses.

—I'll come up, he says: Later today, all right?

❦

But he doesn't come. Zoe considers turning on the phone and calling him, but decides not to. If he said he'd come up, he will. And once night begins to fall, she settles the shotgun by the door, props it into the corner, but then, afraid that it will fall, lays it on the floor against the wall. Nervous, she loads a shell, ejects it, loads another, ejects that, too.

That night, she sleeps uneasily by the fire, stirs at every sound, the collapsing of burnt-through logs, Gus woofing in a dream, the cry of a fox below the house. She shines her flashlight at the shotgun. Still there, playing dead.

The next evening Spark stops up. It's already dark, so he promises he'll come by another day and they'll have a little target practice. He's been awfully busy; there are some leads in her break-in. He won't say any more.

He asks to see the drawing she made of the blue-eyed man.

She throws her palms up.

—Too late. It was in my notebook and my notebook's gone.

Spark frowns, then nods at the shotgun:

—For the time being, keep that right where it is. If anyone comes, call out. And if they don't answer, just point it and pull the trigger.

Zoe's no longer confident about this plan.

—You're sure it's safe?

—Hell no. But haven't you been through enough?

Zoe touches her neck. Just as well she wasn't armed when Adam attacked her. What good would it have done? Even now she suspects she can't pull the trigger.

—Just be sure to call out loud and clear, Spark says: Chances are it will only be me, trying to scrounge a cup of coffee.

For a while, the arrival of the shotgun marks the arrival of a new era; time has now divided into the days before the shotgun and the days after.

One night Spark stops in, and she hears his voice as he comes across the porch:

—Don't shoot! Don't shoot! It's Constable Everett.

They have a good laugh about that, Zoe a little shaky, then he asks some more questions about the break-in, wants to know, for instance, why she called the state police.

—Had to get some use out of that phone.

He asks how she likes it. Is she running up a bill, gabbing to her old girlfriends?

No, she admits. She never leaves it on, then thinks to give him the number.

And then it's clear he's dawdling. He talks about the weather, about her plans for the coming spring, wants to know if she'll ever have people come and stay with her.

Finally he sets his coffee mug down, apologizes.

—I should have just come right out with this.

Zoe's gut turns to water.

—That boy? Spark says.

Zoe stares.

—That boy who. . . .

He rubs his throat as if it aches.

—Oh my god. Adam.

—He's out, Spark tells her: Walked away from his program.

—He broke in here? This was him?

Zoe wants to put her head between her knees, clap her arms over the back of her skull.

Spark shakes his head.

—No, he was still down there at the time. We verified that right off.

—So, where is he?

Spark taps his mug along the edge of the table, as if counting moves in a board game.

—I'm wondering if you want to come down. You could have Unity's old room. He jerks his thumb at Gus: Bring that old galoot with you.

Zoe refuses.

Spark shakes his head.

—You have guts, he says.

—More guts than brains, she says wryly.

It's a lie, of course, and the minute he leaves, she rattles the Xanax in their bottle, counts them. Four left. Then puts the bottle away.

—You're not lost, she tells herself bitterly, quoting the stranger in the woods.

It's probably ridiculous, but she beds down on the couch for the duration. Letting the fire burn down a little, she curls up under a blanket, even conducts mini-drills, flips the cover back, races for the shotgun.

Gus thinks it's a fine way to spend the evening. He's feeling better and he leaps up with her each time, barking madly and racing to the door.

Finally, when she douses all the lamps, she's wired with fear. She tries to lull herself by staring through the tiny tempered-glass window at the flames.

Once or twice, Gus whips his head up, gives a hopeful woof. He shushes on command.

—Only one of us needs to be crazy, she tells him: I have it covered.

In time she dozes, rearranges her hips and shoulders, bobs in and out of sleep. Each time, she sinks a little deeper, stays down a little longer.

And then Gus is up and roaring, charging the door. Zoe flings back the blanket. Galvanized, she rushes on tiptoe, silences Gus, flips him the hand signal for sit. She doesn't remember bending for the shotgun, but there it is, cradled against her shoulder, hammer pulled back. She and Gus stare at the door, Gus horripulated like a grizzly bear.

They hear it:

A footfall, another, on the porch.

She digs the butt of the shotgun into her shoulder, wishes like

hell she'd shot the damn thing before this, then sends her voice
out along the barrel:

—Who's there?

Silence.

Louder now:

—Who's there? I'll shoot.

Another sound.

Gus leaps, snaps his jaws.

The doorknob rattles.

That does it. She holds the barrel an inch or two from
the door, at the last second aiming downward, shuts her eyes
tight, yanks so hard on the trigger that the barrel yanks a little, too.

At first she thinks she's blown off her own head. She's deaf.
Dazed. Disoriented. Sick with the stench of gunpowder.

Gus whines, backs away from her.

Then she hears screaming:

—Oh my god! Oh my god! You fucking killed me.

She can't have blown off her head. She can hear. Her feet seem
to have disappeared, though. She glances down; she hasn't shot
them off either.

In weird slow motion, she ejects the spent shell. It clatters
near her feet. For good measure, she loads another, sets the gun
aside, finally lights a lamp and sets it on the windowsill. Light
slices into the night. Then she picks up the shotgun, opens the
door.

Gus lunges at the figure writhing on the porch, clutching its
thigh and screaming obscenities. Then the dog freezes, wags his
tail tentatively and then, frantic with joy, wriggles in close.

Zoe squints in the pale light, hears herself say:

—Adam?

—Call an ambulance.

The voice moans, begs:

—Please, lady.

—Adam?

—No, it's me. Arnie. Arnie Higby. I came to get Gus back.

Still befuddled, Zoe watches the sprawling boy wrap an arm around Gus's neck, watches Gus shuddering with pleasure.

—Adam? she says again.

CHAPTER 35

꙲

One week later, Zoe's still trying to get back to normal. Whatever that is. She's ordered a new door down at Rileys and this morning, she's trying to replace the porch boards that have been stained with Arnie's blood.

It isn't going well. She knows nothing about woodworking, and despite coaching from her carpentry book, Willis Wagner, she hasn't even been able to pry up the boards with the claws of her hammer; she had been too annoyed and short-tempered to go to Spark's or down to Rileys in search of a crowbar. But the nails are seated deeply, and now Zoe lies underneath the porch, hammering from below to loosen them. Muddy and miserable, she loses some of her sympathy for Arnie, who'd apparently gotten a leg full of buckshot, though it was true he'd brought his beloved dog those mysterious beef bones Gus had carried home to Zoe. All Arnie had wanted that night was some way, any way, to get Gus back.

Especially after he heard about Gus getting his tail whacked off.

She shimmies out from beneath the porch, her back and elbows muddy. Gus digs frantically at the newly exposed roots of a tree, no doubt tormenting some hapless chipmunk. His blunt tail bats back and forth, and she wonders again if she should give him back to Arnie.

No way, said Spark: Not as long as that boy lives with his brothers.

Zoe sees his point. While they'll never entirely sort out the events of these last months, Arnie, at the hospital, biting back pain, had told Spark it was Leland after all who'd sugared the gas tanks at the skete and probably thrown the fireworks at Zoe's. He thought it had been Bart, though maybe Roger, he wasn't sure, who'd poached the deer. Now for the first time he tells Zoe that someone had even driven ten penny spikes into trees marked for cutting at the skete.

That one still gives Zoe the shudders. Imagine the kickback running full-tilt into a spike.

Risk of injury.

Risk of death.

The boards pry up easily now, and Zoe flings them aside onto a rough pile.

When it came to the actual break-in, and the attack on Gus, Arnie had been closemouthed, refusing to say how he knew Gus had his tail whacked off.

The cruelty of it put Spark in mind of Eldon, the oldest, supposedly in Florida, working for an airline. Why he'd be involved, Spark could only speculate.

I wish we had that picture you drew of the man on your land, he'd said more than once.

And then he shuffled and looked away, offered Zoe more coffee when she was already jumping out of her skin, and said that while he still had to get these young folks sorted out, he wanted Zoe to know that the Higbys had learned so much about Zoe from Unity's thoughtless stream of chatter. And he wanted her to know that he was deeply sorry.

Zoe believed him, of course, felt worse for him than for herself to tell the truth, though standing here with the stringers of her porch exposed, the new lumber not even cut to length yet, she wishes she'd thought to extract a promise for a little help. They could fix her porch, erect a gate at the end of lane, and then leave her to hell alone.

She rubs her hands together, considers going inside to warm up with a cup of tea. It's early April, a chill in the air. Her back and elbows are muddy and damp. It's the kind of weather when it seems possible that the gears of the seasons have been stripped, and that it will be chill and dank and raw until the end of time, the Sun watery and distant as if it's lost interest in the Earth and might wander off somewhere else altogether.

In the shed, she finds the hand saws Leland sold her when she first arrived. One is a crosscut, one a rip, and she holds them up, examines them. The triangular teeth of the crosscut fold in past one another.

Leland, she's heard, is either holing up at the Slipney place, or has left town. He no longer works for Callum. Unity is under house arrest at Spark's.

Sighing, she considers cutting the boards to length with the chain saw.

Then smiles.

How crude.

How tempting.

Perhaps she can just leave the porch like this, treacherous and incomplete, so that intruders would fall and break their ankles before they reached her door. Not a bad idea, especially since Adam remains unaccounted for.

Picking up an uncut board, she sights along it, measures, makes a mark. But the T-square slips as she draws a cutting line, and she must turn the board over, remeasure and re-mark it. Wistfully she thinks of cutting brush. Perfect season for it, no leaves, no blackflies.

What was it the man in the storm had said? That she wasn't in charge of what came next?

I sure didn't have this in mind, she tells herself, looking around for a place to rest the board so she can saw it. Steadying it with her left knee, she skids the saw blade back and forth, starts a shallow groove.

It can't be that hard, she tells herself, drawing the saw toward her then letting it glide away again, remembering the feel of the bow saw in her early days, gradually relaxing, when Gus goes into a barking frenzy.

The saw flies up and out of the groove.

She swears, tells Gus it better be good.

He takes off down the road like the Hound of the Baskervilles, a terrible light in his eye. He's been rattled, too, by all the goings-on, though Zoe suspects he's secretly enjoying himself. Clearly he's given himself some kind of a promotion.

She steps out onto the lane, watches Gus down at the foot of it, charging at a stranger in a headlong flight that should scare the bejeebers out of anyone with half an ounce of sense.

The figure comes slowly, Gus leaping up, then away, snapping and barking.

Too tall for Adam, and if it's Spark, Gus has really gone off the deep end.

She holds onto the saw, considers getting the shotgun, but it's daylight, and besides she's still cleaning up the mess from shooting Arnie. Gus keeps the man rounded up, confined to the center of the road. Not a bad moment to have had the helmet on, her faithful chain saw running in her hands. She waggles the handsaw, makes the metal rumble, imagines saying, Watch it, mister, I'm armed.

Vaguely she recalls a salesman who came all the way up here and, even after he'd found out she had neither electricity nor a generator, had gamely tried to sell her a vacuum cleaner.

And then she's staring. The saw grows unaccountably heavy in her hand.

Gus is in full frenzy now.

The man draws closer.

She recognizes the shoulders, the nervous squint.

—That's enough, she tells Gus.

The dog hunkers down, narrows his eyes.

At Dayton.

Nervously, Dayton folds his arms as if to keep Gus from biting.

—That took guts, she says.

—I never figured you for a dog person.

His voice is husky. He coughs, clears his throat.

—An act of charity, she says: He might have been put down otherwise.

Gus wags his hacked-off tail, once.

—So what are you doing here? she says.

Her voice is irritable, annoyed, and she wants to weep at the tone of it.

—Maybe I should have written instead, he says.

He puts his hands in his pockets, shivers a little. She's still standing there with the saw in one hand, trying hard to believe he's shown up, stunned that right this minute she's more annoyed than anything. She taps her boot toe on the lane, looks at the pattern the lug sole leaves.

—I'll just give you this then, and take off, he says.

He looks horrified, as if she's turned into Medusa.

Her hand goes up to her neck. Her scars are hidden by the turtleneck.

Slipping the pack off his shoulders, he unbuckles the flap.

—You came on a bad day, she says, as if they see each other often and perhaps he might drop by tomorrow or next week instead.

—I'll just give you this then, he says again.

Out of his pack he pulls Zoe's notebook.

She glances at it, remote as a childhood toy unearthed in an attic.

—I think you'd better come in, she says.

She doesn't even ask if he wants tea, just assumes he does. He perches on a kitchen chair, keeps his coat on. Locked out, Gus howls on the patchwork porch.

Her returned notebook lies on the table. She hasn't touched it yet.

—I give up, she says: You broke into my house?

He laughs then, a flash of her old Dayton.

—No. You sent it to me, remember? You wrote that note on the inside cover.

Incredulous, she laughs too, shakily:

—Jesus Christ. Someone passed it on?

Defiant, she refuses to apologize for her light use of the name of his lord and savior.

—What kind of tea? she asks, thinking she's ready to lace hers with whisky even though it's only ten in the morning.

He shrugs:

—I'm not fussy.

This, too, is true. About some things, he never was. But now she doesn't even know if he drinks tea, has no memory, yes or no.

He lays a hand on the notebook as she brings the tea, then picks it up, holds it out to her. She doesn't want to take it from him, doesn't want it back.

—I have a confession to make, he says.

Not again, Zoe thinks.

He coughs, clears his throat. His eye squints and his face turns a little ruddy.

—I was the one who went down for the mail that day, and I found it in our mailbox.

—How did it get there?

—Zoe, he says: I read it. All last night.

She lifts it from his hand, holds it a moment, has the urge to throw it in the woodstove, deny its very existence. Instead, she lays it on the shelf beside Saint Barbara.

—I'm surprised you're still speaking to me.

—My father would have been glad to see that you were drawing again. Though a couple of those pictures. . . .

He blushes, then tightens his jaw.

—God wanted you to have that moment, she says, nervous, teasing.

—I never had the impression you believed in God, he says: Weren't you the one who was ready to celebrate . . . what was it? Beltane?

—Dayton, she says: You've been here four minutes. Do we have to get straight to God?

He smiles, shrugs, disarming:

—You're the one who brought Him up.

She laughs then, edgy, perches across from him, trying hard to remember exactly what was in the notebook, equally desperate to blot it out.

He looks uncomfortable:

—I do have to thank you for the taxes. I haven't told any of the brothers yet.

He squints, looks away from her, down at his hands, out the window into her woods, then adds:

—They don't even know where I am.

Suddenly, she's frightened.

—What about this year? I was away.

It's her turn to look out the window. She can't imagine telling him about her visit to the monastery, can't remember if she wrote about it in her book.

—I was away, she says again: Then things started to happen here, and I never got around to calling the attorney.

His face broadens with amazement.

—It wasn't you? This year, it wasn't you?

—It was me the first year, she snaps.

—Yes, he says wryly: Fucking Saint Zoe, as I recall.

She makes a face, laughs at her own temper.

—You won't find her in the calendar, she says.

—So, it was someone else this year, he muses, with wonder in his voice.

He smiles then over the rim of his mug, his eyes briefly bright, mischievous:

—You started a trend.

—Terrific, Zoe says.

—I wonder who it was.

—You have no idea how it pissed me off to hear your little speech at town meeting. As if I wanted your prayers, she says bitterly.

Outside, Gus is roaring again.

Zoe sighs.

—I ought to move to the city. I'd get more peace and quiet.

But Gus is serious and Zoe, wincing, knows she must go out and have a look.

—I can't tell you how tired I am, she says.

Dayton gets up, stands near her.

—Anything I can do? If I keep my prayers to myself?

She scowls at him, furious, then sees he's trying to soften the moment.

—Fix my porch, she says, half-ironic: Go shoot whoever's coming up the lane.

She freezes. Through the window, she catches sight of a state police car pulling in beside her Volvo.

—Oh, shit, she says.

Flinging the door open, she hollers for Gus, afraid he'll bite a trooper and she'll lose him for good.

But it's Spark getting out of the car, coming toward the house, and Zoe can see Gus debating whether he should give Spark a happy greeting or make sure those other strangers stay in their car. Someone's in the driver's seat, perhaps someone else in the back. Some local kid having to do with the break-in, no doubt.

—I'm so tired, she says again under her breath, then says to Dayton: Can you at least stay until they leave?

—I thought you wanted me to fix the porch.

—Right, she says: Sure.

She opens the door as Spark picks his way across the porch stringers. He's wearing a navy blue parka with *Constable* embroidered on the zippered breast pocket.

—My, she says: You look official.

—It is official. Can I come in?

—Don't break an ankle.

Gus meanwhile is out at the trooper's car, keeping close watch.

Spark comes in muttering that he wishes she'd turn on that damn phone so a person could call her once in a while, because he's not exactly comfortable just showing up like this, but there really wasn't a choice. Then he sees Dayton, pouring more water into the kettle.

—I'm Constable Everett, he says.

Dayton holds out his hand, and before he can introduce himself, Spark has placed him.

—You're from that monastery farm.

Dayton nods.

—Zoe and I . . . we grew up together. I'm Brother Dayton.

Spark gives Zoe a canny look.

—I knew there was a tie. Had to be.

Then he cracks a smile, asks if Zoe was always so damn stubborn:

—It takes her a year and a half to buy the blinking phone and then she never turns it on.

Bemused, Zoe waits for an answer.

With a perfectly straight face, Dayton says:

—I'd better not say.

Both men laugh.

Zoe cocks an eyebrow, flirts:

—And you *weren't* stubborn?

Spark watches, waits for more, then runs a fingertip through his chin hairs, says:

—I'm glad you have company right now. There's someone in the car, and I'm going to ask you to come out and identify him. It's a little unorthodox, but the feeling is that we want to get him moved to where he needs to be.

Zoe shakes her head.

—No, she says: I can't do any more. Not one more thing.

Then she catches sight of her notebook by the chimney shelf:

—If it's Eldon, I can show you his picture now. My notebook's back.

Spark's eyes narrow and for a moment he holds very still.

—Dayton brought it, she says, and thumbing through it finds the sketch they both assume is Eldon.

Spark pivots first toward Dayton.

—And how did that come about?

Dayton explains about Zoe's inscription.

—Oh, Spark says, sounding unconvinced, but he lifts his chin, studies the picture through the lower half of his bifocals.

—Not bad. That's Eldon Higby, all right. We're thinking he's behind some of this, might be involved in drug running. Airlines? Florida? Wants a more secluded place up here. Like this one, he says, then looks at Dayton: Or yours.

Then he makes fists in his pockets, squares his shoulders.

—But right now, we need you to have a look at someone. Not Eldon, either.

—I'm not doing it, Zoe says.

Spark's annoyed.

—He's in the backseat of the cruiser. All you need to do is look through the window.

—I won't, she says again: You know all the Shroveton thugs. There's no need.

Spark sighs:

—Then we have to hold him at the jail, a baby John Doe while we try to trace his family on our own. I know he hurt you, but we'll keep you safe.

—My god, Zoe says: Adam?

—He refuses to say a word, Spark says: But that's who we're guessing. Someone found him by the side of the road, half-frozen.

Zoe throws her notebook on the table, skips across the porch stringers as if across the backs of crocodiles.

Ten feet from the trooper's car, she stops, shuddering, pulling at her sleeves, hiding her hands. She tells herself she's cold. That's all. Just cold. Gus comes around the side of the car, wagging his tail, woofing at the parked vehicle.

—Here, Gus, she says.

He sits, stretches tall as possible, leans forward as if to see in the back of the car.

Zoe draws closer, then all at once presses her face to the glass. Her hand shields her eyes.

The front passenger window is rolled down an inch for air.

—Let me in, she says.

The trooper turns in the front seat, eyes the prisoner.

—Let me in, Zoe says again.

—No, ma'am, the trooper says.

—You have to. Look at him.

And then she's weeping, hammering her fists on the glass. Vaguely she sees Adam looking out. His shoulders are small and hunched, and in the halfway house he's gotten a very short hair-cut that makes him look twelve years old. He blinks and blinks, and his lips are tinged with blue.

—Look at him, she says: He's cold.

Behind her, Dayton says:

—Who is it?

—The boy who slashed her, Spark says.

—We need a name, the trooper says, then turns to the still figure in the backseat: You're doing a good job, son. Sitting nice and quiet.

Zoe presses her forehead to the glass again, sobs, and feels horror and sorrow both.

For the boy's life gone so awry.

And for her own life, too, turned inside out.

A hand grips her shoulder.

—You're not helping, Spark says: Just give us his name.

—Adam, she says: Adam Spurling. Now you have to let me in.

—We'd be out of our minds, Spark says.

Zoe pounds on the glass:

—Adam? Can you hear me?

The pale face turns toward her.

—Please, Zoe begs, to anyone who might listen: He's cold. He needs a blanket. He needs two blankets. Three.

She straightens then, looks Spark full in the face, stricken:

—There are blankets in the house, she says: Please.

After a long moment, Spark opens his door, reaches for a latch. The trooper says something sharp, but the back-door lock releases, and Zoe opens the door and dives in, reaching for the boy, as if to console them both for the last eighteen months, two survivors of the same disaster.

Adam leans away, shivering.

He has more whiskers now. His face is puffy, almost moon-shaped, and Zoe knows it must be from medication.

—I hate what happened, she says.

Clearly she's the one who gets to walk away, however slowly, even on some new path. But Adam's life will forever be limited, with illness, diagnosis, monitoring, medication. Perhaps someday even guilt.

—Oh, Adam, she says: Oh, Adam.

—Come on, Zoe, Dayton says: Come on out now.

She sits a moment longer, looking at the boy's beautiful green eyes, the thick lashes that made him so adorable. She remembers the blush in his cheeks as he flirted with the work-study girls, even while the rage and fear brewed up inside him.

—Come on out, Dayton says again: You're scaring him.

—I'm sorry, Zoe whispers: For both of us.

CHAPTER 36

꙳

While the cruiser turns and heads down the lane, Dayton holds her arm. Gus runs back and forth, sniffing the ground in search of interlopers, then catches sight of Dayton, races over, growling.

—Let me take you back inside, Dayton says quietly: If you'll just call off the dog.

—His name is Gus, Zoe says: Throw some sticks for him or something.

—I don't know anything about dogs, Dayton says.

Still staring down the lane, Zoe says:

—And I don't know anything about people.

Then she goes along the path, picks her way across the hop-scotch porch. Dayton wings a stick, and Gus, distracted, charges after it.

Inside, she pokes the fire, then lies on the couch. She wonders how Adam had come so close to finding her, and why he'd made the trip, and she feels sorry for the boy, sickened at the sight of him, cold and small, wonders if forgiveness is a finite act or something that flows in fits and starts, the way a river thaws and freezes.

Footsteps pick their way across the porch, and Zoe stiffens, braces for Dayton's leave-taking, puts a pillow over her head, remembers the man in the storm.

—I am too lost, she mutters.

But Dayton doesn't come to the door. Instead he speaks to Gus, then begins to saw.

Zoe lies still, knowing what she misses is comfort, safety, joy, even the illusion of certainty, things she never had with her fearful, grieving mother, things she's never managed to find since.

She listens to the mumbling of the saw, then the quiet, then more sawing, and she wishes there were some way to tell the difference between faith and delusion.

Later, she calls Dayton in for lunch, a simple meal of soup, bread, and apples. They sit across the table, take turns studying each other, in unspoken choreography, as if it's too unbearable, too embarrassing, to be caught looking at the same time. Zoe tells him about the house and how it's built, how she's just about finished taping the Sheetrock and will start sanding it on rainy days, how someday, if she stays here, she'll have to decide about finishing the floors and ceilings.

He looks at her while she speaks, then she points to something, he looks where directed and it's her turn to study him.

He's still attractive, though more nervous, remote. She figures the nervousness is from the oddness of the day. Apparently relieved to be through eating, he carries his dishes to the sink and says he'll get back to work.

—I'm pretty much finished sawing, he says: So I'll be pounding away out there.

—I'll help, she says.

—You don't have to. It shouldn't take that much longer.

—Then I'm coming out for sure.

—I know you think I left you, he says, his voice hard.

—I don't think that, she says: But you are leaving again.

He turns away, says:

—I came looking for you.

—You came to return my notebook, she says: Or so you claim.

—Back then, he says: I called your mother at least three or four times. I left messages because you weren't answering your phone. I drove to Rhode Island and tried to find you at your college.

Zoe's face and chest turn numb. She pulls up her turtleneck, hides her wrists. This is one piece of the story she hasn't admitted to herself.

—I just couldn't go any farther, she says: You kept pushing and kept pushing, and I just couldn't think straight anymore. I couldn't, Dayton. That's all.

Dayton is quiet.

—My mother died, you know, she says: A few years ago. I don't know if you knew that.

—Come on, he says: Let's get your porch fixed. I liked your mother.

He smiles:

—Even if she was a little batty.

Zoe smiles, too.

—I can finish the porch. If you're in a hurry to get back.

Outside, she sits on the stairs, mug of tea in hand.

—I'm impressed, she says, watching his quickness with the saw as he cuts the last boards.

He tosses a scrap of wood for Gus, who pounces on it, doesn't bring it back.

—It's just a matter of learning a few principles, then getting a lot of practice. I'm no carpenter, I'm what they call a wood butcher.

Zoe smiles.

—Look at us. A couple of town kids. You with your carpentering, me cutting trees.

He's studying the end of a board, laying it in an opening, settling it just so.

—I thought that was interesting in your notebooks, he remarks, paying more attention to the wood than to her: That you turned into a lumberjack.

She drinks her tea, lets herself pretend that she really has him back, tries to saturate herself in the present, the pleasantness of idle talk, of catching up on the news.

—I needed wood for the first winter, she tells him: And somehow I just went on from there. From cleaning up deadfall to tree gardening.

He laughs, repeats:

—Tree gardening. I like that.

—You really should tell me what you're doing, she says.

He holds up a pale golden pine board, sands the rough fringes of the fresh cut.

—You just have to think things through, he says: Measure twice and cut once. All that stuff. And plan to make mistakes.

—No kidding, she says, all at once half-suffocating.

He comes over, kneels, shows her the freshly cut end of the board.

—See the rings? That's the sapwood. Then see the way they cup around the center?

Gus leaps up, barking insanely.

Zoe flinches. Her tea leaps out of her cup, soaks the wood, Dayton's arm and hand.

—I'm going to have a nervous breakdown, Zoe says: That dog.

But there's another vehicle on the road.

—So much for my supposed life as a hermit, she says.

It's Spark again, this time in his own vehicle.

He pulls in fast, gets out, claps his hands at Gus:

—Hello, wild dog, he says, then calls: Can I come in?

Zoe pours the rest of her tea onto the ground.

—Haven't seen you in ages, she says.

—Thought you'd want to know we got that boy a bed in the hospital. The parents are on the way. He's under guard, just to be on the safe side. But he's getting checked over, and fed and warmed up, too.

Zoe lets out a long breath, pulls her arms in tight around her.

—The only thing the boy would say was that he was coming to apologize. Can't quite believe that.

Zoe nods, sadly.

—Actually, I think he did apologize. In his own strange way.

—You look like you need a drink, Spark says.

—I need something, Zoe says: At least Dayton's fixing the porch.

—I would have fixed the porch, Spark says: If you had asked.

—I'm not good at that, she says.

—No kidding, Dayton says.

Furious, Zoe scowls at him, wonders who the hell he thinks he is.

Spark considers Dayton, then starts to speak, stops again, then seems to rephrase his thoughts:

—I have a message for you. There's a certain doctor in Rhode Island who would like to speak with you.

Zoe blushes.

She sees a stillness, an embarrassment on Dayton's face, realizes he thinks the doctor is Zoe's lover.

—My shrink, she tells him: I all but had a nervous breakdown after. . . .

—Who wouldn't, Dayton says quietly, seeming relieved.

—Go on in now, Spark says: Call him or he'll think you never got the message.

Zoe turns toward the door, then turns back:

—Finish that about the sapwood?

—You're looking for the center, Dayton says: The heartwood. Because it's strongest, you always turn it to face the weather, up or out.

—Go make that call, Spark says, then adds: Old carpenter rhyme. Heart-side up, heart-side out.

Back inside, Zoe feels banished. She finds the phone, turns it on, paces, finally goes outdoors.

Spark and Dayton stop talking in surprise.

—The reception's clearer at the spring, she says.

A foolish lie. She wonders if they know it.

Gus follows partway, then gallops back to his guests.

From the spring, Zoe watches the three of them, Spark throwing chunks of wood for Gus, Dayton laying a board in place, reaching for the hammer and the nails. She wants to study his every move, count his breaths, freeze every moment so she can play them back in the years to come. She hates that she must make this call now, waste the precious minutes before his departure. Does Dayton, too, feel time alternately tearing away from them, then holding its breath?

To her surprise, she reaches Zeke's answering machine. Then she laughs. It's not as if he will have cancelled his whole day, waiting for her call.

She leaves a message, tells him she's fine, though things are indeed a little weird just now. In case he doesn't know, Adam's here in the hospital, being warmed up and kept safe.

—I talked to him, she says: It made me feel terrible.

Then she blurts out that Dayton is here, too, that he'll no doubt be leaving soon, and she'll call after he leaves. She walks a few steps on the lopsided stone beside the spring, remembers Spark suggesting she might try to build a springhouse, but warning that sometimes the water vanishes when a human tries to contain it.

Slipping the phone into her pocket, she stoops, plunges her hand into the clear, bitter water. She thinks of the holy wells of Ireland, and offers up a selfish prayer, more like a wish, for the grit it takes to have Dayton here, and for a god who accepts prayers from the doubtful, the unnerved.

Before he leaves, Spark has one more thing to ask.

—Unity wants to come and talk with you. The girl's pretty confused right now, I think it might be good for her.

Zoe sucks in air.

—Not today.

—No, you enjoy your reunion.

He waves then, drives off.

Reunion, she thinks.

Back on the porch, Dayton has two final boards to hammer into place.

From the kitchen, she listens to him banging, looks around for a snack to feed him before he leaves. It occurs to her that she could offer him a ride back.

He raps first, then opens the door. Gus, grinning and breathing hard, comes in at his heels.

—My dog is completely smitten with you, she says.

Dayton gives Gus an amused smile.

—He's his own self, isn't he?

Zoe shakes her head.

—Better than living alone at least.

Dayton takes off his coat.

CHAPTER 37

Up in the cupola, they turn the deck chairs toward the west, and for a long while they sit in silence, looking out at the trees. Zoe remembers times like this, reading together, driving in the car, walking, saying nothing because nothing needed to be said.

She glances at him, sees him smile, relaxed now, somehow taller, younger.

He starts to laugh, asks if she remembers that time they were tubing in the river and he'd decided to show off, jumped from that railroad bridge and sprained his ankle.

And then Zoe's giggling, too, picturing the two of them, wet and filthy as castaways, Dayton trying to be stoic about the pain, yet cursing his stupidity, Zoe feeling sympathetic one minute but then unable the next to resist teasing him about showing off.

It was for those girls driving past, she'd said.

No, no, for you, for you, my love, he'd said, waving his arms, silly and melodramatic, before his face crumpled with pain.

They'd made it out to the road, dripping and filthy, Dayton leaning on their outsized truck inner tubes, Zoe with her thumb stuck out, the two of them alternately laughing then Dayton moaning and Zoe fretting, until she realized there was no way anyone would stop for them unless they left the inner tubes in the underbrush.

But just then a pretzel truck had stopped, and the driver, a young kid, had driven them all the way home, and Mrs. Kuzak, flustered, had bought a year's supply of pretzels in drum-sized tins as a thank you.

—Do you still do that? Zoe asks.

—What?

—Show off, she says, then eyes him: I think you do, actually.

Anger flashes in his face, and Zoe marvels that monasticism has somehow made him defensive. Or maybe it's just being around her.

—Let's just sit, she says.

They drink their coffee in silence. Dayton refills their cups. Zoe pulls off her boots, puts her feet up on the window ledge. Dayton does the same, offers an apologetic smile.

—I stayed in a monastery, she says after a while: Up in Canada. Our Lady of the Snows.

He looks mildly surprised, pleased.

—It was okay, she tells him: In its own way. Except I hated the statues in the woods. Why do you people do that?

—We don't, he says: Not at the skete.

—Yes, you do, she says: I saw the Virgin Mary in your flower garden.

He makes a point of not looking at her, says out of the side of his mouth, trying not to laugh:

—Funny you should mention her. That icon was in the mailbox with your notebook.

Zoe's mortified.

—Were you at the open house? he says: I didn't see you, but a few nights later I started dreaming about you again.

—You dream about me?

—First things first. The Virgin?

—I kidnapped her, Zoe says: But I never could decide on a ransom.

—Do you want her back?

—What?

—Do you want her back?

—Why would I want her back? I'm the one who stole her.

He shrugs.

—She has a way of making herself at home.

Zoe stands, turns her back to him, presses her forehead on the window and looks out into her trees.

—No, she says: I only believe in birch trees. Snow. Coyotes howling on the ridges.

She gulps, nearly suffocates with grief, can't bring herself to say more. Setting her cup on the windowsill, she holds herself tight.

—When I was at the monastery? I read the letter you wrote on the listserv. I read everything about you in the newspapers. Dayton, I still feel this terrible pain. I can't help it. Apparently I'm the weak one.

Behind her, she hears him breathing, steady, deliberate, expects he's angry, thinks it must be inevitable they'll part again in the same way. Her defeated, hurt, in tears. Him silent, annoyed, put-upon.

After a while, he says:

—When someone goes into a monastery, they say it's a kind of death.

His voice drops so low, he pauses and clears his throat:

—For their family and the people who, well, who love them. It's a loss anyway.

—A loss, she says angrily: You didn't even attend your father's funeral.

—There was no funeral, Zoe. The brothers and I sang a Mass for him.

—It's not enough, she says: They scattered his ashes in the gardens by the river. It should have been you, not some cousin and the housekeeper. He loved those gardens. He loved you.

She's sobbing again.

—I loved you.

She turns, forces herself to look at him. Her face is hot, swollen, ugly. She knows her scars are bright red, but for once she'll look him in the eye, just like this.

Pale, he turns his coffee mug back and forth in his hand, stares down at it.

—They don't know where I am, he says quietly: I told you that. I left a note before *lauds* this morning and walked away.

—So, you took a little holiday, she says: You'll go back.

He sighs, says nothing.

—Trust me, she says angrily: Any minute now, you'll put on your coat and walk away. It's what you do.

She gets up, heads down the stairs, says:

—I'm going outside.

Gus follows her to the shed, where she puts on one snowshoe, thinking she'll head into the deep woods, then takes it off again, merely goes and stands in the clearing. The sky darkens, the evening stars emerge, and she turns her collar up. Gus paces back and forth, ready for his supper. When the front door opens, he barrels off, and Zoe wonders just how far he'll follow Dayton down the lane before turning back for home.

Instead, Dayton makes his way along the path to the outhouse, then comes to find her, touches her arm.

—Aren't you cold?

—A little.

—Until I read your notebook, he says: I didn't know how you felt. I didn't know you still thought about me.

—You knew.

Silence then.

—It's not that there haven't been any others, she says: Just that there haven't been others who held a candle to you.

She laughs:

—Poor choice of words.

—Let's go in, he says: You're freezing.

She shrugs.

—I'm fine, I'm used to it.

He laughs:

—Then I'm freezing?

She takes his arm, and standing there in the dark, a litter of stars overhead, the air dry and safe, no snow threatening, she describes the man she met in the storm, tells Dayton everything the man said.

—I want to know what you think, she says: I can't ask anyone else.

Dayton is quiet, finally says:

—It's not for me to say.

—Was he real?

—Zoe, he says: I don't know.

—Fine, then. Was he right?

He looks up a long while at the stars, then with his hands in his pockets, gently bends, kisses her cheek.

—Yes, he says hoarsely: He was right.

Later, she scrambles eggs and vegetables, warms some bread in the oven, hands him a bottle of wine and a corkscrew, says, with a smile:

—I assume you remember how.

While they eat, he talks about the skete, claims they never set out to be rogues.

—We only wanted pure monasticism. We wanted to observe the hours and pray the psalms. We wanted to work and share a small community with nothing between us and God.

Vaguely she listens to him explain they're now at a crossroads. The priest who's been hearing confessions and serving *Eucharist* is being pressured by his bishop to stop coming, and among themselves the debate's been growing about whether or not they should affiliate.

Brother Timothy, in fact, the one with the beard whom Zoe calls Brother Gnome, has decided to see if he can join the Priory at Weston, since he finds the controversy too distracting. And Brother Red will probably be going to seminary after all, although he swears one way or another he'll return to Shroveton.

—We're not lacking for new recruits, he says, sighing: We're up to our necks in volunteers, but we have to be incredibly careful.

Zoe nods.

Incredible care is something she knows well.

He reaches across the table, touches her hand.

—If only I could tell you, he says, aching: The sheer beauty of early Christianity, before all the councils, and the killings over dogma. Mystery, love, light. That's all. Hope in a time of harshness.

—I'll take your word for it, she says, turning her hand over, closing her eyes, feeling the heat of his palm against hers.

He squeezes her hand a moment, takes his away.

—I don't know that it has to do with words.

Zoe leans back in her chair.

—Look at Gus, she says.

He's lying in his spot by the woodstove, keeping a close eye on Dayton's plate, eyebrows working, trying all the while to look diffident.

Before she can stop him, Dayton gets up, scrapes his plate into Gus's bowl. The dog is across the room in a flash, wolfs down the food in two gulps.

—Do all dogs eat like that?

—Shit, Zoe says: He's not supposed to have scraps. He's just gotten over being sick.

Dayton stands there, plate in hand, looking guiltily down at Gus.

—Sorry, pal.

—Don't apologize to him, Zoe says: You made his day.

She fills the sink with hot sudsy water, partly to have something to do. Dayton's coat still hangs over a chair.

Automatically he pitches in, cleaning up the kitchen, bringing her utensils to wash, drying dishes, asking her where things belong. These cups? The plates? The spatula? She smiles at his tidiness and efficiency, wonders if you could get monasteries to train men to be good husbands. She feels the first loosening in her hips, fights the old urge to pat his butt, lean against him, slip her hands into his pockets.

She blushes.

—What? Dayton says.

She blushes harder, changes the subject, asks him to tell her about the other brothers.

—Brother Stephen used to be an accountant, so that's handy, he says: And he can be pretty funny. He does a terrific imitation of himself, listening hard at *lauds* for a bulletin on how the Asian markets performed overnight.

—Does he have money?

Dayton shakes his head:

—Not anymore. It all went into the skete.

—And what about the other one? Brother Luke? He met Gus, you know.

Dayton says he'd heard something about that, actually, and Zoe comments that he seems so lively.

—He glows somehow. There's something about him, isn't there?

—He's in love, Dayton says, matter-of-fact.

—He is? Who with?

—God. Christ.

Zoe fumbles the frying pan. Water slops onto the floor.

—And you? she says, as if watching a car wreck: Are you in love with Christ?

CHAPTER 38

Awkwardness saturates the room, turns the lamp glow harsh, makes the whiff of wood smoke evident in the air. Zoe sees to the stove, orders Gus to lie down and stop pacing, hoping for more hand-outs from Dayton. What she really wants is to wash her face, per-haps bathe, get out of her jeans and turtleneck.

She lays extra wood on the hearth, tells Dayton she's going upstairs a minute, and that the phone is on the chimney shelf if there's anyone he should call.

—Zoe, he says: The way I left them? I'll have to make a formal plea for reinstatement. I don't know what will happen.

—I have to get out of these clothes, she says, then turns back while she's heading up the stairs: They have to take you back. At least twice.

Up in her bedroom, she peels off her turtleneck and jeans, puts on her usual gym tights, camisole, soft wool shirt. At the balcony she listens, hears him take the phone from the shelf, put it back.

—The least you can do is call and say you're all right.

—Okay, he says, but then walks the phone outside, makes his call in private.

When he comes back in, she's sitting in her usual spot on the couch, glass of wine in hand.

—There's more, she says: If you'd like some.

He pours a glass, comes and crouches by the fire, pets his new pal Gus, who looks wary a moment, then gives in to having his belly scratched. Then Dayton straightens, stands beside the fire until Zoe finally says:

—Could you please sit somewhere? You're making me nervous.

He smiles then, sad, bewildered, hopeful all at once.

—Me, too.

He sits beside her, sips a little wine, finally sets the glass on the floor, leans his head back, closes his eyes.

Zoe watches him, protective, considers taking his head in her lap.

—I wish you'd called me, she says.

—Instead of just showing up?

He turns his head, smiles a little sleepily:

—I'd say it turned out all right, taking you by surprise.

—No, before you took your vows.

His face clouds.

—At that point, you'd been ignoring me for years.

She falls quiet, watches Gus fighting to stay awake. After a while, she says:

—Tell me what you're thinking.

He reaches over, takes her hand, says:

—I don't know.

She gets up then, opens the door to the woodstove, throws in another log or two, puts the screen in the door. Heat and light pour out. Gus sighs with pleasure, falls entirely asleep.

Zoe sits again, right up against Dayton, and as if there's been no gap in time, no lost years, he puts an arm around her. She presses her face to his neck, lets her body sag.

After a while, he says:

—Are you all right? Really all right, I mean.

He takes one of her arms, massages the scars. She rolls her sleeves back, offers the other one. He examines both, rubs his palms, dry and warm, up and down her arms. Then he pushes the hair away from her neck, and she lifts her chin, exposes her throat. With a fingertip, he traces the first cut, then the second. She opens her top buttons, lets him follow it to the end.

He kisses the top of her breast, then pulls her in close, murmurs:

—*He will deliver you from the snare of the fowler. And under his wings you shall find refuge.*

—What's that from?

—The Psalms.

She leans away, studies his face in the ruddy light, traces the line of his eyebrow, the nick in his chin. Gently she straddles him, pins his shoulders to the couch. The heat of the fire is on her back, the tide of readiness in her loins.

Gus growls in a dream.

Upstairs she lights a lamp, intends to look at him all she can. They move like two people coming out of a coma, trying to remember the workings of a world long-left.

Dayton unbuttons her shirt, tries to slip it off. Her hand catches in the cuff.

They laugh, nervous.

She shivers, hooks her fingers into the pockets of his jeans. She's not the only one aroused.

Gus trundles up the stairs, lumbers along the balcony, and heaves himself onto the bed. He circles twice in his usual spot, lifts an eyelid at Dayton then falls summarily back to sleep.

Zoe giggles, takes Gus by the collar, drags him off.

He sighs loudly, settles on the floor, tries but fails to keep watch.

—Maybe we should just get under the covers, Zoe says.

There's some awkwardness about peeling off socks, getting Dayton out of his jeans, Zoe out of her tights.

For the first time since the break-in, she dives beneath her quilts, and soon she feels not just safe, but light-headed, half-delirious from all the breathing, the pleasure of having him again. He may have been a monk, but he's forgotten little about lovemaking, and for a man who's AWOL from a monastery right this minute there's no air of guilt about him, only joy.

And Zoe herself feels young again, as if this is one of their first times, somehow eager to recall the exact itinerary of hand and mouth, as if she might never again participate in this instinctively agreed-upon ballet. She offers him the long neglected pleats between her legs. He traces them with a fingertip, watches her, smiles.

Soon she's on top of him, wet and open against the length of him, both of them redolent with pleasure, and with something else. She slides against him, torments him a little, tilts her pelvis just so, catches the tip of him, holds him there, slides away again.

She holds him with her eyes, too, wants him desperately, tilts her pelvis.

He lies utterly still, his hands riding on her hips.

She is who she is. She loves him with her body, too.

Once more she slides forward, sees his eyes close despite himself, feels him tense with ecstasy.

She stills a moment.

—It's true, she says, sorrowful and hoarse: You're the one with the crisis.

He holds her hips just so, angling himself to enter her.

—You're it, he whispers.

She looks down into his face, sees again the rose and green curtains of the northern lights, and lifts herself away, once more gives back what no longer belongs to her.

CHAPTER 39

In the morning, she insists on preparing breakfast, as if they are
an ordinary couple, starting their day. She makes toast and oatmeal, grateful she must confound herself with the doubling of
the recipe. They load their bowls, and Zoe offers butter, maple
syrup, dried fruit.

They barely eat.

Minutes later, they walk out onto the porch. The boards Dayton
replaced are white-gold alongside those that are gray and weathered. Pack in hand, he goes first, steps around them as if not to
dirty them.

—No, Zoe says: Leave me some footprints.

He stands on the new boards then, shifts his weight as if test-
ing the strength of the wood beneath him.

—Heart-side up, he says.

Gus tears back and forth, all rested up, thrilled they're getting
the day off to such a good start, heading out on a hike.

—Gus, Zoe says, but can't think of what she wishes him to do.

Out on the lane, Dayton slips the straps of the pack over his
shoulders, takes her by both arms.

—Did you get any sleep? she says: I could drive you.

Dayton reaches down, finds a stick, tosses it for Gus. The dog
gallops off, is back too soon.

—He did, Dayton says: He crawled in on my other side.

Zoe's eyes flood with tears; her neck turns to iron. Dayton
pulls her to his chest, presses the ball of his thumb into the corner of her eye, as if into sealing wax.

—You're sure?

She shakes her head. Of course, she isn't.

—Aren't you supposed to be carrying a cross, she says.

He smacks his forehead, tries to make a joke:

—How could I forget? And walk down the center of the road.

Zoe smiles, knows they're doing what they never did before.

—It's not the Middle Ages, she manages to say.

Her mouth is dry. She reaches for him again, holds him hard, too hard, releases him.

—We can't send you home with my fingerprints on your back.

She giggles, then gulps back tears.

He holds her chin, kisses her forehead.

—Saint Zoe, he says.

She pulls back, feigns a come-hither look:

—You know where to find me if they don't want you back.

They laugh then, and break apart, and Zoe steps away, as if to give him room. She calls Gus, and he comes and sits, pins her foot down with his paw. She grips his collar tight.

—Ferocious beast, Dayton says, then sets off down the road.

He turns once, makes a show of walking backward, precisely down the crown of the road. Then he blows Zoe a kiss, turns away, picks up his pace. Zoe swallows hard, hangs onto Gus, wishes she knew a prayer for Dayton, for both of them, and she forces herself to watch his progress down the lane, out into the light of the lower field, watches long after he's disappeared.

ABOUT THE AUTHOR

BARBARA DIMMICK's first novel, *In the Presence of Horses,* was translated into five languages. At various times a horse trainer, homesteader, and college professor, she now lives and writes in northern New England, where she's at work on a new novel.

This book was designed by Wendy Holdman.
It is set in Charlotte type by Stanton Publication Services, Inc.,
and manufactured by Friesens on acid-free paper.

Graywolf Press is a not-for-profit, independent press. The books we publish include poetry, literary fiction, essays, and cultural criticism. We are less interested in best-sellers than in talented writers who display a freshness of voice coupled with a distinct vision. We believe these are the very qualities essential to shape a vital and diverse culture.

Thankfully, many of our readers feel the same way. They have shown this through their desire to buy books by Graywolf writers; they have told us this themselves through their e-mail notes and at author events; and they have reinforced their commitment by contributing financial support, in small amounts and in large amounts, and joining the "Friends of Graywolf."

If you enjoyed this book and wish to learn more about Graywolf Press, we invite you to ask your bookseller or librarian about further Graywolf titles; or to contact us for a free catalog; or to visit our award-winning web site that features information about our forthcoming books.

We would also like to invite you to consider joining the hundreds of individuals who are already "Friends of Graywolf" by contributing to our membership program. Individual donations of any size are significant to us: they tell us that you believe that the kind of publishing we do *matters*. Our web site gives you many more details about the benefits you will enjoy as a "Friend of Graywolf"; but if you do not have online access, we urge you to contact us for a copy of our membership brochure.

www.graywolfpress.org

Graywolf Press
2402 University Avenue, Suite 203
Saint Paul, MN 55114
Phone: (651) 641-0077
Fax: (651) 641-0036
E-mail: wolves@graywolfpress.org

Other Graywolf titles you might enjoy:

Trespass
by Grace Dane Mazur

Graveyard of the Atlantic
by Alyson Hagy

The Delinquent Virgin
by Laura Kalpakian

The Stars, the Snow, the Fire
by John Haines

And Give You Peace
by Jessica Treadway

Places in the World a Woman Could Walk
by Janet Kaufman